P9-BVG-916

The Violent Man

The Violent Man

WAYNE C. LEE

Sagebrush
Large Print Westerns

Library of Congress Cataloging in Publication Data

Lee, Wayne C.
   The violent man / Wayne C. Lee.
     p.   cm.
   ISBN 1-57490-098-6 (hc : alk. paper)
   1. Large type books. I. Title.
  [PS3523. E34457V56   1997]
  813'.54—dc21   97-40230
                                                CIP

Cataloguing in Publication Data is available from
the British Library and the National Library of Australia.

Sagebrush Large Print Westerns are published in the United States
and Canada by Thomas T. Beeler, Publisher, Box 659,
Hampton Falls, New Hampshire 03844-0659. ISBN 1-57490-098-6

Published in the United Kingdom, Eire, and the Republic of South
Africa by Isis Publishing Ltd, 7 Centremead, Osney Mead, Oxford
OX2 0ES England. ISBN 0-7531-5835-3

Published in Australia and New Zealand by Australian Large Print
Audio & Video Pty Ltd, 17 Mohr Street, Tullamarine, Victoria, 3043,
Australia. ISBN 1-86340-743-X

Manufactured in the United States of America by BookCrafters, Inc.

CHAPTER 1

DANE BANNING RODE HUNCHED SLIGHTLY IN THE saddle, bone weary, his old wounds aching. But he was fit now, he told himself, tough and hard. He'd gotten off the train in Kansas City, bought this horse and saddle, and had ridden home rather than take a coach just to toughen himself up. It had worked.

He kept reminding himself he was ready for whatever he found but he wasn't at all sure that he was. It had been six years since he'd been home, long years that covered a war, a death-hole called a prison-of-war camp, over two years fighting Indians in Wyoming, and finally a year flat on his back recovering from being gutshot by an ambusher.

His teeth clenched as he thought of it. Home! He hadn't heard from his father or mother or his young bride since he'd been captured at Gettysburg. Five years! His lips thinned over partly bared teeth. What would he find?

Topping the hill, he looked down on the little town of Alpha. It was even smaller than he remembered. The town had been badly located off the main stream of immigrants rushing west and off the railroad. Even Warbonnet Creek flowed half a mile west of it.

He ran a hand over his chin with its three day beard. Nobody would know him. But something in his bones warned him that was good.

He let his horse trot slowly toward town and down the single street. Two or three stores had windows boarded up. Skyrock's general store was still there, open for business. But Dane didn't stop. Keeping his horse at

1

a steady trot, he went on down the dusty street. Across from the store was a marshal's office. That hadn't been there before. He couldn't imagine Alpha needing a marshal. But there was the office and behind it a jail. He saw the livery barn, feed store and a couple of saloons but he recognized nothing else. Alpha was dying although he doubted if those living here realized it.

A half mile south of town, he turned west past the Hatfield place toward Warbonnet Creek. There was home, a place he hadn't seen since March of 1862 when he'd left his bride of two months and his parents to join the Confederate forces to help make the South free to choose its own way of life. Now it was May of 1868, and the last he had heard from any of his family was in June, 1863, just before Gettysburg.

He urged his weary horse to a slow lope. Six years of waiting would soon be over. After passing the Hatfield farm, Dane noticed that the road looked unused and a chill ran over him.

The Banning farm was on the bottomland of Warbonnet Creek. The road running to it topped the low bluffs a quarter of a mile from the buildings. Dane reined up at that spot. The farm was still there, barn, shed, even the broken-down fence behind the barn. But the house was gone.

Touching his heels to his weary horse's flanks, he galloped down the slope to the yard. Swinging from the horse, he walked to the spot where the house had been. Ashes! That fire had been a long time ago. Weeds were growing up in the ashes.

What had caused the fire? When had it happened? And why hadn't his mother or his wife, Charity, written about it? Maybe they had and the letter had not reached him.

Going back to his horse, he stood gripping the pommel, his hand trembling. What a homecoming after six years! It wasn't totally unexpected. He'd had the feeling after five years with no letters that something was terribly wrong.

Staring at the ashes, he tried to think what to do. First, he must find out what had happened. Where was his father and mother? Where was Charity? She likely was with her parents, the Martins. The Martins lived less than a mile from the Bannings, on the other side of the creek.

Mounting, he urged his horse to the creek and across it. The movement cleared his thinking a little. Going around the field that had just been planted, he looked at the house. It was still there but the log barn was gone. Last year's weeds were growing in the yard close to the house.

There was a cold dead weight in his stomach as he reined the horse toward Alpha. He had to find somebody somewhere who could tell him what had happened. A mist filmed his eyes, blurring his vision. Fear, worry and frustration had been building a reservoir of dread inside him for years. Now that dread threatened to well up and drown him.

The road from the Martins' cabin was not so overgrown with weeds. Somebody had used this road coming and going from the field. He crossed the creek again, this time half a mile upstream from the Banning place, and passed the Wieland cabin. No one appeared to be at home but this place, at least, was lived in. A mile directly east from Wieland's was Alpha and Dane followed the well-worn road at a gallop.

The road cut into the north and south Main Street just to the north of Ed Skyrock's general store and Dane

3

reined his heaving horse into the hitchrack in front of the store.

Swinging from the saddle, he walked across the board porch to the door. There was little change in the store from the way he remembered it back in 1862. The Bannings hadn't done much business with Skyrock because he was a Union sympathizer and the Bannings were Southerners from northern Georgia. There had been a store farther down the street where they did their buying. It was boarded up now.

Ed Skyrock was a small man, about five and a half feet tall and weighing well under a hundred and fifty pounds. His light blue eyes fastened on Dane as he came through the door but not until Dane reached the counter did recognition come into them. With the recognition, his mouth dropped open and he stepped back against a shelf of canned goods.

"Dane Banning!" he whispered. "I—I heard you were dead."

Dane leaned both hands on the counter. "When did you hear that?"

"Near the end of the war," Skyrock said, seeming to recover some of his poise. "What—where have you been?"

"It's a long story," Dane said. "Before I tell it, I want some answers. Where's Charity and my folks?"

"Bull Banning and his wife are dead," Skyrock said.

Dane had expected as much and had prepared himself. "What happened to them?"

"Killed," Skyrock said. "We don't know who did it."

"What about Charity?"

Skyrock shook his head. "I don't know. Maybe she went back to Tennessee to live with her folks."

"When did the Martins go back to Tennessee?"

4

"A while before the end of the war," Skyrock said. "Charity stayed here with your folks. Then when they were killed, she disappeared. People figured she went back to Tennessee."

Skyrock seemed to be over his shock now and was talking freely.

"Anybody ever hear from her?"

Skyrock shrugged. "Not that I know of. Who would she write to here?"

Skyrock had a point. Both the Banning and the Martin families were from the south. The Union sympathizers dominated the social life around Alpha and the Southerners were shut out of community gatherings.

"Had she heard I was dead?"

Skyrock frowned as if in thought. "I reckon. I don't recall just when we did get that word."

Dane's eyes bored into the storekeeper. "Skyrock, you're lying about something. You know more than you're telling me."

Skyrock shook his head vigorously. "I'm telling you everything I know. Ask Lon Yockam. Or Atley Logar. Or anybody."

"I'll do just that," Dane said.

Wheeling, he went out onto the porch. He couldn't put his finger on anything Skyrock had said that he was sure was a lie. But the storekeeper was either telling some lies or holding back a lot of the truth. Dane had dealt with enough men to know the signs.

Crossing the street, he walked into the marshal's office. The lawman should know what had happened. Dane almost stopped with one foot inside the door. Sitting behind the desk with a marshal's star prominently displayed on his shirt front was Lon

Yockam. Dane remembered Yockam. He was four or five years older than Dane and he'd always been a bully. Yockam made life as miserable as possible for all Southerners. He had joined the Union army as soon as the war started in '61 and Dane hadn't seen him since.

Yockam's feet slapped down on the floor when Dane came through the door. He studied Dane's face for a moment then lunged to his feet.

"Banning!" he exclaimed. "I thought—"

"You thought I was dead," Dane said. "So did Skyrock. Skyrock tells me my folks are dead. What do you know about it?"

Yockam took his time getting settled back in his chair. Dane had the feeling he was deciding just what to say and his suspicions rose.

"They're dead," the marshal said finally. "I helped bury them. It was just a while after I got back from the army. I got this gimpy leg at Shiloh. Never healed right. The army turned down my reenlistment."

"What happened to them?" Dane insisted.

"They were killed at their cabin," Yockam said, as unconcerned as if he were talking about the death of a stray dog.

"How? Why?"

"Bull was clubbed to death. His wife was shot," Yockam said. "I don't know why. We didn't have any law here in Alpha then. Just the sheriff over in the county seat. He came over but couldn't find anything. The cabin was burned."

"The same time Pa and Ma were killed?"

Yockam nodded. "I suppose the killers thought they'd cover up their tracks."

"What about my wife?"

"Nobody saw her after that," Yockam said. "Most

6

people figure she went back to Tennessee to her folks. The Martins had moved back where they belonged just a month before this all happened."

"Why did they move back?" Dane demanded, his anger growing because he was getting the same feeling from Yockam that he had from Skyrock, he was not hearing the whole truth. Maybe he wasn't hearing any of the truth.

"I suppose they finally saw that they didn't belong up here in Union country. They went back while they could."

Dane leaned forward on Yockam's desk. "Are you saying my folks were killed because they were Southerners?"

Yockam shook his head. "I ain't saying that but I reckon it could have been. This never was Rebel country. And by '64 when this happened, it sure wasn't Rebel country. The Martins saw the light. The Bannings didn't."

Dane went back outside. Maybe Yockam was telling all he knew but he doubted it. One thing was sure. Yockam hadn't regretted the deaths of Bull Banning and his wife.

If Charity had gone back to Tennessee to her parents' home, she surely would have written to him. Unless, of course, she had heard that he was dead and had believed it. He'd go to Tennessee and see if she was there. But first, he had to learn more about the murder of his parents. He couldn't leave without finding out something.

Who would he ask? There were three storekeepers who had been here before the war who would tell him if they knew. But a glance down the street showed him that two of the stores were boarded up and the other was now a saloon. Somebody had done a thorough job of driving out all Southern sympathizers.

Dane got his horse and rode slowly down the main street to the south. The sun was getting low; he'd have to find a place to spend the night. But it wasn't going to be in town. He felt in his bones that he wouldn't be alive in the morning if he stayed in town tonight.

He had ridden a quarter of a mile out of town when he saw a small figure at the side of the road. At first, he thought it was a half grown boy. Then as he got nearer, he recognized Tate Tubulo. Tubulo's parents had been neutral in the war. Yockam and his buddy, Kurt Uhl, who was several years younger than Yockam but just as mean, had made life miserable for Tubulo.

Tate Tubulo had been handed the dirty end of the stick by Nature. Something hadn't developed right in Tate and he had never grown right. He was about two years younger than Dane but he was a couple of inches under five feet tall and barely weighed a hundred pounds. Dane had seen ten year old boys bigger than that. He had been sick most of his younger days, his parents said, so he hadn't gone to school. Everybody looked on him as feeble-minded; some considered him an imbecile. Dane had never thought there was anything wrong with his mind except a lack of formal education and a lot of full-sized men lacked that.

"I saw you in town," Tubulo said in his high pitched voice that would have passed for a young boy's. "You were good to me before you went to the war. I want to be your friend now." He looked up the road toward town. "I don't dare let them see me talking to you. I'll have to go. But you be careful tonight. They'll try to kill you."

"Who will?" Dane asked.

8

"The same ones who killed your pa and ma," Tubulo said then dodged back off the road. In an instant he had completely disappeared.

Dane remembered how Tubulo could vanish like a vapor. It was the one talent he possessed that saved him from a lot of harassment. On occasion when he couldn't dodge Yockam and Kurt Uhl, Dane had stepped in and rescued him. Dane had almost forgotten it. Tate Tubulo hadn't.

Dane rode on slowly, leaving the main road at Hatfield's and going toward the Banning farm. With the house gone, there wasn't much there but it was the only refuge he could think of now.

According to Tubulo, the men who had killed his parents were still here at Alpha and they would attempt to kill him. They were likely trying to keep their tracks covered and they might fear Dane. Dane's lips thinned. They had reason to fear him if he ever found out who they were.

He'd gone off to war a gentle man. His mother had correctly guessed that war would be a terrible trauma for him. But a year of battles and a year of prison topped by two and a half years on the frontier fighting Indians had changed him. He was no longer afraid to face death, not even his own. He'd be glad to see the death of the murderers of his parents and Charity. Maybe Charity was still alive but nobody had seen her since the death of Bull and Mary Banning. Whoever had killed the Bannings weren't likely to leave a witness to tell what she had seen.

Precaution prompted Dane to stake out his horse in the trees along the river several hundred yards beyond the barn. Then he went to the two buildings still standing and looked them over.

9

The barn seemed the logical place to sleep but, remembering Tubulo's warning, he turned instead to the shed. The Bannings had repaired harness and stored winter firewood here. There had been plenty of dead wood in the trees along the creek to cut up and that had been stored in one half of the shed.

The sun was down and deep twilight was on the river. Dane loved this time of day, especially in the spring. He had dreamed so many times of getting home for just such moments as this. But there was no joy in it tonight. Charity was not here to share it with him. Neither were his parents.

Normally, he would have lingered to watch the darkness deepen among the trees and spread out over the land. But he was dog tired tonight. He went inside the shed and found a place in the corner, behind some old sacks that had been piled there so long they smelled moldy. There he unrolled is bedroll and stretched out.

He'd been asleep a while when he heard a noise outside. Slipping out of his blankets, he peered through a crack in the shed. Five riders were out there between the barn and the shed.

As Dane watched, three of them rode toward the barn. The other two dismounted and came toward the shed. There was half a moon that was bright enough to let Dane count the men and see what they were doing but it was not bright enough for him to recognize them. Maybe he wouldn't know them if he could see them. But from what Tubulo had said, he was sure he would.

And he knew what they were doing here now. The two coming to the shed would find him. If they did, another Banning would die here on the farm.

CHAPTER 2

DANE WATCHED THE MEN CAUTIOUSLY APPROACHING the shed. They obviously expected him to be somewhere on the place. Dane wished he had a gun. He had never cared much for guns and he hadn't come home to resume the war so he hadn't brought a gun with him.

The riders had reached the barn and dismounted. The two men approaching the shed were within fifty feet of it. Dane couldn't see a thing inside the shed. Maybe the men couldn't, either. But Dane was sure they'd strike a match before they left to make certain he wasn't there.

Dropping down onto his blankets, Dane remembered the moldy sacks. Reaching over, he grabbed a handful of them and dragged them over him. The mold and dust almost choked him but he settled more over him, hoping they would look like they'd been lying there for years without being disturbed.

He waited for what seemed like an eternity before he heard the rasp of the wooden door being pulled open. There wasn't enough moonlight coming into the shed to penetrate the layers of sacks over Dane's head. But when one of the men struck a match and held it inside, the glow filtered down to him. He held his breath, afraid that even his breathing would move the sacks and give away his hiding place.

The match went out. "He ain't in there, that's sure," one man grunted.

"No place a man could hide in there," the other agreed. "Must be in the barn."

The door swung shut but didn't fit into its frame. The men didn't bother to shove it into place. After they were gone, Dane pushed aside the sacks so he could breathe

11

normally again. Listening intently, he heard men talking over in the direction of the barn. He heard one man say loudly that there was no one in the shed.

Dane got up slowly and carefully, making sure he didn't bump anything that would make a noise. Finding the crack in the back of the shed, he pressed his eye to it and watched.

The five men were clustered at the end of the barn where there were no doors or windows. If anyone had been inside, he couldn't have gotten a shot at them. There was little doubt about their intentions. Dane silently thanked Tubulo for his warning.

"Maybe he isn't there at all," one man said and Dane, listening with all his concentration, could distinguish the words.

"Where else would he go?" another man said. "Cheyenne checked his tracks before dark. They turned off this way by the Hatfield place."

"Well," still another voice said, "if he ain't in the shed, then he's got to be in the barn. Let's burn it. That will smoke him out."

"Who wants to smoke him out?" one man asked. "Let's fry him right there. If we start a fire at both ends of the barn and another one at the door, he can't get out."

"Good idea," another agreed.

Dane watched the men scatter. Within three minutes, three blazes sprang up. The one at the door of the barn blazed up seconds before the two at the ends of the barn. If anybody had been in the barn, he wouldn't have had a chance to get out. Even if he had risked dashing through the fire, one of the men watching with drawn guns would have cut him down.

"Maybe he doesn't have a gun," one man shouted

above the roaring of the flames.

"Makes no difference," another said. "Nothing could be alive in there now."

"Let's vamoose before this fire brings a swarm of curious neighbors."

That suggestion seemed to meet with full approval and the men scurried to their horses. A minute later they were thundering south along the river away from town, the direction from which any curious spectators would come.

After he was sure the raiders were gone, Dane came out of the shed and looked at the burning barn. There wasn't a fire department this side of Kansas City that could put out that blaze now.

He turned to look toward town. This big a blaze should be seen clearly that far away. But nobody came. Either they didn't care what happened to the Banning place or they knew better than to tangle with the men who had set the fire.

There wasn't much breeze so there was little danger that the fire would spread. Dropping into the shadows of the shed where he wouldn't be seen if someone should happen by, Dane squatted down and let his thoughts go back to the good times he'd had here on this place.

He had helped his father build that barn and this shed and the house. Only the shed was left now. His throat tightened as he thought of all the other things that were gone. Six years of his life were gone. His father and mother were gone, murdered. But the deepest pang came when he let his thoughts turn to Charity. Almost a foot shorter than he was, she had come only to his shoulder, her long red hair bobbing in rhythm with the quick moves of her head as if it were alive, her blue eyes laughing at him. It wasn't that she was so little,

13

she'd often said, it was just that he was so big. His six foot two against her five three made quite a contrast.

Then had come the war. The killing had turned his stomach. He hadn't gone into a battle that first year that he hadn't been sick just thinking about it and sick again after the battle was over, remembering.

Finally, for him, Gettysburg. He had become separated from his company in the confusion following a quick retreat from a ridge they couldn't hold against overwhelming numbers of cavalry in blue. He and two companions had been picked up and sent to a prison camp.

A year later had come the opportunity to go west and fight Indians instead of staying in prison. Assured that he wouldn't have to fight men in gray, he agreed. Anything was better than staying in that death hole.

Two years later as he helped set up posts along the Bozeman Trail in Wyoming, he wasn't so sure. If he'd stayed in the prison camp, he'd have been home in '65. It wasn't till early in '67 that he was shipped back east and discharged.

He'd written home to tell his family he'd soon be there. He wondered now what had become of that letter. That had been over a year ago. It was in Illinois that he'd been shot and left for dead. He never really knew what happened. He'd been riding along next to a hedge. It was like the skirmishes in the war that started so often by an ambush from a hedge row. Only he was hit dead center on the first shot and knew nothing until he came to in a hospital where they told him he'd been unconscious for five days. They didn't give him much chance to recover but he did.

He grimaced now as he thought how he'd fought to live so he could see Charity again. How much better if he had died then! It took him a year to recover enough to continue toward home. This time he had ridden the cars to Kansas City, bought a horse, and headed on for home. He'd had a feeling things were not right here. But he'd never guessed how wrong they would be.

Dane's reverie was suddenly interrupted by the sight of a small stooped figure emerging from the trees. Tate Tubulo. Dane stood up beside the shed. Tubulo stopped short when he saw him and appeared ready to run. Then he shuffled on toward Dane.

"I knew they'd try to get you," Tubulo said softly. "I'm glad they didn't."

"They might have if you hadn't warned me," Dane said. "I was watching. Do you have any idea who they were?"

Tubulo looked frightened, glancing up the dark road toward town. "I know. But I can't tell."

"You said it would be the same ones who killed Pa and Ma. When did that happen?"

"Summer of '64," Tubulo said. "The Home Guards did it."

"The Home Guards?" Dane exclaimed. He'd heard of border towns with their Home Guards trying to protect their communities from enemy raids. But Alpha didn't seem like a worthwhile target for any enemy.

"Did you see them do it?" Dane asked.

Tubulo nodded. "I've always roamed around at night. The Home Guards were put together right after Lon Yockam got back from the war. He got crippled so they sent him home. He stirred up people here and got them to organize a Home Guard."

"So Yockam was one of them," Dane breathed softly.

"I didn't say that, " Tubulo said quickly. "I just said he organized the Guard. Most of the men around here belonged to the Guards but only five came out here and killed your folks."

"There were five men who burned the barn tonight. They must all still be here."

Tubulo nodded. "And they won't stop till they kill you. They figure you might try to kill them for what they did."

Dane's mind was racing. "Was Yockam one of the men who burned my house and killed my folks?"

Tubulo squirmed. "I ain't saying. I'd be killed if I did. Anybody in town who squealed would be killed."

"So they've got the whole town treed. All right, no names. Just tell me what happened."

"They'd run out the Martins and several other families," Tubulo said. "But Bull Banning wouldn't run. I knew they'd do something bad. I was roaming along the creek that night when I heard their horses. I hurried up this way and watched from the edge of the trees."

"I heard that Pa was beaten and Ma shot," Dane prompted when Tubulo stopped.

Tubulo nodded. "That's right. Bull came outside when the men rode up. They started beating him over the head with their guns. Mrs. Banning ran out and somebody shot her. Then they finished beating Bull to death."

"What about Charity? Wasn't she here?"

Tubulo nodded again. "One of the men went inside and came out carrying Charity. She was kicking and screaming but she wasn't strong enough to get away. He took her away before the rest of them decided to bum the place."

"Did you see Charity any more?" The words almost stuck in Dane's throat.

"No," Tubulo said softly. "Nobody has ever seen her

16

again."

"Was she killed?"

"I don't think so," Tubulo said.

"Who carried her off?" Dane asked, fighting to breathe normally.

"I don't dare tell," Tubulo said. "They'd kill me."

"I've got to know," Dane said, spitting the words out like bullets. "Nobody will ever know I found out from you. I promise."

Tubulo looked at Dane in the flicker of the slowly dying fire and his face turned ashen. "You got a right to know. It was Kurt Uhl."

Dane's breath exploded from him. He should have known without forcing Tubulo to tell. Kurt Uhl had been the only rival Dane had ever had for the favors of Charity Martin when she first came here.

"He'll never know where I found out," Dane said. "Now who else was here when they burned this place?"

Tubulo looked beaten. He'd told one name. The others spewed out without any hesitation. "Lon Yockam was the leader. He had Uhl, Ed Skyrock, Atley Logar and Cheyenne Fass with him."

"Who is Cheyenne Fass?" Dane asked. "I never heard of him."

"He's a half-breed Indian. Came here shortly after you left. He's a hothead and a thief. I think he joined the Home Guards so he could steal everything when the Guards ran the people out."

Tubulo nervously looked around the shed toward town then down the river. Dane laid a hand on his shoulder. "They won't hurt you. I'll see to that. Those were the same five men here tonight, weren't they?"

Tubulo nodded vigorously. "The same ones. I've got to go."

Dane watched the little man slip away into the shadows. He would have sworn he literally disappeared when he was only half way to the trees. Then he turned his thoughts away from Tubulo.

He knew four of the men who had been on that raid four years ago and had come back tonight to kill him. Lon Yockam didn't surprise him at all. Besides being the marshal, he also owned one of the saloons in town. He'd always been a hater of Southerners.

Ed Skyrock, the storekeeper, was a surprise to Dane. He had never appeared to be such a vicious man although his hatred for the men from the South was no secret.

Kurt Uhl's membership in Yockam's inner circle of Guards didn't surprise Dane at all, especially in the raid against the Bannings. Uhl was a big man, the blacksmith in town. He stood six feet four inches and weighed at least two hundred and forty pounds. Dane knew one thing about him that a stranger would not recognize at first glance. He was a coward. Dane's last memory of Uhl in '62 was his fear of being conscripted for the Union army.

Atley Logar was a trader with the Indians. Not much bigger than Ed Skyrock, he was a colorless man who curried favors with important people. To him, the leader of the Home Guard would be an important person. Logar had had an old team and wagon and hauled loads of goods out to the Kiowa camps before the war. Dane guessed he still did. Most people assumed that a big part of each cargo was whiskey. So far as Dane knew, Logar had few friends anywhere, probably not even among the Indians.

Cheyenne Fass was the only one of the five he didn't know. Tubulo had said he was a half-breed and a thief.

Likely he was a killer, too. Dane would have to be extremely careful until he knew more about him.

He moved his blankets out of the shed and into the trees along the creek. Those Home Guards might come back to make sure they had succeeded in getting rid of Dane. Or Yockam might decide to burn the shed just to make a clean sweep of the destruction.

In spite of his weariness, Dane didn't sleep much during the night. Half his mind was alert for sounds of danger and the other half was busy assimilating the information that Tate Tubulo had given him.

He had no reason to doubt anything that Tubulo had told him. If Dane had a friend around Alpha, it was probably Tubulo.

Still it lingered in his mind as the sun came up that he should check Tubulo's story with someone else. He recalled coming past the Hatfield house as he rode in here. He remembered the Hatfields. They had been neutral on the Secession question. Coming from Ohio on the river just a good frog jump from Kentucky, their background could easily have been either North or South.

As Dane rode toward the Hatfield farm, a mile to the east, he wondered if the Home Guard had let the Hatfields stay. When he arrived, he saw a young man carrying slop to a pen full of squealing pigs.

Dane reined up close to the pen. That would have to be Marvin Hatfield. He'd been going to school in town when Dane left.

"Remember me?" Dane asked. "Dane Banning. Do you know what happened to my folks and my wife?"

The young man stared at Dane, his eyes widening in fear. He shot a glance north up the road toward Alpha then looked back at Dane, licking his lips.

19

"I don't know nothing," he said softly, shaking his head.

"They promised to wipe you out, too, if you said anything, did they?"

Hatfield didn't answer but his almost inaudible gasp told Dane he had hit a nerve. Tubulo had said that anybody who talked had been threatened. This was proof enough of Tubulo's accurate evaluation of the situation.

Dane nodded to Hatfield and reined his horse around, starting back toward the Banning farm. As he thought of the way those few Home Guards controlled the town and the country around it with fear of death, his blood began to surge hotly through him.

His mother had worried about him when he went to war because she said he was a gentle man. Maybe it was well that she couldn't see him now. He was slowly becoming a violent man.

CHAPTER 3

DANE RODE SLOWLY BETWEEN TWO FIELDS. THERE were few places around Alpha where he could feel safe now. His mind grappled with his problem. Instead of home with wife and parents, he found himself surrounded by enemies determined to kill him.

He could not rule out ambush. Last night's raid was proof of that. The raiders had burned the barn, thinking he was inside. And they had made sure that if he had been inside, he wouldn't have had a chance to get out.

Dane could think of only one of the five who might give him an even break if it came to a fair fight. That was Lon Yockam. And he wasn't so sure about him. He hadn't objected to burning the barn last night, hoping to roast him alive.

Uhl would kill him from ambush if he could. Uhl was a coward. He'd be a constant threat to bushwhack Dane.

Ed Skyrock didn't strike Dane as a man who should be involved in this affair in any way. He wasn't a violent man; at least, he hadn't been when Dane knew him before the war. But he did hate the Rebels and somehow he had been drawn into the violent circle by Yockam. There was really no way to accurately assess what Skyrock might do now that he was threatened by Dane's return.

Atley Logar had been considered a worthless specimen when Dane had known him before he went away. Logar had been on the frontier for a long time. He had moved west with the fringe of civilization, always trading with the nearest tribe of Indians. As the Indians settled down on land allotted to them by the government, trading became easier. Dane doubted if Logar ever gave the Indians a fair trade.

Cheyenne Fass was an unknown quantity to Dane. Because he didn't know him, Dane would be most cautious in dealing with the half-breed.

He would settle accounts with every one of them. He didn't make that resolution consciously; it was just there like the dawn of a new day. Those five men were responsible for the deaths of his father and mother and also for whatever had happened to Charity.

He reined his horse north toward the cemetery. There hadn't been many graves in the cemetery northwest of town when he left. There would be more there now.

Reaching the cemetery, it took him only a short time to locate the graves of his parents, just inside the fence. Someone had shown enough compassion to put up wooden head markers at each grave. Apparently no one knew when either was born but the date of death, July 18, 1864, was marked clearly on each headboard.

Dane dismounted and stared at the graves. He was surprised to find them cared for. Who in this community would do that? Then his eye traveled a few feet beyond his father's grave and fastened on another headboard. He leaned over the fence to make sure he was reading it right. The headboard looked like the two on his parents' graves but it was not weathered quite as much. The lettering was very plain. "Dane Banning, March 1865."

Dane stared at it for another minute. There was no sign of a grave beyond the headboard. Was this some kind of joke? Was it an honest mistake? Or was it prophetic?

Turning back to his horse, Dane mounted. There was one thing he had to have. A gun with ammunition. How could he have thought he wouldn't need a gun here? He had to have one if he didn't want to fill the grave beyond that headboard.

Grimly, he turned his horse toward town, not far to the southeast. The only place in town that would have guns would be Skyrock's general store. There used to be a hardware store that carried fine guns made by a gunsmith in Kansas City. But that store was boarded up now. If Skyrock didn't have any, then Dane would have to go to some other town to get one.

Dane rode boldly into town. There was no way he could keep his presence secret if he intended to buy something in Skyrock's store. Dismounting at the hitchrack in front of the store, he tied his horse and went inside.

Skyrock was watching him, eyes wide as if he were seeing a ghost. Dane walked down the aisle until he saw a half dozen guns in a case. He pointed to them.

"I want to see one of those," he said.

Skyrock came away from the counter where he'd been standing as if he'd suddenly been given a shove.

"Sure. Which one?"

"That one," Dane said, pointing to the gun on the right side of the case. His eyes were more on Skyrock than on the gun.

Skyrock reached into the case and got the gun, laying it on the counter. Dane examined it carefully. A .45 revolver. It would serve the purpose. He asked the price.

Skyrock stuttered a little as he said, "Thirty dollars."

Dane guessed that was a little high but he wasn't going to quibble. "I'll need some ammunition for this, too."

Skyrock nodded and set a box on the counter. Dane looked at it and frowned.

"Forty-four shells won't work very well in a forty-five."

Skyrock gasped and grabbed the box from the counter and replaced it with one holding .45 ammunition. Dane didn't know whether the storekeeper had deliberately handed him the wrong ammunition, thinking he'd negate the danger of the gun in Dane's hands or whether he was so flustered he had made an honest mistake.

Dane put some shells in the gun then pocketed the rest of the box. The heavy wooden box made a big lump on his thigh.

"You look like you had seen a ghost," Dane said.

"It's just that we heard years ago that you were dead," Skyrock said.

"You found out different yesterday. Did you expect me to be dead today?"

Skyrock twitched his hands nervously. "Why should

23

I?"

"I asked you first," Dane said. "Let me tell you something, Skyrock. I'm hard to kill. And from now on, I'm going to be even harder to kill."

Skyrock backed against the wall shelf. "Nobody's going to kill you," he said.

"I hope you remember that," Dane said. He started out of the store then stopped. "Who put up the headboards at the graveyard?"

Skyrock shook his head. "I don't know. It was good that somebody did."

Dane thought of the headboard out there with his name on it. "When did you get the word that I was dead?"

Skyrock seemed to think for a moment. "It was in the spring of the last year of the war, if I recollect correctly."

Dane nodded. That fit the date on that headboard. But who had put it up?

Dane went outside. At the door, he almost bumped into a man coming in. One glance told him that he was an Indian dressed in white man's clothes. That was nothing uncommon because many reservation Indians dressed that way. But this one was different. There was a hatred gleaming in his eyes that would have done credit to a brave on the warpath. Dane knew without asking that this was Cheyenne Fass.

"Looking for someone?" Dane asked when the Indian stood his ground, glaring at him.

"I've found him," he said. His eyes dropping to the gun still in Dane's hand. "Are you going to start killing now?"

"The thought has crossed my mind," Dane said.

"You ain't got much time to do it," the Indian said

and backed out of Dane's way.

Dane watched him wheel and disappear down the alley instead of going into the store. Cheyenne Fass was one he would have to watch very closely.

He stuck the gun under his belt and crossed the street to Yockam's office. Yockam was at the desk in the corner of his office. He appeared busy but Dane knew he'd been watching everything that had gone on across the street.

"I want to report that my barn was burned last night," Dane said.

Yockam looked up, his face flushed with anger. Dane guessed it was because the raid last night had failed in its purpose.

"I'm marshal of the town, not the whole county," Yockam grumbled.

"I figure the ones who burned the barn came from town," Dane said.

"Got any proof of that?" Yockam asked testily.

"Just what I know," Dane said.

"Nobody cares what you know. If you accuse some innocent people, I'll have your hide."

"Do I have to do something like that to make you go after my hide?"

Yockam gritted teeth. "No, you don't. You're a stinking Rebel. The only fit place for a Rebel is in the middle of a Georgia swamp. This was a decent place till you came back."

"I thought this nation was trying to pull the two sides back together."

"They can do what they want to in Washington," Yockam said. "But I live here and no Rebel is going to smell up this town."

"That's too bad," Dane said, "because I'm here. And I

figure on staying a while."

Yockam glared at Dane. "If you've got any sense, you'll go somewhere else. There may be some places where Rebels are still welcome. It sure ain't in a town with a Yankee soldier who was crippled by a Reb bullet."

Dane had seen hate in the Indian face but that couldn't match the hate twisting Yockam's face. Dane wondered if he'd be shot down right here in the office. He let his hand rest on the butt of the gun in his belt as he backed toward the door.

Outside, he turned and strode across the street to his horse, the middle of his back prickling with a chill. He didn't think Yockam would dare shoot him in the back right on the street. But he didn't know how tight a grip Yockam had on this town. There were a couple of women down the street and a man was just coming up from the blacksmith shop, witnesses if Yockam should shoot him in the back.

Dane knew he had stretched his luck as far as he dared today. Untying his horse, he leisurely mounted, using all his control to keep from hurrying.

He reined down the street beside the store. It was the quickest way to get out of sight of the marshal's office. Once out of town, he followed the road on to the west. This wasn't the way he usually went home but then it might be better for him not to travel the usual roads.

Since he was so close to the cemetery, he angled off toward it again to look once more at the headboards. Maybe something about them would give him a clue as to who had put them up, especially the one with his name.

Ahead, he saw a rider disappear over the hill beyond the cemetery. He was going the other way so Dane quickly forgot him. He stopped outside the board fence that had been built around the cemetery to keep wandering cattle out. Since the Banning lot was just inside the fence, he didn't dismount.

He couldn't see anything about the three headboards to indicate who might have made them. While he was looking at them, he caught a movement across the cemetery close to a big stone that marked the grave of John Uhl, Kurt Uhl's father, who had died just before Dane left for the war.

His head jerked up. Although he didn't see anything then, instinct sent him diving out of the saddle. A bullet slapped into the board fence just inches to the left of Dane.

He realized now that the rider he had seen must have been getting his horse out of sight in the ravine to the north of the cemetery and then had slipped back and hidden behind the big stone at Uhl's grave.

He thought of Skyrock but ruled that out instantly. Skyrock wouldn't risk laying an ambush while there were others who would do it. His next thought was Fass, the half-breed. Yockam wouldn't have had time to get out here.

Dane pulled the new .45 from his belt. He had planned to test the gun when he got to the trees along the creek near home. Instead, he'd test it here. Lining the gun on the tombstone, he waited for a glimpse of the man behind it. When it came, he fired quickly.

The gun worked well but the bullet only nicked a corner of the stone and screamed off into the valley to the north. Dane waited for another glimpse of the man. When he came, he saw that the man was a hundred yards down the slope, running low, carefully keeping the stone and the low fence between him and Dane.

Dane was sure it was the Indian but he was already out of range. And it was foolish for him to try to overtake him. Likely Fass was better at that kind of fighting than Dane was, anyway.

He saw the other horse come up out of the ravine and gallop off to the north. Dane turned his horse to the southwest toward home. He had a lot of thinking to do.

There was nothing he could do now to help his parents except avenge their deaths. Even that would only help him, not them. But it was more than just revenge; it was self-preservation. If he didn't get them, they would surely kill him.

He didn't know whether Charity was dead or not. If she was alive, then he had to find her. But where would he look? Tennessee seemed like the logical place but Tubulo didn't seem to think she had gone there. He realized he was leaning heavily on Tubulo's judgment when most people wouldn't trust his opinion on anything.

Why would Charity go west, he thought. That was a big country out there with few places for a girl like Charity to go. If there was a clue as to where she had gone, it was bound to be right here around Alpha. He'd have to stay until he found it if there was anything to find.

He rode cautiously. That attempted ambush at the cemetery was proof enough that the Guards would stop at nothing to get rid of him. He knew he had to find a better place to hide out than the farm. They'd try again like they had last night. He wouldn't be lucky enough to escape detection again.

As he approached the farm from the northeast, he saw a horse standing in front of the little shed. His hand dropped again to the gun in his belt. He didn't trust anyone now.

He was almost within revolver range when a man stepped around the corner of the shed, apparently having just heard his approach. This wasn't the direction from which anyone would expect him to come.

Dane didn't recognize the man at first. He saw that he had no gun in sight so apparently he meant no harm. Then Dane suddenly tightened his grip on his gun as he recognized Atley Logar, the Indian trader. He looked very much as Dane remembered him. Small, sloppily dressed, a two day growth of whiskers on his face, his brown hair stuffed carelessly under his hat and his almost colorless eyes showing no expression.

"Been looking for you," Logar said amiably. "Heard about your barn being burned. Thought maybe I could give you a hand in getting settled."

Dane dismounted, never taking his eyes from Logar. "Didn't know you were interested in helping a Rebel get settled here."

"It's the least a neighbor can do for a war veteran, no matter which side he fought on."

Dane looked at Logar in disgust. Last night he had helped burn the barn and now he was offering to help him get settled. He wondered momentarily if he was a spy sent by Yockam. Maybe Yockam wanted to find out just what Dane intended to do. Well, he'd already told Yockam that. As he watched the trader, he realized that Logar was scared. He was trying to escape his share of the punishment for what the Guards had done by getting on the good side of Dane. Right now, Dane didn't think he had a good side. It had been destroyed by what he'd learned in the last twenty-four hours.

"If you want to help me," Dane said, "you can tell me what you know about the Home Guards."

"That was during the war," Logar said quickly. "They disbanded long ago."

"Who was in it?"

"Almost every Union man in the country," Logar said evasively.

"What do you know about Cheyenne Fass?"

"Nothing much," Logar said. "Half Cheyenne. That's why he's called Cheyenne."

Dane had the feeling there was a lot more about the half-breed that Logar could tell but he wasn't going to do it.

"What do you know about Charity?"

Logar shrugged but his veneer of good will was gone. He obviously hadn't expected to be asked a lot of questions.

"They say she went back to Tennessee."

"Is that what you think? Is she still alive?"

"I don't know. I haven't seen her since she left." He turned to his horse. "If there ain't anything I can do, I'd better get back to my own work."

Dane thought of asking him what work he had to do but decided against it. The quicker Atley Logar got out of his sight, the better he'd like it.

As he watched Logar ride away, he thought that he'd have to watch his back when he was around the man. Logar was scared. And a scared man was a very dangerous man.

CHAPTER 4

AS SOON AS ATLEY LOGAR WAS OUT OF SIGHT, DANE turned his attention to finding a place to hide out. Logar, at least, would expect him to be here at the farm. That's where he had found him.

Dane rode on to the creek and turned downstream. He recalled a cave in the bluffs about a mile below the farm. He had stumbled onto it one day when he'd been hunting for a couple of cows that had broken out of the pasture. If that cave was still there, he might make it his headquarters.

The creek rippled through the flat valley here by the farm. Trees lined the banks for ten to twenty yards on either side. Half a mile to the south it curved west until it hit a big bluff that turned it almost due east to meet a bigger creek that would carry it on to the Missouri River.

The cave Dane was looking for was in that big bluff. It wasn't easily seen from any distance and wouldn't be seen at all by a rider passing by on the other side of the creek.

A couple of hundred yards from the spot where he remembered the cave to be, Dane dismounted and tied his horse to a tree. Walking carefully so as to leave no tracks, he followed the creek, finally jumping the little stream.

He found the cave almost exactly as he remembered it. Brush still grew in front of its mouth, hiding it from view of anyone who didn't know where to look for it.

Dane went inside. The cave was dry and dark. He'd be as safe here as any place he could find.

He'd have to be careful about coming or going or someone would track him here. They were looking for him now. They'd be looking harder if he succeeded in the plan that was slowly taking shape in his mind.

Outside the cave, he went down to the creek, which was no more than ten yards in front of the cave mouth, and stepped into the shallow stream. The water was only two or three inches deep. He didn't like getting his feet wet but that was better than having his new hideout located.

Upstream a hundred yards, he stepped out on some rocks that lined the west side of the stream for quite a distance. The water he dripped there would soon evaporate.

Leaving the rocks, he followed a cattle path along the creek bank. Finally he jumped the stream and went to his horse. His hand dropped to his gun as he realized someone was with his horse. But it came away when he saw Tubulo.

"You sure have a way of bobbing up when you're not expected," Dane said.

"That's how I've lived so long and learned so much," Tubulo said with a grin. "Are you going to live in that cave?"

Dane frowned. "How did you know about the cave?"

"There ain't nothing along this creek I don't know about," Tubulo said. "If I was hiding out, that's where I'd stay."

"If you know about it, maybe Yockam or some of those other Guards know about it, too."

Tubulo shook his head. "Nobody ever goes there. I've never seen tracks. Keep your horse out of sight and don't leave tracks. They won't find you."

It was Dane's turn to grin. "Hard to track a man in a creek."

Tubulo nodded. "Good idea. Wet feet won't kill you. Bullets will."

"What do you know about the Indian, Fass, and Logar?" Dane asked. "Logar met me today. He acted like there was something between him and the Indian."

"Maybe there is," Tubulo said. "I heard that Fass is

really Logar's son."

Dane frowned. "I didn't know Logar ever had anything to do with the Cheyenne Indians."

Tubulo shrugged, a characteristic hunch of his small shoulders. "He trades with the Kiowas. They're closer. Fass came here to Alpha just a short time after you left. He said his mother told him his father lived here. He must have been seventeen or eighteen then."

"Didn't he know who his father was?"

"Apparently not. Probably his mother didn't know the real name of his father. Anyway, nobody claimed him and it was Logar who suggested the name Cheyenne for him."

"Is he Cheyenne?"

Tubulo shook his head. "He's Kiowa. He knows it but he doesn't care what they call him. I heard that Fass stole things from his own tribe. He had his choice of taking the tribe's punishment or coming to live with the whites." Tubulo shrugged. "I'll bet the Kiowas think Logan's name is Fass."

Dane was amazed at the amount of information that Tubulo had collected. Prowling the country day and night, he apparently eavesdropped a lot. People might call him a half-wit but Dane wouldn't.

"This is no place to be loafing," Tubulo said, looking around nervously. "You are in greater danger than you were yesterday."

Dane nodded. "Do you know anything at all about Charity?"

"Only what I told you."

"Can you find out anything?"

"There ain't nothing to find out," Tubulo said. "She's been gone for four years. Now you be careful and keep out of sight."

Like a shadow he was gone, disappearing into the trees. Dane led his horse across the stream. In a little notch in the bluffs, he found a tiny meadow with good grass. He remembered the spot because the Banning cows came here often when they got out of the pasture. It always had good grass.

Staking his horse out on the long picket rope he carried, he took his bedroll and supplies and made his way to the creek. Crossing the rocks, he stepped into the water and waded down to the mouth of the cave.

While he was spreading his blankets inside the cave back a short distance from the mouth, he thought of what Tubulo had told him. He was amazed. He doubted if anything important had happened around Alpha in the last few years that Tubulo didn't know. Tubulo lived on the other side of Alpha with his parents. But he was considered too dim-witted to be of any use to anyone.

Tubulo said no one knew anything about Charity, however. Dane couldn't accept that. Someone must know something. If she was alive, he intended to find her, regardless of the odds against him.

Suddenly he thought of Margaret Wieland. Margaret and Bruce lived only a mile north of the Banning farm. And Charity and Margaret had been the best of friends. If Charity had let anyone around Alpha know where she was, it would be Margaret. It was the one stone still unturned. Likely Margaret would know no more about Charity than anyone else in the country but he had to find out. Once convinced that there was no trace of Charity to be found here he'd concentrate on avenging the murder of his parents, then he'd search for Charity until he either found her or found proof that she was dead.

He stepped to the mouth of the cave and watched the

last glow of sunlight on the trees across the creek from the cave. It was already deep shadow at the front of the cave. He'd get the early light from the rising sun in the morning.

He got his supper from the provisions in his sack but he ate it cold. He didn't want to risk a fire. Then he waited until it got too dark out in the valley to see anything. It was time to go. As much as he hated to walk in the water, he stepped into it and waded upstream until he reached the rocks. It wasn't far from there to the cave where he'd picketed his horse.

Saddling the horse, he rode north in the water for a hundred yards then along the creek, keeping to the trees, to a spot opposite the Wieland farm. He had been past here this morning on his way from the Martin farm to the cemetery.

As he dismounted by the barn, he wondered if the Wielands still lived here. So many people had moved; maybe the Wielands had, too.

Crossing the yard, he disturbed a dog that somehow had failed to hear his horse come up from the trees along the creek. His barking announced Dane's presence.

When he knocked on the door, it opened a foot and a woman peered out. She was standing between the lamp on the table and Dane so that her shadow fell on his face.

"I'm Dane Banning," he said. "Is this the Wielands?"

He heard the woman gasp. "It can't be," she whispered.

"Margaret?" he asked.

The woman nodded then slowly backed away so that the light fell on Dane's face. "What—how—we thought you were dead."

"Not yet," he said. "May I come in?"

She stepped back further, nodding. He moved inside and out of the doorway so that he wasn't silhouetted against the light.

There was a man just finishing his supper and two children had just gotten down from the table and now they ran to their father's side as he stood up to face Dane. They all stared at him as if he were unreal.

"I'm not a ghost," Dane said, trying to grin. "Like everyone else around here, I suppose you heard that I was dead."

Margaret Wieland nodded again. "A letter came to your father long after he was dead saying that you had died in a prison camp."

"Did you see the letter?" Dane asked.

"Yes. Mr. Skyrock had it. The post office is in his store, you know."

Dane nodded. "I wish I could see that letter. When did it come?"

"Just a short time before the end of the war."

"I was at Fort Kearny in Nebraska then," Dane said. "Not long after that I was sent to Fort Laramie and the next spring we went up the Bozeman Trail to help establish the forts there."

"How could the army have gotten so mixed up?" Bruce Wieland asked.

"I doubt if the army did," Dane said. "I think that letter was a fake. Certain people intended to make sure that I never got back home. They wanted everyone to forget what happened here in the. summer of '64."

"When did you find out about that?" Margaret asked.

"After I got back here yesterday," Dane said. "I hadn't had a word from anybody since the summer of '63 just before Gettysburg. But I thought the mail just

36

wasn't getting through. When I got out of the army, I wrote that I was coming home. That was over a year ago."

"I thought you just got here yesterday," Margaret said.

"I was ambushed in Illinois on my way home and left for dead. I had no idea then why anybody would try to kill me. Now I know. Was anyone gone from Alpha in April of last year?"

Bruce frowned. "That's so long ago, it's hard to remember. People visit relatives now and then or go to Kansas City on business. Lon Yockam goes to Kansas City two or three times a year."

"Last April he probably went on to Illinois," Dane said. "I came to ask if you know anything about Charity. All I can find out is that she just disappeared. Since you were her best friend, Margaret, I thought she might have contacted you."

Tears dampened Margaret's eyelashes. "We—we can't tell you anything."

"You mean you're afraid to tell me anything," Dane corrected. "Yockam seems to have this entire community treed."

"We tried to remain neutral in the war, you know," Bruce said. "So I guess we were lucky to have been allowed to stay. Most of those who were Southerners, like the Martins, were run out." Going to the window, he looked out into the darkness. "Where did you leave your horse?"

"On the other side of the barn," Dane said. "I won't stay long. I've seen what Yockam does to those who oppose him."

"I'm not exactly a coward," Bruce Wieland said. "But I do have a wife and two kids to think of."

"I'll go as soon as I ask some questions," Dane said. "If Charity is still alive, I've got to find her. Do you know if she is alive or dead?"

Margaret turned to her husband. "It's time to put the youngsters to bed, Bruce. Will you do it?"

"Sure," he said and led the two children into the next room.

Dane didn't miss the significance of that. His hopes rose a little. Margaret must have something to say about Charity. It might not be good news but it would be something.

When the children had disappeared, Margaret turned back to Dane. "I don't know whether Charity is alive or not. I've laid awake many nights wondering about it. But I did get one letter from her after she left."

Dane's hopes soared. "Then she did get away."

Margaret nodded. "I'll tell you all I know. Then you must leave. We all thought that Charity was dead when we heard that Bull and Mary Banning had been murdered. Then a couple of weeks later, I got a letter. It was from Charity but the envelope's return said Sue Flagler."

Dane nodded. "If she'd used her own name, Skyrock would never have let the letter get to you."

"Until I got that letter," Margaret said, "I had no idea that Ed Skyrock was involved in the murders. Charity said that Kurt Uhl took her from the house before the Guards burned it. He carried her off to the Martin place which was vacant then. When Uhl left, he tied her up, then locked the house. She knew of a tunnel from a trap door in the floor to an outside pit that her father had dug so he could fight off Indians if they attacked. She got out of the ropes and escaped through that tunnel."

"Does anyone know you got that letter?" Dane asked.

38

"Goodness, no," Margaret said. "We'd be killed if they knew that."

"Did she sign her own name?"

"In the letter, she did," Margaret said. "Not even the children know about that letter; they might let it slip. Charity said she would never use her real name again. She wouldn't bring disgrace on the Martin or Banning names."

"She hasn't disgraced either name!" Dane said sharply. "But Charity would think of that. She will be hard to find if she's using another name."

"She said she didn't ever want to be found. She was going to disappear forever."

"Even from me?" Dane asked."

"She said you wouldn't ever want to see or touch her again," Margaret said.

Dane bit his lip. "Where was the letter mailed?"

"Topeka. But I don't think she planned to stay there. She's gone, Dane. All we can do is hope that life isn't treating her too bad."

"I'm going to find her if she's alive. I don't care what has happened or what she has done." He turned to the door, then stopped. "I saw the headboards in the cemetery. Did you put them up?"

"Bruce and I did. It was the least we could do for good friends. We'll take yours down."

"Better wait a while," Dane said. "You may need to change the date, nothing else. Thanks for telling me, Margaret."

Dane slipped across the yard to his horse and rode him back into the trees and down the creek to the little cove where he lariated him again for the night. Wading back to the cave, he crawled into his blankets but he couldn't sleep.

He wouldn't believe that Charily was dead. Yockam or Uhl might have trailed her and killed her. But if they hadn't, he'd find her. Margaret had said she had written that she didn't want to see anyone she knew again. That would rule out Tennessee. Then where would she go?

One thing was clear. Yockam was no longer Dane's first target. Kurt Uhl had earned that honor. Dane would get a great satisfaction in slowly choking the life from him.

Dawn found Dane tired but determined to start reaping the revenge due him. After a quick breakfast, he waded up to the cove to get his horse. He stopped just after leaving the rocks where he waded out of the stream. There were tracks there.

Studying the tracks, he could almost picture the half-breed, apparently as good at tracking as his Indian brothers were. Fass had trailed Dane to the rocks. How long before he found the cave?

CHAPTER 5

DANE STEPPED BACK INTO THE TREES AND STUDIED the area, his hand on his gun. If Fass had tracked him this far, he might be waiting somewhere to ambush him.

Satisfied at last that Fass was not here, he moved on cautiously toward the cove where he had staked out his horse. If Fass had found the horse, he likely had taken him. Tubulo had said that he was a thief.

Reaching the cove, he saw his horse peacefully cropping the grass. Fass had not found this nook. Saddling up, Dane mounted and rode out into the stream, keeping to the water where he'd leave no tracks leading to the little cove where he kept his horse.

Leaving the stream, he followed the road between two fields. He'd have to deal with Fass soon or he wouldn't live to take care of the other Home Guards on his list. Heading that list now was Kurt Uhl. It had been Uhl who had taken Charity from the Banning home and he'd pay for that as soon as Dane could find him.

Uhl's father had built the blacksmith shop in Alpha and when he died, his son had continued the work. Dane had seen the blacksmith shop two days ago when he'd ridden through Alpha. But at that time, it meant nothing to him. It did now.

The awkward bulge in his waistband where the gun rested bothered him. If he was going to protect himself and settle accounts with the five Guards, he needed a better way to carry the gun. He also needed a more convenient place to carry his cartridges than having them loose in his pocket.

He swung his horse to the north toward the road running into town from the west. He didn't want to go past the blacksmith shop and alert Kurt Uhl that he was in town. Uhl was a coward; he might sneak away if he knew Dane was close.

He stopped on the north side of Skyrock's store and tied his horse where wagon teams were usually hitched. Walking around to the east front of the store, he glanced along the street. It was almost deserted this early in the day. The only person in the store was Ed Skyrock.

Skyrock's eyes widened when he saw Dane. Dane moved up to the counter, watching Skyrock closely. His hands were at his side but they were also below the level of the counter. A gun could be under that counter.

"I need a holster to go with that gun I bought," Dane said. He lifted the gun out of his waistband.

Skyrock stepped back when Dane touched the gun. If

Skyrock were Kurt Uhl, he'd use that gun, Dane thought. Uhl didn't deserve a fair fight. He certainly hadn't given Charity that option. But Skyrock wasn't Uhl.

"The holsters are back at the next counter," Skyrock said, his voice almost breaking.

He turned that way and Dane followed. Several holsters were hanging on the wall behind the case containing the guns. Dane picked one, tested it, and buckled it around his waist. The gun worked well in it. He paid Skyrock for the holster and went back outside. He didn't expect Skyrock to shoot him in the back.

Getting his horse, he rode down the street toward the blacksmith shop, just south of the feed store and across the street from the livery barn. The door was open so he guessed that Kurt Uhl must be at work. Dane remembered him as a big man. He'd been about twenty-one then. He wasn't likely to be any smaller now.

Reining up in front of the blacksmith shop, Dane dismounted, leaving the reins trailing, and stepped to the open door. He heard a hammer drop on an anvil in the gloomy interior.

Then Dane saw Uhl disappearing through the back door as his eyes adjusted to the semi-darkness of the shop's interior. He was even bigger than Dane remembered, bigger than Dane and Dane considered himself a big man. Uhl was bareheaded as he dived through the back door, his black hair long enough to flutter in the breeze he was creating.

Dane ran through the shop, stumbling over some iron that he didn't see. There was a window by the anvil and forge but only the doors lighted the rest of the building.

Dane was cautious as he went through the back door. Uhl must have heard that Dane was suspicious of

42

Yockam and Skyrock and guessed that he'd been tied in with the crime, too. Being the coward that he was, he was not likely to stay around and find out what Dane wanted.

The back yard was empty. Dane didn't see how Uhl could have disappeared so quickly. Uhl's house stood half a block away to the east but Dane didn't see him in that direction, either. He must have ducked around the corner of the shop itself.

Dane went around the shop but he saw no sign of the big blacksmith. After circling the shop, he turned to the livery barn, still with no luck. He came back and looked around the blacksmith shop once more. Whether Uhl had left town or just ducked out of sight, it was obvious that he didn't intend to let Dane find him.

Mounting his horse, he rode back up the street. Thinking that Uhl might have taken refuge in Yockam's saloon which was the first door south of the marshal's office, Dane dismounted in front of the saloon. Yockam and Uhl had been close friends before the war, even though Kurt Uhl was about five years younger than Lon Yockam.

Dane knew the risk he was taking going into the saloon. But he was depending on the fact that none of his enemies, including Yockam, would risk killing him right here in Alpha where so many people could witness it. Yockam held the town under his thumb but there surely was a limit to what he could do and not stir up a rebellion that he couldn't put down.

The saloon was as quiet as the rest of the town. A man was swamping the floor and the bartender was polishing some glasses behind the bar. There were no customers.

The back door of the saloon opened and Yockam

43

came in. He stopped short at sight of Dane then he came steadily forward until he was within a few feet of him.

"You're thirsty pretty early in the day, aren't you?" he asked testily.

"Not thirsty at all," Dane said. "I stopped at the shop to see Kurt Uhl and he ducked out on me. Thought he might have come in here."

Yockam's eyes flipped toward the bartender and the man with the mop then came back to Dane. "He hasn't been in here all morning. He does his drinking in the evening."

Dane looked at the bartender. "Haven't you had any customers yet today?"

The bartender shook his head, looking at Yockam. Dane saw the two exchange glances. He didn't know what it meant but he knew he was treading on risky ground. He was off the street now and there were no witnesses. If he was killed in the saloon, Yockam could claim self defense. Not even those who secretly sided with Dane could question that.

"I'd suggest you get out of this country as fast as you know how," Yockam said finally. "This ain't a healthy climate for a Banning."

"I thought I might try to change that climate a little," Dane said but he stepped back to the front door.

Yockam's eyes dropped to the holstered gun on Dane's hip. Dane's fingers were only inches away from the butt of that gun. Yockam apparently didn't miss that, either.

"You're lucky, Dane," he said. "I don't usually give warnings."

"So I've heard," Dane said. "Even a rattler gives a warning."

"And he usually gets his head mashed in for his

trouble," Yockam said. "You've heard the rattle now. You can leave or stay permanently."

Dane met Yockam eye to eye. "If I stay permanently, you will, too. Just tell your barkeep that."

Yockam flipped a glance at the bartender then looked back at Dane. "Your choice."

Dane felt he had pushed his luck to the absolute limit. He was gaining nothing by this confrontation. If it came to guns, he might kill Yockam. But that bartender would get him. He likely had a shotgun under the bar.

Dane took two swift steps backward and was on the porch of the saloon. He backed to his horse, keeping his eyes on the door but nobody came through and no shot followed him. Reaching his horse, he mounted and reined him down the street, kicking him into a lope.

He realized he was nearing a showdown with Lon Yockam. That wasn't the way he wanted to do it. A shoot-out with Yockam could very well be the last thing he ever did. He wanted to be sure that Uhl died before he did.

He was still thinking about Uhl and Yockam when he reached the trees along the creek. Catching a movement in the trees, he threw himself from his saddle. No shot sounded and he wondered if it had been Tubulo he had seen. Or maybe it had been a bird or a squirrel.

Leaving his horse, he circled cautiously into the trees. It might be the half-breed, Fass. He had been down close to the cave last night, he might be trying to ambush him today.

Dane moved as stealthily as a vapor until he caught sight of Fass creeping toward Dane's horse, apparently not having seen Dane move away from the animal. Dane inched forward, wondering if he could keep Fass from hearing him. He couldn't bring himself to shoot the

Indian without warning, even though he was sure the Indian would do that to him if the positions were reversed.

When the Indian passed close to Dane, his attention was still on the horse which was moving around nervously as if aware of danger. Leaping like a cougar, his gun in his hand, Dane covered the ten feet between him and Fass in one jump. Fass wheeled but too late to protect himself.

Dane's weight mashed the half-breed to the ground and Dane grabbed Fass's gun hand, pinning it down. The Indian struggled mightily for a moment then re-laxed. Dane was not fooled. If he eased up, Fass would explode with all his strength and upend him.

Bringing his own gun around until the muzzle was pressed against Fass's throat, he said softly, "Drop your gun. You're plain lucky I didn't shoot you on sight."

There was a trace of fear in the Indian's dark eyes but it couldn't override the hatred there. Nevertheless, he let the gun slip out of his fingers.

"Why did you join the Home Guards?" Dane demanded.

The Indian glared at Dane sullenly. "Because they asked me to."

"What were you doing in Alpha, anyway?"

"My father was here. My mother said so. I came to live with him."

"Who is he?"

Fass scowled. "I don't know. There's nobody here named Fass."

"What would you do if you found him now?"

The Indian breathed heavily. "He'd have to pay for not claiming me," Fass said. His eyes fastened on Dane. "Do you know who he is?"

"Ask Logar."

"Atley Logar!" Fass hissed. "Indian trader! It's Logar?"

It was more of a statement than a question. Fass had apparently recognized a connection he hadn't thought of before. Dane suddenly saw a chance to get Logar run out of the country without having to do it himself.

"I'm going to turn you loose," he said. "But the next time you try to kill me will be your last."

The Indian glared at him without saying a word. Dane reached over and pushed Fass's gun out of his reach then moved back himself, keeping his gun centered on him. Fass got up slowly, watching Dane like a trapped weasel. Dane followed him to his horse and watched him ride north.

Dane waited until he was gone then he mounted and rode down the creek, finally turning into the water and going on to the little cove where he kept his horse.

Picketing his horse in the grassy nook, Dane went on to his cave. He saw no tracks along the bank as he waded in the creek. Nobody had found the cave yet.

Sitting on his blankets, he considered his day. He had let Uhl escape. He had backed off from a confrontation with Yockam. He had let the half-breed, Fass, go free. But he'd had a reason for letting Fass go. He might run Logar out. Besides, he didn't hate Fass like he did Uhl or Yockam. He couldn't believe Fass had any personal hatred for the Bannings like the other men had. As a thief, belonging to the Home Guards had been a convenience.

He wished he could talk to Tubulo. The little man might have an idea where to look for Charity if he knew what Margaret Wieland had told Dane.

Topeka might be the place to start if Charity was

47

determined to drop out of sight, she wouldn't mail her letter from a town where she intended to stay. And four years would be a long time for people to remember.

She would be a girl easy to remember, Dane thought, recalling her flowing red hair and bright blue eyes. Closing his own eyes, he could picture her smooth skin and features and that quick smile that always appeared when he came around. That memory had sustained him through six long years. Now it was farther from his reach than ever before.

Dane wandered up and down the creek in the afternoon, keeping in the water, watching for any movement near his hideout. Nothing stirred, however, and he went back to his cave to plan tomorrow's moves. He was fretting to get on the trail of Charity. But first he had to deal with the Guards.

Sunrise found him out of the cave and over in the cove with his horse. Today he was going to begin his vengeful task. Uhl first, Yockam next and then Logar. He didn't feel such hatred toward Skyrock, even though he had been on the raid. And Fass was an outsider so far as Dane's concentrated hate was concerned.

Today Dane rode straight up the road from the south toward Uhl's blacksmith shop. But before he reached town, he noticed the activity in the street more than he'd seen since the news reached the town that Fort Sumter had been fired upon back in April of '61.

He rode forward more cautiously until he reached the blacksmith shop. The door was closed. Uhl wasn't here. Maybe he was up the street where all the excitement seemed to be.

Riding slowly forward, he reached the edge of the crowd in the street between Skyrock's store and the marshal's office.

"What's wrong?" Dane asked a man just in front of his horse.

"The marshal found Atley Logar's body in the alley behind his office this morning," the man said excitedly. "Stabbed and scalped."

Dane absorbed that news. He didn't question who had done it. He had seen the look in the half-breed's eyes yesterday when he'd suggested that Logar might know who his father was.

"Didn't anybody hear anything?" Dane asked.

"Oh, he wasn't killed here," the man said. "He was killed somewhere else and dragged in and dumped behind the marshal's office sometime in the night."

"Know who did it or why? And why was he scalped?"

The man shrugged. "No idea. Some think it might have been that half-breed, Cheyenne Fass."

Dane nodded. Just then Yockam spotted Dane from the porch of the marshal's office. He pointed a finger at him.

"Where were you last night, Banning?" he shouted.

"Sound asleep," Dane said.

"Maybe you killed Logar."

"What reason would I have?" Dane asked.

Yockam started to say something then clamped his mouth shut. He had almost given himself away, Dane thought.

Dane saw Skyrock in the crowd. He was talking earnestly to some other men and looking at Dane. Dane guessed what he was doing. Dane was like a foreigner to the newcomers here. And to the others, he represented trouble because of Yockam and their fear of him. Dane knew a mob might be whipped up in a flash.

49

CHAPTER 6

"I HEARD LOGAR SAY DANE BANNING WAS AFTER him," Skyrock shouted.

Heads nodded around Skyrock. Dane switched his eyes to Yockam. He wouldn't pass up a chance like this.

"I heard that, too," Yockam shouted. "Nobody else had any reason to kill Logar. It had to be Banning. Who will he kill next?"

"Just give me one reason why I would kill Logar?" Dane challenged.

Dane knew that Yockam and Skyrock could give a valid reason. But they wouldn't.

One man in the crowd turned on Yockam. "He's got a point. Tell us why he would kill Logar."

Yockam stalled. If he told them that Logar had helped murder Dane's parents, they'd know that he had taken part in that raid, too. There was no other way that he could know that Logar had been there. Yockam had put the fear into every man, woman, and child who had lived here in 1864 but he didn't have that grip on the newcomers.

While the people focused their attention on Yockam, waiting for his answer, Dane inched his horse around and headed him down the alley south of Skyrock's store. He intended to be far from here before Yockam found a way to get the people excited enough to string him up.

Apparently Uhl was not in town today. He hadn't been in that crowd. There was no way that Uhl could hide his six-foot-four-inch frame in a crowd.

Dane put his horse to a gallop once he was out of town, heading down the road past Wieland's farm to the trees along the creek. As he faded into the trees, he realized that this refuge for him also offered a perfect place for an enemy to lay an ambush. He couldn't forget how close he had come to being bushwhacked yesterday by Cheyenne Fass.

Thinking back to the crowd in the street in front of the marshal's office, he didn't remember seeing Fass there. If he wasn't there, he might be here in these trees waiting for Dane.

Turning south along the creek, he let his horse take its time. He wasn't on the run yet. He didn't think Atley Logar was a popular man so it would be harder to work up a mob to avenge him than if he had been one of the outstanding citizens of the community. Nevertheless, he couldn't overlook the possibility that Yockam, with his grip on so many people, could work up a mob that would come looking for Dane.

He kept his eyes roaming the trees ahead, watching for any movement that might warn of danger. But nothing stirred. Likely Cheyenne Fass was staying out of sight and not thinking about another killing just yet.

Reaching the area of the little cove, Dane put his horse into the creek then brought him out even with the grassy notch in the cliff wall where he kept the horse.

But as he reined his horse into the cove he was aware that he was not alone. His hand dropped to his gun but then Tubulo stepped out into the open. Dane let his breath out in a gush and his hand pulled back to the horn of the saddle.

"You can get shot by surprising people that way," Dane said.

"Didn't figure on you being quite so jumpy," Tubulo said. "Where have you been?"

"Went to town to find Kurt Uhl but I didn't see him."

51

"You ought to know better than to ride into town when things would be steamed up like they are today."

"How was I to know there would be such an uproar?" Dane asked, swinging off his horse.

"A killing always stirs people up," Tubulo said.

"Especially one like this where the murdered man is scalped. Why did you scalp him?"

"Me?" Dane exclaimed. "I didn't even know he was dead till I got to town."

Tubulo studied Dane's face. "Maybe I figured wrong. After I told you who was in that murdering party four years ago, I just guessed that Logar was your first victim." He shook his head. "If you didn't kill him, who did?"

Dane watched the twitching of Tubulo's face as he tried to readjust his conclusions. "Make a guess about that, too."

Tubulo seemed lost in thought then his face brightened. "Cheyenne Fass. There's enough Indian in him to scalp Logar. He believes that a man without a scalp can't go to the Happy Hunting Ground."

Dane nodded. "You're on the right track, I told Fass he should ask Logar about his father."

Tubulo nodded. "That would do it." He turned a deep frown on Dane. "When did you have a chance to tell Fass anything?"

"Yesterday. He was laying for me but I spotted him first. Jumped him and got him down. I was sitting on him when we had our little talk."

Tubulo nodded. "That's about the only safe way to talk to him."

"Where were you yesterday?" Dane asked.

"I was watching what was going on." Tubulo shook his head. "I must be getting careless. I missed what Fass

52

was up to." He looked hard at Dane. "You've got to be mighty careful. Fass loves to kill. You have dodged his ambush twice. That will be like a challenge to him."

Dane nodded. "I figured as much."

"He won't thank you for telling him about Logar. So don't rest easy because of that."

"Do you think he'll find that cave?"

Tubulo nodded. "It's just a matter of time unless you stop him first."

"I'll keep that in mind," Dane said. "I talked to Margaret Wieland yesterday. She told me she had a letter from Charity mailed at Topeka. So she got away from this country alive. Where do you figure she would go from Topeka?"

Tubulo shook his head. "No telling. But how did Mrs. Wieland get a letter from Charity? Ed Skyrock would have seen that letter in the post office and he would never have let it go through."

"Charity didn't use her own name" Dane explained.

"That was smart. Did she mention Tennessee?"

"She said she was going to just disappear from everyone she knew."

"Must have been heading west," Tubulo guessed. "I heard Yockam say one day that half the people west of Hays was using names they wasn't born with. Anybody can lose himself out there."

Hearing Tubulo confirm his own conclusions added strength to Dane's resolve to go west in search of Charity.

"You've got to watch your step as long as Fass is alive," Tubulo warned. "There ain't nothing he won't do to get you if he has his mind set on it."

Tubulo stepped back into the trees and vanished. Dane had the weird feeling that Tubulo could make himself invisible in an open field if he wanted to.

Picketing his horse, Dane moved down to the creek, walking carefully until he reached the rocks then stepped off into the water and waded to the front of the cave. Tubulo was probably right. Eventually Fass would find the cave. He knew that Dane was hiding out somewhere in this vicinity. His tracks along the creek proved that. And yesterday he'd tried to ambush him not far from here.

Going into the cave, Dane studied the situation. He could see no way to protect himself without staying awake twenty-four hours a day. He had to rig up some kind of defense or else go after Fass, determined to kill before he was killed.

From the spot where he had his blankets, he could control the mouth of the cave if he were awake. Perhaps if he moved to one side into that little pocket in the wall of the cave, he would be safe from a frontal attack. But he would still need some warning. Fass had all the stealth of his Indian ancestors. None of the others would track him to the cave, he was sure. Why not? They tried burning him in the barn.

If he had another gun, he could rig it up to fire from that area while he was somewhere else. But he didn't have another gun. Suddenly he remembered the gun he had knocked out of Fass's hand yesterday when they were struggling. He had intended to pick that up but in making sure that Fass left the area without doubling back, he had forgotten it.

Moving to the front of the cave, he checked the area then went down to the stream and waded up to the rocks. It took him only a few minutes to get to the spot where he had pinned Fass to the ground yesterday. But the gun was not there. He searched the area but he couldn't locate it anywhere. Fass must have come back and gotten it.

He had probably wanted it before he confronted Atley Logar. But he hadn't used a gun on Logar. He had stabbed him and then scalped him. Dane had the feeling that Fass was handier with a knife than a gun, anyway.

Dane sat down on the rotted trunk of a fallen tree and thought over his problem. He had settled on the idea of a fixed man in the cave and he didn't like to give it up. But he had to have another gun.

He recalled that after the Bannings came to Kansas, the gunsmith in Alpha had given Dane an old gun. It was in working order and he had taken it into these very trees and tried to shoot birds with it.

But he had found no joy in killing birds. The thrill of hunting was just not in him. He wondered what had happened to that old gun.

He had kept it in the little shed behind the house. It suddenly hit him that it might still be there. The shed was the only building still standing on the farm. It was worth investigating.

He headed for the cove to get his horse. In a few minutes he was riding him up the stream, finally turning him out of the water onto the path that led to the farm.

Near the shed, he checked the area carefully. Anybody looking for him would surely not overlook the possibility that he might be at the home place. Seeing no movement anywhere, he dismounted and went to the shed.

Inside, he began pushing the debris around. The old sacks he had used to cover himself the other night were just as he had left them. He pushed them over into the corner where he had been sleeping. Underneath, he found a bucket full of bolts and burs he and his father had used to repair their few pieces of machinery.

He reached back under the crude bench on one side of the shed. His memory guided his hand to the spot where he had kept the gun. His fingers touched the cold metal and he lifted the old gun out into the open.

It looked usable but it was dirty. He'd have to clean it. He checked it to see if the hammer would cock. It did.

When he began looking for the ammunition for the old gun, he was disappointed. Maybe he hadn't had any when he left for the army. Or maybe something had happened to it. He tried a cartridge from his belt but it didn't fit. This was a .44 and the revolver and ammunition he had bought was .45 caliber.

He made a thorough search of the shed before he gave up. He didn't find any cartridges for the gun but he did find his old skinning knife. He had always liked knives but he had done nothing more lethal with one than skin a rabbit his father had killed for dinner.

Taking the knife and gun, he went back to his horse. He could get ammunition at the store. But remembering the way things had been when he'd left town earlier this morning, he didn't consider it wise to go back to town just yet.

Riding back to the river, he retraced his path to the little nook where he lariated his horse in the lush grass. He headed down to the creek. Just before he reached the rocky shelf along the river bank, he was stopped by Tubulo who seemed to appear out of nowhere to confront him.

"You'd better be careful about riding around in the open like that," Tubulo warned. "There are four men around here who want you dead. And there may be a lot more who would feel more comfortable if you were."

"I went to get this gun," Dane explained, showing Tubulo the gun. "I've got an idea how to outwit Fass if he does find the cave. But I don't have any ammunition for it. I'll have to go to Skyrock's to get some."

Tubulo frowned. "That ain't going to be safe." He thought for a moment. "Skyrock opens his store about seven every morning. I'll meet you in the trees west of Wieland's place about that time tomorrow morning. I'll tell you then whether it looks safe for you to go to town or not."

Dane grinned. "You're my guardian angel, Tubulo. Just be careful that they don't make a real angel out of you."

"I take care of myself better than you do," Tubulo said.

He turned and within ten feet was out of sight. Dane went on to his cave, careful to avoid leaving any tracks. It might take days for the town to settle down so he could slip in and get the needed ammunition. He'd have to hope Fass didn't find his cave in the meantime.

He spent an hour cleaning the old gun until he was sure it would work. Then he turned his thoughts to Uhl. Would he be back at his blacksmith shop tomorrow? Or had he yielded to his cowardly impulses and left town altogether? If Uhl was gone, Dane wouldn't go after him now. If he was going to look for anybody it would be Charity. Even if she had gone west, could he ever find her? Would she be alive after four years of a rough life alone? Maybe she had remarried, thinking that he was dead. Or maybe she no longer cared whether he was alive or dead. The thoughts did little to make sleep easy for him.

True to his word, Tubulo met Dane at the edge of the trees two miles north of the cave the next morning a

57

little before seven.

"The town quieted down yesterday," Tubulo reported. "Not many people believed Yockam when he said you had killed Logar. But you'd better get in and out of town before many people are stirring around."

"What about Uhl? Is he there?"

"Didn't see him," Tubulo said. "I'll check it out. Don't you hang around town looking for him."

"I won't waste any time," Dane promised.

He put his horse to a fast trot along the road that took him past Wieland's and into town from the west. He dismounted on the north side of the store and stepped around to the front, quickly disappearing into the interior.

Skyrock saw him and cringed back as if expecting Dane to pull his gun and shoot him. Dane motioned to the ammunition case.

"I want some .44 ammunition."

"I thought that was a .45 I sold you," Skyrock said, relaxing a little when he saw that Dane wasn't going to kill him.

"There's more than one kind of gun in the world," Dane said. "Let's have that ammunition."

"You bet," Skyrock said and almost fell over himself getting out a box of ammunition.

Dane opened the box and took out a cartridge, broke open his gun, and shoved the shell into the chamber. It fit exactly.

Paying for the ammunition, he backed toward the door. He had seen the wild fear in Skyrock's face. A scared man was the most dangerous kind, Dane reminded himself.

Once outside the store, Dane ducked around the corner, mounted his horse, and put him to a lope out of

58

town to the west. If there had been a trap laid for him in town, he hadn't been there long enough for anyone to spring it.

With his horse staked out in the grassy nook in the bluff, he headed for the rocky bank of the creek.

As he passed under the last trees before hitting the rocky ledge, his eyes were ahead of his path, looking for an ambush. He didn't see the rope loop on the ground until he stepped into it. That triggered the release on a long, bent-down branch and the rope pulled tight on his leg and jerked upward. In an instant, Dane found himself dangling by one foot, head down, five feet off the ground.

His first thought, even before the tree limb stopped bobbing up and down, was that Fass had laid the trap. He was likely waiting somewhere near to kill him. He'd take his time doing it, too. Dane had tabbed Fass as the sadistic kind who would get all the pleasure he could out of a grizzly job like this.

He heard footsteps coming softly toward him but his back was to the sound and he couldn't turn himself to see who it was.

CHAPTER 7

DANE FELT THE SWEAT BREAK OUT ON HIS FOREHEAD as he listened to the soft footsteps come closer. Any second he expected to feel the slash of a knife. He was high enough off the ground that only his head and shoulders would be within range of a man on the ground wielding a knife.

Fass might scalp him before he killed him or maybe use him for arrow target practice. In his agony of

59

suspense, Dane could think of more ways of torture than an Indian would.

Then suddenly the footsteps stopped just below and a little behind him. Dane tried desperately to turn himself.

"Got yourself into a mess, didn't you?"

Dane's breath exploded from his lungs. Tubulo!

"Where's Fass?" he demanded. "He'll be here to kill me any second."

"Not that soon," Tubulo said. "I saw him just a couple of minutes ago out near your old place. He apparently was waiting for you to come back from wherever you went so he could follow you here and see if he caught you in his trap. Only you didn't come down the road he expected you to."

"How am I going to get down?" Dane asked. The blood was running to his head and both his vision and thinking were becoming blurred.

"I'll go up the tree and cut you loose. Be ready to break your fall when you hit the ground."

Tubulo was gone then. Dane heard him scrambling up the tree trunk. Then he came into his upside down vision. He was moving out on the small limb where the rope was fastened. His weight bent the limb a little lower. He had a hunting knife in his hand. Dane spread his hands, ready to catch himself and roll when he hit the ground.

Tubulo cut the rope and Dane landed on his shoulders, only partially breaking the fall with his hands. By the time he had the rope off his leg, Tubulo was down out of the tree. He shuffled over to Dane.

"Break anything in your fall?" he asked.

Dane shook his head. "Hardly felt it. You saved my neck again, Tubulo. We'd better clear out before Fass shows up."

Tubulo nodded. "You've got some rope to use now."

They moved off into a thicket of smaller trees. Dane watched for Fass. It was no longer a game of hide and seek. It was Fass's life or his. That rope trap left no doubt.

"Did you find out anything about Uhl?" Dane asked, realizing even as he asked that Tubulo hadn't had time to go to town since he had talked to him this morning in the trees west of Wieland's.

"Sure," Tubulo said. "I saw Bruce Wieland out doing chores and I asked him. He was in town yesterday. Kurt Uhl has closed up his blacksmith shop and just disappeared."

"Did Bruce hear anything else?"

"Nothing special. He said that Skyrock and Yockam tried to stir up a posse to go out and run you down. But nobody would go. Some thought maybe you had killed Logar but nobody could come up with a reason so they just let it die. Nobody liked Logar much, anyway."

"Tubulo, you're the best friend a man could have."

Tubulo grinned. "Everybody says I'm an idiot. I just let them think it. That way they ain't careful what they say around me."

"Fass ought to be coming to check his trap."

"Even if he does come, you ain't liable to see him," Tubulo said. "He won't just walk out under that tree to see what happened to his rope. Once he sees it is gone, he'll never show himself."

Dane nodded. "Reckon that's right. I'm going to the cave and rig up this extra gun so I'll have some warning if he finds my cave while I'm asleep."

"I hope it works," Tubulo said. "He's tracked you this far; he'll soon find your cave, too."

Tubulo turned and vanished. Dane, used to his sudden

61

appearances and disappearances now, turned toward his cave, crossing the rocks and wading down the stream. Tubulo was right. Fass would find the cave before long. He had determination and the cave wasn't that difficult to locate.

Inside the cave, Dane built a pile of rocks just behind his roll of blankets, leaving a deep notch in the center in which he set his old .44. He stretched some string he had in his roll of supplies across the cave from the gun. He tied one end to the trigger of the gun and braced the butt of the gun so the string would pull the trigger rather than jerk the gun out of its seat in the rocks.

On the side of the cave where he planned to sleep, he ran the string around a big rock so it would slide when pulled. Tying the string to the rope, he unrolled the rope toward the mouth of the cave along the south wall.

Then, making sure the old gun had no cartridges in it, he cocked the gun and went back to the end of the rope toward the mouth of the cave. Giving the rope a sharp jerk, he heard the snap as the hammer of the gun fell on the empty chamber. His contraption would work.

With the rope and string out of the way where he wouldn't trip over them, he loaded the gun and cocked it, making sure the loaded chamber was under the hammer. Now he would wait.

Time dragged. He thought of going outside and decided against it. He was so sure now that Cheyenne Fass would find the cave that he almost expected the half-breed to be outside the cave right now waiting for him to show himself.

He thought about his next move if Fass didn't kill him. If Uhl was gone from Alpha, then Yockam became Dane's main target. He wouldn't forget Uhl. He'd track him down. Somewhere, somehow, he'd catch up with him. After what he had done, Dane would never rest until he had settled the score. But he could wait until he had settled with those Guards still around Alpha.

Rolling his bedroll to look like someone was in it, Dane moved over into the little nook in the south side of the cave and snuggled down, using his jacket to keep warm.

He dozed, thinking about ways of finding Uhl. When he roused up, it was dark inside the cave. Peering toward the front of the cave, he saw that it was dark outside, too.

He hadn't expected to sleep through the day. Nevertheless, he felt that he would have slept longer if something hadn't wakened him.

Without moving, he studied the front of the cave. He really couldn't see much. He waited, the hair on the back of his neck making his skin itch. Surely something was there. That feeling came from some source beside his imagination.

Then he saw the darkness deepen at the cave mouth. Something or somebody was blocking some of the faint light coming in from outside. Dane waited, not moving, scarcely breathing.

It could be Tubulo. He had a way of approaching without making a sound. But he wasn't foolish enough to risk being shot like this. Dane fingered the gun at his side. The hunting knife he had found in the old shed a the farm was there, too. In close quarters, sometimes a knife was handier than a gun.

A little more light seeped into the cave. The figure had moved. Dane listened intently but he heard nothing. He sensed rather than saw the figure moving forward.

Straining his eyes. Dane at last made out the shape of a man pressed against the north wall of the cave. There was no way to identify him but he was much larger than Tubulo's boy-size.

It had lo be Fass. Total darkness was an ally of the Indian in a sneak attack like this. If he had tried to come in during the day, he would have been silhouetted against the daylight outside the cave.

Dane glanced at his bedroll. It was barely visible, looking like a big lump on the floor of the cave. But it would appear to be a sleeping man to someone expecting to see just that.

Fass moved forward as quietly as water flowing over a sand bed. Dane rose silently to his knees and then onto his feet, remaining in a crouch. He had his gun in one hand but he wasn't sure enough of the light to risk a shot, even at this close range.

Then the man suddenly stepped out into the middle of the cave and aimed his gun at the blankets. The moved surprised Dane. He had expected him to keep moving in silently until he could pounce on the blankets. Dan shifted his weight to bring his gun around and his boot scraped across the rocks. It sounded like an avalanche in the cave. The man wheeled toward Dane, his gun swinging around.

Remembering the stationary gun, Dane grabbed the rope at his feet. He gave it a yank and the .44 in the rocks behind the bedroll roared.

The bullet didn't hit the man but he threw himself flat on the ground and his own gun roared in the direction of the shot. The man had landed only a couple of feet from Dane. In grabbing the rope, Dane had lost his grip on his gun. His fingers searched frantically for it now. They came in contact with the knife he had salvaged from the shed.

He couldn't waste time looking for the gun. The

roaring echoes of the two gunshots were still reverberating between the walls of the cave. Clutching the knife, Dane leaped at the man. Fass apparently sensed his presence for he turned just as Dane pounced.

Fass rolled, trying to bring his gun around in line with Dane. Dane swung the knife at the arm holding the gun. If he didn't stop that gun, his knife buried in the middle of the Indian would not keep him from shooting Dane.

The knife caught Fass across the forearm. The half-breed gasped but didn't yell. The gun sagged from his limp fingers. Dane was aware then that Fass had his own knife in his other hand. It was kill or be killed now with no methods barred.

A red haze washed over Dane. There was no hesitation as he plunged his knife at the half-breed. He barely felt Fass's blade slash across his leg. The tail of his jacket caught some of the force of the Indian's knife but at the moment, the cut meant little to Dane. He was barely aware of anything except his drive to put an end to the man he was fighting.

When the haze lifted, Dane rolled back against the wall of the cave, exhausted. He had felt that way only once before in his life and that had been in a battle when he'd had a hand to hand fight with a Union soldier. He had killed the soldier and afterward, he'd been sick.

His mother had said it wasn't in him to kill. But Dane knew she was wrong. The war had brought it out first. Now Fass's attempt to kill him had brought it to the surface again.

He dragged Fass outside the cave. In the light from the stars and the half moon, he looked at the dead man and he wasn't sick. With something of a chill, he realized that no matter how often he killed, it would probably never make him sick again. He was no longer the gentle man his mother had known.

Dane had to get Fass's body away from here. He thought of the way Fass had dumped Atley Logar's body right behind the marshal's office in town. Dane wouldn't do that. But he would take Fass's body some place where it would be found.

He could imagine the uproar that would erupt when it was found. That might work to his advantage. Maybe that would put the fear in Skyrock and he would leave the country. Dane didn't want to kill Skyrock. He hadn't been a leader in that raid. Depriving him of his home and store in Alpha should be ample punishment.

Dragging Fass's body down to the edge of the creek, Dane left it there and went in search of Fass's horse. He knew the half-breed's horse must be somewhere close.

He was about ready to give up the search and go get his own horse when he found Fass's horse tied to a tree two hundred yards from the cave on the opposite side of the creek.

Untying the horse, he brought him to the cave and managed to swing the body across the saddle, tying it there. Then he led the horse up the creek to the cove where his own horse was picketed. Tying Fass's horse, he saddled his own. Leading the half-breed's horse, he crossed the stream, no longer trying to hide his trail, and went north through the trees. It wasn't likely that anyone would try to backtrack Dane now. Fass had been the only tracker among the men on Dane's list.

He turned east past the Banning and Hatfield farms to the main road leading north into town. His watch told him it was almost midnight. There wouldn't be many people out at this time of night.

He stopped at the edge of town, however. A horse going through the streets of town was almost sure to rouse some light sleeper. That would be inviting disaster.

Reining over beside the blacksmith shop, he dismounted and untied the body on Fass's horse. Pulling it off the saddle, he laid it beside the shop wall.

Then he mounted and rode back to the south. Half way to Hatfield's place, he looped the reins of Fass's horse over the horn of the saddle and gave the horse a slap on the rump. The animal trotted off toward the creek. Dane didn't know how far he'd go and he really didn't care.

Riding on to his hiding place, Dane put his horse back on his lariat in the grassy nook in the cliff. Then he went back to his cave, no longer wading in the water. He'd almost ruined his boots already wading so much.

He went to his blankets and tried to sleep but he couldn't. He'd gotten too keyed up during the fight and the excitement hadn't worn off. Besides, he had slept a good portion of the day.

Dane waited until the sun was well above the horizon before leaving his cave. The smart thing was to stay right here today. But he had changed with the killing of Cheyenne Fass. Caution had been replaced with an urgency to finish the job. He wanted to see what Skyrock and Yockam would do when the half-breed's body was found. If nobody else was there, it might be the time for a showdown.

As he rode toward town, he could almost hear Tubulo's warning of the danger he was courting. Tubulo was the only real friend he had found here. Margaret Wieland had made an effort to be his friend, due to the memory of Charity, but it hadn't come off. She was afraid of him and the only thing she wanted from him was his absence.

He was half way between Hatfield's farm and town when he saw the people milling excitedly around Main Street. The body must have been found. There were a lot more people there than Dane had expected.

Someone had loaded the body in a wagon and hauled it to the center of town. Dane could imagine the questions that were being asked. He wanted to hear the answers.

Leaving his horse south of the blacksmith shop where he had dumped the body last night, he went up the alley and slipped out to the edge of the crowd. Yockam was standing at the front of the wagon, scowling at the crowd and roaring that he didn't know who had killed Fass. Dane saw Skyrock on the porch of his store, looking like a rabbit ready to run.

"*Some*body killed him," one man shouted. "He didn't do that to himself.

"I know that!" Yockam roared. "It must be Dane Banning. We haven't had a killing here in three years. Then he comes home and we have two in less than a week."

Dane knew this was no place for him. He couldn't get to Yockam or Skyrock in this crowd. The people were as jumpy as scalded toads. It wouldn't take much to turn them into a lynch mob.

Over near the front of the wagon, Dane saw Tate Tubulo. While no one else had turned an eye his way, Tubulo was glaring at him like a mother who had caught her child drawing pictures in church. Dane could almost read the little man's thoughts.

Knowing Tubulo was right, Dane turned back into the alley between Yockam's saloon and the feed store.

Behind him, he heard a roar. Someone must have seen him just as he stepped out of sight. In the skittish mood the people were in now, they'd be thinking of a rope. He broke into a run.

CHAPTER 8

BEHIND THE FEED STORE, DANE SLOWED DOWN. Listening to the sounds out in the street, he knew that he had no time to waste. He hadn't been able to get to Yockam or Skyrock because of so many people but he had seen their reactions to Fass's death.

Skyrock was as nervous as a cat on a dance floor. He was a dangerous man in his present state of mind. Yockam was still trying to bull his way through things but he wasn't the cocksure man Dane had seen when he first came to Alpha.

The sound out in the street was flowing toward him. He broke into a run again, rounding the corner of the blacksmith shop and grabbing the reins of his horse. Once in the saddle, he turned his horse to the south.

There were no buildings south of the blacksmith shop so he was able to stay on the prairie and get a hundred yards from the shop before anyone in the street could see him. Once in sight of the crowd in the street, he reined into the road and kicked his horse into a gallop.

He couldn't hear the noise behind him because of his horse pounding the road like an excited drummer. Glancing back, he saw the men still milling around in the street. If they intended to pursue him, it would take them a while to get their horses. Most of the men lived and worked in town and none of them would have horses saddled.

Dane reined to the west toward the trees on the creek. Once he reached them, he turned north. If anyone followed him out of town, they would surely turn south in the trees because he had been going southwest from town. They wouldn't expect him to turn back north.

He rode slowly now but he hadn't gone half a mile north until he jerked back on the reins. A rider was coming through the trees directly toward him. His hand dropped to his gun. Then he relaxed as he saw the horse and rider.

It was the first time he'd seen Tubulo on a horse. His horse was really just a pony, a spotted one, maybe bought from an Indian. Tubulo rode as if he was used to the saddle.

Dane took his hand from his gun. Tubulo looked sternly at Dane as he reined up. He reminded Dane of his mother when she was about to scold him for something he'd done.

"Are you trying to get yourself killed?" Tubulo demanded.

"Thought I might get to Yockam and Skyrock before the whole town blew up. They were sure to be pretty jumpy after finding Fass."

Tubulo rubbed his chin. "They're jumpy, all right. But that was plain crazy coming into town this morning. Everybody in town is as skittish as colts. You'd better get moving. Yockam has half the town ready to ride with him to chase you down."

"I suppose he calls it a posse?"

"Sure," Tubulo says. "But he don't plan to bring you in alive. The men going with him know that."

"Is everybody in town ready to see me killed?" Dane asked.

"Enough of them are. Most of the ones Yockam picked for his posse will go along with whatever he says. I think some of the old timers would like to see

70

you get away. But they know they have to live with Yockam so they don't buck him on anything."

"What proof does Yockam have that I killed Fass?"

"He ain't got none," Tubulo said. "But he says you did and that's supposed to be enough."

"Will Skyrock go with the posse?"

Tubulo shook his head. "Skyrock is too scared to do anything but hide inside his store."

"Why doesn't he get out of town?"

"He's too scared to run, too," Tubulo said. "Ain't no place he could run to, anyway. Alpha is the only place he knows."

"Seems like he'd go with Yockam to make sure I was killed."

"Skyrock won't do anything like that if he can get someone else to do it. And he figures that Yockam will."

"Maybe I'd ought to make sure Skyrock runs," Dane said. "He shouldn't be allowed to live high and easy after being with Yockam on that raid on the farm."

"I know what you mean, " Tubulo said slowly. "But I don't see what you can do about it."

"I suppose you think I ought to be running from that posse," Dane said.

"You bet I do," Tubulo agreed.

"Just where would they be least likely to look for me?"

Tubulo frowned then the frown turned to a scowl. "You're a bigger fool than I thought if you ride back into town."

"Can you think of any place they'd be less likely to look for me?"

"Somebody will take a pot shot at you if you go there. That whole town is worked up."

"I don't want to kill Skyrock," Dane said. "But I don't think he ought to be allowed to stay in Alpha and run a store like a respectable citizen. I'm going to make sure he gets out of town—without a penny to his name."

Tubulo shook his head. "If you go to Alpha, your chances of riding out again are pretty slim."

"My chances of surviving this long around Alpha haven't been good, either. One more risk isn't going to make that much difference."

He rode to the edge of the trees with Tubulo beside him and looked out across the fields toward town. Tubulo pointed to the southeast near Hatfield's farm.

"There goes Yockam and the posse."

Dane was surprised at the number of men in the posse. Half the men in town must be with the marshal. He stayed back inside the trees while the posse turned west, following the road that Dane had traveled past the Banning farm toward the creek. He couldn't move until they were out of sight.

"They could still look back and see you heading for town," Tubulo said as if reading Dane's thoughts.

"They'll be looking ahead, not back," Dane said. "Do you think they'll turn south along the creek or go on southwest toward Linville?"

"Hard to say," Tubulo said. "Yockam isn't a man easy to figure. They may look on the other side of the creek for tracks leading toward Linville. If they don't find any, they'll search up and down the creek."

Dane knew he didn't have much time to give Skyrock the scare of his life and make him run. Skyrock had never been a leader so he hadn't been responsible for his parents' death. Dane would feel satisfied if Skyrock was forced to leave Alpha and the store, the only business he knew. It would be punishment enough for his part in the raid to make him go to a strange place and try to start all over.

The posse reached the Banning farm and paused momentarily while one of the men rode over and looked inside the shed. Yockam had probably concluded that Dane had been in that shed the night the Guards burned the barn. He wasn't going to let him escape that way again.

"Does everybody in town think I killed Fass and Logar?" Dane asked Tubulo as he watched the posse.

"Reckon so. Those that were here in '64 know who belonged to the Guards. They see a pattern. Both Logar and Fass were close to Yockam and members of the Guards. They think you are out to kill the Home Guards because the Guards killed your folks."

"Surely they don't think I'll kill every one who belonged to the Guards?"

Tubulo shrugged. "They ain't sure. Most of the Northern men in and around town belonged to the Guards. They know that Yockam took only four men with him on his killer raids. But they don't know that you know that."

Dane nodded. "So they're going to get rid of me just to be safe."

"Something like that. Can't really blame them, can you?"

"I suppose not," Dane said. "How do the newcomers feel about it?"

"All they know is that someone is killing people. They want him caught."

Dane nodded. "I'm blamed if I do and blamed if I don't."

"The only safe thing for you to do is get away from here," Tubulo said.

Dane looked at the tiny man. "You'd be safer if I cleared out, too. Sooner or later, people are going to find out you are the one who has been helping me."

"I ain't worried about that. There ain't many of them who think I'm smart enough to remember what happened during the war."

Dane was watching the posse as it neared the trees half a mile to the south of the place where he and Tubulo waited.

"I reckon it's time for me to be moving," he said. "I'll keep to the trees long enough to make sure all the posse is out of sight. Then I'll head for town."

Tubulo shook his head. "I don't like it, Dane. This ain't a smart move."

"I've got to do it. Don't you see that? Skyrock has to pay something for what he did. I don't intend to kill him."

"It ain't Skyrock I'm worried about," Tubulo said.

"You do the worrying, I'll take care of Skyrock," Dane said.

He reined his horse to the north, keeping well inside the trees. Tubulo stayed where he was, looking to the south. He'd go on down and see just what the posse did do, Dane thought. Somehow he always managed to be wherever the action was.

When Dane reached the road leading to town past the Wieland farm, he reined his horse to the edge of the trees and stopped. Looking south along the river, he watched for any sign of life. There was none. The posse was out of sight.

Lifting his horse to a gallop, he rode past Wieland's to town, leaving his horse on the north side of the store again. Dismounting, he went around the corner to the porch.

The street of the town was deserted as he turned through the door into the building. Skyrock was alone in the store. He looked up as Dane came in.

The interior of the store was not well lighted but Dane could see the fear spread over the storekeeper's face. His eyes widened and his mouth sagged open. He was behind the counter as usual but this time he didn't back off against the shelf. He leaned forward.

"What—what do you want?"

"I came to have a talk with you," Dane said. "You were on that raid that killed my parents. I think—"

He broke off as he saw absolute terror flood Skyrock's face and his hand dived under the counter. The storekeeper must have had a gun hidden there for just such an emergency.

Even though he guessed that, Dane didn't draw his own gun. He didn't want to kill Skyrock. In that moment, it flashed across his mind that the storekeeper was paying a big price for having been on that raid just by living with the terrible fear he had.

Skyrock's hand came out from under the counter with a gun and his other hand gripped the first one to hold the gun steady. Skyrock's first shot was wild, a foot above Dane's head.

Dane reached for his own gun then. He knew that the storekeeper would steady down once he got off that first shot. He wouldn't miss every time.

"Hold it, Skyrock!" Dane yelled. "I don't want to kill you."

Skyrock pulled the trigger again, the bullet snapping past Dane's head and burying itself in a can of fruit behind him.

Dane couldn't wait any longer. Skyrock's next shot wasn't likely to miss. He shot twice, saw the storekeeper stagger back against the shelf behind him then slowly slide to a sitting position on the floor, a silly grin on his face as if he had seen something funny in the last second of life.

Dane wheeled toward the door in time to see an old man step back out of the doorway. The town wasn't as deserted as it had looked when he came into the store. Those shots would rouse anyone else who was still here.

As he went through the door, he heard the pounding of hoofs in the street. From the porch, he saw the posse charging back into town. Someone in the posse must have seen Dane make his ride across the fields to town and called the others back.

The old man Dane had seen standing in the doorway had backed out of the way as Dane charged out. Dane started to wheel back into the store but a bullet slammed into the door jamb just beside his head. Another dug into the porch floor at his feet. Instinct told him to fight or run but reason told him that his only chance to survive was to surrender. He let his gun drop.

"Let's string him up!" one man yelled.

"He ain't had a trial," another man said. "I ain't having no part of a lynching."

Dane turned to face Yockam who was dismounting in front of the store. Others remained in their saddles, their guns trained on Dane. Before Yockam stepped up on the porch, two other members of the posse came running through the store from the back. They apparently had guessed who Dane had come to town to see and had covered the back of the store.

"He murdered Skyrock," one of the men yelled as he came out the door.

"That is trial enough," one man shouted. "Let's string him up."

The old man who had stepped aside to let Dane out of the store shuffled out to the front of the porch while some of Yockam's posse dismounted and two of them grabbed Dane's arms while another one searched him for weapons. Dane recognized the old man then, Russell Conover. Dane had considered him an old man back in '62. He and his son had a farm east of town.

"Hold on, Lon, " the old man said. "I saw that fight. Dane didn't shoot at Ed till Ed had taken two shots at him. He said he didn't want to kill him. He sure didn't or he'd have killed him before Ed took that second shot, anyway. It was self defense."

"What do you know about it, Rus?" Yockam snapped. "He's out to kill every man who was a Home Guard."

"Maybe," the old man said. "But you can't hang him for killing Ed. He was forced to do that."

Yockam looked around at his posse. There were some in the group who were

nodding their heads. Even Yockam's hand-picked posse was not all of the same opinion. Yockam scowled but he strode up to Dane, pushed aside a posseman and grabbed an arm, then started marching him across the street toward the jail.

"He'll get his trial," he shouted. "But it's going to be a short one."

Dane was searched again then shoved into the one cell at the back of the marshal's office. Dane was positive that he'd be shot as soon as the crowd outside disappeared. Yockam could dream up some excuse for killing him and there were enough men who would be glad to see Dane dead that they'd defend Yockam once Dane was out of the way.

Dane went to the one barred window on the south

side of the cell and looked out. He couldn't see what was going on in front of the marshal's office but he could see a part of the street in front of Yockam's saloon. People were gathering there and he imagined there were a lot more around Skyrock's store and in front of the marshal's office.

Several men moved down the alley beside the jail and stopped at the window. Dane moved back from the barred window but he heard them yelling outside. He looked out through the barred opening in the door of the cell. Yockam was in his office with several men. Although he had Dane in jail, there was a worried frown on his face. Yockam's absolute authority had been challenged by the old man, Russell Conover, and Yockam had been forced to back down. It left a chink in his armor and he didn't like it. Dane could see the determination in the marshal's face and he knew what it meant. Somehow Yockam would get rid of Dane before this night was over.

A mob might be the answer. Yockam could say he was overpowered. Outside, men were shouting that Dane should be hanged and Yockam went out to the porch in front of his office and Dane could hear him yelling to the crowd.

"Something happened to him in the war," Yockam shouted. "He is kill crazy. He'll kill anybody who gets in his way. He's killed three times in the week he's been here."

Dane wanted to scream at the crowd that Yockam and Logar and Skyrock had killed his parents. But he knew it wouldn't do any good even if he could make them listen.

Dane went back to the window. There were still some men outside but most of them had left. Back behind the saloon, Dane saw Tubulo. He was always around when Dane needed him. But this time there wasn't anything he could do.

He heard Yockam yelling out in front about the fair trial Dane was going to get but in between his promises of fairness, he screamed that Dane was a rabid killer.

Dane knew what this was working up to. If Yockam didn't find some excuse to kill Dane in his cell, then a mob would appear sometime after dark when men could not easily be identified. They'd rush the jail and Yockam would easily be overpowered. Dane would be dragged out and hanged.

CHAPTER 9

DANE PACED THE FLOOR OF HIS CELL. HE DIDN'T MIND so much going up against big odds. In such a fight, he had a chance, but here, there wasn't a thing he could do.

He looked out the window once in a while. He could still see people milling around in the street. He didn't see Tubulo any more. He felt deserted without the little man in sight. Tubulo had saved him a couple of times since he came back to Alpha but not even Tubulo could get him out of this.

He recalled that Tubulo had warned him against coming to town to talk to Skyrock. The way it turned out, Tubulo had been right. Skyrock must have been suffering plenty just from the fear he felt because he knew Dane was after the Guards who had raided the Banning place.

The two men that Dane wanted most were still free. Lon Yockam had been the leader and Kurt Uhl had taken Charity. Uhl had run like the coward he was but he was still free and unpunished. Yockam was out there in the office now, stirring up a mob to make sure Dane didn't get out of jail alive.

Dane peeked through the barred opening in his door and watched Yockam. Men came and went and Yockam talked to them in low tones. But once when there was no one in the office with Yockam, Dane saw the worried look on his face as he paced the floor, glancing into the street often. Dane guessed he was worried about his authority. That must have been a blow to his prestige when Conover had defied him. Now others in Alpha might rebel against his rule.

The afternoon wore on and dusk settled over the town. Dane was positive that he would not be in this cell when dawn came. If he couldn't think of some way to escape, they'd drag him out and stretch his neck.

Dane listened to the murmur of sound coming from Yockam's saloon just to the south of the jail. As the darkness deepened, the murmur became louder. That was the place where the lynch mob would be born.

Dane went back across his cell and looked out into the office. Yockam was still there. It wouldn't have surprised Dane if Yockam had been over at his saloon giving out free drinks and encouraging the hanging talk. But he had plenty of henchmen to do that. The people of town could see that he was staying on his job. That was just another sign that Yockam was worried about his grip on the town. Dane doubted if he would have cared what the people thought a week ago.

Darkness settled over the cell. If it hadn't been for the light in the marshal's office filtering through the barred opening in the door, Dane couldn't have seen anything.

Then suddenly a light flared outside the cell window. Dane started toward the window then dropped back.

This might be a trick to get him to the window. By the light from the flare, a marksman could kill him.

Dane backed off to the corner of his cell. The light outside flickered then suddenly shot between the bars, landing in the center of the cell. Dane saw that it was a big wad of dry grass that had been set on fire.

He thought of stomping the flame out but then he stopped. That wasn't a big enough blaze to kindle the floor of the jail. Maybe it was meant to light up the cell so anyone standing just outside the cell window could see Dane while he beat out the flame.

Dane scooted down in the corner against the outside wall. Nobody from outside could see him there no matter how light it got inside. The grass flickered and smoldered and the smoke from the dry grass began to choke Dane.

Then he heard Tubulo's voice out in Yockam's office. Needing some relief from the smoke, anyway, Dane moved over to the window and peeked out. So far as he could see, there was no one out there. Then he crossed to the barred opening in the door into the office. There wasn't much fresh air there as the smoke was curling out through the opening.

Yockam was glaring at Tubulo. "What do you want?" he growled.

"I thought I smelled smoke as I was going past here," Tubulo said.

Yockam snorted. Then suddenly he sniffed. "There is smoke somewhere." He looked around then made a dash for the cell at the back of the office. "That prisoner has set fire to the place!"

Dane backed off to a corner quickly as Yockam fumbled with the key then swung the door open. He had his gun in his hand. Tubulo was right behind him.

"I'll teach you to set fire to the jail!" Yockam roared, his gun swinging around in search of Dane.

"He couldn't have set any fire," Tubulo said from immediately behind Yockam. "You took everything from him before he was put in here, even matches."

Dane saw the hesitation in Yockam's face. Light flooded in from the office and the sputtering blaze in the middle of the cell floor appeared even less formidable than before.

Yockam must have welcomed this unexpected fire as an excuse for shooting Dane. But Tubulo was there to watch. He'd have to kill Tubulo, too, if he was to say he shot in self defense or that Dane was trying to escape.

Yockam turned furiously on Tubulo. "You little runt! Get out of here!"

"You can't shoot him for something he didn't do," Tubulo insisted, although he did back up a few feet.

Yockam swore under his breath and jammed the gun back into its holster. Then he charged into the cell, shutting the door behind him. He slammed a boot down on the burning grass and twisted. Bending over, he examined the smoldering mess to make sure the blaze was out.

Dane saw his chance and he realized that Tubulo had thrown that burning grass into his cell for this very reason.

While Yockam was still bent over the grass, Dane launched himself at the marshal, not even taking time to fully straighten up. Yockam saw him coming and slapped a hand to his gun.

Dane hit him then, bowling him over and making him throw out an arm to catch himself. The gun, half out of the holster, spilled onto the floor and scooted against the wall.

Lon Yockam was a little heavier than Dane and solidly built. He was strong, Dane knew, but Dane felt as strong as a bull himself. He had wanted to get his hands on Yockam ever since he had learned from Tubulo that he had been the leader of the Home Guards who had raided the Banning farm. This was the first chance he'd had.

Yockam was used to rough and tumble fighting. Dane had been in very few fights with fists or guns, other than the battles of the war. But this one he welcomed.

After his initial surprise, Yockam recovered quickly and swung a hard fist at Dane's head. Dane pulled his head to one side and the fist grazed past, peeling an ear as it went. Dane jabbed a fist at Yockam's head then pushed him backward to the floor.

He knew he wasn't hurting him much by pushing and shoving but there wasn't room to do much more. He noticed that Tubulo had pushed the door of the cell open so that Dane could get out. But Dane didn't want out. He wanted to beat Yockam to death if he could.

He suddenly backed off to get more leverage on his blows. Yockam came to his feet, too, with surprising agility. He seemed to have forgotten about his gun on the floor. His eyes gleamed with a lust to kill. Dane didn't back off. The same red haze swept over him that had consumed him the night he'd killed Cheyenne Fass.

Yockam charged and Dane met him head-on. Dane knew he was taking some hard blows but he ignored them in his effort to deal out punishment. Yockam was driven by fear; it was in his eyes and in his sobbing breath. Dane was driven by an overwhelming craze to smash the man before him. He dulled his senses to the pain of the blows hitting him and took full enjoyment in every blow that he landed.

83

In the end, it was Dane's drive that overpowered Yockam's fear. The marshal retreated to the wall and there Dane pounded him until his face was a jelly. Slowly Yockam's fists began to sag, no longer seeking to smash Dane's face.

Yockam sank to the floor but Dane kept pounding him as long as he was within range of his fists. Only after Yockam lopped over, his head bumping the floor, did he hear Tubulo at the door.

"Come on!" Tubulo's squeaky voice penetrated the fog in Dane's brain. "You made more noise than two bulls fighting. The whole town will be here in a minute. This is your last chance to get out of here."

The words finally penetrated Dane's thinking and he realized that he had let his craze to beat Yockam to death blind him to the plan Tubulo had worked out for him.

Scooping up the marshal's gun and jerking the belt off his unconscious body, he wheeled toward Tubulo.

"They're coming," Tubulo said excitedly. "Out the back."

Tubulo ran toward the back door as fast as his short legs would take him. Dane overtook the little man just as he jerked the door open. Out in front of the office, Dane could hear men yelling at one another, asking what was going on.

In the darkness behind the jail, Tubulo grabbed Dane's shirt to get his attention. He pointed silently to the south toward the blacksmith shop. Dane nodded.

Glancing toward the street through the wide alley between the jail and Yockam's saloon, Dane could see men running along the street. But the light was very poor. He doubted if anyone would see him or Tubulo as they dodged across the alley to the rear of the saloon.

As he ran, Dane guessed that Tubulo had his horse down at the blacksmith shop. Tubulo wasn't likely to go to all that work to give Dane a chance to break out of the jail without providing a means of escape once he was out.

There was a wide gap between the saloon and the feed store. And another gap wide enough to put up a building between the feed store and the blacksmith shop. Dane and Tubulo negotiated both open areas without bringing a yell of discovery from anyone in the street. But behind them, at the marshal's office, there was an uproar. Apparently Dane's escape had been discovered.

At the back of the blacksmith shop, Dane found his horse, saddled and ready to ride. So was Tubulo's little spotted pony.

"How did you get my horse out of the livery barn?" Dane asked.

"Told the man the marshal wanted him saddled and ready,'' Tubulo said, a touch of pride in his voice. "Then when he went to the front of the barn after saddling the horse, I led him out the back and through the corral gate. He may not have missed him yet."

Dane nodded in appreciation. "Now we've got to make a run for it. It sounds like they have already found out I've escaped."

"You go," Tubulo said, "I won't go with you."

"But Yockam will tell them that you helped me escape."

"Sure he will," Tubulo said. "But I can't keep up with you on my little pony. And besides, your horse is brown. He won't show up in the dark. These white spots on my horse will."

"What are you going to do?" Dane asked, already i

guessing.

"I'm going to ride south. They'll expect you to go that way."

"So they'll chase you, thinking we're together," Dane said. "What happens when they catch you?"

Tubulo gave his characteristic shrug. "Nothing. "I'm an idiot, remember."

Dane shook his head in admiration. "You've got it figured. But it doesn't sound safe for you."

"You look after your own hide," Tubulo said, swinging up on his pony. "My hide's smaller. I can take care of it."

Dane heard the sudden explosion of sound from the rear of the jail as men poured through the back door, knowing that was the way Dane had made his escape.

Dane swung up on his horse and turned him straight east while Tubulo headed south, swinging out into the road where his white spotted horse would be seen. Also, the pony's hoofs on the hard road made a much louder sound than Dane's horse, going east across the unbroken sod.

If Dane had the idea that all the men would follow Tubulo, he was disappointed. Someone had seen him and three riders came after him while the others went down the road after Tubulo.

Dane headed out into country that he hadn't been over in six years. He realized as he came to Tubulo's farm why only a few man had followed him. He had headed directly for Tate Tubulo's home so they must have guessed that Dane and Tubulo had traded horses to throw off pursuit.

Dane turned north just before he reached the farm. The three riders pushed their horses hard while Dane tried to conserve his horse's strength. He doubted if

Yockam was with either of the pursuing groups. It would take him a while to recover from the beating Dane had given him. When he did take the trail, his pursuit would be relentless. These men behind him now likely did not have the heart for the job they had tackled.

Dane had felt the bulge under his leg as he rode. Now he ran a hand along the saddle by his leg. It was a rifle boot and there was a rifle in it. For a man who was supposed to be feeble-minded, Tubulo did some remarkable thinking. Dane had no idea where Tubulo had gotten the rifle but he was thankful to have it.

The pursuers got close enough that one of them fired a shot that fell harmlessly short of its mark. Dane decided to test his conclusion that the men following were not keen on tangling with him in a fight to the death.

Halting his horse and swinging around, he jerked the rifle out of its boot. He hoped Tubulo had thought to put some ammunition in it. Working the lever, he aimed at the little group of riders and pulled the trigger. The rifle bucked against his shoulder and the report crashed against his ears. Levering another shell into the barrel, he fired again.

At the first shot, the riders reined up as if they'd hit a river with the bridge out. At the second shot they scattered, heading for cover. Dane was sure he hadn't hit any of them. They were too far away and the light just wasn't that good. A waning moon, less than an hour high, gave some light but not enough for accurate shooting.

Dane wheeled and rode on. He watched his back trail but he didn't see the three riders any more. Their enthusiasm for the chase had been squelched by those two shots. It was one thing chasing an unarmed refugee;

it was something else fighting an armed man.

Well northeast of town, Dane reined to the west, intending to circle back to his cave. He took his time, making sure he didn't run into the party that had chased Tubulo.

Sometime after midnight he glanced behind him and was shocked to see what looked like a band of horsemen far to the rear. He studied them carefully. But they were far away and the light was very poor. If they had not been moving, he would not have seen them at all.

Dane's guess was that Lon Yockam had revived enough to take the trail. Finding the three men who had turned back, he was sure this was Dane's trail. Now he was following it as fast as tracking eyes could locate it in the weak moonlight.

Dane pushed on, careful now to hide his tracks. He hadn't been careful before. Short of the creek, he turned to the north again, this time making sure his tracks were plain. Then in soft grass, he turned to the creek and reined into the water, wading his horse south. A half mile down the creek, he halted and waited, listening for sounds of pursuit.

The riders were not making a great deal of noise but the spot where Dane had turned north was not far from the place where he waited now in the creek. He heard Yockam's voice snapping orders when the posse reached that point. They turned north.

Dane waited, listening. But the posse did not return. Dane went on south, still keeping to the creek. When he finally reached his cave, about four miles from the place where he had turned his horse into the creek, he reined in to the grassy cove, picketed his horse, and went on to the cave. He took the rifle that Tubulo had put on his saddle and also the revolver he had taken from Yockam.

Through the night he watched and listened at the mouth of the cave. Finally, having neither seen nor heard any sign of the posse, he went to sleep.

He awoke about noon and got something to eat from his dwindling supply. He had to plan his next move. Three of the five names Tubulo had given him were crossed off now. Only Yockam and Uhl were left. He should have finished Yockam in the jail cell. And he would have if he'd had more time. After the beating he'd given Yockam and his escape from jail, he'd be a marked man in town, fair game for anyone with a gun. He had to get away from here if he intended to live. And he still had to find Charity if she were still alive. It was time to go.

Checking his gun, Dane moved out of the cave and went to get his horse. Half expecting an ambush, he saw instead Tubulo standing near his horse in the little nook in the bluff.

"Thought you'd come here," Tubulo said.

"Where's the posse?" Dane asked.

"Ain't none," Tubulo said. "Yockam went out with a posse last night but lost your trail north of town and gave up. This morning he was gone. Took his personal stuff and left. I don't figure he's coming back."

"Why would he leave?"

"Same reason Uhl left. He's scared. He's tried several times to kill you and he can't get the job done. You could have killed him last night and he knows it. He ain't taking any more chances. You going after him?"

"Which way did he go?"

"I think I can find out," Tubulo said. "One thing sure, you can't show yourself around here any more. Everybody in town is scared to death of you. They have all agreed to shoot you on sight."

89

Remembering last night, Dane didn't doubt it. They'd be like Skyrock and start shooting in panic if they saw him. He'd have a hard time getting out of the country without being seen by someone.

CHAPTER 10

DANE STARED OUT THROUGH THE MOUTH OF THE little notch toward the creek and the farmland beyond. This was home. He had looked forward to coming back here for six years. But now his father and mother were gone; his wife was gone. And the people would no longer allow him to live here. Shoot him on sight, Tubulo had said. Nervous trigger fingers would very likely do that.

"Don't they know that I'm only after the men who killed my parents?" Dane asked.

"They're too spooked up to think straight," Tubulo said. "A lot of the men here belonged to the Home Guards. They ain't sure that you won't go after every man who ever belonged to the Guards."

Dane nodded. "If Lon Yockam is gone, there's not much left for me to stay here for, anyway. Yockam and Uhl are the two that deserve killing more than the ones who have already died."

"They'll never come back here," Tubulo predicted.

Dane looked at the little man. "What are you going to do?"

Tubulo shrugged. "What I've always done, I reckon."

"Why don't you come with me? I've got enough for us to live on for a while, anyway. There'll be work wherever we go."

"I ain't much good at work," Tubulo said. "They take

90

one look at me and say I ain't big enough to do anything."

"You're big enough to be a help to me."

Tubulo nodded enthusiastically. "I sure would like to get away from here. It might be nice to go someplace where people would look at me like a human being instead of a dog to be kicked around."

"Let's leave tonight after it gets dark," Dane suggested.

Tubulo nodded. "Not a bad idea. I wouldn't want anybody to know I'm going. Nobody thinks I can survive if I get ten miles from Alpha. And you won't get away if anybody sees you."

"We can be a long way from here by morning."

"I'll meet you on the creek west of Wieland's farm right after dark," Tubulo said. "I've got to look for Yockam's tracks now. He took his horse, the one with the cracked shoe. If I look now, I should find some tracks showing which way he went."

"Which way do you guess?"

"Hard to tell. If he heads for Kansas City, he'll be going east on the train. If he goes west, it will be the tough towns on the railroad."

After Tubulo was gone, Dane went back to the cave to get his few things together. Until he knew that Yockam was gone, he didn't realize how much he had planned on making him pay for his part in murdering Bull Banning and his wife. But it was still Uhl that he wanted most. Dane couldn't think of any punishment bad enough for Uhl to pay for what he had done to Charity.

It struck him that Yockam might go where Uhl had gone. Yockam and Uhl had always been friends. A man on the run always needs a friend. That was one reason why Dane had asked Tubulo to go with him. The little man was a good friend.

It was ironic, Dane thought, that both Yockam and Dane were on the run. Yockam was running from Dane and Dane was running from this community. He didn't expect anyone from Alpha to chase him, however. The people would probably be very happy if he would just disappear and never return.

Rolling his bedroll with all his possessions inside, he tied it, ready to carry it out to his horse. He hoped Yockam's trail led west. That seemed most likely to be the way Charity had gone. Underlying his drive to even the score with Yockam and Uhl was his determination to find Charity if she was alive. It would simplify his task if the trails all led the same way.

Dane waited impatiently for the sun to go down. Now that he had decided on a plan of action, he was anxious to get started. Every minute he loafed around here, Yockam was getting farther away.

As soon as the sun had sent its last shaft of light out over the field to the east of the cave, Dane made a final check inside. There was nothing left. Carrying his bedroll and rifle with the revolver tucked securely in its holster at his side, he stepped outside and down to the water.

There he stopped. He didn't need to wade out this time. Let them find his cave now. He'd never need it again, whether he escaped from here or not.

Walking along the bank of the creek, he came to the cove and saddled his horse. Strapping on the bedroll and sliding the rifle into its boot, he mounted and rode across the creek, turning north well inside the fringe of trees along the creek.

He rode slowly, knowing he was going to get to the

meeting place early. As he passed his old home, he took one last look. Only the shed still stood. That would probably be burned and the ground plowed into a field. Who would get it? Certainly not Dane. And he was the only Banning left.

West of Wieland's, he halted his horse. Thinking of Margaret Wieland, Charity's best friend, he felt an urge to talk to Margaret once more. Maybe she had remembered something that she hadn't thought of the other day. She had been both afraid and surprised when he made that visit. Dane needed every shred of information he could garner if he was to have any hope of finding Charity.

He wondered if Bruce Wieland had sworn to shoot Dane on sight, too. Tubulo had said that the men of Alpha had made that pledge. Bruce had been a friend of Dane's before the war, mostly because their wives were such good friends. Dane had to take a chance on Bruce.

Looking toward town in the deepening dusk, Dane couldn't see any sign of the spotted pony of Tubulo's. He probably wouldn't come for another half hour. That would give him plenty of time to talk to Margaret.

Reining out of the trees and keeping the barn between him and the house, he rode up to the Wieland place. Dismounting behind the barn, he moved around to a spot where he could see the yard. If the Wielands had company, Dane would squelch his urge to talk to Margaret.

He almost grinned as he thought what Tubulo would say if he knew what Dane was doing now. Tubulo reminded Dane sometimes of a mother hen, fussing over a wayward chick.

Dane tried to walk casually across to the house when he saw that there was no rig or horse in the yard. Still he

93

felt a prickly sensation running over him as his imagination put a gun in the hands of a man at the house.

He reached the house and knocked on the door. It opened almost immediately, proving that those inside had seen him coming.

"Don't you know you're a marked man now?" Bruce Wieland asked as Dane stepped inside.

"I heard it," Dane said. "I'm leaving. There is nothing here for me any more."

"Every man who belonged to the Home Guard thinks you're gunning for him."

"I'm after just the ones who killed my folks. I hear that Lon Yockam has left town."

"That's right. Ran like a whipped dog. Nobody in Alpha ever expected to see Yockam show a yellow streak. You came close to beating him to death last night in that cell. He got the message."

Dane's jaw hardened as he remembered his feelings while he was fighting Yockam. "If I'd had time, I probably would have," he said. "He was the leader of the gang who murdered Pa and Ma. He deserves to die a lot more than Skyrock."

"You did kill Ed, didn't you?" Margaret asked, moving in from the kitchen.

"I went in to tell him to get out of town. I figured having to give up his business would be punishment enough for him. But he panicked. Pulled a gun from under the counter and started shooting. He was wild but each shot was getting closer. I had to shoot him to save my own neck."

Bruce nodded. "That sounds about like Ed. He never had much backbone."

Margaret turned to look at the children peeking out of

the bedroom. They ducked back and shut the door. "What about Atley Logar, Dane?" she asked. "Did you kill him?"

Dane shook his head. "Cheyenne Fass did that. Later Fass sneaked into the cave where I was holed up and we got into a battle. I didn't want to kill Fass, either, but I had to."

"You're doing a lot of killing for not wanting to," Bruce said skeptically.

"Maybe," Dane admitted. "If I'd killed Yockam or Uhl, it would have been because I wanted to."

"Are you going after Yockam?" Margaret asked.

Dane nodded. "If I can find out where he went. After what he did, his debt will never be paid as long as he's alive. And I'll never be safe, either. He knows I'm after him."

"You'd better keep an eye open for Kurt Uhl, too," Bruce said. "He won't face you but he'll shoot you in the back if he gets the chance."

"I know. I just hope I can find him. What I came here for was to find out if you had remembered anything else about Charity. " He looked at Margaret. "I'll need every clue I can get if I have any hope of finding her."

"It would be better if you just forgot her, Dane," Margaret said, her voice lowering. "That's the way she wanted it."

"It's not the way I want it. I wonder if she is even alive."

"I wonder that, too," Margaret said. "Every day. The way her letter sounded, I don't think she cared much whether she lived or died."

"You're sure she didn't go back to Tennessee?"

"I'm not sure," Margaret said. "She said in her letter that she never expected to see anybody she knew again.

95

That included her folks. She might have changed her mind later. The Martins left here a couple of months before the Banning raid. So she knew they were back in Tennessee."

"Her folks would have welcomed her no matter what she thinks."

"She might have figured that out after a while," Margaret said. "But when she wrote that letter, she had her mind made up. I think she was too proud to go back home."

"Did she say anything about me?"

Margaret shrugged. "Only that she wanted to disappear where you would never find her. She didn't want you ever to see her again."

"She must have been out of her mind."

"She had a right to be," Bruce said. "She saw Bull and Mary Banning murdered and then she was carried away by Kurt Uhl. I think she showed a lot of spunk to escape from him."

Dane nodded, his fury at Kurt Uhl swelling in his chest and throat until he could barely talk.

"I'm going to find her," he finally whispered, "if she is still alive. I don't care what has happened or what she's done, I want her back."

"I'm glad," Margaret said. "I hope you can find her. What happened wasn't Charity's fault."

"Where do you guess she is?" Dane asked.

"Denver or somewhere between here and there," Bruce said. "She might go to California but she can lose herself in Kansas just as well."

"You think she went west," Dane said, resolving to go west regardless of what Tubulo learned about the direction Yockam had gone. "Do you have any idea what name she will use?"

Margaret shook her head. "She just said she was going to change her name so she wouldn't bring shame on the names of Banning or Martin. I know she wouldn't use the name she put on the envelope. She didn't want to hear from me, either. She was just going to drop off the face of the earth."

Dane nodded then shook hands with both Bruce and Margaret. "You may not hear from me again, either. But if I find Charity, I'll sure let you know."

"I wish you the best of luck," Margaret said softly as Dane went to the door.

Bruce followed him to the back porch and gave him his best wishes, too. Then Dane ducked across the yard to his horse behind the barn.

It was much darker than it had been when Dane had ridden up here. He looked up the road toward town but he couldn't see anything. There were clouds over the stars. That was good, Dane thought. Nobody would likely know that Dane and Tubulo were leaving except for Bruce and Margaret Wieland.

Dane found Tubulo at the meeting place, fretting because he was late.

"Where have you been?" Tubulo demanded anxiously. "I expected you would beat me here. I had trouble following Yockam's tracks."

"Where did they lead?" Dane asked, sidestepping Tubulo's question.

"Toward Topeka," Tubulo said. "I had to ride a long way out to find that split shoe track where it wasn't mixed up with the tracks of the posse. I followed it till it turned into the road leading toward Topeka."

"Topeka is as good a guess as any," Dane said. "And we've got to guess. We can't follow his trail at night."

"We sure ain't going to wait for daylight," Tubulo

said. "They were talking in town about getting up a search party to hunt you down like a mad dog. It was just talk, though. Ain't none of them got nerve enough to actually go hunting for you."

Tubulo led out and Dane followed. They hit the main road leading toward the Kaw River and the road that paralleled the river between the railroad towns.

They rode until well past midnight then Dane found a fine grove of trees and they dismounted, unsaddled, and lay down to sleep the rest of the night. They were far enough away from Alpha now that if the citizens did muster up enough courage to go after Dane, they wouldn't come this far.

The sun was just rising when Dane awoke. He was surprised that he had slept so well. It was actually the first night in a long time that he had been able to sleep without wondering what instant someone would try to kill him in his bed.

Tubulo had brought along a big supply of food and they cooked a good breakfast before moving on. About noon, they came in sight of Topeka.

Most of the town was south of the river but the railroad tracks were on the other side. The road they had followed had stayed south of the river so they found themselves riding into the main part of the town.

"Maybe we'd better split up," Tubulo said. "We can cover the town a lot faster that way."

Dane nodded. They wouldn't tip off Yockam as quickly if they separated, he thought. Tubulo knew that. In fact, Dane was beginning to think that Tubulo knew a lot more than the so-called smart people who called him an idiot.

Tubulo headed for the northern part of town while Dane rode into the southern part. If Yockam was here

98

and he saw Tubulo, he'd know instantly that Dane was nearby. In spite of the fact that Tubulo was a lot smaller, it would be easier for Dane than for Tubulo to lose himself in a crowd.

Dane stopped at two saloons and found nothing. At the third saloon, he asked the bartender if he had seen Yockam. He started to describe the marshal but the bartender stopped him.

"I know Lon Yockam. He comes in here once in a while when he gets to town. Lives over in Alpha. Too far away to come often."

"Has he been here today?'

The bartender shook his head. "He was here last night, though. Rode in all the way from Alpha yesterday. He was really dry. Drank up a bottle like a dried out fish."

"Did he say if he was staying over?" Dane asked.

"Well, I reckon he'd stay over last night. It was past midnight when he had finished soaking up that bottle. He didn't say what he was going to do today."

Dane thanked him and went back outside. He wondered where Yockam would stay overnight. He might still be sleeping off that whisky. If he came back to the saloon for more, he'd probably find out Dane had inquired after him. Dane didn't want Yockam to know he was on his trail.

He inquired at a couple of boarding houses. But they knew nothing about Yockam. He returned twice to the saloon but Yockam wasn't there either time.

Finally, he turned to the north where he would meet Tubulo. Maybe Tubulo had turned up something. He seemed to have a nose for finding out things.

Dane didn't find Tubulo on the south side of the river so he crossed the bridge. The railroad tracks were on the

99

north side. Maybe Tubulo had found Yockam over here waiting to catch a train. Dane doubted it. If he'd found Yockam, he would have come to find Dane and tell him.

Dane was within fifty yards of the depot when he saw something along the side of the road. At the same time, he noticed the spotted pony grazing on a patch of grass a block away.

Dane swung off his horse and hurried over to the little man beside the road. Dropping on one knee beside Tubulo, he felt for a pulse.

CHAPTER 11

TUBULO OPENED ONE EYE A TRIFLE. "I AIN'T DEAD," HE said softly.

"What happened to you?"

"Yockam," Tubulo said. "Is he close?"

Dane stood up and looked around. A train was just pulling out of the depot toward the west. Dane saw a couple of men on the platform but nobody else.

"Don't see him," he said. "Did Yockam hit you?"

Tubulo got up gingerly. "It wasn't a love tap," he said.

"How did you find him?"

"By finding the print of that broken shoe in the dust of the street by the livery barn," Tubulo said. "The livery man said the horse was for sale. He'd just bought him from a man who was going to leave on the train."

"Why didn't you come and tell me?"

"I didn't know if I could find you. And I wanted to know which way Yockam was going. So I came over here to find out. That's when Yockam caught me."

"You didn't have a fight with him, did you?" Dane

100

asked, thinking how ridiculous that would be.

"I fought just like I always do. I played possum. When he hit me, I dropped like he'd killed me. He asked me where you were but I played dead and he ran to the station."

"A train just pulled out to the west," Dane said.

"If he wasn't on it, he'll still be in the station," Tubulo said.

"I'll go look," Dane said, "unless you need a doctor."

"I don't need nothing," Tubulo said. "Playing dead is easy."

Dane hurried on to the depot and cautiously looked inside. If Yockam was here, he'd be alerted since he'd run into Tubulo. But the depot was empty except for the telegrapher. The schedule on the blackboard showed that the next train due in here from either direction was several hours away.

Dane went back to the place where he'd left his horse and Tubulo. Tubulo was leading his spotted pony back from the grassy spot where he'd wandered.

"How did you happen to let Yockam get close enough to hit you?" Dane asked when Tubulo reached him.

"He was in a surrey taking some men to the station," Tubulo said. "I didn't recognize him in the bunch until he jumped out. He grabbed the bridle of my horse and demanded to know where you were. When I didn't answer, he hit me and I rolled off and played dead. That sure saved a lot of wasted words."

"Well, we know he went west," Dane said. "Won't be another train through for hours."

"We ain't going to have much luck trying to catch him now. He may ride that train forever."

"It doesn't run forever," Dane said. "Somewhere out west of Fort Hays, the track ends. We'll catch up with him unless he doubles back on us."

"We'd better get going," Tubulo said. "These horses are going to lose ground pretty fast on that train."

"I've got to look for Charity," Dane said. "Margaret Wieland's letter came from Topeka. It's possible that she might still be here."

Tubulo nodded and said no more about hurrying after the train carrying Yockam west.

Dane spent the rest of the day checking hotels, restaurants and boarding houses where he thought Charity might have found a job. Finally, having found no trace of her, he turned to the saloons. He couldn't picture Charity as a saloon girl. But it was a living and Charity would have had nothing to live on when she escaped from Uhl.

He described Charity to several women. But he realized that the soft-eyed red-haired beauty that he was describing was probably not the Charity anyone here would have seen after the experiences she had been through.

Getting a cheap room in a boarding house, Dane and Tubulo spent the night in town, their horses stabled in a livery barn. Dane was disappointed that they had missed Yockam and found no trace of Charity. He knew that he had no reason to believe that Charity would be here but he had clung to the hope that she had found a good job here and had stayed on.

The boarding house didn't serve breakfast so Dane and Tubulo went to the barn and got their horses, eating their breakfast out of the provisions that Tubulo had brought. Dane would buy more when these ran low. There were towns all along the railroad track.

It was past noon the second day out of Topeka when they reached Manhattan. Manhattan sat on the north side of the river and was only a short distance from Fort Riley. Dane hoped that here he would find Charity. He doubted if Yockam would stop here but he'd check.

Again Dane and Tubulo split up to look over the town. Dane hesitated about letting Tubulo go alone. But Tubulo promised to be more careful and he still had the argument that they could cover a lot more territory if they worked alone.

Dane spent more time inquiring about Charity than he did about Yockam. Again he checked the hotels, boarding houses and restaurants. But none of them remembered any girl who even remotely resembled Dane's description of Charity. He wondered if his memory wasn't describing someone these people had never seen even if they'd been looking right at Charity.

There was no sign of Lon Yockam, either. Somewhere down the line Yockam would have to get off the train.

Dane stopped at a store and bought some canned fruit then went to a restaurant and bought some bread. He still had enough of everything else they'd need for a while. Tubulo didn't eat much. Apparently it didn't take much to fuel his small body.

Before sundown, they rode out of town. A short distance down the tracks toward the next stop, Fort Riley, they found a place to camp. Dane wondered if it was wise for both of them to sleep at once. But the chances of anything disturbing them was remote and they both needed sleep.

They paused only a short time the next day as they rode through one corner of the military reservation around Fort Riley. If there was one place along the railroad where Dane didn't expect to find either Yockam or Charity, it was at the military post. He did inquire of some soldiers near the guard post if they had seen any sign of a man fitting Yockam's description but he drew a blank.

Just before dark, they arrived at Junction City. It was a city in name only, just a cluster of buildings near the confluence of the Smoky Hill and Republican Rivers. The two rivers formed the Kaw River which ran into the Missouri River at Kansas City.

Clattering over the bridge across the Republican, Dane pulled up and he and Tubulo looked over the town.

"Let's live in style tonight," Dane said. "We'll get a room at a hotel and then we'll see who is in town."

Tubulo nodded. "I'll get spoiled, sleeping in a bed so much. Back home I didn't sleep in the house more than once or twice a week in the summer."

Dane found a large building that said hotel. Inside, it looked more like living quarters for a family and perhaps a dozen boarders. Dane got a room for himself and Tubulo for two dollars which also included breakfast.

Taking their belongings up to the room, they went back and took their horses to the livery barn only half a block down a side street.

"I think we'd better stick together tonight," Dane said after supper.

Tubulo nodded. "We've got time to cover this town. Nothing open after dark but the saloons."

Dane led the way down the street. He loosened his gun in the holster. If he found Yockam, he'd need it.

The town hadn't looked like much from the bridge but it seemed to have more than its share of saloons. Dane soon discovered the reason. Over half of the customers in the saloons were soldiers from nearby Fort

104

Riley.

"Yockam had a saloon in Alpha," Tubulo reminded Dane.

"This is a good town for saloons and gamblers. Yockam and Uhl are both mighty good with cards."

"If either one is here, we'll find him," Dane said.

The first two saloons had yielded nothing but soldiers. The third one was full of soldiers and railroad workers. Dane looked over the card games going on at the far side of the room. Nobody there looked like Lon Yockam. Dane wasn't forgetting Kurt Uhl, either. There was always the chance that Yockam and Uhl would get together.

Dane moved over to watch a game in progress, having no trouble picking out the man at the table who made his living with the cards. Between hands, Dane described Yockam and asked if the gambler had seen him.

The gambler looked up at Dane. "Any particular reason you want to know?"

Dane nodded. "He killed my pa."

The gambler pursed his lips. "A man like that sat in on my game a couple of days ago."

"Is he still in town?"

"I doubt it," the man said. "I saw him the next day but not since."

Dane described Kurt Uhl. "Have you seen him?"

The man shook his head. Dane thanked the man and moved on. Yockam had stopped here but apparently only for a day or two. He must be looking for something, too. Maybe it was Uhl. Dane was encouraged. At least Yockam wasn't in full flight. He likely would stop somewhere between here and the end of track. Dane would have a chance to catch up with him if he kept doggedly on his trail.

Dane was in no hurry to leave the next morning. After breakfast at the boarding house, Dane made the rounds of the business places where he thought Charity might have worked when she came west. He had no success. He admitted to himself that he hadn't checked one section of the town's society. But he wouldn't allow himself to believe that Charity had stooped to that level.

They were still in town at noon and Dane found a restaurant where he and Tubulo ordered a meal. When the waitress brought the plates, Dane asked her to wait a minute. She was an older woman and he had the feeling she would know if Charity had ever been in Junction City.

"I'm looking for a girl," Dane said. "She'd be about twenty-five now. Blue eyes, red hair, weighing about a hundred and twenty pounds. She might have been here three or four years ago. She may still be here."

The woman looked at Dane for a minute. "She your sister?"

Dane shook his head. "My wife. I was in the war. They burned out my place. My wife disappeared. I've got to find out what happened to her."

The waitress bit her under lip. "Was that red hair long, down below her waist?"

Dane nodded. "It was when she let it down. She wore it in a big bun on the back of her head."

"It's hard to say with no more description than that. And I ain't got the best memory in the world. But I do recall a red-headed girl who ate here now and then back in about '65."

"She's gone now?" Dane asked.

The woman nodded. "Been gone for nigh onto three years, I reckon. I don't know where she came from or

106

where she went. She likely ain't the one you're looking for, anyway."

Dane frowned at the sudden change in the woman. "Why not?"

"I can see what kind of a wife you would have had. This girl wasn't that kind."

Dane nodded and sighed. The waitress went on and Dane and Tubulo ate their dinner.

They left the restaurant and rode southwest along the tracks. They camped on the open prairie that night and rode into Abilene the next day before noon.

Dane had heard about Abilene before he even got back to Kansas. Somebody named McCoy had built huge stockyards here and was shipping Texas cattle east. The big hotel, Drover's Cottage, that McCoy had built, dominated the town like a giant among pygmies.

"Sure looks like a busy place," Tubulo said as they halted on the east edge of town.

Dust was rising in a cloud from the shipping pens just on the other side of town. It looked like forty or fifty railroad cars were shunted off on a sidetrack beside the loading pens.

The town itself presented a contrast. On the south side of the tracks were buildings that had the looks of some degree of permanency. Across the tracks were dozens of slapped together shacks, offering nothing but partial protection from the elements.

"Looks like a wild town," Tubulo observed. "Yockam might have bought a saloon here or started a game."

"Maybe," Dane agreed. "You can bet there's a lot of money flowing around here with all these cattle sales and cowboy wages."

They rode on into town, following a street along one side of the track then crossing over to Texas Street in the shack town. Somebody had painted in crude letters on one side of an unpainted shack, "Texas Abilene."

"The cowboy part of town," Dane said. "I've heard of it. Yockam is probably here if he's anywhere in town."

They dismounted in front of a saloon called the Alamo. It certainly did no credit to the soldiers who had fought and died at the Alamo but its name probably appealed to the cowboys who were so far from their Texas homes.

Tubulo stopped at the door of the saloon. "Look in there, Dane," he said softly. "Drunks, gamblers and painted ladies."

They went inside and Dane searched the faces around the gambling tables at the back of the saloon. Kurt Uhl could be here, too. Dane remembered how well he liked to play cards. He might consider himself good enough to try his hand against half drunk cowboys who had far more money than judgment.

As his eyes swept over the room, they were caught by a red-headed painted girl standing behind a gambler at a table. For an instant, his heart almost stopped. Then he got a look at her face as she turned half around. There was no resemblance to Charity in those hard lines and sharp features. Maybe this was the girl that the waitress in Junction City had seen.

His eyes moved on and barely caught a glimpse of a man hurrying out the back door of the saloon. In that instant, he thought he recognized Lon Yockam. But he hadn't seen enough of him to be sure. He had been so intent on finding Yockam that he might mistake any big man for him when he got only a quick glimpse.

"Did you see that man leaving through the back door?" Dane asked Tubulo.

Tubulo shook his head. "I can't see much but legs in

a crowd like this."

Dane realized that Tubulo wouldn't be able to see beyond the few people closest to him. He didn't reach much higher than the waist bands of some of the cowboys.

Dane moved over to the bar. Catching a bartender who seemed more inclined to visit than work, Dane asked him about Yockam, describing him.

The man nodded. "I think maybe I've seen him. I see an awful lot of people going and coming so I can't be sure. This is the first big year for Abilene as a cow town. It sure ain't going to be the last."

Dane described Kurt Uhl but stirred no memory in the man. He thought of asking about Charity but didn't. She wouldn't be in this element and, even if she was, he wasn't sure he wanted to know.

Dane moved outside with Tubulo clinging to him like a burr. Tubulo had probably never seen a mob like this. Dane was guessing there must be a thousand cowboys in some stage of drunkenness racing or roaming up and down Texas Street, the main street on this side of the tracks. He saw no sign of any lawman and an inquiry revealed that there was no marshal or law of any kind in Abilene this summer.

Dane and Tubulo went into a half dozen saloons with no luck. When they got out of the last one, Dane suggested that they ride out to the loading pens. He'd had enough of Texas Abilene.

The noise was even worse down by the pens but here it was mostly angry bawling from aggravated cattle and shouts and curses from equally aggravated cowboys.

Dane rode slowly around the pens while Tubulo dismounted and climbed up on the heavy board fence to watch in awe as the cattle were loaded. Dane looked at every man he saw. He didn't really expect to see Yockam but he might have come down here if that had been him he'd seen disappear out the back of the Alamo. Dane expected Yockam to try to keep out of his way.

Reaching the far end, he started to swing back up the other side. As he crossed the tracks, he thought he saw a big man near one of the holding pens. It looked like Yockam just as every big man reminded him of the man he wanted so much to see.

Nudging his horse forward, he reined in toward the holding pen. Again he thought he saw him climbing a fence ahead of him. Dismounting, he tied his horse. He couldn't chase a man through pens of cattle on horseback.

Dane ran forward, planning to climb the fence of the next pen to get a look at the big man to see if it was the Alpha marshal.

As he ran past one of the crowded pens, the gate suddenly swung open and cattle poured out onto the prairie like water out of a bucket. Dane was almost directly in front of the wild-eyed steers and he had no chance of getting out of their way.

CHAPTER 12

DANE HAD NO TIME TO WONDER WHY THAT GATE HAD suddenly sprung open and the cattle turned loose. He knew he couldn't escape the wild charge of the frightened steers. All he could hope to do was divert them.

Jumping up and down and waving his arms wildly, he tried to scare the wild-eyed lead steer worse than he already was. The steer snorted but when Dane didn't get out of his path, he lunged to one side, slamming against another steer and pushing him aside. Others followed the lead steer's move until all fifty head in that holding pen had gone past Dane and streamed out onto the prairie.

Dane was choking on the dust the steers had stirred up. He stared at the pens, wondering if any more cattle would be coming at him. But he saw only the one gate open.

Then through the dust, he saw a man leap up to the top of the fence of the empty pen, a gun in his hand. Dane dived headlong into the dust as the gun roared. The bullet snapped through the air above his head, hitting the ground several feet beyond him.

Rolling frantically, Dane tried to get his gun free. He expected a hail of bullets now. One of them would surely hit him. That had to be Lon Yockam on the fence. It must have been Yockam who had opened that gate, hoping the steers would trample Dane to death in their dash to freedom. As soon as he saw that his plan had failed, he had leaped up on the fence and started shooting. Dane was out in the open. For Yockam, it would be like shooting a crippled rabbit.

Dane clawed his gun free and rolled to his knees, facing the pen. But he didn't shoot. There were three men up there on the fence now. Yockam was clawing at a whip lash wrapped around his neck while one cowboy jerked the gun from Yockam's hand.

Dane still held his gun in his hand but now one of the cowboys pointed a gun his way.

"Don't do it, mister, or you're dead!"

Dane dropped his gun back in his holster and stood up. Yockam wasn't going to do him any damage now.

He started walking toward the pen but one man jerked Yockam off the fence and pushed him down a runway between pens while the other cowboy stayed where he was, his gun still trained on Dane.

"Stop right there, fellow," the cowboy said. "There ain't going to be no more shooting unless I have to shoot you. These critters are spooked enough."

Dane realized then that the cowboys weren't interested in keeping either him or Yockam alive. They wanted to keep the cattle from breaking down these heavy pens and stampeding.

"I want that man who shot at me," Dane said.

"You'll have to get him somewhere else," the cowboy said.

The cowboy held his gun on Dane and Dane knew better than to crowd his luck. He'd be dead if he did.

"Are you going to let Yockam get away?"

"Sel may kill him for turning that pen of cattle loose," the cowboy said. "I wouldn't blame him. It will take two or three hours to get them back in here."

Dane thought of arguing longer but knew it would be no use. No matter what he told the cowboy about Yockam, he wasn't going to let Dane go after him.

The cowboy kept an eye on Dane but he did flip a glance backward once in a while to see where the other cowboy had taken Yockam. Finally he put his gun away.

"You can go. If you find that jasper now, you'll be far enough away from here that your shooting won't spook the cattle."

Dane went back to his horse and untied him from the fence. Riding around to the other side of the pens where he had left Tubulo, he found the little man still on the fence watching the activity. Dane climbed up beside him.

"See where Yockam went?" he asked.

Tubulo nodded. "That cowboy escorted him half way to town then gave him a kick in the pants." Tubulo grinned. "You should have seen that. Yockam didn't even turn around and swear at him."

"Probably afraid to."

"I reckon," Tubulo said. "I thought every critter in all these pens was going to stampede out of here when Yockam fired that gun. Ain't cattle supposed to be used to guns?"

"About the only time they hear a gun is when the riders are trying to turn a stampede," Dane said. "Anyway, they're plenty spooked by these pens. I doubt if any of them have ever been in pens before. They're as jumpy as cats at a dog show."

"Where will Yockam go now?" Tubulo asked.

"I wish I knew. Let's get back to town and see if we can find him."

They rode back to town. Although they searched every place they could imagine Yockam might be on both sides of the tracks, they didn't find him.

A train went through town going west. Dane hurried that way. But it paused only briefly at the station than moved out. Dane didn't get close enough to see whether Yockam got on or not. A few minutes later the cattle train, fully loaded now, puffed slowly onto the main track and went east. Dane couldn't see into the caboose. Yockam might be there but he doubted it.

"I'll bet Yockam is gone, one direction or the other," Tubulo said.

"I won't take that bet," Dane agreed. "I'm guessing he went west. He has had enough of cattle and cowboys."

"Are we heading out right now?"

"Let's wait till morning," Dane said. "Yockam knows we expect him to take the train out. He might have stayed to throw us off his trail."

Tubulo nodded. They crossed over into Texas Abilene once more and toured the saloons where Dane thought Yockam might be. He checked the boarding houses but found no trace of him there, either.

Dane made some inquiries about Charity but didn't turn up any clue. He was beginning to doubt that she had come west at all. She might be dead or she might have gone east from Topeka.

The town was well filled so Dane and Tubulo slept in the hay mow of the livery barn that night. Dane had never seen anything like Abilene. Over in the wild half of town, the lights never went out. There was yelling all night and a couple of times shots rang out. When Dane and Tubulo got up the next morning, there was still some activity across the tracks.

"That place never shuts down," the livery owner said, shaking his head sadly. "Abilene is a nice town in the winter. But look at it now. I reckon there won't be a quiet minute until all the cattle are gone this fall."

Dane didn't say anything but he could sympathize with the man. He wouldn't want to live here where night was the liveliest part of the day.

Once outside Abilene, Dane and Tubulo rode past herds of cattle being held on the grass to fatten before shipping. Dane was sure they were at least ten miles out of town before they passed the last herd. And a couple of columns of dust to the south told of new herds still coming. He wasn't surprised that Yockam had stopped there to make a killing off the cowboys.

It was almost sundown when they came within sight

114

of another town sprawled along the tracks. The one building that stuck up here was a hotel, something like Joseph McCoy's Drover's Cottage had stuck up above the other buildings at Abilene.

"Let's get a room there," Dane said.

"How about money?" Tubulo asked.

"I've got enough yet," Dane said. "A good bed feels good after a long day in the saddle. I can find a job if our money runs out."

Salina wasn't much of a town. There was only one place where they could leave their horses where they would be fed. The man who owned the barn said that the big hotel belonged to Mother Bickerdyke. The soldiers she had nursed during the war had given her that name. Last year she had come out and picked the place for her hotel before the rails had reached the town. Now she had as good a hotel as there was west of Abilene.

Dane and Tubulo headed back toward the hotel. The hotel was a good one and the supper there was the best meal Dane had had for a long time.

Dane and Tubulo went out on the street after supper but they found that Salina, in sharp contrast to Abilene, had little activity after dark. A short tour around town convinced Dane that neither Yockam nor Kurt Uhl would stop here. There was nothing in Salina to challenge their talents.

They rode on the next morning. Late in the afternoon, they passed Brookville with its big roundhouse for the repair and maintenance of the locomotives. But there again Dane saw nothing that would attract men like Yockam or Uhl.

Dane and Tubulo rode on beyond the town about four miles and camped for the night. It was sometime in the afternoon of the next day that they came to Fort Harker. Riding on to the town of Ellsworth a few miles to the west, Dane called a halt for the night.

"He might be here," Dane said to Tubulo. "An army camp close by means lots of soldiers and they usually have some money."

Tubulo agreed. They looked around Ellsworth. It was a fair sized town. Most of the buildings were new or just moved up from the river bottom where the flood the year before had inundated the old town. But Ellsworth had been in existence almost as long as the fort had been, which was four years, first as Fort Ellsworth and then as Fort Harker.

Their search here proved fruitless and Dane wondered if he would ever cut the trail of Yockam again. So far he had found no trace of Kurt Uhl, either. And he had almost stopped looking for Charity.

Impatiently, Dane pushed on the next morning. They had been riding leisurely. But Dane was beginning to feel he had to hurry or he might never find the men he was after.

Dane guessed they covered about forty miles before sunset. Tubulo was pretty tired when they halted for camp. The little man couldn't take the long days like Dane could. Still, Dane wasn't sorry he had brought Tubulo along. He was good company and he had sharp eyes. He didn't miss much.

"When will we get to Fort Hays?" Tubulo asked before they went to sleep.

"We should make it about noon tomorrow," Dane said.

"Maybe we ought to go around that place," Tubulo said. "I don't like the feeling I have."

Dane studied the little man. Tubulo seemed to have

116

premonitions about people and places. But instead of considering Tubulo's suggestion that they pass up the town of Hays City, he felt an urge to get there quickly. Tubulo's feelings might mean that here they would catch up with Yockam.

It was a little after noon when they reached the town of Hays City. The fort was off to the southwest of town a short distance. It, too, was fairly new. The flood of the year before had washed over the old Fort Hays, several miles down Big Creek. Some soldiers had died in that flood. The army had moved the post up here close to the railroad and the town of Hays City.

Dane and Tubulo rode around town cautiously then Dane reined west to the little town of Rome. Here they found the rough element. This town had been started by the scout, Bill Cody, and a man named Rose. They had been here before the town of Hays City had ever been thought of.

But when the railroad put its depot in the new village of Hays City, most of Rome moved across the railroad grade to the new town. Rome faded rapidly. The cholera epidemic of the year before had almost wiped it out. But it was still there, smaller but rougher and tougher than its neighbor.

Dane and Tubulo went back to Hays City and got a room for the night. Then they prowled the streets after dark. There were no Texas cowboys here like there had been in Abilene but Hays City was not a quiet place. The fort was close enough that soldiers were everywhere. Saloons were busy and the gambling tables were never empty. Dane felt that he might find Yockam or Uhl here.

"Do you still have that bad feeling about this place?" Dane asked Tubulo.

The little man nodded. "I don't like it, Dane. There's trouble here."

"Do you think we'll find Yockam?"

Tubulo shrugged. "I don't know. I just don't feel right about this place. It's even worse over in that town of Rome."

"Maybe that's the place where we ought to be looking," Dane said.

"Not unless you want something terrible to happen," Tubulo predicted solemnly.

Dane looked through the saloons in Hays City. But he found nothing. About midnight, the saloons closed down.

"We'll look the whole place over tomorrow," Dane said as they went to bed. "Yockam must be here. There's nothing much west of here."

"I'll feel safer looking in the daytime," Tubulo said.

Dane started with the hotel and the stores the next morning, asking if anybody had seen a man fitting Yockam's description. Last night, he'd thought he might find Yockam in person. Now he was depending on questions to tell him if he was still on Yockam's trail.

Only one storekeeper responded favorably to Dane's description of Yockam and he wasn't sure. Dane doubted if the man had seen Yockam at all. A lot of big men could fit the best description Dane could give of him.

The saloons opened a short time before noon and Dane checked with a couple before going to dinner. One bartender nodded when Dane described Yockam.

"I think he was in here just a couple of days ago." He pointed to a table in the back of the room. "He played cards there with some soldiers three or four nights in a row. But he hasn't been in the last day or two."

118

This time Dane felt confident he had found the trail of Yockam again. The bartender had seen Yockam enough times to recognize him. Further inquiries at other saloons, however, brought no favorable responses.

Late in the afternoon, Dane headed his horse toward Rome in spite of Tubulo's reluctance. Rome had few businesses except saloons and a big dance hall. Dane headed for the saloons. He doubted if the girls at the dance hall would admit seeing Yockam if he'd been there. Their customers were their private business.

At a saloon right across the street from the dance hall, Dane inquired of the bartender and got an affirmative nod.

"He's been here several times."

"When was the last time?" Dane asked.

"Yesterday," the bartender said. "Said he was leaving."

"Where was he going?"

The bartender frowned. "Mister, I don't ask questions like that. He didn't volunteer any information. There's Lizzie. He was with her yesterday. Maybe he told her."

Dane saw the girl who had come into the saloon. He didn't have to be told she had come from the dance hall across the street. He spoke to Lizzie and asked about Yockam.

She shrugged. "I see too many men to remember what each one says. I think he did say he was leaving. But I didn't ask where was he was going. Didn't make any difference to me."

Dane left the saloon. Tubulo was ahead of him and Dane could see the relief on his craggy little face when they were outside.

"We're still on the trail," Dane said. "He may have gone back east from here but I'm betting he went west.

119

We'll go on and find out."

It was almost sundown and Dane led the way a couple of miles up the track west of Rome before finding a good camping place. He was thinking more of Charity than Yockam. He was becoming convinced that Charity was either dead or a long way from here. She would never stay in a place like Rome or Hays City.

"We'd better get going early tomorrow," Tubulo said uneasily as they were spreading their blankets. "I still don't like this place."

"We'll be riding early," Dane promised.

They were far enough from the twin towns that no sound reached them. It seemed to Dane that they were cut off from all civilization. He was thinking of Charity when he went to sleep.

It was pitch black when running feet awakened him. He realized in a flash that those boots were coming toward him. Dane rolled out of blankets just as a big man hit him.

CHAPTER 13

DANE WAS BOWLED BACKWARD LIKE A FEATHER IN A wind gust. He jerked himself sideways and managed to avoid the full impact of the big man's weight. He believed the man had intended to crush him in that first fall.

Dane saw another man behind the first. And from Tubulo's terrified squeal, he knew there was still another one after him.

Lunging backward away from the reaching arms of the two men, Dane felt a fury building inside him. These men were jackals, trying to kill without risking any injury to themselves. The bruises Dane had already sustained only added to his fury.

Dane lurched to his feet as the two men charged at him again. He couldn't make out much about them except that both were big. From the pain that streaked through him when one of their blows landed, he knew they were powerful.

He heard Tubulo's squeal as the man attacking him scored a hit. A red mist swept over Dane. Tubulo had certainly done nothing to deserve a beating like this. And he had saved Dane more than once. It was Dane's turn now to save the little man. He'd have to do something fast. These men had come to kill.

Tubulo squealed again. Ignoring all precaution, Dane charged toward Tubulo. But the two men were between him and the little man. Dane didn't hesitate. He had been trying to avoid the punishment the two were handing out. Now he ignored the punishment and waded in.

Dane's sudden attack surprised the two big men but they didn't retreat. Dane felt the pain of their blows but he shut his mind to the pain and concentrated on bulling his way past them. He landed a fist in the middle of one of the blurred faces before him and that one sagged back. But then a blow from the other man caught him on the cheek bone and spun him around. Before he could recover, another fist smashed into his side.

He felt himself falling but even as he fell, his fury threatened to burst his chest. As he hit the ground, he saw the man lunging toward him. Rolling to one side, he avoided the main force of the blow but he was still struck in the side.

He didn't think so much of dying himself; he was thinking of Tubulo. Tubulo shouldn't even be here. He had come along to help Dane. Now he was dying because of it.

The thought gave Dane new strength. Once more, he ignored his bruises and rolled around to meet the attack. Both men were on the ground with him now, apparently feeling they could kill him more easily with their hands if they had him down.

A hand reached for his windpipe but a thumb got into Dane's eye instead. The little finger of the hand brushed down across Dane's mouth. He clamped his teeth on that finger and felt the bone crush. The man screamed and lunged backward.

Dane wheeled his attention to the other man who was hammering his chest and face, apparently trying to knock him unconscious. Dane clawed at the man's face with both hands, getting a finger in one eye and twisting. The man howled and tore at Dane's hands.

As the man backed off, Dane lunged upward, upsetting him. He rolled him to the ground and lurched to his feet. The man with the crushed finger was coming toward him now, both hands above his head. Dane saw that he had something in his hands, probably a rock.

Dane dodged to one side and the force of the man's downward swing carried him to the ground as he missed his target. Dane landed on him, his fingers clawing for the rock. He found it and jerked it from the man's hands. Before the man could roll around to throw Dane off his back, Dane brought that rock down on his head. He hit him again and again as a red fog clouded his reasoning.

He was finally thrown off the man's back by a body block from the other attacker. But he held onto the rock and swung it around, hitting the man on the arm. The man screamed in pain and Dane was sure he had broken that arm.

Lunging to his feet, he started for the man then heard Tubulo squeal again. He wished he had his gun but that was under the coat he'd been using for a pillow. He lunged toward the sound of Tubulo's squeals.

The man beating Tubulo was not as big as the other two but he was a monster in comparison to Tubulo's size. Dane hit him with the force of a charging buffalo bull, knocking him spinning. Dane leaped over Tubulo and followed the man. The man came to his feet and lunged to meet Dane. Dane swung the rock which he still gripped. The rock stopped the man with a crunching thud. He went down and Dane knew he wouldn't get up.

Wheeling back, he found the man he had hit on the arm writhing on the ground. Dane ran to him, the rock poised above his head. The man held up one hand to ward off the blow, half screaming that he gave up.

The red mist slowly faded from Dane, leaving his heart threatening to burst from his rib cage. A wariness swept over him. He lowered the rock but didn't drop it from his hand. Tubulo came shuffling toward him.

"Are you all right?" Dane asked, not turning his head.

"I'm alive," Tubulo said. "That's better than I expected."

"Can you get a fire started?" Dane asked. "I want a look at these sidewinders."

"Sure," Tubulo said.

Dane kept the rock in his hand and watched the man squirming in pain before him. There was no stir from either of the other two attackers.

The fire flickered to life as Tubulo started it with dry grass and some buffalo chips. Dane looked sharply at the faces of the three men. He didn't know any of them.

"What was the idea of jumping us?" Dane demanded

of the man with the broken arm.

The man glared at Dane through his pain. "You looked like you had money," he muttered.

Dane looked at Tubulo and shook his head. "That won't go down. You wouldn't have had to kill us to get our money."

The man scowled. "A man hired us to kill you two," he finally said sullenly. "He said there would be a big man and a little runt."

"Yockam?" Dane demanded.

The man glared at Dane and finally nodded his head. "That's the name he used."

"Where did he go?"

"Somewhere to meet a friend. Said he couldn't wait to do the job himself."

"He was afraid to try it himself," Tubulo said. "Look what it got you." He looked at Dane. "Those other two have cashed in."

Dane nodded and concentrated on the one survivor. "Who was this friend he was going to meet?"

"He didn't say," the man said sullenly. "What are you going to do with me?"

"Dead men tell no tales," Tubulo said.

"We were just doing what we were hired to do," the man said, fear twisting his face.

"Don't take jobs you ain't man enough to handle," Dane said. He looked at Tubulo. "Get the horses?"

"No more sleep?" Tubulo asked.

"Not here, anyway. Do you feel like sleeping?"

Tubulo shook his head and disappeared into the darkness. Dane looked again at the wounded man.

"You were in the saloon at Rome, weren't you?"

The man nodded. "We all worked there."

Tubulo came with the horses. Dane let Tubulo watch

124

the prisoner while he saddled up. Then he handed the reins of the spotted pony to Tubulo. He looked at the man on the ground. From the fear in his face, it was obvious that he expected to be killed before they left.

Dane swung up on his horse. "I reckon you can walk back to Rome and brag about how you beat up two travelers," he said. "Come on, Tubulo."

Reining around, he led the way into the darkness, heading west up the railroad tracks. He knew they couldn't go far as badly beaten up as they were. But he also knew they had to get out of here. Those three might have friends who would come looking for them.

"How far are we going to ride?" Tubulo asked.

"Only far enough so nobody from Rome can find us," Dane said. "I'm boogered up pretty bad. How about you?"

"More bruises than a swatted fly," Tubulo said. "You killed two and broke the arm of the other one." There was awe in his voice. "I don't ever want to get you mad at me."

Dane turned his horse in under a trestle that crossed a deep gully. he tied his horse to one of the heavy poles holding up the trestle.

"They won't find us here," he said.

He had ridden about as far as he could go until he let those bruises heal a little and he imagined Tubulo was in no better shape.

Dane barely stirred the next day. If anything, Tubulo was bruised up worse than Dane. Dane was glad neither had any broken bones. Just getting out of that ambush alive was something to be thankful for.

Dane took the horses out a short distance from the railroad and picketed them where they could graze then came back into the shade of the trestle. He and Tubulo ate only once during the long day, shortly after a train rattled over the trestle, waking them up.

By the next morning Dane felt able to move on and Tubulo agreed that he could ride. They didn't go far but Dane realized they would have time to let their wounds heal. If they caught up with Yockam at all, it would surely be at the end of track, Sheridan. There wasn't much between here and there, he knew from what he'd heard.

They took three days getting to the fading town of Coyote, which had been the next end-of-track town west of Hays City. Dane and Tubulo didn't even stop.

They passed another little town called Carlyle a couple of days later. The soreness was mostly gone from Dane's bruises now and Tubulo was again acting like himself.

At the next station, Monument, Dane turned in. It was little more than a telegraph station. He asked the man there how much further it was to Sheridan.

"About twenty miles," the man said. "But if you ain't looking for trouble, you'd better stay away from there."

Dane nodded. "Maybe I'm looking for trouble."

"In that case, just keep riding. Good luck."

As they neared Sheridan, the next day about noon, Dane resigned himself to the fact that he'd either find Yockam and Uhl here or he would probably never find them. If they had gone on west, it would have been by stage and there wasn't any place for them to stop till they reached Denver. And a man could lose himself in a town that size where nobody could find him.

Tubulo twisted uneasily in his saddle as they followed the railroad which curved to the north then pointed back southwest. Sheridan was sprawled out before them on both sides of the track, most of the tents

126

and dugouts on the south side.

"Something bothering you?" Dane asked.

"I don't like the feel of this place," Tubulo said.

Dane grinned. "Glad to hear that. You seem to feel trouble before it touches you. In this case, trouble is probably spelled Yockam."

"Maybe," Tubulo said, frowning. "But I don't like it."

Dane knew he would find a boisterous bustling town at the end of track but he hadn't expected anything quite like this. They rode into town along the tracks and Dane reined in at the Cross-Tie Saloon next to the Perry Hotel. They went inside. The bartender scowled at Tubulo then waited for their order.

"A couple of lemonades," Dane said.

The bartender frowned again then shrugged. "Guess it is a little early for the good stuff."

"Need a clear head to look over the town," Dane said. "How many people are here, anyway?"

"Nobody knows. They're guessing over two thousand. Besides the usual people in a town at the end of track, we've got a lot of railroad workers with no jobs, Mexican freighters from Santa Fe, buffalo hunters who sell their hides to Otero & Sellars and W.H. Chick and some other buyers and a company of soldiers from Fort Wallace to handle army supplies coming in on the rails." The bartender shrugged. "Makes a lively town."

"What kind of law do you have?"

"The only law in this town is the law you carry in your holster, mister. If you can't live by that law, you'd better get out or you'll get a high lot in a hurry."

"High lot?" Dane asked.

"Sure. A six by three hole in the ground up on the hill north of town."

The bartender laughed at his own joke. Dane and

Tubulo finished their lemonades and went back outside.

"We'll stay at the hotel tonight," Dane said. "If I don't land a job pretty quick, we'll have to find a place outside town to camp."

They turned back to the east and went into the Perry Hotel. Getting a room and carrying their belongings up to it, they went back and rode on down the tracks. A lot of the town was sprawled to the south on the gentle slope leading down to the North Fork of the Smoky Hill River. Somewhere in all this turmoil, Dane was sure he'd find Lon Yockam and maybe Kurt Uhl, too. As always, he thought of Charity. But he had decided some time back that she had not come this far. He couldn't shake the feeling that she was probably dead.

At the west end of town, they found a livery barn on the north side of the tracks and they left their horses there. Walking back, Tubulo suggested that they split up and see what they could find.

Dane agreed but with a warning for him to be careful. Then he headed down into the lower end of town. There were no street markers; in fact, there were hardly any street delineations. He found a hodge-podge of saloons and dance halls and little else. He had the feeling that life was dirt cheap down here.

Going back to the tracks, he stopped at the Section House. If the railroad had any jobs available, they should know about it here. It didn't look to Dane like any other kind of work would be available unless it was a bartender or gambler. He'd be no good at either.

The man surprisingly nodded when Dane asked if the railroad was hiring. "We ain't hiring many men," he said. "But we got orders to go ahead with the grading north of the Twin Buttes. All our former hands are either making more money gambling or else found out they weren't gamblers and went broke and left. We can use a man who can drive a team on a scraper. Can you?"

Dane nodded. "I was a farmer in eastern Kansas." He didn't add that that had been six years ago.

The man nodded. "Be ready to go to work at seven in the morning."

Dane went out to find Tubulo. He finally located him standing just inside the Bullhead Saloon, watching people going and coming through the door.

"See anybody you know?" Dane asked.

"Not yet. But I think everybody west of Hays City is right here in this town."

"Let's go to the hotel and rest up," Dane suggested. "We'll have plenty of time to look for Yockam and Uhl. I got a job working on the railroad so we can eat well. We'll spend the evenings looking for Yockam. I figure he'll show himself more at night than in the daytime, anyway."

Tubulo nodded. "He's probably aiming to get rich at the gaming tables."

"Plenty of gambling here," Dane said. "This is wilder than Abilene."

Dane hoped the soreness of his bruises wouldn't flare up again when he began working. At supper time, he went downstairs with Tubulo and found a table in the hotel barroom where they could eat.

Before they had finished their meal, a girl came in, blue eyes flashing over the room. Dane barely noticed her but Tubulo kicked him under the table.

"Look who's got her eyes on you," he whispered.

Dane looked up. The blue-eyed girl with the silver blond hair was coming straight toward his table, her eyes fixed on him. Dane laid down his fork. He had never seen the girl before. Yet she was coming as if she had just seen an old friend.

"Mind if I sit down?" the girl asked quietly when she reached the table.

Dane shrugged. "Pull up a chair. I don't believe we've met."

"Please don't let anyone else know that we're not old friends," she said softly. "I want somebody to believe we are. My name is Mamie Zehr."

"I'm pleased to meet you, I think," Dane said, suspicion running through him.

Maybe the girl was really in trouble. But he couldn't bring himself to trust anyone in this town. He kept thinking that Mamie Zehr might be the bait in a trap. He could be dead before he found out.

CHAPTER 14

DANE STUDIED THE GIRL IN THE CHAIR BESIDE HIM. She was very small, not much bigger than Tubulo, although she didn't look under-sized like Tubulo did. Dane had to admit she was pretty, something he hadn't expected to find here in Sheridan. The women he'd seen on the street down in the lower part of town had left their beauty far behind, if they'd ever had any.

"Any reason why you want to appear to be good friends with us?" Dane asked finally.

"There's a man who has been pushing his attention on me," she said softly. "I told him I had all the friends I needed. He was following me down the street and I stopped here, thinking maybe I could make him believe some big strong man here was the friend I was talking about."

"Why me?" Dane said. "There are bigger, tougher-

130

looking men in here than me."

"Not the kind I had told him was my friend."

Tubulo spoke up, his voice squeaky with apprehension. "Dane has had all the fighting he needs. He ain't taking on somebody else's war."

"Dane?" The girl turned her big eyes on him. "That's a pretty name."

"His name will be mud if he listens to you," Tubulo said.

"Dane Banning," Dane said. He looked at the door. "I don't see your would-be friend."

"He won't come in here," Mamie said. "This is too high class for him. But if he sees me sitting with you, maybe he'll let me alone."

Dane considered what the girl was saying. It could be true. There were twenty men here for every woman. And there must be a hundred men for every decent girl. He wasn't sure what kind of a girl Mamie was. But she gave the appearance of decency.

"Do you live here in Sheridan?"

"Of course," she said with a shrug. "Where else could a person live around here? I stay in a boarding house down beyond Otero and Sellar's warehouse."

"Isn't that a rough part of town?"

"Every part of this town is rough," she said, lips grim. "I work at the Antelope Restaurant. I was going to work just now but I was afraid I wouldn't get there before that man caught up with me."

"Looks to me like you'd better catch the next train back east," Dane said.

Mamie sighed. "I've got to make enough money for a ticket before I can leave."

Dane finished his meal. "We'll walk you to your job."

"Thank you."

131

Dane had expected her to refuse the offer. Something about the way she had come straight to his table smacked of a trap. He couldn't get it out of his mind. He hadn't caught her in anything that he could prove was not true but he didn't trust her.

Paying for the meals, Dane and Tubulo went outside, Mamie walking between them. Mamie was only a little taller than Tubulo and not as heavy. Yet she looked cute and petite while Tubulo looked like what he was, a dwarf.

"Which way?" Dane asked.

She motioned west. "The Antelope is down this way."

Suspicion soared in Dane's mind. That was the same direction as Otero and Sellar's warehouse. How could she have been going from her boarding house to the restaurant and still go by the Perry Hotel?

Dane kept on the alert as they went down the street. They passed three saloons. Then they came to the Antelope Restaurant, across the tracks from the railroad Section House. Dane and Tubulo followed Mamie inside. He expected her ruse to show up here. But the man behind the counter yelled at her the instant she appeared.

"It's about time you showed up, Mamie. We've got more business than I can take care of alone."

"I'll be right there," Mamie said. She turned to Dane. "Thanks for walking me down here. I'll be all right now. That man will go down on Rat's Row to spend his evening."

"Where's Rat's Row?" Dane demanded.

"Down on the slope toward the river. If you go down there after dark, you're liable to get shot or stabbed."

Dane nodded and went outside. He turned to Tubulo.

132

"What do you make of her?"

"She's tricky," Tubulo said. "Somebody put her up to something."

"Sort of what I figured," Dane agreed. "But who knows we're here?"

"Somebody must have recognized us," Tubulo said. "And the only people who would know us are the ones who want us dead."

"Let's take a swing down along Rat's Row," Dane said.

Reluctantly, Tubulo agreed. They cut down the little side street beyond the warehouse. The din coming from that section of town was enough to warn any person valuing his life to stay away. Dane realized this was the same street he'd been on this afternoon. Now it was all noise and confusion. Men were staggering along the street, going in and stumbling out of saloons. Perfumed girls were sitting or standing on dimly lighted porches of the dance halls. They were attracting as much attention as the saloons and would draw even more as the evening wore on.

Dane kept an eye open for a glimpse of Yockam. They moved down the length of the street and turned back to the railroad tracks without seeing anyone they knew. This had seemed like a noisy street today but it looked calm to Dane now after coming from Rat's Row.

Dane and Tubulo sat on the hotel porch and Dane planned their days. Tubulo would move cautiously around town while Dane was at work. If he found anything worth investigating, he would tell Dane when he got off work. He would take no chances. Tubulo agreed.

Dane went to work the next morning and found that it wasn't hard. The railroad was not hurrying the construction. Dane found himself working on a cut through the shale slope north of the Twin Buttes that looked down on Sheridan from the southwest.

The North Fork of the Smoky Hill River came down from the northwest, running east of the buttes, then swinging almost due east as if putting a southern limit of the expansion of the town. East of town a ways, the creek cut sharply to the southeast again, meeting the South Fork of the Smoky Hill River about eight miles southeast of Sheridan.

The trestle for the railroad to cross the creek had already been made. But it would take a lot of work to make the cut through the northern edge of the bluff north of the buttes. Beyond this cut, Dane was told, the grade would run smoothly to Fort Wallace about seventeen miles to the southwest.

With only a little money to hire men and no firm contract to go ahead with the road, there was no urgency to get the cut made and the men worked lackadaisically. Dane felt that he had hardly earned his wages when they went back across the creek to town while the sun was still well up in the sky.

Tubulo was waiting for Dane when he arrived at the hotel. He looked as if he'd had a harder day than Dane had.

"What did you find out today?" Dane asked.

"Not much," Tubulo said. "But I figure I will if I keep watching."

"Let's wash up and go down to the Antelope for supper," Dane suggested.

Tubulo nodded. "Maybe Mamie will tell us something. I went by there twice this afternoon and she was working both times. I think she works there afternoons and evenings. So she wasn't going to work when she bobbed in on us last night."

"I know that," Dane said. "This hotel is not on the way between her boarding house and the Antelope Restaurant."

Mamie saw them as soon as they stepped in the door. "I'm glad you came here," she said, face beaming. "We'll feed you better and for a lower price than the hotel."

"That's what we're here to find out," Dane said.

Mamie seemed completely open about everything this evening. Dane found himself attracted to her in spite of his suspicions. When they had finished their meal, she invited them back.

"I suppose we'll eat there from now on," Tubulo said as they left.

"The grub is good," Dane said. "And it is cheaper. Why not?"

"You just want to look at Mamie," Tubulo accused. "Are you forgetting Charity?"

Dane shook his head. "I'll never forget Charity. But I'm having doubts that I'll ever find her. She may not even be alive."

Putting his thoughts into words took the glow off the evening. Mamie had given him a lift, but it was gone now.

It was two nights later when Dane came in from work that he found Tubulo pacing the porch of the hotel, anxiously waiting for him.

"What did you find?" Dane demanded before he reached the top of the steps.

"Kurt Uhl," Tubulo said.

"Where?"

"He's a gambler down in the Dew Drop Inn Saloon on Rat's Row."

"Let's go have a talk with him," Dane said.

"You'll have to talk with guns," Tubulo warned.

"That's all right with me, I've come a long way to find him. I don't want to miss seeing him now."

Dane checked his gun. He was the only man on the crew who wore his gun. Several had rifles in case of Indian attack but Dane wore his revolver on his hip and the foreman didn't object.

The sun was still a half hour high when Dane and Tubulo got down to the street that people referred to as Rat's Row. Tubulo led the way toward the saloon where he had seen Uhl.

"You didn't let Uhl see you, did you?" Dane asked.

"No. Uhl and Yockam both know me. They'd kill me on sight."

Ahead of them a man suddenly burst out of a saloon, waving a shotgun. Dane stopped and caught Tubulo's arm. The man was drunk and he was waving the gun around without any regard to the direction it was pointed.

"That's the Dew Drop Inn," Tubulo said.

"Who's the man with the gun?"

"Never saw him before."

The man was yelling that he was king of the whole town, challenging any rivals. Most people were getting out of his way.

The man's voice rose to a scream. Jamming the gun butt against his shoulder, he fired first one barrel, then the other. The shots went just above the level of the crowd but it made every man either drop flat in the street or streak for an alley, bending low. Dane pushed Tubulo down and dropped down himself.

When Dane got up after the two blasts, he saw men rushing out of the saloon. Grabbing the man's arms, they jerked the empty shotgun out of his hands then began propelling him down the street, his feet barely hitting the ground.

"We don't want to see you in town again!" one man yelled as they shoved him into the dust.

A man close to Dane chuckled. "Old Neb's been put out to grass again."

"You mean he's done this before?"

"Maybe not just exactly this but he's always causing trouble. Everybody calls him Neb, the devil's own. Named for that Bible character, Nebuchadnezzar. They tell me he had to eat grass for a living, too. Old Neb sure ain't going to get much else to eat for a few days now."

As the street quieted down, Dane and Tubulo went on to the Dew Drop Inn. Dane posted Tubulo at the door while he stepped inside.

Dane looked around for Kurt Uhl. There were three tables in the back of the saloon where cards were played. Two of them were just settling down to business again after the shotgun interruption. The other table was empty.

"Who works that empty table?" Dane asked the bartender.

"A great big fellow," the bartender said. "Must stand nearly six and a half feet tall and weigh about two hundred and fifty or more."

"Didn't he come in tonight?"

The bartender scowled at Dane. "Yes, he did, if it's any of your business. But he lit a shuck out of here when Neb started shooting."

"He wasn't shooting into the saloon."

"That don't make no difference to Uhl. He's a good man with cards but he's got a yellow streak down his back wide enough to carpet this floor."

Dane nodded. That sounded like Kurt Uhl. He was sorry he had come in now. It would have been better if he'd waited until a time when nothing had happened to scare Uhl away. He turned and went outside. Maybe the bartender would forget that he'd even asked about him.

"Let's go get supper," Dane said. "Uhl ran like a scared coyote when he heard those shots. He won't be back tonight."

Tubulo shook his head. "Likely not. We should have known he'd run if he thought there was any danger."

They ate at the Antelope Restaurant again. Mamie asked about the shotgun blasts. They had echoed over the whole town. Dane explained but he didn't say why he and Tubulo were down there. While they ate, Dane and Tubulo planned another excursion to the Dew Drop Inn tomorrow night after supper.

Dane found it hard to sleep that night. He was getting so close to cornering Kurt Uhl. Right now that was far more important than catching up with Lon Yockam. If Kurt Uhl hadn't run off with Charity, she would have been waiting for Dane when he got home from the war, whether that had been in '65 or '68. He had a big score to settle with Uhl.

Dane worked through the next day with his mind ahead of himself, planning his moves tonight. He had to catch Kurt Uhl by surprise or he would run again. He could hardly wait for the sun to sink toward the west. He wasn't anticipating the fight as much as the satisfaction of making Uhl pay for what he'd done.

Work ended and Dane hurried to town even though he and Tubulo had agreed that they wouldn't go down to the Dew Drop Inn until after supper.

Tubulo was waiting and Dane cleaned up hurriedly, then the two of them headed for the Antelope

Restaurant.

"See Uhl today?" Dane asked.

"Only a glimpse," Tubulo said. "I didn't want to risk letting him see me. He went in the back door of the saloon. Maybe he doesn't use the front."

"He evidently went out the back way yesterday," Dane said.

"Maybe you ought to go in the back way, too," Tubulo said.

Dane considered it then shook his head. "I don't want to sneak up on his back side. He'll get his chance to fight."

Mamie met them just inside the door. Her usually smiling face was pulled down in worry.

"I heard some talk today, Dane," she said. "Somebody is out to kill you. I couldn't find out why."

"I already know why," Dane said. "It's nothing new. So don't worry your pretty head about it."

"You just go around as if everything is all right when you know somebody is trying to kill you?" she exclaimed in exasperation. "In this town, they could shoot you down right in front of a crowd. There's no law to stop them."

"I know," Dane said. "How about supper?"

"Oh!" she said in frustration, whirling around toward the kitchen.

When supper was over, Dane and Tubulo headed down toward Rat's Row. Darkness was sweeping over the town but that only seemed to be a signal for most of the town to come to life.

"I'd better watch the back door," Tubulo said.

"You can watch," Dane agreed. "But I don't want you taking any part in the fight if Uhl tries to get away. He's all mine."

Tubulo nodded. "If he runs, I'll see which way he goes."

They separated half a block before reaching the saloon. Tubulo ducked into the alley while Dane continued toward the front of the saloon.

Checking his gun, Dane pushed through the doors. His eyes swept over the back of the room. Kurt Uhl was at his table. But there was something different tonight. There were three big men standing in front of the table where Uhl was playing cards with two other men.

The three men were watching the door and their eyes riveted on Dane the moment he stepped inside. Dane knew that someone had tipped off Uhl that Dane had been inquiring about him. It had to be the bartender.

But regardless of how Uhl had found out, it meant now that Dane would have to wade through three big tough men to get to Uhl. The odds were next to impossible. But Dane didn't hesitate. He had to try.

CHAPTER 15

WITH THE THREE MEN WATCHING HIS EVERY MOVE, Dane crossed in front of the bar and moved through the tables toward the spot where Uhl sat. Uhl had stopped his game, his eyes on Dane.

Dane was close enough now to see his face. He was afraid but he wasn't running. He had faith in his three bodyguards. None of the three were as big as Uhl himself but they were big enough. In Uhl's place, Dane would have felt safe, too.

Dane knew the deck was stacked against him. But he'd come too far to get to Uhl to pass up his chance now that he had him in his sights.

140

Pulling his gaze from Uhl, he looked closer at the three men. He guessed that they might have worked on. the railroad when the crews were working full time.

One had a deep knife scar across one cheek and under his chin. He had little pig eyes that watched Dane with the anticipation of an alligator waiting for a chicken to be thrown in his pen.

The one on his right had a mop of bushy red hair and light blue eyes that gave the appearance of having no color at all. Only the tiny black pupils showed.

The one on the left of the scar-faced man was the biggest of the three. He had one hand missing and another scar on his forehead proved that he was no stranger to conflict.

All three seemed to anticipate the chore ahead of them. Only the thought of what Kurt Uhl had done to Charity drove Dane to challenge such odds. If Dane let Uhl get away this time, he might never get another chance at him.

Dane moved closer to the table, walking slowly now. Uhl laid down his cards and stood up. The two men he'd been playing with swept up their money and scurried over behind the other tables. The chatter in the saloon slowly died until the silence seemed tomb-like.

"Not another step, Dane," Uhl warned.

"I suppose you're going to say you don't deserve killing," Dane said, his fury rising with each step he took.

"No Johnny Reb is going to lay a finger on me, " Uhl said, his voice almost breaking as he put the table between him and the men forming the barricade in front of Dane.

The man with the scarred face turned to look at Uhl. He seemed to hold the leash on the other two. When he gave the word, they'd come for Dane. But he had to get his orders from Uhl.

Dane moved a step closer, thinking that there must be some way he could get around the three to Uhl. But deep inside, he knew that he wasn't going to get around them. If he got to Uhl, he'd have to go through them or over them.

"Stop!" Uhl screamed, his voice pitched as high as Tubulo's.

Dane kept moving. Uhl stepped back, panic in his face.

"Kill him!" he screamed.

It was the signal the three men had been waiting for. They didn't pull guns or even knives. They surged forward like an irresistible tide. Dane's hand dropped to his gun. But he knew he couldn't kill all three of them; in fact, he was too close even to use the gun effectively on one.

He felt the red haze sweep over him. These three had nothing at stake in this but the money Uhl was paying them. But they were keeping Dane from getting to Uhl. It flashed across Dane's mind that nobody had the right to keep him away from Uhl.

Instead of backing away as the three men obviously expected him to do, Dane leaped forward, driving a fist directly into the teeth of the scar-faced man. He felt the man's teeth cut his knuckles but he also felt them yield to the force of his blow. The man staggered backward, blood squirting out over his face as he spit out two teeth.

The redhead caught Dane a blow on the side of the head, making it ring like a hollow drum. Dane kicked with all his might, catching the man on the shins. The man screamed and dived backward, his hand dropping to rub the bruised spot.

Dane caught his balance just as the third man swung his handless arm like a club. Dane knew if that club hit him, he'd be knocked senseless. He ducked under it, taking the blow on his shoulder. Using all the momentum he had generated in ducking under the blow, he drove a fist and his head into the man's stomach. The breath exploded from him and he reeled backward, upsetting the table where Uhl had been playing cards.

Scarface had spit out another tooth and with his sleeve wiped the blood off his mouth, smearing it from ear to ear. He grabbed a gun from his belt.

Dane lunged forward, catching the gun before the man had a solid grip on it and wrenched it from his grasp.

Before Scarface could recover from his surprise, Dane swung the gun, smashing the barrel across the side of his head. He slumped down as if he'd been hammered with an ax.

Dane swung around as the redhead leaped at him. He had no chance to use the gun. He was smashed backward, striking a chair and splintering it, the gun flying from his hand. The broken chair threw him to one side and the redhead came down beside him instead of on top.

In trying to scramble away, Dane's fingers closed around one leg of the broken chair. He wrenched it free as the redhead lunged toward Dane, intent on pinning him to the floor where he and the club-armed man could finish him off.

Dane swung the chair leg with all the force he could muster from his prone position. The blow caught the redhead across the face, smashing his nose and spurting blood over Dane and the floor.

Dane rolled to his knees, bringing the chair leg down

again across the man's head. He slumped forward, unconscious.

Dane was knocked flat again by what felt like a foot thick pole. Then a body thumped down on him and he knew it was the club-armed man. It must have been that handless arm that had hit him.

Twisting, he avoided another blow from that arm aimed at his head. Bringing an elbow up with full force, he hit that already sore stomach and the breath whistled out of the man's lungs again. He reeled backward and Dane hunched his back like a bucking bronco and unbalanced the man.

As he toppled to one side, Dane brought the chair leg around, hitting the man on the stub arm. He howled in pain and lost the grip he had on Dane. Dane wiggled free, coming to his feet along with the other man.

That handless arm came at Dane again just as Dane swung his chair leg. The arm hit Dane, knocking him sideways, but not before the chair leg had delivered its blow on the side of the man's head. The man reeled sideways, hitting a table that had so far escaped the melee. It tipped over with the club-armed man draped over it.

Dane saw things through a haze but it was no longer the red haze of fury. This was the verge of unconsciousness. Staggering to his feet, he looked around. Uhl was gone but all three men he had fought were down. One was groaning but the other two were unconscious.

He saw Tubulo near the back door. He had a gun in his hand, the one he'd brought with him but up till now had never displayed.

Wheeling, Dane looked at the men in the saloon. He wondered why the bartender or one of the other

144

gamblers hadn't taken a hand. Now he knew. Tubulo. The bartender's hands were flat on the bar and the other two gamblers were back against the wall, their hands spread out along the wall at their sides.

"Where's Uhl?" Dane asked.

"This way," Tubulo said, jerking his head toward the back door but not taking his eyes off the bartender and the gamblers.

Dane lifted his gun out of the holster which had somehow stayed there through the fight. "Go on outside," he said. "I'll be right behind you."

He looked over the room but no one even hinted at trying to stop him. Most were looking in awe at the three gladiators on the floor.

The violence was seeping out of Dane but then he thought of Kurt Uhl. He had to get him. He had another reason now to kill him. A coward who would hire three pit fighters to go after one man didn't deserve to live even if he hadn't committed other crimes.

Dane felt every bruise as he backed out of the saloon. But he couldn't stop. If he didn't catch up with Uhl tonight, he would never catch him.

"He went toward the tracks," Tubulo said. "Are you going after him?"

"Got to," Dane said. "I won't get another chance. He'll never stop running."

"I'll go up the street to the west," Tubulo said.

Dane nodded and turned up the street. He hurt too much to run. Looking down an alley, he thought that Uhl wouldn't go up the street. He'd sneak along in places where no one would see him.

Ducking between two buildings, he turned to his right behind the haphazard row of shacks and tents. It could hardly be called an alley. There had to be a hundred hiding places back here. A coward like Uhl might hide in any of them.

Dane moved along, wondering if he was wasting his time here. But if Uhl had kept running, he could never catch him, anyway. He had to hope that the coward in Uhl had made him hide and that he could roust him out of his hiding place.

Although he had tried to prepare himself for it, the shot came as a surprise. The gun had been fired from only thirty feet away but the darkness had been deceiving. The bullet hit Dane in the side, digging along the ribs but not going between them.

Dane staggered but kept his feet. Seeing that Dane didn't go down apparently completely unnerved Uhl. He broke from his hiding place and ran down the alley. The light was bad but Dane knew from the size of the man that it had to be Uhl.

He yelled at him to stop. Instead, Uhl kept running, half turning to fire another shot at Dane. Dane brought up his gun and fired three times. He didn't trust his luck to one bullet. Uhl staggered at the first shot and was down by the time Dane fired the third time.

Dane ran forward. Uhl was dead when he got to him. Slowly the fury drained out of Dane. Uhl had died too easily to pay for what he had done. But he had died a thousand times while he waited for Dane to catch up with him. A coward's life could be worse than dying, Dane thought.

Men poured into the alley. One brought a lantern. Some grumbled ominously when they saw Uhl sprawled in the dirt. But one man from the Dew Drop Inn nodded his head. "He got what he deserved." That seemed to satisfy the dissenters. Dane turned toward the street along the tracks.

146

Tubulo appeared from between two buildings to help Dane as he staggered along, holding his side. He guided him to their room in the hotel then left again. He was back in five minutes with Mamie.

Mamie looked at Dane's wound and his bruises with horror. But she poured water from the pitcher into the bowl and began washing the wound. In a few minutes, she had him bandaged.

"You'll have to keep quiet for a few days to let that heal," she said. "You seem determined to get yourself killed."

"Just if that's the only way I can get to the men I'm after," Dane said.

She shook her head and went out the door. Tubulo helped Dane get to bed. Then he repeated Mamie's orders.

"I'll be out on the street tomorrow," Dane said.

His resolve to go out died the next morning when he tried to walk across the room. The walls danced before his eyes and his knees buckled. He crawled back into bed and stayed there.

The first thing he heard when he did go down to the street three days later was the story of what he had done at the Dew Drop Inn. Uhl had hired three of the toughest in-fighters in town. Each one had boasted that he could lick any two men who ever walked. Dane had whipped all three of them at once. His reputation as a vicious fighter was all over town.

Dane fretted at the interruption in his search for Yockam. He had found Uhl here so he was willing to bet that Yockam was here somewhere, too. But he couldn't do anything about it now.

Tubulo, however, was not confined to the hotel. He wandered over town and Dane worried about him.

Tubulo had plenty to tell Dane but nothing about Lon Yockam. Maybe Yockam had decided to leave after Uhl was killed. But Dane couldn't believe that. Yockam had run from Alpha but Dane felt that was partly because he had lost his grip over the people and not all because he was afraid of Dane.

Mamie came by every day. She had brought a doctor who had dressed Dane's wound and told him emphatically to stay off work for at least ten days. Dane was sure he wouldn't have a job by then. Mamie's visits were the highlight of Dane's existence.

Dane had just started to walk along the streets, re-gaining the strength he had lost from his inactivity when he witnessed an unexpected gun duel. A man named Frank Rush, a big blond man with colorless eyes, got into an argument with another tough hand in the Bullhead Saloon. This was less than a block from the hotel. Tubulo had told Dane about the argument and how those in the saloon had pulled them apart. Each had vowed he'd kill the other and there was speculation in the saloons about what would happen when they met. Dane had given it little thought but he happened to be on the scene when the two did meet in the Cross-Tie Saloon right next to the hotel.

Dane had stopped in, nursing the faint hope that he might see Yockam. Rush was at the bar this day. Dane recognized him but paid no attention.

Before Dane left, another man came in. Dane didn't recognize him but he knew from the way silence fell over the place that others did. A path was cleared between Rush and the newcomer. There wasn't a word said. Each man was carrying a gun and they both dived for their weapons. Rush was much faster and killed the newcomer right in the doorway. Dane couldn't leave until someone had pulled the dead man out of the way. He wouldn't forget the gunman, Frank Rush. He looked as if he had actually enjoyed the killing.

Dane had recovered from his wound enough that he was considering going back to his job if it was still open when Tubulo brought word that an Irishman was going on trial the next morning at the Golden Eagle Saloon. The Irishman had shot a man named Hank who ran a dance hall down on Rat's Row. Hank had survived and was to be on hand to testify. Since Sheridan had no lawman or legal court, this would be a civilian jury and judge. But the verdict would be just as decisive as any legal court. The railroad trestle out east of town had served as a gallows for many a misbehaving rowdy.

Dane and Tubulo got there just as the trial was about to begin. But before the judge could rap for order, Hank, faced twisted in fury at the sight of the man who had shot him, moved over to him, pressed a gun to his head and fired. Even the jury which was set to hang the defendant thought this justice a bit premature so they demanded that Hank be hanged instead. There were plenty of witnesses ready to help the jury and judge carry out the sentence.

Dane watched them drag Hank, yelling and cursing, from the saloon and down the tracks to the trestle over the gully and there drop him off on a short rope. From there they went to the cemetery on the hilltop northwest of town and buried both Hank and the Irishman he had killed in the same grave.

On the way back to the hotel, Dane and Tubulo stopped at the Antelope Restaurant for dinner. Mamie served them but her eyes were clouded with anxiety. Dane noticed it and demanded to know why.

"Somebody followed me home last night," Mamie

said. "I heard his footsteps behind me. I hurried and got to the boarding house before he caught me. But I—I guess I'm too scared to think right."

"Do you have to work late tonight?"

"I work late every night," she said.

"I'll come over tonight and walk home with you," Dane said.

Relief swept over her face. "I'd appreciate it. Maybe it was just a drunk who won't show up again. But I'm scared of this town."

"Nobody can blame you for that," Dane said. "It scares me, too."

Dane checked the time when Mamie would get off work and he and Tubulo came back to the restaurant just before Mamie's quitting time.

"I'll stay well behind," Tubulo said with a sly grin. "But if I see anybody following, I'll whistle. Like this." He placed two fingers to his lips and sent out a shrill whistle that could have been heard for five blocks.

Dane nodded. "That should scare anybody who is following."

Mamie was ready to go when they arrived. It wasn't far to the boarding house where she stayed but it was well back from the street. Dane didn't expect trouble but he welcomed the chance to walk Mamie home.

They crossed the street and walked along the front of Otero and Sellar's warehouse. A short distance beyond, Mamie turned down a path that led to a house set far back from the street. It was very dark, the light from the buildings along the street cut off by the dark wall of the warehouse.

Dane heard Tubulo's shrill whistle and stopped to listen. His muscles tensed. Someone must be following them.

150

"Let's run," Mamie whispered.

"Let's find out what we're running from," Dane replied softly.

Suddenly out of the deep shadows less than thirty feet away, two men charged. Dane had a sinking feeling. He wished he had followed Mamie's advice and run. He was in no shape for another fight.

CHAPTER 16

DANE'S FIRST THOUGHT WAS TO SHIELD MAMIE. THEN he saw the two-by-fours that the two men were holding above their heads like clubs. They wouldn't attack a tiny girl like Mamie with clubs. They were after him.

They were coming as fast as they could run. He knew that he couldn't take another fight like the one at the Dew Drop Inn. Besides, these men had clubs; he didn't.

Jerking his gun out of the holster, he leveled it, thinking as he did that if this had been a gun fight, he'd have been too slow against anyone but the rankest amateur.

The light wasn't good enough for accurate shooting but that wasn't worrying him. The two men weren't wielding guns. Apparently they intended to keep this fight quiet.

Dane spoiled those plans. His first shot missed both men but a direct hit wouldn't have been any more effective in stopping their charge. The two-by-fours were dropped as if they had become angry rattlesnakes. One man dived each way into the shadows.

Dane held his fire. He didn't have any desire to kill them and he had already taken all the fight out of them. In a moment, even their fading footsteps were gone.

Tubulo came running up through the darkness but Dane recognized the rapid patter of his short legs.

"Kill anybody?" Tubulo panted, stopping in front of Dane.

"Just scared them," Dane said. "They were coming at me with clubs. Let's get Mamie home."

She was frightened and thanked Dane repeatedly for escorting her home. Dane and Tubulo returned to the street.

"Were they after Mamie or you?" Tubulo asked.

"Me, I reckon. They wouldn't come after Mamie with clubs. I can't figure how they would know I'd be with her."

"They probably guessed you'd try to protect her if they had scared her enough last night for her to tell you."

"Maybe," Dane said. "At least, we can't blame Uhl for hiring these thugs to kill me."

"Could have been Yockam if he's in town," Tubulo suggested.

They went into the hotel and up to bed. Dane was still thinking about the attack. Had Yockam hired those men to kill him? They certainly hadn't been after Mamie. Had Mamie been the bait for their trap? Not knowingly, Dane thought. This town was one that destroyed faith in everybody. But a man had to trust someone and he wanted to trust Mamie.

A day later, he felt ready to go back to work. After breakfast, he went to the Section House and inquired if his job was still open.

"We found another driver," the man said. "But we're still short. If you want to work, we'll put you back on."

Dane nodded and an hour later he was west of the creek working at the trench that would eventually be the

152

roadbed for the rails. He was tired at the end of the day's work but he felt fine.

At the restaurant that evening, Dane saw Frank Rush. He frowned. What was Rush doing here? He belonged down on Rat's Row. Dane knew he was being unreasonable. There were no social barriers in Sheridan. But he felt uneasy around a gunman like Rush.

Rush didn't pay any attention to Dane and Tubulo but he paid plenty of attention to Mamie as she moved around serving the customers.

As she passed him on her way to Dane's table, Rush reached out and caught her hand. She jerked away but Dane had noticed the action.

"Is he bothering you, Mamie?" he asked when she reached his table.

"I can handle him," she said softly. "Don't you tangle with him. You know his reputation."

"That reputation doesn't give him the right to do anything he wants to."

Mamie moved on and Dane and Tubulo finished their meal. Dane was just pushing back from the table when Rush made another pass at Mamie, catching her arm and holding it. She was brought to a stop beside his table. Dane strode over and glared down at the gunman.

"Did she say you could hold her arm?" he asked softly.

Rush looked up, his pale eyes focusing on Dane's face. "Who's asking?" He still clutched Mamie's arm.

"Let go of her!" Dane snapped.

Rush dropped her arm. "Now that's a language I understand." He stood up. "Have you got nerve enough to try to make me let her alone?"

"Nothing your size has ever stopped me yet," Dane said.

"You're wearing your gun. Let's see if you can back up your big mouth with that."

"I don't fight with guns," Dane said. "Let's see if you've got guts enough to fight with your fists."

Rush laughed nastily. "That's the squawk of a chicken scared of a hawk. Whenever you are ready to use your gun, let me know." He sat down to his unfinished meal.

Mamie was tugging at Dane's arm. He let her lead him to the counter. "Don't fight with him. He's the fastest gun in Sheridan."

"I'm not about to fight him with guns," Dane said. "But if he doesn't keep his hands off you. I'm going to mess up his face with my fists."

"You can't," Mamie said. "He won't fight except with guns."

Dane and Tubulo left the restaurant but Dane knew he hadn't left that fight behind. Rush was not one to let an opportunity like that drop. At the hotel, he was still wondering why Rush had pestered Mamie. Would he have done it if Dane hadn't been there?

The next evening Dane and Tubulo ate at the hotel. An hour after supper, Dane went to the restaurant. It was almost empty. He crossed to the counter where Mamie waited.

"Was Rush here tonight?" he asked.

She nodded.

"Did he bother you?"

She shook her head. "But he made all kinds of remarks about how yellow you were. Afraid to eat here any more."

Dane nodded understandingly. "It's me he's after then. I stayed away tonight to see if he'd make a pass at you when I wasn't here."

154

"Don't come back until he gets tired of showing up," Mamie begged.

"I won't be back until tomorrow night," Dane said. "Have a good supper ready for me."

Turning, he went outside before Mamie could argue. He wished he knew why Rush was challenging him. Maybe it was because Dane had earned the reputation of being the most violent man in town, even more violent than Rush. Rush was not a fighter; just a killer. Sheridan had all of those it needed.

Dane wasn't sure what would happen but he knew he had to meet that challenge. Something would happen to Mamie if he didn't. Rush must know that Dane would come after him with a gun if he bothered Mamie enough.

Tubulo was waiting for Dane when he got to the hotel from work the next day. "Let's eat here," he suggested.

"We're eating at the restaurant," Dane said.

He washed up but left his gun and gun belt in his room. Tubulo had his gun. He had taken to wearing it everywhere lately, even though it looked like a cannon strapped around his tiny waist.

A hush fell over the restaurant when Dane and Tubulo came in. Dane didn't even look for Rush. He knew he was here. Finding a table, he sat down.

"Came back to see me kiss your pretty girl?" Rush called from three tables over.

Dane ignored him. He knew he wasn't going to be able to ignore him much longer. Mamie came to take their order, going out of her way to avoid Rush.

"I wish you'd go somewhere else," she whispered, her face white with fear.

"You'd rather have Rush for a customer?" he asked.

Irritation showed in her cheeks and eyes. "You know

155

he's just here to make you fight."

"Maybe he'll get his wish," Dane said and gave her his order.

Mamie went back to the kitchen. When she came out again, Rush was standing by the counter and he grabbed her wrist.

"Now, honey, you're going to be nice to me whether you like it or not."

Dane took a deep breath. Rush grinned as he saw Dane get up.

"Going to fight for your girl?" Rush asked.

Dane nodded. "I'm unarmed. If you want to shoot me, that's your privilege. But there are plenty of witnesses. I imagine that rope is still dangling from the trestle where they hung Hank for shooting an unarmed man."

The grin left Rush's face. "You ain't making me fight with fists. You come any closer and you get it."

Rush still had a grip on Mamie's wrist. Dane moved swiftly, hitting Rush before he could let go of Mamie and grab his gun. Rush staggered backward, catching himself against the counter. His hand darted down to his gun but stopped as Tubulo's squeaky voice shrilled over the room.

"You touch that gun, mister, and you're dead."

Dane shot a glance at Tubulo. He had his gun on the top of the table, cocked and aimed directly at Rush. Even Rush had to know that the little man could kill him before he could get his gun out. He hesitated and another man spoke up from across the room.

"You started a fight, mister. Now take off that gun belt and go outside and fight like a man."

"I don't fight with fists," Rush growled.

"You will this time," the man said. "Any coward can shoot a man with a gun. But it takes a man to stand up

156

and fight with fists. Let's see if you're a man or just a blow-hard."

Reluctantly Rush unbuckled his gunbelt. Dane went outside and the men inside, leaving their meals, pushed Rush through the door.

Rush, seeing he couldn't escape the fight, made a dive at Dane, intent on grabbing him in a bear hug. But Dane stepped back quickly and lashed two hard fists to his head, snapping his head back like a broken single-tree.

It wasn't much of a fight. Dane hadn't expected it to be. Rush depended on his reputation with a gun to keep him out of fights like this. He knew nothing about fist fighting. Dane cut him down quickly, actually enjoying it when he thought of the way Rush had been baiting him.

Rush finally went to the ground and showed no signs of getting up. He spit some blood and swore viciously.

"I'll catch you someday when you've got your gun on and you're going to fight my way. I'll break both arms and legs before I kill you."

Dane turned and went back into the restaurant. He knew beating Rush with his fists hadn't settled the matter. But he had gotten some real satisfaction from it. In the eyes of those who had watched, he had won a decisive victory. Rush could never regain any stature until he beat Dane. For a gunman, there was only one way to do that.

Dane didn't expect trouble from Rush for a day or two. He was badly pounded up. No gunman would look for a fight when he had sore muscles.

Dane felt none the worse for his fight with Rush. His work at the grade west of town kept his muscles loose and he felt as good as he had before being shot by Uhl.

157

A couple of nights after his fight with Rush, Tubulo met him on the porch of the hotel, excitement plain on his face.

"I saw a man today that I want you to see," Tubulo said.

"Yockam?" Dane asked instantly.

"I don't know," Tubulo said. "This may not be him. But it does look like him."

"Why can't you tell?"

"He's wearing a full beard," Tubulo said, "and I didn't get too close. They told me his name is Samson. He owns the Dew Drop Inn but he isn't there much."

Elation pounded through Dane. This all fit. Kurt Uhl had been a gambler at the Dew Drop Inn. Yockam and Uhl had been friends. Dane didn't doubt that Yockam had brought enough money with him to buy a saloon.

"You'll have to be mighty careful," Tubulo said. "When I peeked in there this afternoon, it looked like he had a lot of rough men around him."

Dane nodded. "Could be. We're going to have to find out for sure if it is Yockam. We'll go down right after supper and see."

Rush wasn't at the restaurant that night. Dane was glad. He had other things on his mind. If Tubulo had located Yockam, Dane would have to find some way to catch him without his bodyguard. Then he'd have his mission completed except to find out what had happened to Charity.

Thoughts of Charity brought a sharp pain. Mamie's friendship had done much to erase the pain but nothing would ever do it entirely, he knew. Mamie worried him in a way. She seemed to like him but sometimes there was an aloofness about her that he didn't understand. And he didn't understand his own feelings, either. He was trying to make her take the place of Charity; he knew she never could. If he could make himself accept the fact that Charity was gone, maybe he could center his life around Mamie.

Supper over, Dane and Tubulo went down on Rat's Row. Half a block from the Dew Drop Inn, Tubulo touched Dane's arm.

"Let's look in the back door. Nobody will see us and maybe you can sneak a look at Samson."

Dane nodded and they dropped back into the alley. They were moving silently along toward the back door of the saloon when a man leaped out from the shadows as though he had been waiting for Dane.

Dane tried to dodge him when he saw another one coming from a different angle. He had walked into another trap.

CHAPTER 17

IN THE DARK ALLEY, DANE COULDN'T BE SURE HOW many men were charging at him. He barely saw Tubulo duck low and dive against the building. The men may not have even seen him; they seemed intent on getting to Dane.

Dane had dodged the first man's lunge but the second one caught a shoulder against his side and spun him around. Fury raced through him. It seemed that somebody was always trying to beat him up or kill him. Even though he had come to Rat's Row prepared for trouble, it wasn't this kind of trouble.

Dane caught his balance and wheeled to face the charge of the first man. He ducked under his wild swing and hit him with all the force he could muster directly under the ribs. The man gasped and backed off.

While Dane turned to look for the other man, he realized the first one was rushing back at him in spite of the blow he had taken. It was then that the gun exploded like a cannon in the narrow alley.

Dane saw the man he had just hit stagger sideways and fall. He couldn't see where Tubulo was but that shot must have come from him. Pounding footsteps told the rest of the story. The second man was running for his life down the alley.

"Did I get him?" Tubulo squeaked.

"You did," Dane said. "Now let's get out of here before everybody in that saloon shows up. They'll hang us for murder."

"It was self defense," Tubulo said. But he was already running back the way they had come.

Dane paced himself to keep even with Tubulo. Tubulo had gotten him out of trouble again. He wasn't going to desert him.

They turned from that alley into another one in the next block, although Dane wasn't sure these haphazard buildings could be divided logically into blocks. They headed for the hotel on the north side of the tracks while an uproar rose in the alley behind the Dew Drop Inn.

"We got away," Tubulo panted.

"But we didn't get a look at Samson," Dane grumbled. "If he is Yockam, those might have been his guards posted to watch for me."

"Could be," Tubulo agreed. "They know you're in town. You flushed Uhl out of that saloon."

"Maybe they saw us turn out of the street into the alley and went back to meet us," Dane said. "We'll be more careful next time."

"Maybe we'd better try to catch Yockam away from

160

his bullies at the saloon."

"That could take a long time," Dane said. But he saw the wisdom of Tubulo's suggestion.

Back on the job the next day, Dane heard talk of the killing down at the Dew Drop Inn the night before. The rumor was that Dane had killed the man in the alley. Dane denied it but it proved that someone at the Dew Drop Inn was watching for Dane or he wouldn't have been blamed. That must have been Lon Yockam.

When Dane got in from work that evening, there was a gathering in front of the Bullhead Saloon. Finding Tubulo on the porch of the hotel, he asked what was going on.

"A couple of big braggers got into a fight down on Rat's Row," Tubulo explained. "One of them came up to the Bullhead and when the other one showed up, the argument started again. I just heard a fellow say they were going to settle it with a gun fight."

"Let's get off the street so we don't get shot," Dane said.

"They're going up to the graveyard," Tubulo said, "Each one will dig a grave for the other one, and then they start shooting. The winner buries the loser."

"What kind of idiots are they?" Dane asked.

"At least, nobody will have to clean up the mess after the fight," Tubulo said. "Let's go up and see how they come out."

Dane glanced at the sun. There was still quite a bit of daylight left. It looked like half the town was going to follow the two fighters up the hill to the cemetery. This was just the kind of thing that might attract Yockam.

Dane nodded. "Let's go. Do you know who those two men are?"

Tubulo shrugged. "Only what they call them. The one

with the scraggly beard is called Sour Bill. The other one is Gunshot Frank. The town won't miss them if they kill each other."

Dane and Tubulo fell in with the crowd that trudged up the hill. All around him, Dane could hear wagers being made on which one would kill the other. It was a festive event for most of the people, especially for the gamblers.

At the cemetery, one man picked out a spot that wasn't occupied and gave each man a shovel. Digging was easy in the loose gravel and both men seemed anxious to get his grave dug first. According to the agreement, when they were finished, each combatant was to stand by the grave the other one had dug and then begin shooting.

While the two were digging like badgers, Dane looked over the crowd that had followed the men up the hill. He wished Tubulo was taller so he could see everybody. Tubulo would recognize the man called Samson. Dane might not.

"I don't see anybody who looks like Yockam," Dane said softly. "Do you?"

Tubulo shrugged. "Everybody's legs look about the same."

Dane did see Frank Rush in the crowd. He knew the issue between them was not settled. But this certainly was not the place to do it. Sour Bill and Gunshot Frank had center stage here.

As the two dug, they yelled angrily at each other. There seemed little chance that they would work off their anger.

Then, just as the graves were almost done, Gunshot Frank made some nasty remark to Sour Bill that Bill apparently couldn't take. Lunging over the rim of the grave he was digging, he grabbed his revolver. Before anybody could stop him, he fired twice, killing Gunshot Frank instantly.

An angry roar came from the crowd. This wasn't what they had come up here to see. Sour Bill had taken the sport out of it.

"Make him bury Frank," one man yelled and others agreed. That suggestion met with Bill's approval. After all, that's what he'd been digging the grave for.

So Sour Bill buried Gunshot Frank. But the minute he had finished, a dozen angry onlookers leaped at Bill and two of them grabbed the shovels the men had been using. They bashed in Sour Bill's head and toppled him into the other grave. Within minutes, after making sure Sour Bill was dead, he was buried and the crowd headed down into town to celebrate the double funeral.

"Nice peaceful town," Dane said softly as he and Tubulo followed the crowd back down the hill. "Do you see Samson anywhere in that crowd?"

Tubulo shook his head. "I can get a pretty good look while they're strung out like this but I don't see him. Rush is there, though."

"I saw him," Dane aid. "Let's go to the Antelope and get supper."

At the restaurant, Dane and Tubulo found a table where Dane could watch the door. He expected Rush to come in one of these evenings and challenge him again. He might not be able to avoid a gun battle again.

Mamie came to take their orders and asked bout the excitement she'd just heard about up at the cemetery. Dane explained what had happened then asked a question of his own.

"Do you know anything about a man named Samson? I hear he owns the Dew Drop Inn."

"I've seen him," Mamie said. "He doesn't mingle much. He came to Sheridan a while after I did. He was growing a beard when I saw him."

Dane nodded. That could be Yockam. He would have arrived sometime after Sheridan erupted into the wild town it was now. It had been just a camp for the railroad workers until the end-of-track settlement moved here from Coyote.

"Did you know Kurt Uhl?" Dane asked.

"Saw him a time or two. Nobody liked him very well."

Dane and Tubulo ate their meal and went out into the street. Without a word, they headed down into the Rat's Row area. Circling the Dew Drop Inn, they approached from across the street. Two well-armed men were standing in front of the saloon. Dane and Tubulo stayed across the street from the saloon for two hours but, although dozens of men came and went, none of them was Samson.

"Just watching for him may not work," Dane said as they went back to the hotel.

"It sure won't be safe to try anything else," Tubulo warned. "I'll keep an eye open while you're working. Maybe I can figure out what hours he spends at the saloon. I've seen him there only a couple of times. Didn't suspect him of being Yockam the first time I saw him."

The next evening when Dane came in from work, Tubulo had some news for him.

"I watched the Dew Drop Inn all day," he reported. "Didn't see Samson. But I did see Frank Rush there."

Dane whistled softly. If Samson was Yockam, that put a different light on all the people who came and went from the Dew Drop Inn.

164

"Maybe Rush is working for Yockam," Dane said. "That would explain why he is so set on getting me into a gun fight, using Mamie as bait."

Tubulo nodded. "Makes sense. Yockam is too scared to fight you himself. But he has enough money to hire a killer to go after you."

"It isn't Rush I want to fight," Dane said. "It's Yockam."

"Ain't it supper time yet?" Tubulo asked just before sundown. "I didn't stop watching the Dew Drop Inn long enough to get dinner."

"I reckon Mamie can take care of that. Let's go."

As usual, Dane picked a table against the far wall where he could watch the door. Now that he had guessed that Rush might be working for Yockam, he was more alert than ever. Rush probably had money as well as personal antagonism for reasons to draw Dane into a fight.

Mamie came and Dane and Tubulo gave their order. "Haven't seen Frank Rush around, have you?" Dane asked.

"He came in last night a while after you left," Mamie said.

"Did he bother you?"

She shook her head. "He just got his supper, watched the door all the time he ate, then left."

That convinced Dane that Rush would keep looking for him. Last night Dane and Tubulo had been in the restaurant early for they'd come here right from the shooting at the cemetery. Tonight they were not early.

Tubulo, looking out the window, nudged Dane. "Rush is coming across the street now."

Dane leaned forward where he could see. Rush's eyes were darting up and down the street. He didn't miss much. He'd see Dane the second he stepped into the restaurant.

"Go tell Mamie to bring us our coffee right away," Dane said to Tubulo.

Tubulo frowned. "She always brings it right after we order," he said.

"Tell her to hurry it up."

"You just want to get rid of me," Tubulo accused.

"Maybe," Dane admitted. "No sense in two of us getting hurt."

Reluctantly. Tubulo got up and moved over to the counter. But he didn't call for Mamie. He turned where he could watch the door.

Dane quietly slipped his gun out of the holster and held it in his hand under the table. His eyes were on the door when Frank Rush came in. Rush paused just inside the restaurant, his eyes sweeping the diners. When they hit Dane, they stopped.

Rush moved inside where he had a clear view between tables across the room to Dane. His right elbow bent as he moved his hand above the butt of his gun.

"You got a gun tonight, yellow belly?" he asked.

Dane nodded. "I've got one."

Rush crouched a little. "Stand up and draw. Or die right where you sit."

Dane bunched his muscles and suddenly lunged to his feet kicking the table away. His hand swept up, gun aimed directly at Rush. Rush had started to draw but suddenly stopped as he stared at Dane's gun.

Dane's move had been smoother than he had hoped for. To anyone in front of the table, it must have looked like he had stood up and drawn his gun in one motion. From the startled expression on Rush's face, it was evident that's what he thought. His hand suddenly came

166

away from his gun as if it were red hot.

Dane held his gun steady. "What happened to you, yellow belly?" he asked, throwing the words back at the gunman. "I thought you wanted to have it out."

"It—it wasn't fair," Rush mumbled. "I didn't see you start to draw. There'll be another time."

"Do you think you'll be faster next time?" Dane pressed.

"You can't do that again," Rush blustered, evidently realizing that Dane wouldn't shoot him now.

"Willing to bet your life on that?" Dane asked.

"There'll be another time," Rush repeated, backing to the door.

He probably had never been outdrawn before in his life. His nerves were shattered; he had to reorganize himself.

Rush backed out the door and walked hurriedly down the street. Slowly Dane righted the table and sat back down. He wouldn't see any more of Frank Rush tonight.

"You should have bored him while you had the chance," one man over in the corner said. "He's a killer who ain't particular how he kills. You beat him to the draw; now he'll look for some other way to kill you."

"Maybe," Dane said. "But I didn't want to spoil everybody's supper by putting a dead man on the floor."

Tubulo came back and Mamie brought their meals. The restaurant quieted down. Dane found that he wasn't hungry. His stomach was so tight he couldn't force anything down into it.

Tubulo was not affected by what had happened. He ate his meal with a relish. Dane picked at his food and when Tubulo was finished, he got up and paid for the meals.

"You watch yourself," Mamie warned as Dane started

167

to leave.

"Especially your back," a diner nearby added.

Dane and Tubulo went outside.

"Let's go down and look for Yockam," Dane said.

"I suppose you'll want to waltz right into the place now," Tubulo said. "You're tough as they come but you ain't that tough. How did you beat Rush to the draw?"

"I didn't," Dane admitted. "But he thinks I did and that's what counts. If I have to barge into the Dew Drop Inn to get to Yockam, then that's what I'll do."

"You'd be wiped out before you even got to the door," Tubulo said. "I've had a good look at the guards around that saloon."

"I'm sure Rush works for Yockam," Dane said. "He's so shook up tonight he won't be worth anything in a fight."

"You won't be tangling with Rush," Tubulo warned. "He ain't a regular bodyguard. Evidently he has been assigned to get you into a fight and kill you. These guards Yockam has at the saloon are there just to protect him."

"That's assuming that Samson really is Yockam," Dane countered. "I've got to find out for sure."

"Let's wait a day or two," Tubulo argued. "If Samson is Yockam and Rush is working for him, Yockam probably knows by now what happened in the restaurant so he'll be expecting you tonight."

Dane saw the wisdom of Tubulo's reasoning but waiting was straining his nerves to the breaking point. He was constantly having to fight the men around Yockam. He wanted to get to Yockam himself.

"The longer we wait, the more chance Yockam has of finding someone or some way to kill me."

Tubulo nodded. "That may be right. But if you go

down there tonight, you'll be walking right into an armed camp. There's got to be a better time."

Dane yielded to Tubulo's argument. He was still tighter inside than a sailor's knot. Even if he got to Yockam, he wasn't sure he'd be able to handle him.

Work the next day drained the tension out of him. He realized he would never make a gun fighter even if he could handle a gun well enough. Last night's encounter with Rush had rattled him more than any fist fight he'd ever had.

The work on the trench north of the twin buttes was going very slowly. With no contract to continue on to Denver, there seemed no incentive among the contractors and the feeling passed on down to the workers.

While Dane worked, his mind searched for ways of getting into the Dew Drop Inn without fighting the guards posted around the saloon. Suddenly he was jerked over against the steel handle of his scraper as if by an invisible hand.

A split second later the flat spang of a rifle echoed over the cut. Men dropped their reins and dashed for cover. Dane had already dived around behind his team. He'd had the reins looped over his head and one shoulder so his hands would be free to handle the scraper. The bullet had cut the reins six inches in front of his face. Before the reins gave way to the force of the bullet, they had jerked him over against the scraper.

Dane's scraper was closest to the spot where the bullet had come from on the bluff that ran out north from the buttes. Dane couldn't see the ambusher but he knew that he meant to kill him and he had an excellent chance of succeeding.

CHAPTER 18

THE TWIN BUTTES WERE LITTLE MORE THAN weathered bluffs southwest of the bend where the creek turned east. North of the two buttes was a gully washed by the rains. A long ridge ran north from them toward the cut being made for the roadbed for the rails. The end of the bluff overlooked the trench the men were cutting. It was from the edge of this bluff that the ambusher had fired. It was just luck that the bullet had struck the lines in front of Dane's face instead of hitting him in the head.

The second shot from the rifle slammed into the steel scraper and ricocheted off across the cut. The mules Dane had been driving jumped nervously. At the third shot from the rifle, they bolted, leaving Dane out in the open.

Before the mules hit full stride, Dane had dived up against the wall of the cut. With the dirt bank for protection, Dane began searching the top of the bluff for the ambusher.

From the other side of the cut where the crew had stacked their rifles, a rifle boomed and dirt spurted from the top of the bluff. Dane saw a flash of metal as the ambusher jerked his rifle back and rolled away from the edge of the bluff. He likely knew that the crew had rifles to stand off a possible Indian attack and now he must think that he was taking twenty men instead of the one he had tried to ambush.

As soon as he disappeared, Dane leaped out of the cut and started scrambling up the steep north face of the bluff. The rock looked like layers of shale but it was not hard and crushed under his step so that he got good

170

footing.

It was foolhardy to go after a man with a rifle when the only weapon he had was the gun in his holster. But he'd been shot at and jumped on so many times in the dark that he'd lost count. His patience was exhausted; he had to strike back.

He guessed that the man was either waiting back where he was safely out of sight of the riflemen in the cut or else he was running for his horse, which surely was in the gully north of the north butte. That would be back a hundred or more yards from the lip of the bluff.

Dane was puffing when he reached the top of the bluff. He saw the man more than half way down the ridge, heading for the wash near the north butte.

Looking back, the man saw him and wheeled, firing the rifle without taking aim. The bullet was wide of its mark. Dane looked around for a place to find cover. The nearest place without retreating was a small gully washed in the east side of the bluff. That was only fifty feet to his left.

But the man wheeled back after firing that one shot and dashed on toward the gully, apparently convinced that Dane was just the first of the twenty men working in the cut who would come over the hill.

Instead of seeking cover, Dane dashed after the man. The ambusher wasn't a good runner and the ground was strewn with rocks in the thin grass. Many of the rocks were mica or some kind of silica, reflecting the light of the sun, glistening in spots along the ridge.

As he ran, Dane kept looking for low spots where he could find protection if the man wheeled on him with the rifle again. He was still out of effective range of his revolver. But the man apparently had almost panicked after failing to kill Dane in his first barrage of shots.

Dane guessed that he wasn't used to running and probably didn't do much work of any kind. The uneven ground caused him to tumble every few steps.

Wheeling, he fired once more. Dane didn't have time to find a place to hide. But again the bullet went wild. Dane was close enough now to recognize Frank Rush. He was surprised. A gunman like Rush ought to have a cool head but he showed no sign of being the cold-blooded killer everyone in Sheridan thought he was.

Dane was estimating Rush's speed and the distance between Rush and the gully where he surely had his horse and he doubted if he would get within range of his revolver before Rush reached the gully.

Then Rush wheeled again, jerking up his rifle. But he hadn't stopped running and his foot caught on a rock. He fell backward, hitting the ground hard. The rifle hit the ground and fired into the air but Rush lost his grip and the rifle flipped away.

Half screaming, Rush scrambled to his feet but he couldn't seem to see where the rifle had gone. Meantime, Dane was running forward as fast as he could.

Rush gave up looking for the rifle and jerked out his revolver. The range was too long but he fired twice, anyway. Dane had his own gun in his hand but he didn't fire. He knew that Rush still had the advantage. He was used to shooting at men; Dane wasn't. Both were out of breath. At this range, only a lucky shot would hit its target.

Rush's fourth shot nicked Dane's sleeve and he realized he was flirting with disaster getting this close without shooting back. He stopped suddenly and leveled his gun, holding it with both hands. He was breathing so hard it was almost impossible to hold the gun steady. He fired twice. The second shot staggered Rush but Rush fired again, the bullet snapping past Dane. Dane dropped to one knee and fired again.

Rush sat down like a startled baby then slowly toppled to one side. Dane got up and moved forward cautiously. When he reached Rush, he saw the battle was over. He dropped his gun into its holster and turned wearily back toward the north end of the bluff. He thought of finding Rush's horse and tying the gunman onto the saddle. But he was too exhausted to do it now. He was just thankful to be alive.

When he got back to the work site, he found that someone had caught his mules. Dane answered the few questions asked about the identity of the ambusher then he went back to work.

The weariness clung to Dane through the day. One man rode into town with a report and someone came out with a wagon and got Rush's body off the ridge and hauled it back to town, leading Rush's horse. Dane wished that had been Yockam instead of Rush. Yockam was the last of the Home Guards who had killed his parents. He had the feeling he'd been fighting the men Yockam had hired ever since he got to Sheridan. Tonight, if possible, he was going to find Yockam and settle the issue one way or another. He had reached the point where he didn't care much whether he won or lost just so it was settled.

When he got back to the hotel that evening, he learned that the story of what had taken place on the ridge north of the buttes had preceded him. Since Frank Rush had run his bluff on most of the town Dane's accomplishment was all the more impressive.

"You're almost a celebrity," Tubulo said as they went down to the restaurant for supper.

"I was almost a dead man," Dane corrected. "It took a lot of luck to keep me alive today. Tonight I'm going to find Yockam if he's in town and have it out with him."

Tubulo nodded. "I reckon if you get Yockam, you'll be rid of all these ambushes and beatings. Somebody is paying those thugs to go after you. I saw Samson again today coming out of the Dew Drop Inn. I'm positive it is Yockam."

"We'll find out," Dane said grimly.

After supper, they went down to their post across the street from the Dew Drop Inn. While they were watching the men come and go, Tubulo suddenly poked Dane in the ribs hard enough to make him jump.

Following Tubulo's pointing finger, Dane saw a bearded man coming along the walk and turning into the Dew Drop Inn.

"Looks like him, doesn't it?" Tubulo asked.

"It is him," Dane said positively. "Didn't you see that limp? That's what he brought home from the war."

"Sure," Tubulo said. "I was so used to that little limp of his that I really didn't think about it. So now we know where he is. How do we get to him?"

Dane was already wrestling with the problem. There were the two men with guns sagging at their hips standing carelessly in front of the saloon. There would be more inside.

"You'll have to help me," Dane said softly. "I'm going around and come down the street toward the saloon. You stay here and watch for me. When I get as close as I can without being seen, you shoot into the air two or three times. That should bring some of those trigger happy guards over to see what is going on. I'll have to take my chances on what is left in the saloon."

Tubulo nodded vigorously. "Might work. Those two

174

in front of the saloon are sure to come over. Maybe those inside will come, too."

"You just make sure you disappear after you fire those shots," Dane warned.

"You can depend on that," Tubulo said. "I ain't hankering to get into any shoot-out with those gun slicks."

Dane dodged back into the alley and checked his gun. It was fully loaded and loose in the holster. Running down the alley a half block, he moved back to the street. Looking toward the Dew Drop Inn, he saw the two gunmen lounging in front of the place but they weren't looking this way. Carelessly, he sauntered across the street as if he were heading for a saloon directly ahead of him. There were several men moving around as the evening traffic began to pick up.

Once on the same side of the street as the Dew Drop Inn, he turned toward the saloon. As men moved along, he moved with them, trying to keep himself hidden from the two gunmen on the porch of the saloon. He got to the alley beside the saloon and stepped back into the shadows. The two guards hadn't seen him.

He waited, looking across the street. He couldn't see Tubulo and he wondered if the little man had seen him. Then two quick shots echoed from the alley over there.

The two guards on the porch came alert, their guns leaping into their hands. Several more men came out of the saloon and looked across the street. Another shot roared over there followed by a piercing scream. That would be Tubulo putting in a little added inducement to bring the men over.

They took the bait and crossed the street on the run, guns drawn. Dane could imagine Tubulo running back down the alley and finding a place to hide. He wasn't easy to find when he wanted to hide.

When the men reached the other side of the street, their attention on the alley, Dane dodged around the corner of the saloon and moved quickly to the door. Ducking inside, he scanned the interior of the room in a quick sweep.

There were only four men left, two of them were playing cards in the back and another had a bottle at a table, too drunk to know or care what was going on outside. The man called Samson was standing at the bar, his eyes riveted on the door, waiting for a report on the shooting across the street.

He was so intent on finding out what was going on that he seemed to look right through Dane when he saw that he wasn't one of his own men. Dane moved quickly to the bar. He had to be sure that this was Lon Yockam. A full beard could really change a man's appearance.

Then as he reached the bar, the man called Samson suddenly seemed to recall something he'd seen a moment before. His eyes flipped from tile door to Dane's face and recognition flooded his eyes. His lips sagged open.

"Banning! How did you get in here?"

"Walked," Dane said, watching Yockam's eyes. "We've got some things to settle."

Yockam didn't hesitate. His hand dived for the gun at his hip. Dane made the same move. Dane was not swift with a gun but neither was Yockam. Dane usually fought his battles with fists. Yockam usually hired his battles fought for him. Neither had an option now.

Dane fired but he knew he'd been a fraction of a second behind Yockam. He felt the blow in his chest. But he fired a second time before the room began gyrating and he hit the floor.

Looking up through eyes rapidly clouding over, he saw that Yockam wasn't standing, either. Hunching himself up on an elbow, he located Yockam sitting on the floor, his back resting against the bar. His hand was slowly raising his gun for another shot.

Dane lifted his gun. It weighed more than anything he had ever tried to lift in his entire life. He managed to squeeze the trigger once more just as Yockam did the same.

Dane was slammed back to the floor and the gun dropped, too heavy for his hand to hold.

Dimly he heard men running back into the saloon. Somebody lifted him somewhere. He wasn't sure where and it no longer made any difference. But he clung desperately to the thread of life left him. He had to know if Yockam was dead.

Through a swimming mist, he saw Tubulo move up beside him. He tried to form words but could mange only one. "Yockam?"

"He's dead," Tubulo said softly. "Don't try to talk. The doc will be here soon."

Dane dropped his head. Dimly he heard another man say, "No sense in sending for a doc. This one ain't going to make it, either."

A calm settled over him. He had finished the job he had started out to do. Yockam was dead.

Dane had another dim waking moment. He couldn't put things together. He had to be dead; he had received his death wound. Yet there was pain in his chest and in his side. There shouldn't be pain once a man was dead.

It was impossible to grasp any thought and hold it. He heard a woman's voice from somewhere in the past before he left for the war. It was his own Charity bidding him good-by. He tried desperately to cling to that one wonderful moment. But it slipped away.

Sometime later the dream came again. Neither time nor place had any meaning now. He was with Charity again. She was telling how she had missed him after he went to the war.

Dimly a thought came to him. His mother had said they'd all be together again someday after they died. That had to be it. He had died and so had Charity. Now they were together. He tried to hold to that moment. But it, too, slipped away.

The dream came again, spurred by Charity's voice. He couldn't tell what she was saying but he knew he had to touch her, cling to her, or she'd slip away again. If they were going to be together forever, why did he have to fight so hard to stay with her? And why did he hurt? Did he have to take his wounds with him into the hereafter?

A cold cloth on his forehead made him open his eyes. It was difficult to focus them on anything. But he thought he was seeing the girl he had left when he went away to war. The face wasn't quite the same but the blue eyes and long red hair were the same.

"Charity?" He managed to whisper the name.

"Yes," she said softly.

But he slipped away again without getting the grasp on her that he knew he must have if he expected to stay with her.

When consciousness came to him again, Charity wasn't there. His first thought was that he had failed to hang onto her. But this time, his senses returned to make him realize he was not dead. No dead man could hurt like he did.

He relaxed, letting his mind clear like the water in a muddy spring. He was alive. But where was he? He saw the crude room he was in. It wasn't even as well built as that old shed back on the farm. There were rough boards on the floor and a cobbled-up stand by the bed. There was a broken table and a small stove that would never heat this place in cold weather.

Then the vision came again, floating through the door, the red-headed picture of Charity. Only this time he knew she was real.

"I'm so glad to see you are awake," she said, the voice the same as he remembered over those years.

"Charity!" he whispered. "I—I tried to find you. Where—?"

"I live here," Charity said softly. "After what happened to me, this was the only way I could make a living."

He tried to talk but couldn't find the words or the strength to say them. She pressed a finger against his lips. "As soon as you're able to take care of yourself, I'll get out of your life."

He pushed her hand aside. "Never again," he croaked.

Another girl came through the door. Dane recognized her instantly, Mamie. She came to the bed and smiled down at him.

"You are a tough man," she said softly. "You're going to make it."

"Somebody tell me what happened," Dane said.

"I will," Mamie said before Charity could speak.

"Charity found you practically dead and brought you here and nursed you back to life. That was ten days ago. She found me six weeks ago, the first day I came down on this street. She took me back up on the main street and found me a job."

"This was no place for you," Charity said to Mamie.

"She also saw you when you first got to town,"

179

Mamie said to Dane. "She told me about you. And she sent me after you."

"You deserve a good girl like Mamie, Dane," Charity said.

Dane looked at the two women, his mind being forcibly cleared by the things he was hearing.

"You're my wife, Charity."

"Not any more, Dane," Charity said, her voice barely a whisper. Tears welled into her eyes and ran down her cheeks. "Not after what I've been for the last four years."

"I'm no angel, either," Dane said. "I've killed a lot of men. Some call me a murderer. We're both tarnished, Charity."

"But what about Mamie?" Charity asked, apparently still trying to grasp a situation she had long ago given up as an impossibility.

"I like Mamie," Dane said, finding talking almost more than he could do. "But you're mine, Charity."

Mamie turned to Charity. "Don't be pig-headed, Charity. You've got something good. Take it." She leaned down and kissed Dane on the forehead. "You two will always be my best friends. " She turned toward the door. "I'll tell Tubulo he can come in and see you now."

"What happened to us," Dane said when Mamie was gone, "was caused by the same crime. Things like this happened to a lot of people in the war. Let's start new."

He lay back, sweating from the effort of talking. Charity dropped on her knees beside him, her eyes shining as he remembered they once had years ago.

"We'll do it," she whispered. "We'll go forward from this day and never look back."

A Year
by the
Sea

Thoughts of an Unfinished Woman

A Year
by the
Sea

JOAN ANDERSON

MJF BOOKS
NEW YORK

Published by MJF Books
Fine Communications
322 Eighth Avenue
New York, NY 10001

A Year by the Sea
LC Control Number: 2014930530
ISBN 978-1-60671-235-1

QF   10   9   8   7   6   5   4   3   2   1

*To my role model and best friend—my wondrously
unfinished mother—who continues to evolve
and transcend herself.
Her wisdom, and that of her mother,
whispers throughout these pages.*

ACKNOWLEDGMENTS

I am deeply indebted to my friend Cheryl Lindgren, who gave me *Women Who Run with the Wolves* with the inscription: "Never forget our roots." She was referring to our femininity, which, back in 1992, was tattered and unraveling. Together we formed a group of women to share our mutual plight and attempt to get back to our authentic selves. To these original *soul seekers* and *pathfinders* I owe the deepest gratitude: Virginia Dare, Joya Verde, Joan Daniels, Judy Greenberg, Hazel Goodwin, Julie Hansen. We worked toward growth and change for several years and this story is theirs as well as mine.

Local Cape Codders Marilyn Leugers, Nancy Cole, Geri Appleyard, Loni Ebersold, Marcia West, and Judy Corkum added encouragement and insight as the journey continued. Their feedback is sprinkled throughout subsequent drafts. Still others—the Snyders, Emmerlings, and Bormans—

offered their hideaways and cottages where I retreated to sort out my journal notes and formulate this manuscript.

There are no words to communicate my gratitude to Nicholas Monsarrat, Barbara Curcio, and Rebecca Anderson, three intuitive and discriminating editors, writers in their own right, who fine-tuned each chapter, fussed over my grammar, insisted that I not cut out on the truth, prodded me for more when I wanted to give less. Thank you for being incredible coaches during my literary marathon!

And a special thanks to Hannah Andrychowski, who transcribed notes, typed draft after draft, met strenuous deadlines, and cheered me on, for she believed the message.

Of course this book would not have been possible without the clear and steady vision of my agent, Olivia Blumer . . . her sense that I was compelled to write this book, her faith that I could achieve it, and most significantly, getting it to the desks of Patricia Mulcahy and Harriet Rubin, venerable editors who know the market and were able to direct me to write for it, and special thanks to Denell Downum, who navigated the manuscript into port.

And then there is family: my cousin Judy, a sounding board and voice in the wilderness who prodded me from far-away Texas to finish the job; Wendy, her sister, who stood in admiration and cheered; my sons, who continue to push me toward authenticity, and their wives, whose independence and striving determination to become their own persons within the bounds of marriage continue to inspire me. But most of all I have enormous gratitude for my husband, who gave me license to share the hard truths and sought his own in the process. He never once interrupted my writing time, always ready to read the next chapter with a critical eye and encouraging words.

Many have provided a cheering section from afar: the Geigers, Chertoks, Jan, Dan, and Martha Masterson, especially Pamela Borman, a staunch supporter and good friend who believes in my message and is the best public relations person I could have.

Finally, I was so blessed to find my mentor and playmate, the late Joan Erikson, who committed to the task of dishing out her Eriksonian actuality day in and day out until it took hold.

CONTENTS

There is a tide in the affairs of men,

Which, taken at the flood, leads on to fortune;

Omitted, all the voyage of their life

Is bound in shallows and in miseries.

On such a full sea are we now afloat;

And we must take the current when it serves,

Or lose our ventures.

—*Shakespeare,* Julius Caesar, ACT IV, SCENE 3

A Year
by the
Sea

EBB TIDE

September

*Be patient toward all that is unsolved in your heart
and try to love the questions themselves.
Do not now seek the answers, which cannot be
given you because you would not be able
to live them. And the point is to live everything.
Live the questions now. Perhaps you will then
gradually, without noticing it, live along some
distant day into the answers.*

—*Rainer Maria Rilke*, LETTER TO
A YOUNG POET

The decision to separate seemed to happen overnight. My husband came home from work one day and announced that he was taking a job hundreds of miles away. As he yammered on about the details, I sat blank-faced, hard-pressed for an excuse not to accompany him. After all, our two sons were grown, the big old family house in which we had resided for seventeen years had long since outlived its usefulness, and my job was portable. So where was my resistance coming from? Why was I frozen, frightened, and full of anger?

It didn't take long to realize my uncomplicated truth. I simply did not have the inclination or the energy to move with him. Trying to start a new life, in a strange place, when the marriage had gone stale was simply too overwhelming. I surprised myself when I blurted out the only alternative I could think of: retreating to our Cape Cod cottage to figure things out. I was alarmed by my numbness, my seeming lack of compassion, but there it was staring me in the face.

Consciously, I wasn't thinking this would be a legal separation, just a little breathing space that would be a sort of time-out, a vacation from relationship. For all intents and purposes, we would be back together again in a few months.

My husband met my challenge with little or no emotion, becoming remote, even blasé. We went about making plans for our futureless future with a frightening politeness, casually announcing the decision to friends who gathered after a garage sale in our living room, now emptied of stuff, extraneous and otherwise. While most of them stood aghast, one quickly filled the stunned silence with "Well, what kind of memories do you have about this place?"

I felt myself shudder as one of our sons began recalling celebrations I had created. Others followed, and the remembering continued until the room reverberated with nostalgia. Just then it seemed all right that this chapter of our life was closing. We had lived hard and loved this place much and, perhaps most important, shared it with others.

As we turned out the lights and flopped onto our mattress, now on the floor because we had just sold the four-poster bed, I panicked about my immediate destiny. Mellow moments have a way of erasing all the others. I turned onto my side and draped my arm around his portly middle, reaching out for I-don't-know-what. I would miss the comfort of familiarity, I thought, snuggling closer to the back of him. He stirred, and for a moment I thought he might turn over, say something, perhaps even take me in his arms. But in seconds he fell into a deep sleep, and I was left to be lulled by the pattern of his breathing.

So many nights I had lain beside him wondering what his dreams were made of, what haunted him so. I had known from the beginning that his childhood was harshly lonely, raised as he was in an alcoholic family, sent away at the tender age of twelve to an Episcopalian boarding school he hated. As we were falling in love, he made sure I realized the strikes against him, the baggage he carried, but I, the ultimate caregiver, was all the more challenged by his shadows. I found a sort of comfort going into a marriage where my role as resident nurturer was already defined, and thought I'd fix his melancholia somehow, lifting him above the darkness he had grown so used to carrying.

But alas, over the years I wearied of his pain, which seemed impossible to exorcise. Too often I translated his emotional unavailability as rejection and began pleading for attention: "I have needs, too, you know," I would reiterate, hungering for connection and affirmation. He would look up from the book he was reading and inform me that "Needs are a roof over your head and food in your stomach. Period." That kind of answer generally shut me down, as well as other remarks that always sounded accurate enough to make me feel the fool for asking. He would trivialize my outbursts with a practical saneness, as befits a pragmatic man who favors semantics. Over the years, being on the other side of strained reasonableness became more than frustrating.

Still, there were a few times when he was actually jealous of me. After a dinner party where I had regaled the guests with stories and jokes, as he remained typically quiet and withdrawn, he said, "You're Technicolor and I'm black and white."

"So?" I retorted. "Why not add some color to your life?"

My answers were rarely that clever, and humor was seldom a part of our discourse. I found myself feeling more and more oppressed by a role I had undoubtedly created. My twisted sense of loving was about giving and giving and giving until I saw the pleasure of my efforts on the other's face, so my own happiness was wrapped up in making him feel good. I think he thought I was nicer when I forgot myself. My needs so often must have sounded like demands that he would choose not to meet. When he did try, his attempts fell short of my expectations. In any case, the joy of living had been sucked out of him, and I had given up any resuscitation attempts.

A relationship to me was supposed to be about adventure, having fun, sharing. He saw his primary role as breadwinner and occasional participant in the periphery of our family life. I would fill the weekends with people and parties, hoping to ignite his spirit, but often such occasions made him retreat all the more. When I would try to pry him out of his shell, his retort would be "When will you ever be satisfied with what is? If it's excitement you want, then go get it!"

So I did, promptly developing a crush on a married man—running away from the intensity of those feelings to a writer's conference in Maine, returning with new contacts to energize my career, signing up book projects, thus burying my personal needs in the glamour of the writing profession. Although each escapade offered momentary titillation, all of them failed to bring me what I craved—intimacy and relatedness.

So here I am, with the only alternative I have left: refusing relationship for the time being, or perhaps seeking relationship with myself. It is late. Tomorrow is a big day. I roll over on my thoughts and sink into sleep.

It was 5 A.M. when I awoke, an hour later for him, and we scurried to finish packing both cars before he took off for his new job and I for a new life. "I can't believe we're doing this," I said, complicating the leave-taking and knowing what could come back to me in response.

"*You* can't believe it," he retorted, through clenched teeth. "This was all *your* idea!" My words infuriated him, as usual, and his body language conveyed anger as he crammed the last few bags into my already cramped trunk and slammed down the lid.

"I gotta get going," he said, softening his bluntness with a smile, "getting on with my life just as you are getting on with yours." I prepared myself for more punishment as he walked away, not even looking back. But then he turned, and his dark gaze, though pained, was eerily peaceful. "See ya," he said, and that was it.

The weight of his departure was stunning. I leaned my forehead on the roof of the car and began to cry, having no other remedy for my pain, and then stifled my sobs when two friends stopped by with a Thermos of coffee, food for the road, and hugs. These celibate wives, whose marriages had grown angry and cold long ago, stood there with longing in their eyes. They said I was brave, that they wished they had the guts to do the same, that they dreamed of being able to stand on their own. I raised my chin and placed a finger under my nose to keep more tears from flowing, wanting so badly to protest. "Desperate" was the operative word to describe me that very moment. I could hardly categorize my move as brave. I had been trained to believe in "whither thou goest, I will go . . ." and now I was running in the opposite direction. Each minute that I lingered was bringing me dangerously closer to changing my mind.

Female friendships have been my panacea, always a salve on dark days. But this time I was in a crisis that needed my full attention, not the distraction friends would provide. Staying with the familiar would only serve to prolong my inertia. And so I climbed into my rusting old Volvo, stuffed mostly with books, papers, unfinished manuscripts, and other writer's paraphernalia, and took off, gazing at the FOR SALE sign on the front lawn. My last stop would be the bank, where I would clear out what was left of my savings, $3,782.42. He was to cover the big bills, but I was to take care of myself, a fair deal, since over the years my writing income had paid for such things as the boys' education, taxes, and most of the extras.

As I drove out of Nyack and headed for the Tappan Zee Bridge, I repeated not once, but many times, "You're making the right move—keep going—you're making the right move." Once I paid the bridge toll and saw the sign for New England, my shoulders began to drop and my back molded into the seat. I was finally on my way, and it felt as though this move had been in the works for a long time.

Perhaps it had. There had been other false starts, times when I had run away on impulse but then learned if you run away too often it loses its dramatic effect. This time was different, monumental even. I had tied up significant loose ends before bolting. I felt suddenly Machiavellian, a master planner, or like someone about to die, putting her affairs in order. The lives of everyone I had been responsible for were in place. I fear sometimes, that in my impatience for my own freedom, I had hurried the boys along, encouraging my older son to take the plunge into marriage long before any of his friends had even considered such a move, giving my own engagement ring to the younger one so the diamond could be made into a ring for his bride.

What should that have told me? If I no longer had a handle on my own happiness, perhaps I wanted to ensure theirs. Their weddings, coming as they did at the height of our disillusionment, served to distract us for a time. I've seen many of our friends get into the "wedding machine," with all of its accompanying minutiae. My husband and I were no exceptions. If we were no longer to experience the headiness of romance, then maybe our consolation prize was to get a brush of it vicariously. I often wondered if that was the reason so many people cry at weddings. They see love and want some for themselves, all the while knowing that such a dream eludes them. It felt good being the proud mama and papa at our sons' weddings, being part of the pageant. Was the hope I held for them the hope I still had for us?

But the magic evaporated as soon as the rice was thrown and it was back to business as usual. Even the cat, who was our last dependent, conveniently died, dropping dead of a stroke in our basement one Sunday while we were at church. Nothing seemed to be holding us together anymore.

My head was spinning as I careened onto the Merritt Parkway, and I reached for a pen to jot down my thoughts. "One of these days you're going to die writing in the car," a good friend once warned. "I know, I know," I said, never heeding her warning.

❊ ❊ ❊

Cocooned in my Volvo, heading away from everything that was, I now find myself thinking more clearly, feeling miraculously light. I tune the radio to a classical station playing Vivaldi's *Four Seasons*, music I used to run to, a good omen, as I am running to a new life. I once heard that Olympic coaches play baroque music in the locker room before big meets to quell their athletes' anxiety. I take a deep breath and wish for such a calm to overtake me.

Still, I feel naughty, even bad. The one who leaves is always wrong, while the other partner, who passively goes along, gets all the sympathy. Most men, I've noticed, are reluctant to walk out. They may want out of their marriage, but set it up so the wife actually does the walking. Surely, when the boys begin to question what is going on, they will worry far more about their father than about me. They have rarely seen his faults, perhaps because his usual persona is rational, responsible, honest. I, on the other hand, am the one who flails, who has the big mouth, the outrageous moods, who ends up screaming at situations—but rarely at the man who might have caused them.

I'm barreling north now on Interstate 95, far away from anything that resembles city, speeding to the racing violins in the allegro portion of Vivaldi's "Spring." Yet, I can't get away from the negative voices that say I am a spoiled brat. After all, my husband is not a wife beater, he's never called me a bitch (although he has called me bitchy), and he seems so forlorn. "You've really done it this time, Joan!" I say, hitting the steering wheel as if to smack myself. I wish I could have a drink, or some Valium, or even a punching bag!

Just then I am distracted by a sign: NEW HAVEN. God, I've passed this place hundreds of times and never bothered connecting it to my past. This is where we met. Yale was the beginning. I slam on the brakes and skid onto an exit, hell-bent on seeing the past, finding an old haunt or two.

In minutes I'm staring at the White Tower Diner, right across from the Green, where free refills of coffee had kept us talking long into the night when we were first discovering each other. Trusting my rusty memory, I turn onto Trinity and see the Drama School, its garish red doors just as I re-membered them, and nearby, the alleyway where we used to neck. A couple of kids are leaning against the stone wall doing much the same thing. I drive around the block and spot the dump of a house where I had a basement apartment and where we dry-humped but didn't dare try much more.

There is purpose and excitement everywhere, just as there should be in autumn at the beginning of a school year. I see students with beautifully scrubbed faces, some in spir-ited conversation, others walking with jaunty determination toward class. Just like us back then, except I suddenly remem-ber his running away when our relationship was getting seri-ous. Perhaps I should have let him go, but I was determined to get a husband, and he seemed a most likely candidate. So I chased him until he caught me, and soon thereafter we were engaged, with a ring handed to him by his mother, given to me moments later. An "arranged marriage" it was, or so it seems as I think back on it now. I had already known he had brought other women home, but as far as his mother was concerned, I had taken the prize. My mother, on the other hand, was duly impressed because he was the son of a doctor, therefore well heeled. She overlooked his parents' heavy drinking in favor of the fancy house and beach club, stuck as she was on appearances, hardly the best manure to spread over a marriage bed.

A car behind me honks as I stall at a green light. I turn the ignition key and gun it, lifting a finger at the guy's impatience and remind myself that I'm trying to move forward and leave the past behind. Once on the highway I open the car window to let the air blow through my hair and feel a rush as I begin speeding toward my future.

I never feel legitimately in New England until I've crossed the border from Connecticut to Rhode Island. That's when I become giddy, excited even, knowing the journey's end is only a couple of hours away. Going home or to a place that feels like home evokes an unmistakable aura of settledness. The Cape permits such feelings because it's where I've spent every summer since I was a child.

A new beginning in an old place. I like the sound of it. Posted over the sink in our cottage is a Wendell Berry quote: "If you don't know where you are, then you don't know who you are." Once there I always feel more secure about who I am, perhaps because its well-worn paths are familiar to me. What's more, I can indulge in a kind of knowing that doesn't involve my head but rather engages my senses. There is not a channel or dune or marsh that is not associated with a time or event or person from my past, and I think I am counting on these memories to remind me of who I was before—that raw-material person I seem to have lost.

I suppose it became truly home after my father died and was buried in the cemetery beside the First Congregational Church, circa 1746, along with one grandfather, two grandmothers, an aunt, and a cousin. I was startled at first upon seeing the gravestone marked ANDERSON, but soon thereafter felt somehow grounded by it. All the other towns and cities in which I had previously resided became mere temporary stops on my way home.

Change occurs slowly on an elbow of land where there is just so much earth surrounded by sea. I know where to find huckleberries in August and bittersweet in September, where the sand dollars nestle and the starfish cling. Even my feelings of anticipation about getting there are no different than they were years ago when my brother and I sat huddled in the backseat of our father's old Buick, watching for the telltale signs that indicated arrival was imminent. First we'd notice the soil at the edge of the highway turning sandy; then spot a gull or two hovering overhead; eventually we'd see the Sagamore Bridge, gateway to our paradise. Once over and onto the other side, we'd open the windows, rain or shine, sniff the moist air with its aroma of dried pine needles, knowing that before long we'd be wending our way through town, past the church whose steeple bell rings every hour, past the soda fountain across the street where we would slurp coffee frappes, past the harbor where our little boat is moored, and finally to the sandy trail that leads to our cottage door.

Lost as I am in my thoughts, I am startled to actually see the bridge so soon. It seems as though I've just left New Haven, and it is barely noon! The sun is welcoming, yet I feel as disoriented as a gull circling overhead before a storm, uncertain where to put down. I seem to want to delay landing, settling in too soon. I remind myself that I have no schedule. After all, no one is at the cottage waiting for me. That thought alone creates anxiety. I'll head for the shore, give myself time to ease into the move here, and think what it might mean—let the rhythm of the ocean cradle me and bring me to a state of simply being.

Once in the parking lot of my favorite beach, I slip out of my shoes to feel the moist sand on my feet and then run to the top of a dune as if to claim my territory. Since I am wholly unprepared for what comes next in my life, I am forced to content myself with that which is before me. I think it was Thomas Merton who said that the easiest way to rid yourself of neurosis is to surround yourself with nature, or more specifically trees. "You can't be neurotic in front of a bunch of trees," he claimed; nor, I hasten to add, in front of dunes or sea or humble scrub pine. Standing here at the edge of the world shows me how exaggerated my own emotions seem to be. This strong, silent place interrupts confusion, rage, and depression, and just now I feel more at home with the landscape than with people.

I'm staring at the autumn-brown beach, taking in the aging white lighthouse towering to my left, the gently lapping water to my right, and under my feet the sienna-stained dune grass. Circling my head is a monarch butterfly, which long ago should have been on its way to Brazil. "Perhaps you, too, need some extra time by the sea," I say, as it flaps its wings and settles on my shoulder. I eventually wander down from the bluff toward the calm surf, where the water is not going anywhere, neither coming in nor going out, ebb tide, I suppose—the sea at a standstill, as am I. It was always the nothingness of ebb tide that drove me to distraction—when the wind stopped breathing and the water was still—when there wasn't enough depth to have a good swim and not enough current to make it a challenge.

High tide was the one my cousin and I liked best. Her family owned a cottage at the edge of a marsh near a wonderful channel that wound its way out to the open sea. When we were kids, it was there that we would swim, but only when the tide was just right, when the whitecaps were churning and the ocean was charged with energy. We would run to the end of a very long jetty, plunge into the cool salt water, and let the current carry us all the way back to her cottage door.

On stormy days, when the boat traffic was light, we would slip off our bathing suits and skinny-dip, letting the rush of water and sea lettuce caress our bodies. Our glee was punctuated with high-pitched squeals as one or the other hit a cold spot or chanced a foot on the sandy bottom, where crabs lay in wait to nibble on our toes.

We tolerated low tide only because it provided us with plenty to do in the way of shelling and clamming or just general mucking about. But it still beat ebb tide, when you couldn't do anything but sit passively by and watch while the sea turned itself around. It occurs to me, just now, that perhaps ebbing can be a rest time, a "psychic slumber" from a lifetime of learning to be a woman. I never thought about just being still, caught up as I was with escape and all it entails.

I'm tired of swimming upstream, against the current, only to arrive at unnatural destinations with little sense of where to yield, when to sow, what to ask, how to find. More than anything I wish to be carried out with the surf and be buoyed by the salt water. But reality keeps me beached for the time being. I need to hunker down like a nesting crab or a plump clam and take stock while the tides wash over me.

It is eerily quiet. My soul is as drab as the September beach upon which I sit. I must be still and listen to the primitive squawk of birds and breathe, breathe deeply of the moist, clean air and be open to whatever comes my way.

The Call of the Seal

Early October

When one is freshly informed, has a serendipitous experience, one's mood is changed, one's heart is changed. That is why taking time to see, hear, be present to images and language that arise from new experiences have the power to change one from one way to another.

—*Clarissa Pinkola Estés*, WOMEN WHO RUN WITH THE WOLVES

It *is* morning—an early, dark morning. I listen for the birds who usually begin chattering at four-thirty. There is silence, only the pitter-patter of rain hitting the skylight above my bed. Do I roll over and fall back to sleep or get up? This is always the dilemma.

I've been here for three weeks now, one day folding into the next. Without goals or routine, I am losing track of time. There isn't even a calendar around in case I want to know what day it is—but I don't. Still, I fight playing the dilettante. My instinct tells me to lie low, to process the grief that is the partner of change, but I am also aware that I should begin to do something.

My only regular undertaking is a daily trip to the post office, where I hope to find a check or two, this being royalty month. With no new projects in the offing, I'm counting on my old books to carry me for a while. The postmistress, whose cat ZipCode lounges on the counter, knows me as both a writer and a summer person. She's mystified that I am back in town, imagining that I'm working on some sexy novel.

A new kind of loneliness is setting in as I lie here with flicker-flashes of hard truths, failed beginnings, mostly dark thoughts that come after phone calls from my husband reminding me of some family matter or friends inquiring about my well-being. With no pat answers for anyone, I'm left frustrated after the calls. Contacts with the world I've left behind confuse me and make getting up not terribly appealing.

Long ago I lived for such rainy days, when I would make myself a cup of cocoa, climb back into bed, snuggle under the comforter, and just listen to the storm outside. Perhaps I would benefit from doing the same today. Recently, when I sought counsel from a minister friend, she affirmed my conclusion that I was stuck. "You're in the desert," she said, "and you're parched, but not dried out." As she talked, I pictured myself sitting on a stump in the middle of a vast wasteland, surrounded by nothing save miles of adobe-colored, hardened soil, with no escape route in sight. "You've no alternative but to simply sit still and listen. In time you'll hear the answers."

I swing my legs over the side of the bed and get up carefully. My lower back has seized up in the past few days. I'm not surprised, as a massage therapist once told me we store our visceral energies there. It has been a long time since I've indulged in earthy desires. It figures that my back should rebel.

My bare feet on the cold floor awaken what vestiges of me are still asleep, and I head for the kitchen and coffee. Alas, the coffee can is empty. I have been living off the staples in the pantry, avoiding the grocery store, turning my back on any reminders of domesticity. But now I want some coffee, and the only place to get a cup at this hour is Larry's PX, a fisherman's hangout. I've been wanting a legitimate excuse to go there for years, and now I have it. I pull on jeans and a tattered blue sweater retrieved from the floor beside my bed, grab the car keys, and head out.

A pea-soup fog makes the ten-minute drive fifteen, but the parking lot is as welcoming as a lighthouse, loaded as it is with pickups, fishing gear, and faithful dogs waiting on the front seats for their masters.

My entrance halts all conversation. I pretend not to notice, and breathe in the smell of simmering bacon. The only available seat at the U-shaped counter is at one end, and I slide onto the revolving stool, plopping myself beside a burly man with a permanently tanned face and a thick, blond beard. I feel awkward barging into a locals' hangout, but a morning fix is a morning fix. The waitress is quick to pour me a cup of coffee while I lose myself in the simplicity of the place— starch-white walls, red linoleum counters, plastic-covered plates holding stacks of doughnuts, copies of the local paper piled neatly nearby.

In a minute or two the chatter starts up again, and I bury my head in the menu, pretending not to listen. They are talking about weather and catches and the poisoning of seagulls, when someone brings up the subject of seals crowding the harbor. I order a couple of fried eggs in order to hear the rest.

Seals here? Couldn't be, but the locals go babbling on about how they number a thousand, and they're eating up all the fish! I look up now, my head bobbing from one fisherman to another, as if I am watching the ball at a tennis match. They know I'm listening. Perhaps they are starting to embellish, I don't know, but their conversation has got to be the best show in town.

Seals belong in Baja or Patagonia, exotic places, not in my little fishing village. I am fascinated as they talk of gray seals and harbor seals and how they used to migrate back and forth to Nova Scotia. But now they seem to be sticking around right through the winter, and it's bugging the fishermen. My cheeks burn with excitement. It's as if someone has plunked a package down in front of me that I can't wait to tear open.

I stop eating and drinking, not wanting my chewing or swallowing to interfere with my hearing; I picture a sea full of seals, and suddenly I want to be swimming with them. Ridiculous as it sounds, I am more than intrigued, I am crazed. I need only a way to get out there. Without missing a beat, I muster my nerve and promptly ask the guy next to me if he'll take me out.

"You're kidding?" he says, taking a gulp of coffee. I stare back with a determined look, although I surprise myself that I am being so bold. "Y'mean today?" he drawls, turning on his swivel stool to the man sitting next to him as if to get some confirmation that he's hearing right.

"I'll be out there for seven or eight hours," he continues, sure, I suppose, that this information will dissuade me. "Gotta see how long I can make the tide last," he adds with a wink. The last comment really gets to me. Imagine timing my day not to a clock but to the cycles of the sea! "All right by me," I answer.

Everyone around the counter is watching our exchange, ready for the next move—his or mine.

"Y'best get yourself some warm clothes and a sandwich," he suggests, calling my bluff. But I don't flinch. "Meet me at the pier in half an hour. The name of my boat is *Seal Woman*."

I shove my plate aside, leave a couple of dollars on the counter, and tear out, racing home in record time, where I grab a jar of peanut butter and a stale bagel, throw a slicker, a towel, and another sweater into my canvas bag, and hurry back to the pier with just minutes to spare.

"You made it," he says, sounding surprised, as if it were all just a big tease. "Toss me your gear and hop aboard."

I'm suddenly tongue-tied, blushing even, as he offers me a hand and helps me onto the deck. I'm shocked at how his touch electrifies me. Has it been that long since I've been touched?

Get a grip, Joan, I think as clouds of doubt quell my adventuresome spirit. What the hell am I doing, going off with a total stranger? I look around at the other boats, also readying themselves for a day at sea, and take note of a grin on the face of the fisherman in the next slip. Nothing goes unnoticed in small towns, particularly in the off-season. I wonder what kind of a scandal I'm starting. I don't even know if this guy is married or not. Well, I still am, I remind myself, although I'm finding this ruse fun. Yes, fun—the "F" word, my friends and I would call it, chiding one another to make sure to have some fun each day. We rarely succeeded; the needs of everyone else always got in the way.

It occurs to me that I've picked up this man! Unbelievable at my age, and yet why not? I remember picking up only one other guy in my entire life, an "older man" I got to talking to on a flight from New York to Dallas/Fort Worth. He offered to drive me to my hotel, as he was renting a car and I was not. When we got to the Hertz desk, however, and I double-checked the location of my hotel, he was headed for Dallas and I was going to Fort Worth and that ended that. The only other pickup, which also fizzled, began on an international flight after I got bumped up to first class; I was seated beside a man who looked like a football player I had dated in high school. We talked all the way across the Atlantic, to the dismay of those sitting around us, and planned to have dinner at some point during our mutual stays in Seville. But his unconsummated business deal got in the way of his having a free dinner slot.

"Would you untie that knot?" my clamdigger asks, breaking into my daze. "Sure," I say, eager to please. I perform the task like a well-trained deckhand as he puts the key into the ignition and the motor starts up. "I don't even know your name," I say, extending my hand. "I'm Joan."

"I'm Josh," he says. "Joshua Cahoon."

We glide out of the harbor with an escort of gulls overhead flapping their wings. Two white herons, perched on a piling, turn their heads in our direction with neither fear nor interest. It appears we are headed toward a long strip of sand held together by a dome of sky. I suddenly feel the pleasure of being exactly where I want to be. My heart is racing. I can barely recall when last I relinquished control to another—took a dare, really, and went off to a place I didn't know, trusting a stranger to take me there.

Once we clear the channel, he cranks the engine and motions for me to take protection behind his tiny windshield in a space big enough for only one. We stand shoulder to shoulder, and I get a sense of his well-built chest and broad back and feel another charge. Oh, God, how pathetic! Even so, I confess that I find him sexy. After my years of living in the white-collar world of pin-striped suits, horn-rimmed glasses, and *The Wall Street Journal*, a rough-hewn type is quite appealing.

I might have a WASP name, but I could never quite behave like one. Such a persona demands that one be demure, pale, thin-lipped, expressionless. I remember seeing Catherine Deneuve in a movie for the first time, and I wanted to be just like her. I tried on her mannerisms all the way home from the theater, acting cool, composed, delicate, like the petals of a soft coral rose, and even attempted to draw my husband out, to get him to do whatever I wanted, the way Catherine could always do with the men in her movies. But I failed miserably.

I must have been a lusty barmaid in a past life—probably lived in some Mediterranean town where the seafaring men were hard-drinking and tough, yet full of bravura and humor. Perhaps that's why I love being here right now. I need to be more wild and earthy.

The combined sounds of wind and the engine make talk impossible. I stare at his large strong hands as they grip the wheel and peek at his cool blue eyes, squinting now as we face an orange ball of sun. His boat is humble yet sturdy. It has the barest essentials, yet it gets the job done. Fishermen don't indulge in excess. They can't afford it. This impresses me. Men who make do undo me. They remind me of my father, a frugal genius who could make anything out of nothing.

We are flying over the surface of the water, bucking wave

after wave. I'm not sure whether I'm running away again or simply taking myself to a momentary refuge. Who cares? The adventure is intoxicating. It amazes me how my perspective changes when I'm in a boat looking back toward the shore. Out here are myriad invisible paths that only Josh seems to know, and we're free to move at whim. No clutter, no control, no boundaries, no societal constraints.

In the distance I spot an island, a grand mound of tan rising from nowhere with a darkened spot in its center. Within minutes Josh cuts his engine. "There," he whispers, pointing straight ahead. And then I see them—hundreds of beached blimps, smooth blobs of gray, brown, and beige, bespeckled creatures that blend into their space.

"How close can we get?" I ask. Just then a whiskered face pops up from beneath the sea. "Is this close enough?" Josh asks.

"Hello," I say spontaneously. It seems a natural reaction to speak back to a face that holds my gaze, eyes never blinking. And then, just as quickly as the seal has appeared, it disappears under the water, reemerging some fifty feet away, looking back to see if I'm following. As the motion of the water pushes us nearer to shore, several of the colony begin to stir, raising their heads, sniffing and surveying. Finally a large bull rolls over, stretches out his plump body, and awakens another. Like dominoes, one after the other turns over until the once-velvety blanket that covered the beach comes to life. *Thud. Thud. Thud.* The sound of hundreds of flippers crossing the hardened sand is thunderous, and I get goose bumps. They begin sliding off the embankment, where they seem awkward and unsure of themselves, and into the crisp, blue water, where they are sleek and in control. They swim to us, curious about our boat as well as our intentions, bobbing up and down like jack-in-the-boxes. Each time they surface, they make eye contact, then crane their necks, as if to say, "Follow me." I am transfixed.

Joshua breaks the spell. "Time for you to disembark," he says abruptly.

"What? You must be joking," I blurt out.

"You can wade in from here," he continues. "They're used to the occasional visitor."

"You're leaving me here... alone! I thought you were going to clam?"

"I go on down to the point—that's where the flats are. Like I said, I'll be back when the tide changes."

There is no arguing. I've signed on for the day and whatever it may bring. I quickly roll up my jeans, straddle the side of the boat, and splash into the icy-cold water. "Neatly done," he quips as he hands me my stuff. "See ya in a bit," and with that he puts the boat in reverse and takes off.

Yeah, sure, I think. Judging from the angle of the sun, it couldn't be more than eight or nine in the morning. With the tide still high, it'll be at least eight hours before he's back. And yet isn't that what turned me on? Spending a day timed to the tides?

I plow on, holding my canvas bag above my head. Fortunately the water grows shallower— Oops. I hit a drop-off. Now I'm wet up to my crotch. Damn him! You'd think he could have pulled closer to shore. Jeans were a dumb thing to wear. They don't stretch, they cling, and they're heavy. I should have stripped them off back on the boat, but that would hardly have been appropriate in front of a stranger.

Finally, my last step. I reach the embankment and collapse on the shore to catch my breath, overcome by the primitive beauty of this place that has no edges. For sure, I've been stuck in worse places. I think it's going to be a good day. In any event, I'm quickly learning to relish whatever comes to me by chance.

SEAL SENSE

Same Day

*Animals may aid us in our everyday lives, in our dreams, medi-
tations. Since they were created before humans, they are closer to THE
SOURCE and can act as allies, guides and familiars
in our search for wholeness.*

—An Inuit woman

It *is* one of those Indian-summer days when you are lured to the shore for one last taste of summer. Yet today I have come for other reasons, without beach chair or umbrella, and suddenly feel as though I don't belong. I am a misplaced person, unceremoniously dumped with a colony of seals on a strange stretch of beach.

I don't know what I had expected. Come to think about it, I didn't have time for any preconceived notions. For once I had acted on impulse and am now left to deal with the consequences. I feel strangely alone, wishing for Josh's company. Do I want to have a fling with him? I don't think so, although perhaps I'm hoping for a flattering spark.

I'm not ungrateful to be here. God, no! This has got to be the most extraordinary beach in the whole world, and what's more, hardly anyone knows about it! When will I ever learn to accept what is given instead of always yearning for more? My lavish expectations too often tarnish my blessings. Right now the seals, at least forty of them, are staring me down as they tread water. I suppose they want me to move so they can reclaim their space and sun themselves. Never comfortable in the role of intruder, I give up this spot to explore the rest of the island. My mother taught me well the importance of accommodation. I developed the knack for selfless behavior because we moved so many times when I was growing up. "The way to fit in," she would say, "is to play by their rules, ask questions, and contribute something." I mastered her advice, since I was forever the new kid on many different blocks, constantly giving, in order to be accepted.

It's getting hot, and I'm sticky. I need to peel off my wet jeans, now thoroughly caked with sand. I place them on a clump of dune grass to dry out and grab my lunch. As I spread peanut butter on my bagel, I wish it were a turkey club with avocado and sprouts. Here I go again, never satisfied with the blessings before me. Of course, I could have come better prepared, but too often I've used up precious time *preparing* for experiences rather than just having them. I must learn to surrender to the moment, but the very word "surrender" evokes giving up and giving in, not an easy task for a demon planner like me, who has spent the better part of my life stage-managing everyone else's show while waiting in the wings for my own time to come. Yet look what happened! Destiny won, as it always does. I'm no longer in control of my marriage, the children, or my future. Nothing is certain.

Actually, there is a sense of relief in admitting that everything is out of my control. It's hard trying to be right all the time, to be a good girl. On occasion being dead wrong and human offers some solace. I'm reminded of the last time I got a speeding ticket. The moment I spotted the patrol car, its lights spinning in my rearview mirror, my heart sank. I quickly took my foot off the gas pedal, not wanting to admit to speeding, and pretended that it wasn't me he was after. But when he turned on the sirens, I knew I had to ditch the charade. I'd been caught, and giving up was the easiest alternative.

Perhaps I've held on to control out of fear that if I didn't, the whole family would go down the drain. I've been labeled strong, even resilient, two admirable traits that have been my undoing. But one day I caught on to the burden that goes with control: The controller does most of the work! Oddly enough, it was just this quality that attracted my husband to me. "I never thought I would need to take care of you," he said nonchalantly, twenty-five years into the marriage, as I stared utterly dumbfounded at him. "You've always appeared so strong and in control." Ever since that statement, I've come to despise being called strong, being the one everyone counts on to pick up the slack.

I need to stop this incessant chatter and work up an appetite for just *being*. Gently lured by the sea's distant roar, I begin to stroll to her music, tiptoeing over newly sprouted dune grass, trying not to destroy its work of holding together, via miles and miles of root, this very beach. Dune grass is admirably self-sufficient.

I remember a family picnic long ago on a similar remote beach, to which we carted babies, toys, bassinets, grills, food, everything needed to spend a day away together. We had only one son at the time, and he immersed himself in sand-castle building with assorted cousins and uncles, while my husband and I wandered off to make love in the dunes. The naughty danger of it created an unforgettable thrill. Sad to say, it was an isolated moment. Reaching adulthood before the Pill made me cautious, cool, not wild and free.

Before marriage I had played a kind of "sexual Russian roulette," doing everything except going all the way. This offered me the vicarious thrill of witnessing the man's pleasure, while my prize was the power of knowing I had contributed to his euphoria. Such safe sex or half sex kept me pure, but less than satisfied. Wild abandon was all but impossible on my wedding night. I couldn't suddenly let go just because some minister had sanctioned the once-forbidden act. I was trapped in a vicious cycle that led my husband eventually to label me frigid.

I'm walking faster now, through warm white sand, realizing even my feet are starved for stimulation. The entire island is sunning itself, and I am embracing its warmth. Although I cherish this time alone, I have a momentary craving to share it with a passionate lover. Instead, I receive a succulent substitute from the welcoming sea, its foam and crystals spewing high into the sky like a fountain, inviting me in to play.

A dark cloud obscures the sun, and I hug my shivers, running toward the water, not planning to plunge in, but doing so anyway. After the initial shock, I realize the water is warmer than the air and decide to stay in until the sun reappears. This is serious surf, though. I can't just drift. I must move with determination to ward off the undertow. *Never swim without someone watching from the shore* was always the rule; I'm breaking that one now, along with so many others. A gentle wave suddenly rises and towers overhead. Impulsively, I dive under, coming out the other side. I haven't dared that for years. In fact, I've had a phobia about going underwater for some time. Why am I more cautious as I age instead of the other way around? I wonder if it's all tied in to failure. I tend to forget my gains and remember only the losses. The failures have piled up, wreaking havoc with my confidence until, as an adult, I've become afraid to take chances.

Maddeningly, though, I watch my sons take risks. One has biked cross-country several times, and the other is a stand-up comic. They aren't afraid to fail, which they frequently do. I suppose I was just as bold at twenty: I got myself into drama school as the only undergraduate to do so, worked in the bush in Africa, became the secretary to the American ambassador's wife when I could hardly even type, talked my way into an editor's office to sell a magazine story without ever having been published before. Hell, I thought I was invincible for a long time, and then suddenly I stopped taking any risks. Inexplicably, there was a gradual erosion of faith in the essence of myself, as the habit of deference grew like a cancer on my soul until what I had become was out of my hands.

I think it was Picasso who said he spent the first half of his life becoming an adult and the last half learning to be a child. Is that why I have spent the last few summers gazing longingly at wide-eyed children? I was utterly entranced by one such child at the beach whose mother kept calling to her, "Victoria, do this . . . Victoria, do that." Victoria would have none of it; she was simply too immersed in her environment to eat or take a nap or be part of her family group. No, Victoria was in her own world—breaking all the rules, naked to the waist, hair caked with salt and sand—the embodiment of bliss.

I think I'm having some of that bliss right here and wish my kids could see me. They would applaud, no doubt, as I believe that our children want to see their parents happy, playful, even carefree. Once they gave me an Emerson quote about success, reading it aloud, flattering me by saying that it seemed to have been written about me. *"Successful people live well, laugh often, and love much. They've filled a niche and accomplished tasks so as to leave the world better than they found it, while looking for the best in others and giving the best they have."* "I'm working my way back to such success," I shout, as if the boys are watching from the shore, and gulp a mouthful of salt water.

I hear a snuffle, followed by a snort, and I dive under and swim into deeper water. The seals are here—not one, but many! Did they follow me from the other side? They must be trusting my presence now; in any case they are inspiring a momentary trust in myself. I dare to swim a bit closer as they pull at me like a magnet. I am under their spell and begin mimicking them, dipping in and up, rolling with the swells, then floating easily, the seals and me, suspended in time. Unexpectedly, a large breaker scoops me up, and I ride it on up to the beach, my thighs rubbing against the rushing sand granules. I am thrust ashore laughing—alone and laughing—lying spread-eagled, staring up at the vast sky, feeling delightfully foolish. Boy, have I ever allowed too many days to go dull and permitted too many parts of me to go unused. Perhaps in my next life I'll return as a seal and be forced to use all of me. Unless, of course, it's not too late for this life!

Just now I wish for a seal's extra coat of flesh. It's chilly, and I run up the beach for a towel and sweater, then huddle into a small hole of hollowed-out sand, wanting to stay with the seals and watch their antics. They are taking me by the hand and leading me back to my childhood, altering my sense of time, speaking to me with their bodies. One dives and reemerges with a large fish, which he devours while two others frolic aimlessly. They are masters at play, gazing back at me before taking each of their delicate, arching dives, as if to say, "This is what it's all about."

A concert of sounds engulfs me now—gulls honking, seals sniffling, waves spilling themselves farther and farther up onto the shore. It's a full-moon tide and should be higher than normal; maybe it will flood this entire spit of land. Will I be marooned, I wonder? I steady my nerves, knowing the moment of high tide is just that, a brief time that will always reverse itself and diminish. And so it is with me as I stand between my former life and the next stage. I rush to higher ground, trying to stay in the moment.

I envy how the seals handle their fat, furry bodies, instruments that truly work for them. Why am I not at home in my body? Probably because I am a large woman, and society only applauds the slight ones. What a waste to feel only shame and disgust for something that should be celebrated.

The loathing of my body started long ago, when I began turning chubby at nine or ten. My mother hid the snacks and tasty food and rationed my portions. I came to realize that my shape embarrassed her as we shopped for a winter coat and she refused to buy me the flashy aqua one I liked. "Not with *your* body," she said. "The camel-hair, double-breasted coat would suit you better."

In early adolescence I thinned out and was thrilled with my new circle skirt and pink sweater, which I tucked in to show off my waist. "What do you think?" I asked my father, pirouetting about the living room. "It's nice," he said, somewhat embarrassed, "except for that business on top."

My bulging breasts were the "business on top." Finally something acceptable was expanding, but in that moment I wished they, too, would shrink. My body image only worsened as I grew. Mothers in the fifties were determined to create finished products by the time their daughters were of marriageable age. Cut off from my body, I learned to play sophisticated games of flirtation, feigning submission in order to be more attractive.

My best friend told me that on her wedding day she felt like a piece of USDA Certified beef being led to slaughter. She had been inspected by doctors and dentists, then handed over to her groom like a prize animal.

Women's opinions of their bodies haven't changed that much. Emaciation is rampant. Starving is in! You can never be too rich or too thin. Not only do mothers push their daughters to be thin and beautiful, but they continue to push themselves, far into old age. No one seems as real or free as the seals in front of me. What a pity.

What attracts me to these adorable creatures most is their vulnerability and lack of constraint. Domestication seems to force women into such an unnatural state. Yet I eagerly and willingly played house throughout the sixties and seventies; the role of wife and mother was a virtuous endeavor. I baked bread, created healthy meals, orchestrated memorable parties; I was the perfect nurturer. I even slammed down the phone when I heard my husband's car pull into the driveway so I could greet him appropriately, matching his mood if it was good, perking him up if he was down.

Nobody asked me to behave in this fashion. It was more or less expected that a woman would create relationship first and herself second. It's beginning to occur to me that we got it all backward—that we need to attend to ourselves first. If I worried that my flight to the Cape was somehow narcissistic, I should abandon any such thoughts from here on out. Of primary importance now is for me to retrieve the buried parts of me—qualities like playfulness, vulnerability, being at home in my skin, using more of my instincts. Like so many pieces of a puzzle, I need to find a way to create the whole once again.

The tide rushes up like some unannounced visitor and washes over my feet, threatening to swallow me. I back away, rescuing my beach bag, and retreat to the sliver of dune, allowing every last sensation to sink into me.

I walk with clearer intent now, back to the place on the island where this adventure commenced, the great blue blur of ocean wavering behind. I'm recognizing happiness as it arrives.

Josh had promised to return at high tide, and sure enough, as the day wanes and the setting sun paints the sky orange, pink, and purple, his little boat rounds the point. I run to slip into my jeans, and wave him down. Wading out, I haul my body headfirst into the hull, now loaded with burlap bags bulging with freshly dug clams. Josh has harvested much, and so have I.

As we push off, the seals raise their heads to mark our departure. A few slide off the embankment and swim toward us, playing in the wake of our boat. But as we near town, they stop. Their soulful eyes meet mine one last time; they dive and swim away.

"So," Josh asks, "did you get what you wanted?"

I don't know what to say. How can I explain to this

practical man that I have spent the day swimming with seals? He may think I have lost my mind, as would half the other people in my life. I go for the easy answer. "What an incredible place," I say. "To think I've been summering here all these years and have never been out there."

He smiles and nods, as I shrink back into silence. A wave of melancholy sweeps over me, because I know such a day cannot be duplicated. So many compressed desires have been unleashed. I only hope I can nourish the resulting passion. I have found guidance through life's passages in books and lectures, but never before from a colony of animals.

In a very brief time, too brief, Josh is cutting the engines, and we are drifting into his slip. I gather my belongings and climb onto the dock as he unloads his clams and gives me a basketful of steamers and cherrystones. "You've worked up an appetite—enjoy 'em," he says.

"My favorite," I say. "You've given me so much today. Are you sure?"

"My pleasure."

I walk away, imagining a raw bar of cherrystones, salivating, and realize suddenly that I don't know how to open them; that's always been my husband's job. No time like the present.

It's a shock to be behind the wheel of a car, driving through a town, being part of its collective busyness. I am grateful to be heading home to my quiet place, tucked as it is in a scrub-pine forest a short way inland, at the end of a narrow, sandy path.

The cottage is cozy, womblike: beamed ceilings, seasoned wood that smells of salt air, kerosene lanterns I use more than electric lights. It is especially inviting after a day outdoors. I toss my wet clothes into the tub, put on some sweats, and take a bottle of wine from the refrigerator. I stop to gaze at a family picture, focusing on the fifty-year-old woman. I barely recognize her tight jaw, forced smile, eyelids drooping, hair streaked, more gray than blond.

They say you get the face you've earned by the time you're forty—all those sorrowful, angry expressions, long hidden behind makeup, become the naked truth. It mirrors who you are, who you've been, a kaleidoscope of endless patterns. Oh, well, for today at least I'm beginning to loosen up and like who I could be.

I uncork the wine and pour a glass. Settling into the window seat, I prepare to stare at a moonlit night. Today's adventure taught me how simple it is to be involved and uplifted by nothing more complicated than the unexpected. Me, the programmed woman with the low tolerance for boredom! I raise my glass to the future, just as the phone rings. Few have my number here. I consider letting it ring, but my curiosity gets the best of me. I dash for the receiver.

"Hi, it's me," my husband says. His hollow voice flattens my upbeat mood.

"Hi," I say tentatively. I've learned from several previous calls to listen hard and talk later. As the reality of our separation sinks in, he has become less friendly, more businesslike. The tenor of his voice tonight makes me uncomfortable.

"How are you doing?" he asks, a benign yet loaded question. If I say fine, and he is not fine, there will be hell to pay. I'm finding that unhappy people despise hearing good news from the contented ones. I stifle my impulse to tell him about my day, choosing to offer as little information as possible, waiting to hear the real agenda.

"The house sold," he announces matter-of-factly.

"Wow," I respond, realizing that as a couple we are now down to two homes—his and mine—with no old homestead to return to.

"We'll have some extra money," he continues. "I can rent a really nice place out here, and you can move in."

I pretend not to hear. He doesn't understand that I'm not interested in moving, period. Still, the wife in me feels obliged to offer something. "Perhaps I can visit some weekend," I reply, remaining as noncommittal as possible.

"Well, whatever," he says, backing off. Having made no specific arrangements when we parted, he probably thought after a couple of weeks I'd come to my senses and join him. The trouble is, I'm getting used to my solitude and, after a day like today, not only liking it but also seeing the worth of it.

It's not what he says that unnerves me but what he doesn't say. I have a habit of filling in blank spaces and make the grievous error of mentioning the seals.

"Seals," he says testily. "Where are they?"

"Monomoy."

"Who took you out there?"

"A fisherman friend."

"How did you meet *him?*"

No matter how I try to rescue the conversation, our moods begin to plunge. Now I'm feeling guilty and begin justifying my day, explaining more than I should. I feel strangely in his debt.

He allows that he would give anything to be wild and

free, "but one of us has to be practical, after all," he says. I stifle the urge to banter further, my spirit broken. The reality of my amazing day has dissolved, the comfort of my seclusion has been disturbed. How often have I allowed someone to spoil a perfectly good mood? I struggle to breathe as I hang up. Then, in a flash, I know why I'm here. I return to the pillow on the window seat and talk to the moon.

RIPTIDE

November

*Woman must come of age by herself. She must find
her true center alone.*

—*Anne Morrow Lindbergh*, GIFT FROM THE SEA

I've *taken* to chasing the light, which means rising when it is still dark and driving to the fish pier to view the fiery dawn. I'm always amazed to find others there, people who care to pay homage as one planet bows to the other, to see first a narrow pink stripe dividing water and sky, followed by a broad splash of pungent orange. As the sun now casts a glow on the faces nearby, I take a sip of coffee from my Thermos and inhale the crisp morning air.

It is one of those Cape Cod mornings when no sooner does the sun appear, bold and undaunted, than the clouds roll in. What was at first clear blue sky is suddenly dappled with fluffy pink clouds, which gradually become lavender and then a sullen gray, until the original picture dulls, as if someone has pulled a shade down to shut out the light. The Technicolor of dawn has lasted all of eight minutes, and now the sky is black and white. Fishermen are able to adjust to such mixed signals, checking the weather's subtle signs while preparing to launch their boats. Although the sky has changed, the sea remains calm, at least here in the harbor. It's different at the outer bar, where protected water meets open sea. Still, venturing out each day is a necessity for these men. They make their solitary decisions, sensing what's best for themselves and those they leave behind. Overcast skies don't call for them to scrap their day—they just proceed with more caution, taking nothing for granted. So it should be with each of us as we begin a new day.

I'm reminded of a hot August afternoon a few years back, when my husband and I took a picnic to the outer bar. The surf was inviting and the sun brutal, so we kept dipping in and out of the refreshing water. On the last dip we became more aggressive, swimming farther away from shore, unaware at first that a riptide was pulling us apart. No matter how hard we tried to swim together, we seemed stuck in independent courses. As wave after gigantic wave began crashing down, it became clear that getting back to safety would be an entirely individual issue. We each would have to swim for it or drown.

The same seems remarkably true of our lives now. Having drifted off course, we have no choice but to find our way back, with or without each other. There are no lifeguards, no inner tubes to save us—inner strength and *will* our only lifelines. I watch now as the fishermen maneuver their boats slowly, carefully, in and around buoys as if on some slalom course. It is a craft, an art form, just to get out of the harbor, but the distant roar of the sea beckons, and they seem driven to follow. Some go it alone, but most venture out with a crew, each possessing a well-developed skill that will serve him best when all the men pool resources and work in tandem. Such is the way to land a sizable catch. Such is also the way to lead a successful life.

If only my husband and I had learned to work more in concert! I sensed a need for a deeper sharing from the beginning. Perhaps our Peace Corps life in Africa worked well because we had to depend on one another for virtually everything. Certainly our son and his wife, on their biking tours, are establishing a bond stronger than most of their peers possess. Yet many of us entered marriage as only half a person, expecting to be completed by the other. We held dear to the fantasy that the man waiting at the end of the aisle had all the answers.

Once, when my husband and I had a disagreement, he blurted out, "We're not making it, sweetie." The truth of those words terrified me, and I quickly denied them, redoubling my efforts to make right whatever was wrong. Those were the days when the children were young and the stakes were high—becoming a single mother was unthinkable. Underneath I harbored doubts. Underneath was where I had been trained to keep them. I was obsessed with relationship and held high my illusion of what marriage should be. Perhaps now I grieve the death not of my marriage but simply the illusion of marriage.

It has grown cold and drizzly. Most of the boats have cleared the harbor. I wish I were out there with them, with some goal for the day. Being alone doesn't come easily to someone who has always liked inclusion. Stepping outside marriage is as difficult as not coming to the rescue of a needy child. It has taken more than a month to understand what I've done—what I still need to do.

But every time I replay the phone call of the other night I feel relieved, even privileged, to be apart from those who have for so long looked to me to make everything work, to be without duty or schedule. Instead I stand here and dream and wonder and watch as the sea empties and fills itself up again.

Just now I'm among a collage of people all of whom seem to be in varying degrees of seeking. I wonder about my fellow dawn-worshippers, imagining their lives to be more interesting than mine. Whatever my life lacks, I fantasize these strangers already have—wild sex, cozy evenings beside a hearth, perfect jobs, capable children. However, while such visions initially entertain me, they soon depress me, until I remind myself of all the clandestine chats I've had with friends who tattle on their truth and tell their secrets— women who've been made to have too much sex, or who never have sex, or who have put on naughty black nighties and played "dirty" to enliven a man, or participated in a ménage à trois, or are victims of passive aggression, or must endure someone who cheats, or someone who is simply dull.

Still, it's hard now to watch the passion of two young lovers leaning against a nearby pickup truck, enveloped in a blanket and each other, or the hard-bodied jogger running to stay fit for what I imagine must be some equally gorgeous partner, or a couple ensconced in a Mercedes, not talking, just being together at peace.

I'm overcome with envy and momentarily wish to be held, until I'm distracted by a middle-aged couple. He's staring straight ahead, stone-faced, hands stuffed into his parka pockets, alone with his thoughts. His wife has wandered off, hiding her face under a hood, equally alone, estranged. I remember an evening with my husband, years ago. We had escaped to a romantic inn in hopes of refueling our sagging spirits. There we sat, in a picture-perfect setting, sharing a bottle of Pinot Noir. My husband turned the spotlight on me. Flattered to be asked about my reading and research at

47

that time, which involved sensuality and sexuality, I waxed poetic about the meaning of eroticism. There was a method to my madness. I hoped he might catch on and we would proceed in kind. But what ensued was a debate. I heard a man hungry for sex and fed up with a woman who lived too much in her head. I became quiet, and he became stony. A curtain came down between us.

For now I must take solace in watching the solitary walkers as they pass, mostly middle-aged women like me. Their faces display a determined power and seem free of encumbrances, no longer stranded in others' lives. Their strides suggest confidence and self-respect; they are relieved, perhaps, to be away from the turmoil of relationship. I suffer less pain alone, it seems, than in the presence of an indifferent partner.

Still, there's a price to pay for such self-indulgence. I stand here holding freedom in one hand and guilt in the other—guilt not only for failing my husband, somehow, but for having hidden thoughts that do not include him. I felt compelled to make sure we were roughly similar and worked hard to bridge every gap. Our differences frightened me. Surely they were signs on my part of some vague infidelity. Even now leaving him seems to have been a grievous sin—a silly attempt at belated adolescence. The critic in my personality continues to blame me for stepping outside the norm. Why should I be allowed to indulge myself in such wild abandon when he cannot do the same?

Poor fellow! He comes from that generation of men who counted on wives to be wives, who needed a wife not only to take care of things but for the sake of respectability. It doesn't look good for us to be living apart. My sense is that only if we get back together and restore our life will he stop being angry.

And so I wonder how long I can extend this separation and hold the guilt at bay while I repair and revive. I remember the words of a friend who insisted, at a dinner party no less, that anyone who claims to be in love all the time is a liar. "I have been blissfully happy for five or six years," she announced, "felt tolerable in the relationship for ten, was semi-miserable for four, and mildly contented the rest of the time." I marveled at her honesty, considering that her husband sat beside her. But I, too, have come to appreciate that I can't fake what I don't feel, and that too much vitality is used up trying.

Doesn't change occur only when we stop living the expected life? For sure, marriage, like any other institution, cannot contain and should not restrain anyone. Hell, every marriage needs community relief. How could one partner, no matter how remarkable, be everything to the other? It's ludicrous to believe so. I've no choice now but to fall in love as soon as possible—not with a man but with my immediate life and eventually myself. I'm free to make my own decisions and equally free to take the consequences. For once to be harsh, indifferent, unfeeling is liberating. At the very least, being so permits me to cultivate the other half of my whole. So I've declared my freedom and am somewhat at peace with it. What's left is to make sure there's no residual guilt.

It is eight in the morning, and the day is in full swing.

Action surrounds me. I am awake to my immediate reality: I need a job, not only to augment my savings but to save my sanity. Asking my husband to meet even my slightest financial need seems preposterous. I want to pay for my own lipstick, underwear, and entertainment; I don't want to feel beholden. Before me in the window of Nickerson's Fish Market is a HELP WANTED sign. I head for the door and walk in without a moment's hesitation. The owner is busy cutting fish on a marble slab. He peers up at me over his half-frames, as the doorbell jingles.

"May I help you?" he inquires, expecting me to buy fish, I suppose, not ask for a job. Strong men in yellow rubber aprons are in the backroom hauling giant boxes of fish packed in ice; there is not a woman in sight. What kind of a job could there be for the likes of me, I wonder?

"I need . . . I mean, wish to apply for the job advertised in the window," I blurt out.

"You want to work here?" he asks, chuckling at such an idea. I'm middle-aged and not even officially local. The fish pier is staffed almost entirely with locals. "Why would you want to work here?" he asks.

"I love the waterfront," I say, and then add without thinking, "I'm a writer always in search of a story." The words again areout of my mouth before they are formed.

He puts his knife down, wipes his hands on a rag, and comes closer, peering at me behind his glasses. "It's tough work, y'know—hauling and weighing fish, climbing up to the lobster tanks, dealing with the customers."

"I'm up to it," I lie. "Besides, don't you close at Christmas for the winter? If I don't work out, you can get rid of me then, without any hard feelings."

"I suppose you're right," he says. "How bout reporting for work in the morning?"

And so I become part of the job force. I have found a lifeline, for now.

WATER THERAPY

Late November

We cannot write in water . . . we cannot carve in water. Water's
nature is to flow and that is how we should
treat life . . . emotion, negative or positive. Do not deny it
but always let it flow through and then away.

—*Anonymous*

Driving to work under cement skies makes my arrival there all the more heartwarming. The fish market itself is ablaze in light, everything inside painted a white enamel that shimmers on even the darkest days. The trip is brief and uneventful, along winding country roads until I reach the sea and weave along the shoreline for a few more miles. Today it is bitter cold, with a wind from the northeast stirring up ruffles of whitecaps that decorate the surface of the water as far as I can see. The ocean is charged with energy, which in turn charges me. As I enter the market, the side door is seized by the wind and slams shut behind me. The backroom is bustling as the floor is littered with freshly caught cod, sole, and halibut, waiting to be filleted. I tiptoe over the fish bodies, their fixed eyes staring up at me, hang my coat on a hook, and report to the front, where several customers are waiting.

"May I help you?" I ask two men who seem mesmerized by something in the lobster pool.

"We're wondering if you have a dead lobster in there," one of them replies. I peer down. A two-pounder is huddled in a corner, isolated, totally still. On closer observation, I detect a subtle undulation—its shell appears to be hovering slightly above the body.

"It's molting," the owner says nonchalantly, "shedding one skin to grow more flesh and become larger."

"Amazing," I whisper, still staring. It occurs to me that you don't often get to witness growth and change. I respect the instincts of a molting lobster, hiding out while it is raw and vulnerable until it becomes tough and resilient once again.

Working in and around water, with its gushing, splashing, and slurping sounds, transforms an otherwise mundane job into a sensuous experience. It's like water play. Being here day after day is beginning to relieve my spiritual drought, the routine of work staving off depression, reinvigorating me.

I'm into my third week, and there is still the sense of novelty. The very mention of where I work raises eyebrows. I'm amused by people's reactions. "You're doing what?" a neighbor asks. She thinks the fish business is men's work. I get a kick out of proving myself—hauling and weighing buckets of lobster, shucking scallops and clams for chowder base—all the while knowing that the men in the backroom, no less than my neighbor, are looking me up and down and wondering where the hell I've come from.

What no one knows, and I had forgotten, is that I've been drawn to this place for years. This ramshackle shed, which sits on the water's edge and hasn't changed for as long as I can remember, is a comfort to me. In past years I'd watch fishwives shuck scallops on the dock while others baited hooks and mended nets nearby, but I could never have guessed that I would one day be doing similar things. Being the opposite of what I was before is opening up new vistas.

Even so, there are drawbacks. The dress code, for one—jeans or khaki pants, with a tucked-in navy-blue top. Never having had a decent waist, I usually hide my figure in oversized baggy sweaters. I hold on to my vanity, however, by donning the yellow plastic bib apron worn mostly by the men. Then there's the temperamental cash register that beeps and buzzes whenever I hit the wrong key, which happens to be several times a day. The noise heralds the owner's wife, who sighs at my stupidity as she voids my error, while the impatient customers watch and wait. I then begin these transactions all over again, feeling as embarrassed and stupid as I did back in college, when I'd take on part-time jobs that were over my head and end up failing or getting fired.

When, if ever, will I get it? Still, I remain the good sport, trying to cover up my insecurity by being more eager and enthusiastic, even though my flushed cheeks and perspiring face suggest shame and distress.

I try not to take myself or the work too seriously, but I do have utility and other bills to pay. I'm addicted to perfection and need to please, but more often feel as though I disappoint. Too proud and needy to quit, I make up for my inadequacies by arriving early and leaving late, not taking pay for the extra hour or so I work. Why is it I always feel that when someone hires me, they are doing me a service instead of the other way around? How quickly I'm reduced to feeling like a child, craving praise and appreciation, needing reassurance about my performance. My father used to tell me I was supersensitive. Well, who likes to be found wrong all the time? Who enjoys criticism?

I've always wanted to be like my brilliant older brother, who stood by the phone one April day in his senior year of high school taking call after call from Ivy League colleges offering him assorted scholarships and awards. When my turn came, a guidance counselor told my concerned mother where nonachievers such as myself were being accepted. I was sent off to a junior college—a finishing school, as they were called back then—intended for attractive, dumb blondes to be groomed and polished and sent out, not to a bigger world but to the confines of marriage. The trouble was, the school fell short of finishing me. Instead, it left gaps in my heart and soul that I am now trying to fill.

My ego is what is really being tamed in this job. It's taking some getting used to being a servant, not a master. The Yankee natives give me orders without looking me in the eye, or they insist on being served by the proprietor, who they are certain will give them special favors. At first I was insulted by these people of means. I'm of value, too! Like them, I've traveled the world, been educated, even written a couple of books. But who cares what they think? What I'm trying to do here is not about impressions. Instead, I mind my own business, speak when I'm spoken to, cut their fish, and pretend to like serving them.

My only pretense involves the owner's wife, who thinks I'm a happily married quasi-bohemian, hanging around the waterfront in order to write a book. If she only knew. But I'm not going to confess my ambiguous marital state to her, especially since she and her husband seem a close-knit team, equally dependent, one with the other. Besides, I'm fast becoming aware that married women don't much trust unmarried ones. She and I banter back and forth, mostly about husbands and children, when she's not listening to customers' tales of woe. The market is a veritable town hall. People don't come in here just to buy fish; they seek affirmation and come to pass news. We always know who is getting married and who is getting buried.

Seeing the same faces day after day, I can just about guess the truth of their lives. There are the widows on fixed incomes who come for just a few ounces of cod, and the working-class wives, young mothers, who want to buy swordfish but can afford only catfish. There are those that ask for fish heads and lobster bodies, claiming they want them for bait; I figure they're making chowder they will need to stretch for two meals. There are the wealthy ones, "kept women" I call them, who live in rambling oceanfront homes with wicker furniture on the porch, flowers delivered weekly, expensive casual clothes from Neiman Marcus, who bask in soaking tubs and use bidets and order whole fillets of salmon, instructing me as they breeze out the door, "Put it on the tab."

I've never had the privilege of being "kept," if, in fact, it is a privilege. I look at the scrupulously scrubbed faces of these mannequinlike women and wonder, Does having it all make you happier or sadder? Does it make you free?

My back is aching, but several lobster tanks need to be scrubbed. I think I'm more than a tad bit jealous of them. Still, there are ground rules I'm certain they must live by, rules set up by their husbands and society that they must obey. Earning one's own keep has a great deal of merit.

I remind myself each time I want to quit that this job is about my independence as well as learning to rise above criticism, honor my ignorance, and deal with my occasional arrogance. And, having surrendered to a simpler life, I am finding excitement in little things that others might think dull.

Tonight it's about hanging out. I wasn't looking forward to an entire evening alone. One of the guys in the back stops me at the door. "Want a beer?" he asks as he does every night.

"You know I don't drink beer," I answer. "Now, if you were offering wine . . ."

"As a matter of fact I am," he says, lifting the lid on the ice chest and producing a bottle of Gallo Chablis. Not my brand, but the invitation to stay awhile seems delicious. Besides, I'm a sucker for anyone who presupposes a wish or need. Hungry for connection, I dare to dally, throwing my coat aside and sitting down on the nearest overturned bucket. There's no need to hold myself aloof anymore. These guys are all the community I have right now.

The unpretentious wine is as refreshing as the conversation, sprinkled with off-color remarks and jokes. I'm laughing, something I haven't done for weeks. Laughter requires company, unless, of course you're laughing at yourself! It feels good to linger—not to be running home or racing off to an obligation. Of course, I have none of those here, not as in my former life, which was driven by the calendar. I'm relishing these weathered men of thirty who look forty, who make time for one another and value their camaraderie.

I gulp one glass, then another. They wonder about my family, my life alone, but hesitate to ask too much. Fishermen are loners. They keep to themselves and accord the same privilege to others. I sense they like me, even respect how well

I work. I love being the voyeur, seeing behind the scenes, knowing more about unknown lives. Sitting here with these young men makes me miss my boys. I wonder what they're up to, wish we could hang out together like this. These guys have no idea how much their letting me in delights me. I feel a part of something. For now, I'm one of them.

WAVES OF TRUTH

Late December

To arrive where you are, to get there from where you are not, You must go by a way wherein there is no ecstasy.

—*T.S. Eliot, "East Coker"* FOUR QUARTETS

The $chill$ of the house awakens me each morning, and I hustle to put another log on the wood-burning stove before the red-hot coals turn to ash, after which I place a kettle of water on top of the same stove and sit huddled nearby to wait for its whistle.

Such is my morning ritual, nothing terribly complicated unless I've forgotten to bring logs in from the woodpile the night before. I'm deep into my time-out season of life, where it seems best to be actively passive, involved in little, aware of much. Instinct told me to take myself away and look at all the unwrapped gifts nature has to offer. The natural world is hibernating, and so am I.

In former years, winter days and nights meant hunkering down, gathering in, the fireplace crackling, chili bubbling on the stove, and the boys sweaty and energized from basketball games, filling the house with the magic of their youth. Now I'm down to dinner for one, conversations with myself, hauling and chopping wood, and continuing on my private pilgrimage as I grapple with darkness, in hopes of seeing the light. This remote peninsula, extending into the sea, makes it easier for the pilgrim to stay true to her quest even at this most festive time of year, because here the spirit of the season is contained somehow.

I've always loved the intention of Christmas, but lately

I've been overwhelmed by its excessiveness. When I see the exhausted expressions on women's faces as they run around trying to please, I realize that modern-day Christmas seems to happen at the expense of women. We have taken on the job of infusing our homes with joy, whether the family wants it or not. In past years I was so consumed by this imperative that I staged a holiday party for twenty or so families, complete with crafts, carols, and buffet dinner, importing people and their accompanying merriment to ensure that we would be full of joy.

And even if I had been a woman who entertained effortlessly (which I'm not), I was always the last to catch the spirit, so caught up was I in creating it for everyone else. My old book club always ended up canceling the December meeting. "We've no time," the women would say, "no time to meet, much less read." What a pity, I thought. Surely the producers of Christmas needed time off more than anyone. A few of us did manage an evening last year. We sipped sherry and shared Christmas memories. It turned out to be the most magical night of the season.

I'm glad I have that simple memory to recall just now, as I'm shunning anything seasonal, instead gliding solo like a skater from one part of the pond to the other, a stark contrast from the usual holiday clutter.

This is definitely not the year for engraved cards or Christmas letters. I've received few and am sending none, letting the answering machine hold both wishes and questions at bay. Since I'm still unclear as to my future, I've come to hate inquiries that make me produce logical answers. In place of talk, I record ideas in my journal, then cling to the thought, "To live is to change, and to strive toward a more perfect life is to have changed often." But really, do I have to go to such extremes?

I decide to leave for work early today in order to stop at a tiny chapel I've been frequenting. It is nestled in a hollow of pine trees at the end of town, and once inside, I take to my knees in the darkened sanctuary, asking whomever will listen to forgive me for such things as leaving my husband, wanting more than I deserve, and choosing a course of action that continues to seem narcissistic.

Churches have a humbling effect on me—sometimes they even stabilize me. I wouldn't think of trying to sell a story or a book without first stepping into a church on the way to a meeting with editors. Today I seem to want to just sit and absorb any message the spirits care to bestow upon me. I become haunted by the empty crèche that sits on the altar waiting to be filled with the Holy Family and their visitors. By leaving my home and husband, have I emptied our personal crèche for good? I hope not, but the trouble with Christmas is that it brings such reminders and triggers such questions.

I take my leave, feeling troubled instead of calm, and hope that the drive through town will brighten me up. There are wreaths adorning gray shingles, electric candles lighting up windowsills, and a hardware store bursting with shiny red wagons and Flexible Flyer sleds. Fortunately this quiet enclave lacks most of the glitz and glitter that never fail to depress me. I'm able to avoid the psychic bombardment. Still, I can't shield myself from seasonal nostalgia each time a customer at the fish market places a large order. You can tell by how many pounds of lobster and oysters they order, just how many people they're entertaining and when the family will arrive. A melancholia overtakes me as I realize that my boys won't be home. I was such a good sport when they told me about their Christmas plans that did not include us, but secretly I felt abandoned. Not wanting to appear pushy, I accepted their decisions and hoped they would be home next year. I knew that after they were married we'd have to share their time, but knowing it and experiencing it are different things. We haven't enjoyed this holiday as a family for three years. The rituals just seemed to stop, like all the other natural endings—such as the last time one of the boys crawled into bed with us, or I carried them on my hip, or saw them naked, even. Such moments evaporate so quietly that you don't realize it's the last time until long afterward. I envy divorced people who are forced to divvy up time with the kids and are made to stick with it.

Just now the fish-market radio is playing "I'll Be Home for Christmas," and I am overcome enough to duck into the bathroom and have a good cry. My husband will be coming, which makes me all the more teary. Are we up for a reunion just yet? I don't know, but the alternative of each of us being alone seemed unthinkable. Tears come easily when I'm needy. I dab my eyes, gulp my grief, and head back toward the customers, where I spot a white-bearded man wearing a hand-knitted stocking cap. He's peering at me through metal-frame glasses. "You must be Santa Claus!" I say, forcing a cheery greeting.

"Been called that," he answers.

"I bet you've played him, too," I say.

"Just yesterday," he says with a twinkle.

"Well, I've been naughty *and* nice," I continue, enjoying the charade. "Know what I want for Christmas?"

"You have everything you want," he says, not missing a beat, and with that, exits the store.

What was that all about? I wonder, momentarily dumbfounded. What does he know about me? How could he possibly claim that I have everything I want? I am agitated, testy even, and I don't know why. It must look to people that I have everything—good health, creative career, time away, solid kids, a loyal husband. What else is there?

Plenty, I think as I sling a tray of filleted cod into the ice case. I want to be happy, that's for starters, to feel again and not just be numb, to laugh more and have someone to cry with. The nerve of that Santa character, laying such a trip on me. I suddenly have this gagging sensation that says I have everything I was *told I should want*, but that's a far cry from what I really desire! It's hard for most of the women I know to state what they want, because they've gotten used to wanting only what's available.

At least I'm beginning to see what *I no longer want:* things like making life pleasant for others while forgoing my own desires, writing the script for the last act of our marriage without my husband's participation. I don't want to have to deal with my partner's bad moods, his stony silences, wondering if they have anything to do with me while my own spontaneity is squashed.

Still, I hate myself for never being satisfied. I should be more grateful and accept the status quo, but obviously I wouldn't be here if I could. Perhaps the encounter with Santa was fortuitous. It's high time I ask myself the tough questions before my husband arrives with questions of his own.

A blizzard is brewing, and the market is closing early. "You'd best be on your way," the owner warns, knowing I don't have four-wheel drive. "Don't forget our Christmas party, Friday night," he adds. "It will be a last hurrah before we batten down the hatches 'til Memorial Day." A party! The last thing I want to do is make an appearance alone, socializing with people I barely know. What will I wear? I've left all my good clothes in storage. I'll check the minute I get home, I say to myself, making a quick exit into the blustery wind, pulling my jacket collar up as high as it will go and huddling in its warmth.

As the lights of the village drop behind me, I am momentarily lost, like the astronauts during the blackout period when they're returning to the earth's atmosphere. The snow is blowing across the empty road. I shift into second gear and creep. The noise of ice chunks scraping against my windshield wipers creates a sort of eerie music. I can barely see in front of me, yet I can see everything. I am inside a glass ball, those Christmas toys that children shake. Being in the storm is scary but invigorating. I just manage to find my own driveway through the whirling snow, and savor the relief when I'm finally home.

Once inside, I slam the door, bolt it as if to shut out the world. A cup of cocoa and a newly stoked fire will be my tonic for the moment. I will sit with my journal and just be, yet even in the silence my mind chatters on. I ponder that most-asked question of the season: What do you want? We usually answer with some material object. Imagine if we said something like a better state of mind, or togetherness, or simply to be surrounded by laughter. Last year my son asked for my Christmas list over the phone. I promptly responded by saying, "A tape of you singing holiday music." He laughed at my request, but it was my real desire, to hear his voice as smooth as maple syrup, the sound more soothing for me than an aria by the Three Tenors.

C. S. Lewis spoke of something he called "felt satisfaction," which he interpreted as "a quality of fullness ... an immediacy worth perpetuating." I try to imagine what that might be. Sitting here alone is satisfying enough, but the night would be far better if shared with another—with someone whose mood meets mine, who relishes moments, whose wonder remains untainted, who appreciates simple things and says so, who laughs much, indulges heartily, is spontaneous in spirit, is quick to embrace, and sees joy as a duty!

Oh, dear, now I've gone too far. Who could ever be that way? Still, just a few of these qualities would be enough. Isn't this what's missing in my marriage? I am astonished that my wants are attainable. What's more, they don't take money or power, just a little attitude change. So why isn't this within my grasp?

Aha, because grasping isn't the way—reaching perhaps, but not being overt about it. That's how I've failed in the past, wanting others to be a certain way and trying to push and cajole them in that direction. Good things seem just to happen along. The state of feeling satisfied occurs most often when I haven't sought it. If only I can break with fixed notions, I might see new possibilities in relationship.

I'm beginning to grasp some idea of what I want. For starters, I want to take no action, "pursue that which is not meddlesome," says the Chinese philosopher Lao Tzu. Having taken myself away, I am in a frame of mind to wait and see rather than manipulate and direct. Living with nature has taught me the dignity of being without motive. Occupying this tiny cottage with no clutter, only barren essentials, has served to help me find more in less.

Speaking of less, I need to find some decent party clothes. My all-but-empty closet looks bleak. There's a green velour pantsuit, several pairs of khakis and blue jeans, a tweed blazer, plaid culottes, and, hidden under a plastic bag fresh from the cleaners, my black crepe pantsuit, which I've all but forgotten I owned. Perfect, I think, stripping down to my underwear and stepping into the pants, only to find them impossible to button. Damn! I wasn't aware I had gained weight, but living under layers and eating whatever I pleased has obviously added some unwanted fat. Panicked now that nothing will fit, I begin grabbing at tops and bottoms, mixing and matching in an effort to put something together, experiencing several hot flashes in the process. Up till now it hasn't mattered how I dressed, and I don't like suddenly worrying about it. Mercifully, the velour pants with the elastic waist work well with a black cowl-neck sweater. A little jewelry and I'll be presentable. Phew! Now back to the quiet business of the season.

My grandmother used to say, "As the hands toil, so the spirit is raised above the troubled motions of the mind." There's stollen to make, mince pies, Newburg sauce, and butter cookies. What would December be without the smell of cinnamon, nutmeg, and cloves? I reach for a saucepan, pour in some aging cider, add the nostalgic spices, and let it bubble away on the stove to create the aroma I've been craving.

Next I put Pavarotti's Christmas CD on the stereo, open a bottle of wine, and choose happiness over righteousness for now. Being right almost always ends in splendid isolation anyway. 'Tis the season to put the past away—I'm feeling a bit like the recovered Scrooge—new and happy and grateful for a few waves of truth.

SILENT SEAS, SILENT NIGHTS

Christmas

For a few days, once a year, the atrophied souls of grown-ups are filled again with that spirit which inspires the wisdom of fools and children.

—*Michael Harrison*, THE STORY OF CHRISTMAS

It is the day before the day before Christmas. He'll be here in a few hours. I've nailed a homemade wreath onto a tree at the end of the lane and will light the kerosene lanterns and candles before he arrives. I am nervous, afraid that I will revert back to the wife role just when I'm getting used to being happily single. I've prepared all our traditional food in an absolute orgy of domestication, to please our palates as well as to soothe our souls. Soul food for Christmas—I like the sound of it. Figuring we get to experience only seventy or eighty Christmases in a lifetime, I am determined to enjoy this one my way, no matter who is or isn't around. I read somewhere that the Frenchwoman's role is to please others, but to please herself in the process! This concept is new for me, that my own joy is my responsibility. Only I can receive it, and, likewise, only I can allow others to take it away. Not this Christmas! I've had my fill of bleak midwinters and now set my sights on joy.

I hear his car, see the headlights through windowpanes etched in frost. I throw on my coat, toss a scarf around my neck, and head out to greet him. For three months I've been testing aloneness. Now I face awkward togetherness. This is real life moving right along and high adventure as well—Christmas and the two of us, alone!

There is a tentative embrace that unnerves me, and so I

grab his suitcase and hurry back inside, reminding myself that he has had a long drive and hasn't spent these last few months pondering as I have—or has he? How has his bachelor life taken shape? He's been a loner most of his life. I wonder if he is enjoying his solitude all the more. I will refrain from asking questions just now and let the evening develop its own rhythm.

It has been his habit to inspect every inch of the cottage each time he arrives, and tonight is no exception. I fix him a scotch, which he carries with him from room to room. Once he learns that all is well in his lair, he settles into a rocking chair and places his long legs on a stool in front. I sit on the couch, legs curled under me. He sighs, sips his drink, and seems mildly content. I'm frankly petrified, empty of agenda, so I wait to see what transpires. It will take some time, I fear, to locate the tender and live spots in each other. He has grayed considerably since the fall, and his face looks weathered and drawn. I wonder how I appear to him? Do I look rested and bright-eyed or tense, like the day we parted? Stingy as he is with both compliments and criticisms, I'll probably never find out.

His drink disappears too fast, and I offer to refill it. "Please," he says, as I walk briskly for the ice, leaving the weight of silence behind. Silence is a good friend, I repeat, as if saying a mantra. It allows for the natural progression of things. Still, I remain nervous, anxious to fill the void as I used to with the interesting questions, chitchat, sweet nothings that nice girls like me were taught to utter. I sure did have that nice-girl persona down pat. Now, what takes the place of nice, I wonder?

"How are you?" I ask. "I mean really."

"Things are okay," he says blandly. "I've joined a health club, playing some indoor tennis, trying to reduce this." He points to his portly middle. "It's all those TV dinners."

I feel a pang of guilt; he's touched the mother in me. I suddenly want to cook for him, send him back to his place with a cooler full of casseroles.

"You'll have to come down some weekend. You'd like my place," he continues, teasing me with a description. "It's an old barn that looks like Ralph Lauren designed it."

"Maybe next month," I answer, wanting to offer some gesture of goodwill, "now that I'm finished at the fish market."

"The fish market," he says. "Joan the fishmonger!" He's lighthearted in his sarcasm, actually fascinated. "What did you do there?" he wonders, and asks more, as if he's really intrigued about the fishermen, the waterfront, everything. We are on our best behavior, yet it doesn't feel artificial or contrived. I'm thinking how pleasant it is when two people try to be gentle with one another.

"Would you like another glass of wine?" he asks, noticing that my glass is empty. I nod, and he goes off to fetch the bottle. My mind wanders to a friend who trained monks in ritualization. "When they started Communion," she explained, "they would pick up the chalice without giving it any thought, purely an object to be used, not treated as holy. What they needed to learn was the importance of developing a relationship with liturgical things and become involved with them. Only then would the ceremony have meaning." Listening to her, I couldn't help but imagine what my world might be like if I looked at the human beings I was closest to as holy and treated them with that same sense of respect. These thoughts flash through my mind as he returns. I try to look deeper into his heart, at the human being behind the roles of husband, father, educator. Seeing him apart from mortal agendas permits a sort of genuineness of spirit to float about the room. Whatever toughness he brought home with him seems to be melting away. Perhaps we'll be able to find some neutral ground.

After soup and bread I suggest a game of cards. He says he's tired, ready for bed. I feel my first pang of rejection. Tired, to me, has always been synonymous with boredom. Still, I agree, it's late. I blow out the candles and head for the loft, wondering if we'll fall into the same bed. He gives me a peck on the cheek and heads for the guest room. Wind howls outside our thin walls. I wonder about sex, even though I'm not at all sure I'm interested. Is there another woman? Is he in contact with his college sweetheart, who constantly keeps in touch with us, or the woman to whom he sent flowers last year, the bill inadvertently coming to me. I sigh and go into what has become my own room, pushing away such thoughts. This has been an eventful evening, an evening that had the potential to be hard but was soft. Perhaps a Christmas is in the making.

He is up long before I am. I can hear the scrape of the shovel as he attempts to dig us out of several inches of snow. The aroma of coffee permeates the house, and for the first time in months I don't have to make it myself. He's left me a cup on the bedside table, an old habit. I had forgotten what a treat that was. The house is toasty. I can hear the logs crackling in the stove and linger in bed a while longer before dressing and going downstairs. He's still outside, so I knock on the window and mouth a good morning.

It's overcast but no longer snowing. I prepare a breakfast of bacon and eggs. Over a second cup of coffee, I say, "Want to go to the beach?"

He stares. "You've got to be kidding."

"No, I mean it. I've never been to the beach after a snowstorm. It would be an adventure!" At the beginning of our marriage he was always quoting a line from *The Matchmaker* about the importance of having adventures.

"Hell, why not," he says, surprising me.

Within minutes we are in the car, skidding down our icy road. I can't believe it. He hates the cold, frequents the beach only in the best of circumstances. Perhaps this gesture is an olive branch—maybe he's ripe for anything—perhaps the gambler in him doesn't want to let the dare go by. No matter, we're outside, and somehow nature always seems to generate unity.

I hold the wheel tightly. Once at the beach, on the narrow track that cuts through the dunes, we head out toward the edge of my world. Some say the next stop is Portugal! I'm certain he thinks I've lost my mind as I drive onto the semihard sand. He says as much: "What if we get stuck?"

"I do this often," I say. "We've had freezing weather for the past week—we should be fine." Still, I sense his uneasiness. As usual, I'm the one who wants to throw caution to the wind while he plays it safe. We are ensconced in a white world, snowy heaps upon snowy heaps blown smooth, scalloping the dunes as if with marshmallow topping. I exclaim about the majesty, hoping to initiate a response from him, some welcome affirmation.

"Shall we stop here?" I ask.

"It's your call," he answers, absolving himself of responsibility. We stop at a spot wide enough for me to turn back around. "C'mon," I say, eager to get out and explore. All is quiet, eerily so, a dead-end world, yet bright and beautiful. I walk ahead, coaxing him toward the top of a dune. In front of us lies Nantucket Sound, appearing like an open field, a seascape frozen in place with icy strips decorating its surface, looking like whitecaps on a restless summer sea. I've never seen it like this, a normally restless body of water now a silent picture, a still life—the ocean seeming still and frozen, like our marriage. The danger, I think, lies in refusing to admit to being frozen, keeping dissatisfaction a secret, so that one day you end up sitting in the middle of a frozen surface not knowing when the ice will crack and thaw.

I can tell he's less moved. He has a detached look that tells me his thoughts are elsewhere, not here with me. I take his arm and nudge him closer to shore. We are amazed to find that all is not still. Thick sheets of ice move gently to the rhythm of the tides, a subtle undulation. This slow-motion sea, usually roaring, is now whispering. I hear a quiet splash from somewhere under the glacial surface that sounds like the rustling of a taffeta skirt. Then I spot a seal, not swimming, but sitting upright on a raft of ice, drifting at the whim of the waters. "Can you see him?" I say, pointing with one hand, squeezing my husband's arm with the other. He shakes his head in wonder. A broad smile spreads across his face. For one brief moment we seem kindred spirits. Then a burst of arctic air and a sudden snow squall interrupt our momentary enchantment. "I'm heading back," he says. "Take your time. I know this is your thing." He disappears into the flurry of snowflakes, looking to me like a phantom on a spatter-painted postcard.

Turning back to the sea, I notice two boats and a dinghy iced in. They will remain so until the thaw. Their owners can no more loosen them from the grip of ice than I can unthaw our marriage. I'm reminded to simply stay *in* the season and stop trying to play God. In time the tide will turn, and thawing weather will replace the arctic chill. I start back to the car, thinking there is much to garner from frozen flats and icy seas.

A veil of snow blocks all that is beyond me. Shy, unsure, I put one foot in front of the other, not unlike our wedding day when he was waiting for me at the front of the altar, then smiling and tearful. Now he is disguised behind a steamed-up car window and a blanket of snow. The image is as blurred as our future. I am suddenly wistful and weary, but nevertheless I take time for one last indulgence, making an angel in the snow, flapping my arms and legs while staring up at the white sky, pausing for just a moment in hopes of hearing the angels speak.

"What are you doing, you crazy lady?" he calls from the car, sounding puzzled but amused.

"Can't you see my angel?" I say, lifting myself carefully off the spot so as not to disturb the shape.

"C'mon in here where it's warm," he says, opening the door and brushing snow off the seat.

I'm grateful. He's turned on the engine, and the car is warm. He gives my shoulders a gruff rub, stifling my chattering teeth. As we leave, I manage a precarious turn and get the car back onto the frozen tracks of a previous driver. His mood is lighter.

"You've changed, you know," he says, his observation coming out of nowhere. "I mean, really changed."

"How so?"

"I don't know exactly," he continues, "just freer. That's it, a free spirit! It's becoming," he says, sounding wistful, as if he wished the same for himself. "How do you do it?"

"There's hardly a choice living here," I say. "Few distractions, no people really. I've been forced to make friends with the outside. Makes you kind of wild."

We're out of the tricky part of the drive, heading across the parking lot, when he asks me to stop the car. "Back up, just a little." He hops out, running into a small wooded area, scarf whipping, hair blowing. When he reappears, he is carrying a pathetic-looking pine tree.

"Don't you think we need a Christmas tree?" he asks, before stuffing the tree inside the trunk. "This one kind of reminds me of us right now."

We both laugh. One spontaneous gesture, and the void begins to fill.

"But we don't have any ornaments," I say. "Oh yes we do," he says, pulling a handful of seashells out of his pocket. "I picked them up while you were still walking."

Together and separately we are making things up as we

go along—a patchwork Christmas-in-the-making. And so the day goes quickly, like most Christmas Eves. There is much to do, even though it's just the two of us. He busies himself jury-rigging the tree while I work on dinner and the stollen. There are various ways to hide from one another, and we've managed to do it in the past—keeping busy, our heads behind books, other people—but today, although working apart, we are collaborating. I feel as playful as that cocky seal, unabashedly floating here and there, drinking a hot toddy and humming holiday tunes. Have I finally used up all my despair? Is all not irretrievably lost?

The Christmas tree is in a flowerpot full of sand. I watch him struggling to string the seashells. His job was always to do the lights, while the boys and I hung the ornaments.

"Want some help?" I ask.

"My fingers aren't as nimble as yours," he responds. He seems happy to hand me the pile of shells and ball of twine.

"So what's tonight's program?" he asks, and immediately I feel resentment. Why is it always my job to create the event and set the scene? "I suppose you want to go to church," he adds. What a stupid statement, I think. Christmas Eve and church are synonymous, aren't they? Why must he even ask? Why doesn't he know what I want?

I could turn his question into a tiff, but I don't, not tonight.

"There's a sweet church nearby," I say, "a simple place. We wouldn't even have to change our clothes."

He takes a swig of his hot toddy. It seems all right with him. We decide on the early service, saving dinner for later.

Even in the best of circumstances, entering a church on Christmas Eve can often distress my psyche, as I am frequently reminded of better and brighter holiday moments. But tonight it looks as if there's going to be a pageant, which might help bring out the child in me. I choke up during the first strains of "O Come All Ye Faithful," its very words suggesting that we all be "joyful and triumphant," but recover quickly upon seeing the Virgin Mary processing past our pew—sneakers on her feet, a wad of gum stuffed in her jowl, and a live baby Jesus slung on her arm as if she'd been a mother forever! Following her are three kings and a queen, assorted bathrobe-clad shepherds, and some fishermen complete with slickers and poles, an obvious gesture for children who know nothing of deserts in the Far East and much of oceans and fish.

I have been in need of something to break in upon my numbness, and the assembling manger scene is doing it. It only gets better as I watch the yawning acolytes who keep forgetting their cues and the little boy who, when the lights are dimmed and the candles lit for "Silent Night," exclaims loudly, "It's Christmas!" Being so disarmed, my guard down, the boy's delight in turn unleashes the child in me.

We exit before the benediction, not wanting the moment to evaporate into bright lights and people chattering. I tuck the bulletin into my pocket in order to read and reread the evening's prayer:

"Forgive our foolish and wandering ways. Open us
anew, stir us and move us to grow . . ."

My cheeks are glowing from the warmth of it all, and what settles over the cottage upon our return are uncomplicated feelings of tenderness. We exchange gifts: He offers his mother's diamond earrings made to fit my pierced ears, a wall hanging displaying business cards of ten accomplished women with a blank space left for my card, and a ceramic seal with a Christmas wreath around its neck. I give him a simple watercolor of our home back in New York, complete with the boys playing basketball in the driveway and our cat on the front porch.

Even our conversation is peppered with a redemptive spirit. When he utters a throwaway comment about our bad marriage (meant to be a joke), I scoop it up before it hits the trash basket, saying, "It's the relationship that soured; the marriage has been a success. Look what we've accomplished as a team: the people we touched, raising boys who had the courage to commit in an age of no commitment, being good children to our parents—need I go on?"

We've been temporarily relieved of tension, as if the tide had changed and the water were rushing in to quench us both, just in time. Yet I would be a fool to jump into his car and return home with him. While this Christmas has been a gift, the new year and its accompanying resolutions remain a challenge. I don't want to return to the way we were, but welcome the unknown of what we could become.

GETTING MY FEET WET

New Year's Eve

Each first of January that we arrive at is an imaginary
milestone—at once a resting place for thought and meditation, and a
starting place for fresh exertion in the performance of our
journey. The man who does not at least propose to himself to be
better this year than he was last must be either very good
or very bad indeed.

—*Charles Lamb*

I*t is* the first night of the new year and the last night of the old, and I'm standing in the center of town wearing number 76, surrounded by a hundred or so lean and mean runners, reluctantly waiting for a two-mile road race to begin. Whatever possessed a nonathletic, overweight, middle-aged hypochondriac to do such a thing? It must have been the ad I kept seeing for this event, the one that dared me to greet and meet myself in a new way. I've known for some time that I needed to get out of my head and into my body, and this race seemed to offer me a perfect starting point.

Not only is it a road race, but to add to the element of fun it is a costumed event. I'm dressed in a red warm-up suit with a Christmas tablecloth dangling from my shoulders to look like Little Red Riding Hood. I even brought along a basket to hold and a bonnet to wear. To say I look ridiculous is an understatement. The more experienced runners have donned pitiful accessories such as baseball caps, signs on their shirts, and eyeglasses with plastic noses; nothing that will impair their running prowess.

I've never been in a race before and am more than self-conscious. I move my leaden body away from the crowd so as to consider how I might flee, making comparisons with the other runners, seeing my imperfections, envying their trim physiques, noticing their well-worn sneakers. The few times I remember feeling comfortable in my skin were when I was three or four, all round and dimpled, or during pregnancy when the lack of dips and curves was acceptable. But no sooner were the babies born than my abdomen went from taut to soft, like bread dough, and I reverted to hating my body. No matter that the stretch marks I now boast have my children's names imprinted on them or that I had just finished carrying and creating new life! All that was reflected in the mirror were sagging breasts, minimal waist, a pear-shaped person who was no longer sexy or desirable.

Well, today I am here to face my gross negligence and mend the breach between body and mind. I retire to a nearby parking meter in order to lean on it while I do some stretches. It has always been an annual resolution to work on my body, but resolve usually fades by the end of January. This year seems different, though, and I no longer intend to hide my feelings and aspirations in fat. I want to stand whole in my skin and fly. I'm in a race against time. I need my body to catch up with all of me, to test my will and endurance.

Just then, as I am pulling my foot up to my buttock, my right knee gives out. I shudder in spasm, freezing for a moment to allow the joint to relax before letting go of my foot.

God, I've missed a lot. I should have loved my body better before this race. But physical prowess was not something I was taught to seek. Both my mother and grandmother put limitations on their bodies (or was it done for them?). Hell, when they gave birth, they were thoroughly drugged, such meager faith did doctors place in the workings of their bodies. Imagine, they were denied the one really glorious moment when a woman's body can truly shine. It's no wonder my forebears gave me so little support for my own physical being.

I stopped using my body after the hopscotch period of life, avoided gym class for fear of messing up my hair, wouldn't be caught dead sweating, as it was considered un-feminine. My body became a stranger I chose not to know. Although attached to it like a Siamese twin, I paid it no attention, disgusted as I was with its smells, covering up its eruptions, denying its effluvia. My body became no more than a piece of granite to be chipped away at until it became an acceptable shape. I tucked all my insecurities and unresolved emotions into muscles and joints, which now ache from atrophy.

The various doctors I saw along the way contributed to my bodily aversions. One internist, after hearing a functional heart murmur, sent me off for thousands of dollars' worth of tests that resulted in nothing except a severe case of anxiety. Then there was the obstetrician who told me to cross my legs when I was in the final stages of labor while he delivered a woman's twins in the next bed. And my children's pediatrician, who enjoyed feeling up his patients' mothers every time they came to the office. These men hardly evoked a sense of trust in themselves or in my body. After a time I simply began to deny I had a body at all and stopped going to doctors, which only served to fuel a much more insidious kind of denial that resulted in less maintenance and care.

But then my body began sending me messages, pounding clues about its needs into my bones and flesh. The first signs attacked my lower back, forcing me to take to bed for days until the spasms subsided. There were frequent headaches that hit each time I became obsessive or unrealistic about deadlines. And finally shingles that attached themselves to my ribs and hips and appeared each time I suffered a loss or rejection. Years of denial, coupled with increasing pain, eventually made me take notice, as if a child were tugging at my sleeve pleading for attention. My body was telling me to stop living one way and start considering another. I suppose that's the real reason I'm standing here shivering in the cold, choosing to do something ridiculous or at least downright embarrassing. I need to give my body a mind of its own, to lift the restrictions I have placed on it, to try for once to treat it as if it were all right and normal, whatever that might be.

I move back into the crowd of runners and take a position on the side, near the back of the pack. The day is mine, seize it or miss it altogether. Then this stunning bit of math: I'm fifty. I'll be lucky if I reach eighty. I have 360 months left!

Just then the starting gun explodes and I tentatively push off, muscles trembling, employing a queer bounding gait. But with ample cheers from the crowd feeding the thrill of the moment, I soon become like a horse in a stampede, wanting to run fast, following the leader. The first half mile is a gradual decline, thank God, hardly taxing. I make a pitiful attempt to leap ahead, keeping my stomach tucked in, spine straight, as long as the crowd is watching. But in a matter of minutes my body retaliates from the abuse and neglect; my hamstrings fail to extend, and my calf muscles cramp. As I round the corner of Main and School Streets and spot the hill I must climb, I tell myself I can't.

Still, I'm distracted from the pain by the jungle of

bodies around me. I focus on fannies as they shift and jiggle with each step, observe the ripened, swaying breasts on the larger women and the pancake-flat stomachs on the slight ones, wondering how they can contain their insides in such svelte shells. In contrast, I run in a body I deserve, and just now I feel gravity tugging at me, inches of fat slivering downward from stomach to pelvis to thighs until it settles into my feet, making them feel like five-pound bags of sugar.

I'm following the leader, many leaders, and by now most of them have passed me by as I trip over my feet and slow to a crawl. It's a relief to be running alone, no more comparison, no more competition.

I hate competition. Once I was waiting to appear on a television show to promote a book I was sure would be unpopular, when I gazed at the monitor and heard another author profess that her book had already sold half a million copies. I turned to a stranger nearby and asked, "How can I possibly follow her?" She took me by the shoulders, looked me square in the eye, and said, "Don't compare!"

Okay. Okay. So today I won't compare either; I'll find my own style. But then another hill! I thought this damn town was flat! Only when you meet the road, foot to pavement, do you really become acquainted with the terrain. I'm overwhelmed with the need to quit as the blood carries messages across my pulse points, and I think I may die. The loneliness of the long-distance runner is becoming clear to me. What a dumb idea this was!

But like a woman about to give birth, who doesn't want to do it just yet, I am faced with the reality that I must finish what I started. I gulp some cold air, thinking it will freeze inside me, and run on. A lady cop in a patrol car cheers me on. "Way to go!" she shouts, honking her horn, flashing her lights. She looks about my age, a bit overweight. Maybe she's wishing she had tried to run as well. As I feel her encouragement, I decide to continue for both of us. I nod and wave, amazed that I have enough energy to do so, and think I can't *become* unless I *do.* Then the words from my favorite children's book, *The Little Engine That Could,* pop into my head and give me a subtle rush: *"I think I can, I think I can."*

I've worn too many clothes, a sweatsuit no less. Even so, I'm sure my perspiration will soon become icicles dangling from my armpits and upper lip. How could I know that running in twenty-degree weather would make me hot? Relax your shoulders, Joan, widen your stance a bit, forget your fanny and breathe. What a mean trick I'm playing on this body! A tight body can't suddenly be loose. I've kept it chained and constrained for so long, that suddenly released from its bondage, it is spastic. You can't just one day order a body to do what you need at the moment; a relationship must develop. I must make friends with this stranger that is speaking to me with whines, creaks, and groans, coming to life after thirty-five years of slumber, a woman turned inside out, just now in touch with what once was invisible.

Real fatigue is setting in, but there is mercy. I spot the finish line, pull my shoulders back, throw my chin to the sky, and relax my hips. As I hammer toward the finish, I experience a gush of energy, instead of the strain and tension of the start.

Then it's over. I stagger to a nearby bench, briefly register the genuine applause from the remaining spectators, and collapse. Lost in exhaustion, coughing the chill from my chest, I try to breathe rhythmically again. If I entered this race to escape numbness, I've certainly succeeded.

It's a strange victory I've won. What began as a dare has now become a breakthrough. My father always said that if it wasn't tough, then it wasn't right. Today I had a choice: to grab the day or to be victimized by it. The gift was being given a chance to go beyond my perceived limits. I trusted the unknown, relied on a body I had been taught to fear, and it more than surprised me. I shall give up the idea of having a fashionable body, or an Olympian body. I just want a body that works, that is durable and resilient, that can climb a mountain, carry grandbabies on its back, be vital and energized even after a long day.

A noise parade is assembling in the adjacent park, a motley group of revelers carrying pots and pans, cymbals and sticks. They will create a crazy clatter, their purpose being to drive away that which is old, to let go of the old demons and make room for the new. It occurs to me that I have just been initiated into the second half of my life, crossing the threshold of my past, heading toward unknown frontiers that will inevitably lead me to myself.

I used to feel sad on New Year's Eve, clinging to the old year, never wanting it to be over. I avoided good-byes for the same reason, clinging to what was, simply because it was *known*, whereas the future was *unknown* and therefore to be worried over. How much fear has controlled my life. No longer!

My cheeks sting, and my fingers prickle. I duck into a nearby watering hole and order a hot cider, comfortable this day sitting among strangers. I pat my firm thighs and promise to banish further negative thinking. Smug about my New Year's resolutions, I raise my glass to being big, beautiful, feminine, and forever changing, promising to work with my bones and flesh. After all, bones make new bones if they are exercised, skin sheds itself to make room for fresh flesh, muscles untangle and restore their strength. I truly have rejoined the human race.

FOGGED IN

February

I wake to sleep, and take my waking slow.
I feel my fate in what I cannot fear.
I learn by going where I have to go.

—Theodore Roethke, "The Waking"

I am sitting at my grandmother's wobbly old kitchen table, nursing a third cup of coffee after the high point of my day—a brisk four-mile walk. I'm generally contented during my walk, with its simple goals of getting my pulse up and trying to beat yesterday's time. Activities with beginnings, middles, and ends spur me on and offer an adrenaline rush, but when they are over, my mood plummets. Having no clear objective dulls my spirit, and then lethargy sets in, stopping me altogether.

This is a lonelier journey than I expected. In the past few days I've spent inordinate amounts of time watching sand slip through an hourglass—it takes fifteen minutes for the sand to empty out of one end, and then I turn it over and watch as the process begins again. I'm reduced to simply watching time pass me by.

My excuse for today's paralysis is a snowstorm which hit two days ago, knocking out both the power and phone lines. I used to like snow days when the kids were little—when they'd snuggle in bed for an extra hour until I lured them into the kitchen with the smell of bacon and crepes. But being alone and holed up on a dirt path that the town doesn't plow is hardly fun, especially since my firewood is dwindling and I have taken to stealing from the neighbors. I tried to hack away at an old fallen tree in the backwoods, but there weren't enough hours of daylight to chop the amount of wood I would need to keep the stove burning for even one night.

My anxiety increases with each passing day—what do I have to show for my half year of seclusion anyway? I'm putting the finishing touches on two children's books, but after that my professional future is uncertain. My collaborator of twelve years up and left, moved cross-country with little or no consideration for the reputation we had developed or the amount of money we generated together. If I hope to salvage my career (which I'm not at all sure I do), I'm left to find myself a new photographer. It feels like a divorce, yet another of last year's many losses, which have left me with a raw, lingering ache.

Certainly the most devastating blow was my father's death, after which I had no time to cry. My mother and her widowhood took precedence over my grief. What's more, I lost my relationship with my only sibling along the way—a brother whose second wife had no use for any part of his family history that did not include her. I hated my brother for not coming to our father's funeral, which sparked a series of arguments that culminated in his throwing me out of his house and his life forever. Stale marriage aside, so much unfinished grieving must surely contribute to my stagnation now. Perhaps I shouldn't chastise myself so much for wandering from room to room, nibbling on stale Christmas cookies, starting projects but not finishing them. I want to trust the hours, but waste them instead. I've never been so close to myself, but somehow we can't seem to make friends.

I did make an attempt to find me last week when I came across a box of childhood snapshots, the box top startlingly labeled THE PAST. I spent an entire day mesmerized by my metamorphosis—spreading the little black-and-white photographs the length of the living-room floor, arranging them in chronological order, looking sometimes with a magnifying glass for telling expressions. Until I was six or seven I appear the epitome of innocence, security, and wonder: frolicking in the snow, at the beach, in the backyard; climbing trees; hanging from jungle gyms; riding my tricycle—always with my brother by my side.

But then we moved—away from our childhood home of Buffalo, New York, to the hills of Pennsylvania, then seventeen more times, each move eliminating more of our history, further uprooting our formative selves until a permanent outsiderness set in. Suddenly, as I gazed at my life on the living-room floor, I saw a little girl with a distant look in her eyes, one who was once tiny and perky, now chubby and sad, a forced smile replacing the earlier easy one, a tense, fearful, yet brave look on her face—as if it was taking every impulse she had to keep herself together. Eventually, in the teenage pictures, I saw a pretty yet rigid person I did not remember, but a persona I recall acting out. Not only did moving catapult me into strange lands, it also wrenched me away from a neighbor lady—a childless woman who loved me unconditionally—who had become a veritable second mother.

Being displaced time and again must contribute to a deeper inner displacement, so that after a while familiar images and values all but slip away. I saw in those pictures that I fitted in and survived by being what those around wanted me to be, leaving the real me by the wayside with permanent scars on her self-confidence. I need to grab her by the hand and make up for lost time, or at least honor her determination and stubbornness—attributes that she displays in the pictures.

"Surely I am lost enough to find myself," I say, repeating the words from a Robert Frost poem. Enough dancing around the edges of newness, Joan! No more treading softly on the back roads of consciousness—circumventing the issues, hoping they will go away. I shake my dismal thoughts and sit Indian style on the floor, eyes closed, rocking back and forth, closing my eyes, shutting off my mind, which too often tempts me into the games of deception I play with myself.

I reopen my eyes and see hanging in front of me a cross that I bought in New Mexico. It's made of scraggy mesquite, crooked and ragged, not straight and narrow. I like its undefined edges. I stare at its hammered-tin center, thinking that at this moment I am at a crossroads that offers three paths (the one behind me represents the past to which I cannot return). The shorter arm to the left leads to my husband, clearly not a place I choose to go. Two other possibilities remain, their destinations unknown. A quiet presence overtakes me, and my pulse slows. My hands relax, and my palms open spontaneously as I am reduced to blessed clarity. I feel a subtle yearning for adventure, similar to the way I felt last fall. Haven't I been counting on seeing new paths? Don't they abound everywhere, out here?

I'm reminded of the words of a Jungian analyst who spoke to a group of women about just such crossroads.

"Many of us would just as soon have our choices made for us," she said, "but the heroine, when at a juncture, makes her own choice—the nonheroine lets others make it for her."

Somewhere in all this muted splendor there must be something that wants me to find it. Why do I dally? I gaze out the window at a thick fog—the Gulf Stream must be blowing its warm wind across yesterday's frozen land, replacing the stark whiteness with a murky gray. The mounds of frozen snow have turned to slush. Perhaps escape is possible.

A foghorn beckons—it's been moaning all morning. Perhaps I'm meant to answer the call, give some value back to my day, leave the safety of the center. I don my yellow slicker, hop into the car, and plow through piles of slush, skidding my way out onto the main road, following the sound as if it were a mother calling her children home, the depth of her howl guiding even the most hopelessly lost back to safety. I'm being pulled toward town and the beach. Once there, I walk gingerly, barely able to see my hand in front of my face. When I round the bend in the road where there is usually a clear view of the sea, I can hear the surf and follow the sound of the water's motion, picturing her foamy waves, soon plunging my boots into the thick, slightly frozen sand.

Trust takes over in the fog, making me think about each step, demanding that senses be finely tuned. I move with determination, though, as I know this place and carry an invisible map in my head. Just now there is no past, no future, only the present. I push on toward the shoreline, planning to follow its lead. I am at the periphery of nowhere, enveloped in heavy mist, moving to the rhythm of undulating water, heading toward a jetty that protrudes far out to sea—a sacred place, really. It is a strong arm of protection for the harbor, an isolated peninsula, perfect for contemplation, a place where no one is likely to find you and try to change your course. I accomplish the mile-long walk in no time and climb upon the rocks, tiptoeing from one to the other, treading carefully as the splashing high tide creates a slippery surface. Utterly alone and feeling devilishly free, I begin to relish my solitary adventure, when suddenly I am startled by the chiseled profile of an aged woman standing tall, a black cape flowing behind her.

She turns her sparkling blue eyes on me as I approach. "Well, hello there. Are we the only ones in this town in a fog?" she quips, laughing at her own joke.

"I guess so," I answer. "How do you do? I'm Joan Anderson."

"I'm Joan, too," she answers, feeling no need to add a surname. "I'm new here. Isn't this a wonderful place?"

I only nod, entranced by her gracefulness—delicate face, high cheekbones, a patrician nose. I'm mystified to find such an elderly person perched on the edge of the world. My sense tells me that she is eighty-five or ninety—her right hand clasps a gnarly wooden cane, partially hidden by her long indigo jersey dress.

"Shall we walk?" she asks, already moving, beckoning me to follow. A few gulls squawk at our invasion, but we march on, drawn by the sound of the channel marker that sits at the very tip of the jetty. The farther we go, the less we can see of the harbor or beach. A small dory has broken away from its mooring and is being smacked against the jetty with each roll of a wave. "I feel a bit like that little boat," I blurt, not meaning to speak my intimate thoughts out loud.

"How's that?" she asks.

"I feel loosened, even free, but with no oar to steady the boat just now."

"I'd say I'm at sea as well," she admits, "but I just keep going. Don't look back—look out. I've left lots of stuff back on shore, hoping I'll find more out here."

"The fishermen think like that," I add. "They go out day after day, trusting the voyage, casting their nets on a whim, and always seem to come up with something."

"It's about action and touch," she says, as if she knows. "That's where the wisdom is—in the senses—stepping out on a gray day, daring to be different. There's no one as foolish as us right now. Thank goodness! We can be in a fog all by ourselves! I love the grayness of it. The mist sort of wraps itself around our thoughts, so they can take hold."

"Never thought about it that way," I say, navigating more cautiously, as waves now splash all about us. The formlessness of the fog encompasses us. We are without shape and design, simply fluid and expansive. To be walking with a fragile dowager, in a precarious spot, challenges me to dare to go farther.

"Sometimes I think women are like the fog," I comment.

"How do you mean, dear?"

"We have a knowledge of what is underneath, but our real selves are obscured by what others think of us."

"Well, I suppose that's so. The mysterious female—we'd best keep it that way."

I laugh at her gentle feminism. "I've been out here a hundred times and never come across the likes of you," I say, reaching out to help her across a gap in the rocks.

"It's all right, Mommy," she says, rejecting my help. "This old body hasn't failed me yet," she adds puckishly, all but dancing over the rough spots.

"How do you keep so well oiled?" I ask.

"Oh, my dear, that's easy. Movement, lots of movement. I walk a couple of miles each day. My body's my main strength, so I'm diligent about taking care of it."

We arrive at the end and lean against the base of the channel marker. Her thoughts are delicious. I want to know more—could listen to her all day. *When the pupil is ready, the teacher appears,* so the saying goes. And to think I hesitated before venturing out today.

She seems to share my feelings and surprises me by saying, "I like you! What do you do, anyway?"

I fill in the blanks of my life—married, two boys, a writer of children's books—and tell her that I've come here to find myself.

"Well, you sure can find a self out here, I should think. I've never been able to substitute words for experience—just got to get out and do it, like we're doing now." Her words are as soothing as the lighthouse beam that now cuts through the fog—steady, strong, alive—a focal point amid the gray.

Eventually we begin to make our way back from where we came, walking single file. "I'd be delighted if we could meet again," she says. "Perhaps have some port, late one afternoon."

"I'd like that," I say, as we approach the parking lot where a taxi is waiting to take her home, wherever that is.

"I hate not having a car," she says, clearly not happy having to be driven around. "I'm looking into getting a golf cart this spring—that and a three-wheel bicycle."

I shake my head in disbelief. Never have I seen such determination in someone so old. "Your last name—tell me how I can find you," I say, as she gracefully ducks into the backseat. "Erikson," she answers. "Joan Erikson. I live up Bank Street on Parallel. Call me, will you, dear?" And with that the door slams and she is gone.

I am smitten. For such a long time I've been wishing to stumble upon someone who might point the way, or at least hint at it. It occurs to me that being in the fog does not have to mean being altogether lost.

SEAL WOMAN

March

In the beginning there was thought and her name was woman.
She is the OLD woman who tends the fires of life.
She is the OLD woman spider who weaves us together.
She is the eldest God and the one who remembers and
RE-MEMBERS.

—Anonymous

S*he appeared* in my life like a full-moon tide whose frothy waves smack upon the shore, trickling upward, refreshing the toes of the beachcomber. After our first encounter, our next—complete with an orange-and-purple sunset and several glasses of port—sealed the friendship, lifting the fog that had encapsulated me.

I was reticent, even shy at our first few meetings, having noticed her late husband's picture on the cover of *Time* hanging over her desk—the famed psychoanalyst Erik Erikson, who coined the term "identity crisis." Celebrity unsettles me, making me wonder if I can measure up. I had to stifle the desire to impress and, instead, strive to give in to just being me, with all my inadequacies. Fortunately, Joan reassured me that perfection had also eluded her. In any case, I had no choice as to whether or not I would be her friend; she had attached herself to me, as I had to her, like an oyster to a rock. We would be "stuck" as long as no storm came along and tore us away—me and an old woman with the heart of a young girl, opening her heart because she thought us kindred spirits.

Real connection seems to happen that way—two like-minded souls meet and sniff around one another like puppy dogs, then *whoosh*, a moment of fission occurs, pleasantries are dropped, closely twined feelings surface, and a relationship is born. It's been six weeks since that afternoon on the jetty; we're past the beginner phase of friendship, eager to jump into the deeper places where intimacies and vulnerabilities lie waiting to be shared.

"If we can't share our real feelings, we might as well be men," she joked one day last week, dropping one of her verbal nuggets. "Everybody is soooo serious, when actually we're all a joke."

Being "stuck" with my new friend is like having Tinker Bell or Cinderella's fairy godmother stop by and insist on being of service. I have always had an affinity for magical creatures, for their power to transform mundane individuals into liberated spirits. It is as if I've been kissed by a muse— not of the Prince Charming variety, but rather, a ninety-two-year-old lady who spins out her wisdom, expecting me to catch the vibrations.

"Leave room for yourself," she insists as we spend several afternoons working together on handheld looms. She has taught me how to weave, and now we are creating small tapestries that represent the stages of our lives. I was characteristically rushing the process, combining the colors too quickly without really absorbing what each one meant: qualities such as autonomy, initiative, industry, intimacy. "You must look more carefully at what it means when one color meets another," she says, "to see how many strengths you have to work with and lean on."

Through her I am beginning to see that every thread is significant. To think of pulling out a color here or adding one there would be to alter the fabric of who I am. She is teaching me that the delight is in the continuum—to take all that I know and am and weave that wisdom into the fabric of everyday life, remembering always to leave room for myself. "Please, dear," she's had to say to me more than once, "keep the weaving tight so that you have space for what you're becoming. You've covered two thirds of the loom, and you still have half your life left."

Every woman should have a mentor—not her mother, but someone who doesn't have a stake in how she turns out, who encourages her to risk, who picks her up when she falls flat on her face. Joan prods, pokes, and coaxes me each time we're together, like a mother trying to waken her sleepy child to get her off to school in time. Her phone calls come early, during the twilight state between dreaming and waking.

"Hi, dear," she says, her voice as soothing as warm maple syrup. "Want to get into some trouble today?"

"What did you have in mind?" I ask, smiling at her devilishness.

"Oh, I don't know—just getting out and gathering up some experiences!"

Today's outing will be a hike through a nearby moor. Around noon I drive to her tiny house, which is nestled beside a marsh, and bow to a statue of St. Francis, whose duty is the safekeeping of the multiple species of birds that come to eat at one of her various bird feeders. In lieu of a doorbell she has a metal triangle hanging from a hook beside the front door, with written instructions dangling from its wand: RING VIGOROUSLY. Several clangs later she appears, comfortably dressed in her at-home uniform—tights, sensible black sneakers, and a jacket that she made out of her husband's old ties.

"Hello," she exclaims, opening her arms, pulling me into

a hug. I embrace her gently, fearful of brittle bones. "Oh, no, you don't," she whispers, sensing I'm holding back, and she hugs me more firmly. "Come in. I've something to read to you." She takes my hand, leads me down a hallway, past the treadmill and a makeshift altar for her dancing Buddha, then into the sparsely furnished living area, where a giant piece of driftwood is the only adornment.

I settle onto a wicker stool near her feet, as she straddles a swivel seat near her desk, which is awash in a glorious confusion of cubicles stuffed with notes, lovely stationery, fountain pens, and a sign pasted to her lamp that says, SMILE ANYWAY. "Now, let's see, where's the damned thing?" she says, fumbling through papers until she locates the one. "I wrote a poem for you last night. Tell me what you think."

RECOMMENDATION

Impatient lady, eager now to know
To traffic with that bird of night
Before even early frost has touched your hair.
An open mind has depths that grow
Only as shadows to the light,
Let be what is Becoming—slowly
Slowly grow and know, Patience.

I squirm a bit, knowing she has tapped into my haste—my need to find answers *now*. Although she hasn't pried into my life—what I'm doing here without a husband—I'm sure she senses my struggle. "Patience isn't your virtue, is it, dear?" she says, filling the quiet moment between us. "You mustn't fret. There is no arriving, ever. It is all a continual be-coming."

Tears fill my eyes as I recognize that she is seeing the real me.

"So much of you is waking up," she adds. "I see you bubbling all over the place—you're yeasty, and I think it's grand!"

I suppose she's right, although I still can't shake the stagnation that overwhelms me every time I think about the future.

"You must have been so careful with what you did and said in your former life, so as to stifle the very essence of you. No wonder you're here, and in a hurry."

Tears trickle down my flushed cheeks, as I am relieved to be found out. I've always wanted to know someone who would bother to see beyond the surface of me, without my giving many clues.

As if she knows what I'm thinking, she says, "It's the way they want us, you know—predictable and appropriate. Trouble is, we end up being apropos of nothing!"

We both laugh, dispelling any gloom. This is the first time since coming here that I feel affirmation for my decision. "It was so hard to leave home," I tell her, "but instinct told me to travel to where nature might take its course."

"Me, too," she offers. "I came here, leaving friends and Cambridge behind, to deal with my husband's infirmity without interference. You are never free to do as you please when you stay with the familiar."

I find our situations curious. She ran away *with* her husband, I *from* mine. I wish my inclination had included him, but it didn't. Before I can sink into disdain, she rescues my mood.

"Being here is a sound choice, dear—not hiding under the covers like so many wives do, sniveling, afraid of losing their security. So many women believe that love is a feeling of being dependent. Sometimes having a husband can be a sort of alibi for a woman. Look, you've slammed one door, but oh, how you've opened another! People develop in aloneness and are only led to the truth after being disillusioned."

My panic subsides as she continues.

"I've been running away, all my life," she says. "When I was little, I ran to the woods—only place I could be my-self—then off to Europe—unheard of for a woman of twenty-one—changed my name and became whatever and whoever I wanted. You've got to be your own person. In any case, it's pretty deadly not to be! Honey, it takes action to create change. Everything we talk about isn't worth a dime if we don't actualize it."

"So what are we waiting for?" I say. "You keep talking about overdosing on the senses. Shall we get going?"

"It's high time," she agrees, grabbing her coat, hat, and gloves in order to face the cold, gray afternoon. We are in the car and at Stage Harbor in no time. I park near the light-house, and before I can lock the doors she hops out, heading straight for the desolate moor at a catch-me-if-you-can pace. It's a desolate place, but we think it beautiful, overflowing as it is with hearty lichen, bayberry shrubs, grasses—a place abundant with signs of beginnings. Here the visitor is tempted not just to stretch, but to grow new as well.

We pretend we're on a treasure hunt for our souls,

looking for nothing in particular but hoping to find that piece of shell or rock or driftwood that speaks to us. The winter's storms have deposited inordinate amounts of seaweed everywhere, which makes navigating feel as though we are walking on a giant sponge. I see her in the distance, bending down to pick up a handful of weed. She turns to see if I'm looking, then drapes a bunch of it over her head. "I always dreamed of being a mermaid," she shouts, wryly amused at her own folly and her new mass of tangled hair. "What do you suppose people would say if they could see what passes between us?"

It occurs to me that she is a native of these elements—familiar with them in some intimate way. Just now her manner reminds me of the seals. They hear what others cannot, have knowledge of what is underneath, are energized by the wild. Is that who Joan is, after all: a seal woman who traverses the worlds of humans and animals alike? In any case, her antics never fail to strip away adulthood and reduce me to childishness. Suddenly there is playfulness and light. Who cares where water stops or wind begins?

I spot a red fox staring into a puddle not ten feet from where we stand and grab Joanie's arm to alert her. Within seconds the creature notices us, and we stand eyeball to eyeball for a solid minute, after which the fox turns back to the puddle, more interested in her own reflection than in the likes of us. "Good for you," Joan says, applauding the fox. "We could all stand a little more reflection."

We move toward a hollow where thousands of bleached shells and other souvenirs of sea life are scattered about.

Poking with her cane, she loosens one object, then another—the more broken and ravaged, the better. I sit contented on a nearby log and peruse this solitary place. "Would be a great place for a vision quest," I think out loud.

"What's that?" she asks, continuing to scavenge while I talk.

"I had it explained to me by a Navajo elder a few years ago. He takes to the wilderness once a year and spends twenty-four hours in one solitary spot, while nature offers itself to him. He told me that even the most cluttered mind is emptied of extraneous thought after the first hour, and that a true language comes out of silence."

"This would be a fine place," she agrees, sounding eager to participate in such a thing, right now.

I move away, withdrawing into my own space, having found some beach glass and now want to look for more. As I finger the pieces in my pocket, I realize that once they were part of a whole. Now they are cracked and broken, but time has softened their edges, each becoming new on their own—a nice metaphor for a woman who has evolved through various passages, integrating the soft and the hard sides of her personality, now beginning to relax into understanding what her life is all about.

Today a quahog shell, complete with a hinge holding a fragment of its other half, teases me to pick it up. It has a regality about it, a triumphal purple band embedded in its edges. I imagine the juicy center it once had and think such a shell is like a woman who spends years holding her family members together, then becomes unhinged when they're gone, like the clam, no longer needing to be so attached to the other half; not unlike a husband and wife in a long-standing marriage, both pursuing that which is unlived about their lives.

My nose directs me next to a cluster of toenail shells wilting on the drying sand, clinging to one another. I am struck by the stench that comes from such clinging, holding on when it might have been better to let go. How many people have I clung to or let cling to me long after it ceased to be a healthy thing to do? Part of the freedom I feel today comes from letting go.

After a while Joan comes to me, taking hold of my hand without asking, and we stand facing the sea with all the vastness it offers. We are helping each other be real people; her need for companionship, so she can have freedom and adventure, forces me to go after the same. Our treasure hunts rarely reveal a single insight of great importance. Rather, we come away with new attitudes. As for me, my energy is redirected, my humor returns, body and mind are stretched.

Eventually we head home, two wash-ashores who have taken a seaside cure, more refreshed than when we arrived.

Ebb and Flow

April

If you can talk with crowds and keep your virtue,
Or walk with Kings—nor lose the common touch;
If neither foes nor loving friends can hurt you;
If all men count with you, but none too much;
If you can fill the unforgiving minute
With sixty seconds' worth of distance run—
Yours is the Earth and everything that's in it,
And—which is more—you'll be a Man, my son!

—Rudyard Kipling, "If"

I *am* standing in the kitchen on an early-spring morning, hands in soapy water, tackling a sinkful of dirty dishes from last night's feast, one of many I've prepared this month for the smorgasbord of people that has appeared on my door-step, melting my carefully drawn boundaries as quickly as the ice has dissolved on the pond.

These random intrusions began innocently enough, with day visits from an old college roommate and a distant cousin in search of a cottage to rent for the summer. Soon thereafter the entertaining got more serious: relatives of Joan Erikson for a weekend, a visit from my good friend Hazel, and eight days of dinner parties for an independent film crew. I am being forced to stop being in solitude!

As I stack the plates, hand-dry the glasses, and sort the flatware, I keep glancing at the little weaving Joan and I did, which hangs on the wall over the sink, and wonder if, as she so often urges, I've left room for myself during these visits or given in to the demands of the crowd?

Although I was apprehensive about company of any kind, Joan's description of her cousin and his wife, coming east to attend a conference, was thoroughly tempting; he is a psychoanalyst and she an Episcopal priest. How could I not take them in? I felt it was time to open my door anyway, to let in fresh thoughts. There was a special appeal to playing hostess to a shrink as I began to imagine all the questions I could ask him about my psyche.

His wife unnerved me at first, until I realized that she was merely studying my character, making sure that Joan had fallen into good hands. He, on the other hand, stripped away my armor in no time, an affable sort of guy eager for involvement, who asked *me* questions, rather than the other way around.

They arrived after dark, and as we shared wine, cheese, and our life stories well into the night, I remembered how good conversation has forever been an aphrodisiac. Our talk turned to Jungian philosophy, as we discussed balancing the feminine and masculine in our personalities, working with one's shadows, and other such erudite topics.

"At our ages and stages we should be going for the gold of our shadows," he said. "Look at the dirt in your life and work with it, instead of avoiding it."

"Wait a minute," I inserted, not holding back as I often do to hide my ignorance. "First things first—what the hell is my shadow?"

"Your dark side, the evil stuff about you," he answered. "Here's an example: I might be attracted to a twenty-one-year-old client, not an unusual occurrence for a man my age, and yet if I acted on my lustful fantasies there might be all hell to pay. But simply denying these thoughts is sheer repression. I might have had to turn off such thoughts when I was newly married and we were raising our children, but now I have more freedom and will gain nothing from denying my fantasies. Rather, it behooves me to bring them to the surface, look at what I might be missing, and then move ahead to incorporate, say, more passion in my life, within the bounds of my marriage."

I was sitting cross legged on the floor and changed positions, a bit self-conscious now, wondering what he really thought about my leaving my husband, living alone, trying to find myself. I dared to ask, not for his opinion of me, but how someone in my situation works with her shadow.

"You're actually embracing your shadow right now," he said, "by doing something out of the ordinary pattern, looking at stuff you've probably been afraid to unleash for years."

He was right, of course, but I didn't want to say what I was unearthing, because I didn't feel comfortable just now, spilling such thoughts to a relative stranger, no matter how quickly we've become intimate. Even so, each evening with these two was intense and invigorating.

Still, I remained aware that I was the entertainer—the hostess who had the dinner ready when they returned every evening from their conference and vacation time, the one doing most of the planning and work for them, dues I obviously still think I should pay in order to have such experiences. So it was shocking when I sat down to record our conversations in my journal and search for the answers we surely must have arrived at after all the talk. When I drew a blank and had nothing to write, I began to wonder if any hard truths had passed between us. Was our talk mostly theory, lacking feeling? Both concerned and then agitated, I went to Joan to discuss why so much effort brought so little return.

"You can't find answers from authorities, silly, especially when they are men!" she said, somewhat disappointed that I hadn't gotten that already. "It's only going to come from here," she insisted, pointing to her heart, "not out there. It's about give-and-take, pulling and tugging, working it through, like our weavings."

I chastised myself all the way back to the cottage for having dumb expectations. Suddenly I was cranky and irritable from all the effort I put forth. Solitude eliminates servitude, that's for sure. Although I love the idea of an open-door policy, and am coming to realize that some helpful lessons can be learned from new people and experiences, I must remember to be kinder to myself. I will launder the sheets and towels, close the door to the guest room, and reclaim my unencumbered space.

Just as I was again getting used to walking around in my underwear and not flushing the toilet if I didn't want to, I heard a car disturbingly close to the cottage. I peered out the kitchen window, expecting a fuel truck or the mailman, only to discover the pixie face of my good friend Hazel behind the windshield of her car. Both anxious and excited about this new interruption, I went out to greet her.

"Your voice sounded awfully flat to me the last time we talked," she confessed, explaining her unannounced arrival. "I was in Boston visiting my aunt Bessie and couldn't resist seeing for myself if you were really all right."

I let her caring sink in. Her coming was a brave move. Despite our eight-year friendship, she still does not trust the fact that I love her unconditionally and would never say no to a visit. Still, there she stood: in a loose-fitting Putumaya dress, her arms loaded with food and gifts, looking more like an aging flower child, complete with Birkenstocks and granny glasses, than the well-established pediatrician she is.

Always paying her way, more than generous, Hazel gives too much, compensating, I suppose, for what she thinks she lacks in personal attributes. How could such an accomplished woman be so short on self-esteem? I wondered, then laughed. We are the same. Perhaps that's the reason we're friends, why I wasn't put off by her arrival. Hazel is as hungry for approval and affection as I am; we both have much to give each other.

"I last saw you as you drove away from New York," she said wistfully when we settled into an evening of catching up. "I was so jealous. I still am, come to think of it, now that I see what you were going to."

"But you couldn't run away if you wanted to," I reminded her, "married as you are to your pediatrics practice and that husband of yours, who you can't stop trying to please."

She only nodded, offering no comment. We usually save husband and children talk for last, after we've covered the details of our own lives. "How long can you stay?" I asked, hoping maybe for a couple of days.

"Just the night," she answered, "although once I take residence in that cozy loft guest room of yours, I may never leave. It feels like a tree house."

We got into the pissing-and-moaning phase of the evening while making dinner and getting a little drunk. I'd forgotten how much fun it was to have someone to complain and gossip with, to make those inevitable comparisons between our lives and those of mutual friends. We like our rebellious friends best and have less patience for those who hesitate to risk. We cheer on the ones who stumble regularly, endure false starts, and couldn't be perfect if they tried.

The next morning more of the same chatter continued over the breakfast Hazel had whipped up, blueberry pancakes "full of bran and whole-wheat flour," she insisted, "not at all fattening."

"Next time you've got to stay longer," I told her as she prepared to leave. Tears, partially hidden behind sunglasses, stained her cheeks as we said good-bye. There is so much relief and comfort in sharing truths with a dear friend—being with someone with whom you don't have to justify everything.

Her visit affirmed the life I have chosen to live and the limits I have set. She did not stay beyond her welcome or ask me to play hostess. She offered me time and companionship and, as usual, left behind a pile of books I was supposed to read for discussion the next time we met. I was eager to settle back into seclusion just as the phone rang.

"Hey, Joan," my oldest nephew said, "I'm on the Cape, about to shoot a film, and I need to talk to you. Can I come over?"

"Why not?" I answered, even though I sensed he was after money, shelter, something like that, the operative word being "need." I had half expected to hear from him, as the entire family had been following his fledging film career and I knew his latest script was set by the sea. Still, I was curious as to how I might fit into the picture. He's a master persuader, and I've always been a sucker for his requests since I was actually present for his birth. I braced myself.

A few hours later he arrived with his problem. "The woman I had lined up to cook for the crew got another job," he said. "I need someone in a hurry. Is there any way you'd consider doing it?"

I was momentarily flattered that he had such confidence in me, and I quickly felt that old adrenaline rush that comes from greasepaint. The romance and excitement that surround production are pure heaven for me, a form of speed that always fires me up, taking over my entire personality. Still, he was not asking me to hold the lights, design the set, act in the production. I was, after all, only the cook. I tamed my initial enthusiasm and asked for more details.

"I've got a thousand dollars budgeted for food," he continued, "and minimum wage for the cook. That would be you," he added, pointing to me with an impish grin.

Should I or shouldn't I? Two gorgeous guys, crew members, stood nearby as we talked, their raw ambition contagious. I was about to acquiesce, tempted by the lark of it all and the prospect of some extra cash.

"Is your place large enough to handle the whole crew?" he asked.

"My place!" I hadn't thought where they'd be fed.

"We'll be shooting for the next six days. Lunch is served on location, and then we crash for dinner wherever you prepare it," he added.

My enthusiasm waned the more I contemplated the logistics, as well as the invasion of my carefully calculated privacy. He offered further details, assuming now that I was his for the asking. "Three are vegetarian, six don't eat mayonnaise, one's lactose-intolerant, another is allergic to nuts.

Actually, most of them are into health food," he added, "so have lots of juices, yogurt, and salad stuff."

"Wait a minute," I said, now clearly annoyed by all the restrictions. "You're in a jam and I happen to be available to help out. But I've got my own parameters. You'll get your basic Yankee fare—chowders, fish stews, corn pudding, baked beans. Those with dietary idiosyncrasies will have to fill in with their own stuff. There are limits to my good graces," I countered, surprised, yet pleased for speaking up.

He was pensive for a minute, concerned, not so much for me, but rather with pleasing those in the crew. Still, what choice did he have but to agree with my terms?

"Okay. It's a deal. Thanks for helping out, Joan," he said with a sense of resigned relief. "I've set up an account at the market," he told me. "Sign my name along with yours." And with that, they were off.

My mind raced with menu possibilities as I contemplated the shoestring budget as well as the pampered palates. Tacos with beans and rice instead of beef will be the first meal—a do-it-yourself dinner with very little cooking and a lot of chopping. Other entrees: pizza, vegetarian lasagna, bouillabaisse. I made a list in the car on the way to the market: noodles, cheeses, salad stuff, spaghetti sauce, sour cream, drinks. Drinks! Other than juice, what should I get? I settled on seltzer and cheap wine. One hour later, dragging two grocery carts into the checkout line, I had the ingredients for four dinners and several lunches, and had spent only $492.43.

Mornings were the most hysterical, filled with preliminary dinner preparations and lunch fixings that had to be packed for transport and driven to location, then set up as a buffet in the back of a borrowed Jeep.

But the payoff was being the voyeur, drinking in scene after scene, watching two actors, a director, a female cinematographer, and sound, lighting, and set designers work their magic, some doing it for as little as room, board, and love of the craft. Mostly I was struck by how finely tuned their senses were, all having their own specialties, and how they blended their sensitivities to bring about a unified creation.

How do my sensitivities measure up? Do I truly hear? Am I really aware of the subtleties of light? Do I notice color and form? Perhaps the next time I do something as simple as go to the beach I should take note of what I'm seeing and hearing as if these sights and sounds were to be immortalized on film. In any case, eight days of watching people dig beneath the surface of things, striving to get into the soul of the materials, was nothing short of inspiring.

Beyond that, I saw these troubadours living out their dreams—albeit from hand to mouth, but traveling wherever their next job takes them, working with the unknown and thriving. I don't think I regret leaving the theater business some thirty years ago, but I am glad to be reawakened to the delight of it and reminded that it is never too late to dream.

As I wipe down the counters and take out the garbage, I'm amazed that I survived this social month fairly unscathed. Perhaps that's because I went with the ebb and flow of each visit, allowing for some give-and-take, offering and retreating, weaving myself in and out of each encounter.

I'm not anxious to play bountiful hostess to anyone. But

I will welcome family, good friends, and creative people in small doses and as often as my energy permits.

For now, though, I'm glad to have my time and space back. Tonight I shall open a can of soup and dine happily alone. I'm learning to sponsor myself, no longer the servant but a master of my own time and destiny. It's all about intention—knowing when to open the door and then when to close it again.

LOW TIDE

May

One is not born a woman, one becomes one.

—*Simone de Beauvoir*, A WOMAN'S JOURNAL

I've *taken* up clamming, not because I yearn to battle the fickle spring elements of the outer bar, but because I am in dire need of some cash.

The crisis occurred a few weeks back when I went to do a sinkful of dirty dishes and realized that there was no hot water. I headed for the cellar, hoping that the pilot light had been snuffed out, and promptly stepped into an inch of water. The plumber confirmed my worst fear: a leaking water heater. The cost of a new one would be twelve hundred dollars. It has always been difficult for me to ask for help, but I had no choice. I would have to swallow my hard-earned, self-sufficient pride and telephone my husband.

There have been a few friends I've been able to call on because they give without condition, but not my husband, and certainly not now. "If you'd been living with me as I had planned, this wouldn't have happened," he said upon hearing the problem. "Obviously you've overtaxed the water heater. I told you the cottage wasn't properly winterized."

"I know," I say shriveling into silence, feeling weak with surrender, guilty once again for all I'm not doing.

"Look," he continued, "we don't have the money right now. The deal was, I'd keep paying the mortgage on the cottage, and you'd do the rest. This house I rented down here for the *two* of us is draining me financially." Then, with his

Scorpio venom, he added, "Why don't you call on one of your fishermen friends? They seem to be coming through for you."

There was more than a hint of jealousy in his voice, which completely turned me off. My mind flooded with memories of other times he hadn't come to the rescue—the onset of a miscarriage when he left me in pain to attend a board meeting; forgetting to renew the Triple-A card when he knew my old car was constantly breaking down; waiting for me once at the wrong door of the train station while I stood for three hours as my period trickled down my legs.

I wanted to kick myself for calling him, clinging to the infantile fantasy of being rescued, wanting him to feel sorry for me. But as his litany of excuses continued, I simply interrupted. "Never mind. I'll figure something out," and then hung up the phone, determined not to sink.

"I can move through this storm," I repeated under my breath, defiant now. I might crave consensus, but chaos and rejection, filled as they are with fear and hope, offer a high of their own. At the very least, anger incites me to action, which in turn forces me to be creative.

As I ponder my options, I'm inspired by the stories of others in my gene pool—strong women who faced a good deal more than not being able to pay their bills. My grandmother, who left her womanizing husband after an argument and wheeled her two babies in a pram from Brooklyn to Manhattan to take shelter with an aunt; my mother, who lied about her age in order to get employment and move up the ladder on Wall Street; and an aunt who, when her father made her reject a scholarship to a good university, thinking she would only get into trouble, disregarded his dictum and ran off to Europe, where she was free to do as she pleased.

Their collective stories rescue me from any remaining vestiges of victimhood, getting me out of the cottage and heading toward the fish pier with a mind full of job possibilities. I could become a fish baiter, baiting miles of line in order to lessen the fisherman's labor; or pack and ice fish at the cooperative; or get some other odd dock job. The closer I get to the harbor, the more eager I am to *do something*, hopefully something remarkable.

The very act of seeking sets things in motion, my father used to tell me, and he is about to be proven right. No sooner am I in the parking lot than I spot Joshua Cahoon. "I don't believe it's you," I shout out the car window, excited to reconnect with my clamdigger friend. "I haven't seen you since the market closed. How have you been?"

"Not bad, not bad," he mumbles in his slow Yankee drawl. "Now that the weather's turned, I'm getting out to the flats almost every day. And you? Thought you'd be back in the big city by now."

"Nope, not me," I answer smugly. "It has been a good winter, except for right now. I'm a little short of cash."

"You could always try clammin'," he suggests. "Just need to get yourself a license. I'd be happy to loan you a rake and basket."

"What's a license cost?" I ask.

I'm shocked when he says a hundred dollars. "But you'll make that back in a day. Just gotta dig eighty pounds or so. I do that in a couple of hours."

"Sounds like an awful lot to me," I say. "Do you really think I could do it?"

"There's lots of lady clammers," he informs me. "Just takes some will and fortitude. You seem to have plenty of that," he says with an impish wink.

I'm taken aback, not only because he's being unusually communicative, but because he's trying to solve my money crunch.

But with no HELP WANTED signs anywhere in sight, I figure I'd better seize the chance, very much like the surfer who catches the crest of any wave in order to ride to shore. My mother had religiously preached the old adage "Nothing ventured, nothing gained." Without further discussion, I spring for the license and commence digging for my fortune.

Two weeks have gone by. I've been out to the flats now six or seven times, a certified clammer almost, complete with my own rake and a brass growth ring I wear on a leather string around my neck.

The first day was a disaster, with high winds and heavy mist. I tried to learn how to clam while wearing several layers of clothing and a slicker. I was not only discouraged but demoralized, with nothing to show for my labor after the first hour.

Joshua paid me no attention, intent as he was on digging his three hundred pounds' worth. Mercifully, sometime before noon he noticed my predicament and came over to give me some pointers. "First of all, you've got to stomp around a bit—get the clams to spit, which makes holes in the sand. See what I mean?" he said, pointing to all the holes he was generating. "There's clams underneath here." In seconds he was digging briskly with his short-handled rake and popping them out one after another. "You've got to picture just where you think they are and then scoop 'em out. Okay, now you try."

Down I went, body bent over as if to pray, and plunged the rake into a spot with tons of air holes. Then I lifted the wet sand out of the muck—and with it a clam!

"Go on," Josh coaxed, "do it again." Soon I had created several feet of sand mounds, and a string of clams decorated the surface.

"I think you've got it," he cheered, genuinely happy for me. "It won't be so easy in an hour or so. Your arms will hurt, your back will ache, but keep your mind on the money. A basket of clams is worth fifteen or twenty dollars! Set a goal—a bucket would be great for today—and then go after it."

A quick calculation that first day told me this wasn't going to make a dent in my crisis. The plumber would install a new water heater if I put down a third of its cost. At that rate it would take a month of working every day just to get the down payment! I had to dig at least two buckets that first day and then try to increase my haul each time I went out. Desperate, I began digging relentlessly. Beginner's luck was with me. Every strike with my rake rendered a clam or two. I grew exhilarated. "Nothing ventured, nothing gained," I repeated again and again.

An hour of steady work, and I ran out of steam. Having never used my upper body like this, my arms were in spasm. I retreated to the dunes for a sandwich and some coffee. Josh had long since eaten his first lunch—he brings three. "I lost thirty pounds the first year of clamming," he said. "Doesn't look as strenuous as it is."

"So I'm finding out," I quipped, stretching out on the dry dune and raising my arms above my head, careful not to get too comfortable, as I had a bucket and a half still to fill.

"You don't want to stop for very long," Josh warned. "Motion is the only way you'll stay warm."

I rallied and began stomping around like an Indian at a powwow, becoming giddy when I realized that hundreds of clams must be spitting underneath. Back down I went for round two, this time praying to St. Anthony, who finds lost objects, and sure enough I began popping up the little buggers. It was addictive, like eating peanuts; the more I found, the more I wanted to find. By midafternoon I was topping off basket number two.

It took a while to find a slow and steady rhythm, but the more comfortable I became in the role of clammer, the more I relaxed into the flats. Josh sees the flats as his office. To me they feel more like church. There's something spiritual about a span of beach that appears out of nowhere for a limited amount of time and then disappears again, never to resurface in exactly the same way. I'm learning to surrender both to the grueling work and to the isolation. When I need centering, I sing a favorite hymn, "Spirit of God descend upon my heart," which also allows me to eavesdrop on my spirit and pick up on its mumblings.

On bad days what bubbles up is self-loathing. Working in the muck tends to make me focus on my dark side, on all the faults and vices that my husband and others have had to put up with. It depresses me to think that my desire to seek clarity this past year has probably only further complicated my relationship, harmed my husband's ego, and distanced me from my sons. But on sunny days, when my haul is good, my spirit is buoyed. I feel a pride that comes from problem-solving and genuine hard work. Each time I venture to this eerie place, I become a little less of the me I once was—that controlling, stubborn person—and more of the spontaneous person I want to reclaim.

Joan Erikson applauds my new job. She says work should be play, that anything else is a dead end. "I'm glad you're getting out of your head and into your body, dear. That's when you learn. Theory doesn't mean a damn if you don't actualize it," she repeats. She's right. I hadn't realized how much I enjoy using my hands. Clamming reminds me of when I was a child building sand castles, everything within my grasp and the range of the eye. A task that was at first monotonous has become more creative as I focus on what's before me: uncountable gradations of tone and hue—mauve, black, brown, gray—a world of reflections created on wet sand from the slanted light of a cloudy sky. I'm put into a Zen-like state, often transcending who I was when I arrived at the beginning of each day.

I'm learning that what's important is not so much what I do to make a living as who I become in the process. Simple labor is smoothing my edges, teaching me to crave work not just because it might make me special or wealthy but because the job pleases my spirit, makes me a more pleasant person, and meets my immediate financial needs. These days satisfaction comes from seeing wire clam baskets filled to the brim, three-quarters submerged in a nearby tidal pool some six hours after I arrive at the flats.

Just as the sea has withdrawn to offer us its floor, ever so subtly it returns. At first I notice the dry spot where I stand becoming mush. Then water begins pushing up from underneath, creating rivulets, which grow into tributaries of the mighty ocean. Within minutes water swirls around me.

"Here comes the tide," Josh yells. Sure enough, his little boat, which had been beached, leaning on its side for several hours, has now righted itself and stands ready to take us back to the mainland. I grab my baskets and gear and wade out, ready for the day's end. Timing my day to the tides has helped me stop the frustrating practice of forcing and manipulating my life. I understand now why I was annoyed when a neighbor stopped by the other day with a bunch of forsythia. "Something to brighten your day," she said cheerily, speaking with pride of how she had gathered the branches over a month ago, brought them in to the warmth of her house, and forced the buds to blossom early. I listened, all the while feeling unsettled about what she was telling me. Clamming has taught me that all will be mine in its time and season. Forcing things works against instinct and the elements. It is an art form I was taught to perfect—forced conversation, feelings, orgasms even, prayer—but it is no longer a comfortable way for me to be. Working within the tides and the rules of the universe is fast becoming my preference.

I take one last gulp of the clean air and exhale slowly as Josh starts up the engine. Surrounded by sea life, picking the grit from under my fingernails, licking the salt off my lips, I know, *truly know*, the value of a day, which is made even more apparent when my pockets bulge with cash, soon to be stuffed into a coffee-can bank, partially hidden among food-stuffs in the pantry.

I am cold, wet, achy, yet eager to call the plumber. Today's haul put me over the four-hundred-dollar mark. If he can schedule me for tomorrow, I can finally take a blessed bath! I've made do by leaving a lobster pot full of water on the woodstove in the morning and then dumping it into the tub at night. Tiger balm and cheap wine are the other indul-gences that repair my body in time for the next dig. I wel-come a real cleansing.

TREADING WATER

Memorial Day

It is easy in the world to live after the world's opinion;
it is easy in solitude to live after our own; but the great
man is he who in the midst of the crowd keeps with perfect
sweetness the independence of solitude.

—*Ralph Waldo Emerson, "Self-reliance"*

Memorial Day is upon me, with its annual family reunion. Once the boys were married, we picked one weekend a year to gather as a family. This early-summer holiday fits the bill because it lacks ritual and presents no divided loyalties with the in-laws. I considered canceling it this year, given my tenuous situation, but I see the boys so seldom that any chance is a gift, no matter what the cost.

I used to be nervous enough greeting them as they returned from college, new jobs, travel; each had changed a bit since the last time we had been together. When you see those you love infrequently, it takes time to reestablish an honest connection. I liken it to adjusting the level on the stereo, turning the bass and treble knobs in search of perfect harmony.

But greeting their wives unnerves me even more, especially since I have had my inevitable slips with both of them. Each faux pas has made me cautious. As much as I want to be natural with them, my manner invariably becomes forced, and I find myself adjusting to *their* rhythms and ideas.

When I was first introduced to my sons' women, each was on her best behavior. There would be thank-you notes after visits, little gestures of appreciation, gifts even. After thirty years in a household of men, I became entranced by the notion of having women around. But once each was married, a subtle power shift took place; eager openness was replaced by guarded politeness. In each case I sensed competition between us, two women involved with the same man. Fearing the reputation of clingy mother and the sting of all those awful mother-in-law jokes, I distanced myself. But that only exacerbated my feeling that everything had suddenly changed.

"I thought I would be gaining a daughter!" I moaned to my cousin's daughter one day.

"That's unrealistic," she replied. "When I get married, why would I want another mother? I already have one."

Her point was well taken and set me straight. My sons' wives relish their autonomy, even flaunt it, and so I've stopped trying to be anything more than a supporter and am grateful to participate when asked. They make it simple, with their carefully drawn boundaries and well-orchestrated activities. But staying on the periphery of their lives takes some doing for someone who has spent much of her adult life being indispensable and responsible.

I used to probe, wanting to know more than they chose to reveal, until one daughter-in-law stopped me in the game. "You always ask how I feel about this or that," she said firmly but with a convincing smile. "Don't you know feelings aren't thoughts? They're not always something you can talk about or explain. They're just what they are—feelings!" I could only guess that she had arrived at this opinion because she is a dancer and emotes with her body, not words. In any case, I now refrain from either asking them about their feelings or showing mine.

Still, I long to be close to my sons and their wives and

find myself wondering why. My friend Joan tells me it's pretty hard just to drop what you enjoy so much. "That's why you walk on eggshells, trying not to hurt or misjudge," she says.

"True," I agreed, as we talked about my apprehension around this impending reunion weekend. "But I no longer want to edit my behavior, twisting myself up like a pretzel."

"You won't," she assured me. "Now that you've tasted the other, you won't go backwards. It'll be better than ever, you'll see. Just let whatever comes flow through you and then away. Everyone is after the same thing, y'know. It's called intimacy. The only way to experience it is to be yourself."

Anyway, I've hardly had time to fret. Yesterday was my last day of clamming, and I haven't had the energy to do more than tidy up the place. For once, financial pressures and simple existence have taken precedence over self-inflicted anxiety. I did make a bouillabaisse for dinner, full of hand-picked steamers, but I'm counting on everyone to pitch in for the other meals. I shake my head in amusement, thinking back to the ridiculous culinary productions I used to orchestrate, turning the household into a fantasy of impossible perfection, only to end up exhausted and irritable.

I look at the clock. Two hours until they arrive. Oh, God, let me enjoy the pleasure of being graceful! As I gaze about the patio at the flowering perennials that endure year after year, I do myself a favor and recognize that I am no more or less than the perennial that provides the bulk of the lush backdrop for her family and those around her. It has taken years of growing and expanding to become as colorful and abundant as I am. I'm not some hothouse flower, forced into bloom, but rather a ripened woman who is getting to know what she's about. There's no need for me to fret over the young seedlings.

My instinct is to approach the weekend as if I am treading water, keeping my body upright, watching the action, calling on my instincts, remaining centered, not going in one direction or another. I intend to listen more, talk less, receive whatever it is they offer, and then, like the woman I've become, let the ripe fruit fall where it may.

My older son arrives first. He's the traditionalist, the enthusiast, the one who will set a celebratory tone for the weekend, which takes the pressure off me. Our younger son and his wife come next, as if they have choreographed their arrival, appearing during a lull in the action, making it possible for me to welcome them all in measured doses.

The boys greet one another and begin talking as if they had never been apart. I think back to the rehearsal dinner for our older son's wedding, when he lifted his glass and toasted his younger brother, borrowing a sentiment his paternal grandmother held for her sons: "No woman will ever come between me and my brother." I wonder, as the years go on, if he will be able to keep his promise.

Within the hour my husband arrives, and the quiet cottage wakes up, as if from a Rip Van Winkle slumber. This place, which has been used as a retreat for life's richness, can't help but glow with good energy from times well spent: nights of song and games of charades, pine floors permanently tarnished from those who spend days on boats and in sand, late-afternoon homecomings with a line of salty people waiting by the outside shower. There is a central spirit that everyone shares, not unlike the cozy connectedness of a Christmas Eve. It feels right to surrender my isolation. I'm hungrier than I thought for family.

My husband is imbued with an unusually generous spirit, wide watery eyes, hugs for everyone, even me. I automatically pull away from his embrace and then wonder why, since the touch feels good. Practiced repression has no room in my new life, so I slip my arm through his.

The repartee between the boys and their father makes me sense that they have been communicating frequently. There's no doubt the boys bring out his best side. Their affection for him is more readily apparent than their feelings for me, and he responds as anyone would who is being loved. I'm comforted that he hasn't allowed a void to develop between them. Whatever conversations they've been having don't seem to have involved me or the marriage. I surprise myself by feeling relieved.

There are few secrets in a tiny cottage and precious little privacy, yet I'm taken aback when my younger son appears in the kitchen carrying my clam basket and rake. "Who's the clammer? Don't tell me you've taken that up as well," he says, already embarrassed by my job in the fish market.

The others wander in, their curiosity piqued by the conversation. "So that's how you got your tan so soon," says one. "Gee, Mom, what happened? We weren't under the impression that this was one of your lifelong career goals."

"The hot-water heater busted," I confess. "Clamming was a way to get some quick cash."

"But your bad back." One of the girls asks, "How did you manage?"

"The work has actually strengthened my muscles," I answer. "Anyway, you mostly use your upper body."

I am getting the impression that my kids view me as old and finished. They mostly see me in the role of mother, not Joan, the person. Standing here, answering their questions, I feel a certain smugness, triumph actually. I'm proud to be seen as one who pulls her own weight.

My husband, who is leaning against the kitchen sink sipping a glass of wine, has been listening intently with a bemused look on his face. He says nothing, but when he catches my eye, he raises his glass to me.

Slowly, this most ordinary day begins to glow, and the weekend commences. The curtain opens, the drama begins— three whole days, like a three-act play that will never be performed quite the same way again. There is a sense of expectancy in everyone—the daughters-in-law who have never spent a span of time together; the brothers, bonded by blood but changed by transitions; the parents, tainted by separation, strengthened by solitude. Everyone appears hopeful, excited simply by the ritual of the weekend itself. My shyness is further assuaged when a daughter-in-law hands me a gift, a hand-painted sign that says TRADITION. I hang it on the kitchen wall and know that my desire to bring us all together each year is right, that we are intertwined in some indefinable way. Her gesture starts me breathing again, steadily, rhythmically.

As if the cottage were not enough to bond us together, the weather cooperates by being warm for May and blesses us with a beach day. Not that we couldn't have gotten by with mist and rain, but somehow being out under the big sky with the sensuous sounds of water and wind ensures fun, frolic, and freedom.

"Which beach?" the boys ask, as I am now the native. I choose South Beach, built by a storm, now to be our playground. Big ocean beaches were always my preference when the boys were small, busy, and loud. I counted on the sea to soak up their sounds and wildness.

We pile into the Volvo, my husband motioning for me to climb into the front seat beside him, and it feels like déj à vu, all those years of driving to the beach in a car stuffed with food, drink, Wiffle ball, and bat, and, most of all, an eagerness to get there and stay all day.

We choose the shelter of a dune and unpack our belongings, right next to a colony of sandpipers seemingly unperturbed by our presence. After a time one, then another, lifts off, and each of us, in our own way, follows suit. One of the girls chases a white heron, as a child would a kite, while the other searches for bleached shells. "The more broken the better," she says, "because then you can see right through to the center."

By noon the towels and blankets that have been protecting us from the morning chill come off, and we peel away layers of both clothes and pretension. Manners melt as we fall under the spell of this wild place. The gift of such a day is sinking into a seamless world of uninterrupted time, where the endless hours allow something to grow from nothing.

I watch, as if peering through the lens of a movie camera, shifting from one frame to another. Truths, once held as secrets, slip out. Similarities and differences become comfortable companions in this primitive place where violence and peace go hand in hand.

I overhear my husband confess his anger and lethargy, for which he is getting therapy; a son admits to making a fool of himself at work; the other confesses to a conflict in his marriage. I like watching them share, not just the good stuff but the bad. Men rarely talk to each other as women do. Although my boys are feminists, we raised them to grab the brass ring. By doing so, they are reticent, I fear, to share their hard times, eager only to report the successes, which makes really knowing their grown-up selves all the more difficult.

As a young bride I sent my parents letters filled with lies, wanting to convince not only them, but myself, that I was happy. It occurs to me that I will continue to know my children less if they think I want them to *be* more. Seeking perfection is a terrible thing when it robs you of truth. I wonder if role-playing and being careful are the chief causes of loneliness.

It is only a matter of time before the boys are swimming in the cold spring sea, not because they were once sailors and raised near the water but because one has dared the other. I sit chilled, knowing they are romping about in fifty-degree water and marvel at the glory of their youth, just as my husband takes a running dash and joins them. Minutes later a wave spills all three onto the shore, and the boys rush to roll around on a mound of warm, soft sand. If there had been an ounce of tension left in any of us, it has been banished.

At times like this I find myself wondering how I came to have these particular children. Are they what I expected? Am I totally responsible for what they've become? One is a teacher, the other an actor. I fear for the financial security of the latter and worry that the teacher will get bored in his job. I know I've both spoiled and repressed them, contributed to their neuroses, encouraged their sensitivities, pushed the limits of their goodwill. Yet with all of their foibles, I remain enchanted by their essence, their individual lives, and awfully curious about all I don't know about them, especially their interaction with their wives, who have settled on another mound of sand, sculpting a mermaid. Bent over, digging diligently, they are joined by their men.

My husband and I wander off with the excuse of looking for scallop shells to create the mermaid's fin, but actually we want some time alone. We are two people who have taken steps toward selfhood this year and are in need of sharing what we are becoming.

He seems to be appreciating family as never before; having withdrawn for a time like a hibernating bear, he returns, eager for rediscovery. I find myself walking along a beach with someone who feels like an old friend. We have chosen to walk on firm sand near the surf, where waves splash around us, rinsing the sand from our feet time and again.

I've come to believe that love happens when you want it to. It is an intention, rather than a serendipitous occurrence.

Only when one is open to receive and absorb love can it occur.

"You know, I'm beginning to think that real growing only begins after we've done the adult things we're supposed to do," I say.

"Like what?" he asks.

"Working, raising a family, doing community things—all that stuff keeps you from your real self, the person you've left behind."

"So . . . ?" he asks, waiting for more.

"I don't ever want to be finished. Now that I'm catching on to real living . . . the formlessness of it . . ."

He doesn't understand the concept of unfinished, nor does he see it as a positive word. Part of him wants to be finished, away from his dull job and the need to collect the weekly paycheck. He wants to have that behind him. And yet, what would he be without that definition? This is what he finds scary.

"We're as unfinished as the shoreline upon this beach," I tell him. "Isn't that exciting? Up until now we've done what everyone else wanted us to do, and now it's our turn. I hope to continue to transcend myself as long as I live."

I realize as I speak that my words might be falling on deaf ears. Neither of us has any idea of where we're headed. We've never been as unsure of our future as we are now. And yet, there is a degree of excitement to not knowing, like the young couples we have just left behind. What is clear about their future?

He stops walking now, and I turn to meet his gaze. Tears are streaming down his cheeks. The thawing of a relationship takes hard work. I find it curious that our time is occurring in the spring, when everything else is waking up. It occurs to me that nothing ever really comes to an end. Being by the sea has taught me that.

"Look," I say, breaking the silence, "all I know is that I have spent the bulk of this year unlearning all the rules, the conditions and goals that were set for me by someone else. Finally I feel mature enough to recover myself—that person I was born to be."

He takes my hand, and we walk back to the others, collecting scallop shells as we go. It is one of those walks when, after it is over, you know something has changed.

We see the family, and the flurry of activity that occurs when one must race against the tide to construct a work of art. Just as we are finding various pieces to create the perfect mermaid, so we must dedicate as much time to carefully putting back together the pieces of our own lives. An artist has endless possibilities when the medium is sand and water. So it is also with human sculpture. We are as malleable as the mermaid in the sand—unfinished men and women making new creations out of our old selves.

I relish the passion that bubbles up in this family when we all work together. "Vital lives are about action," Joan Erikson tells me. "You can't feel warmth unless you create it, can't feel delight unless you play, can't know serendipity unless you risk." I'm trying to bring more of the spontaneous beach back to the cottage and incorporate it into my everyday life.

Perhaps the delight I feel right now has to do with the

display of diversity as two generations of men and women evolve, change, and grow. Suddenly the issue of *how* we're all changing seems irrelevant. The fact that we're all striving toward unknown ends is what is so grand. Although I see the essence of my sons, what they become will forever be a surprise. The task is to applaud each surprise as if it were a birthday package plunked in front of me, enjoying the fictional flair of our life stories as they evolve.

The boys are constantly chiding me about my idiosyncrasies. I'm supposedly nosy, loud, inappropriate. You name it, they think it. I, too, see characteristics and attitudes in them and their wives that could stand adjusting. But what makes them interesting are their imperfections. They are perfect in their imperfections! Could that be?

Although the rosy glow of the late afternoon tempts us to linger, the sun will set all too soon, and it is time to gather our belongings. Having arrived at high tide, complete with the ocean's applause, having watched the sea turn itself around during the ebb, and now preparing to leave as the water retreats, I feel full up. To experience the whole of the tide cycle is to view change, to watch time actually pass by. In the process, I feel the pull and tug of the universe.

We don't get dinner on the table until way past nine. I say "we" when in fact the girls take on the duty while I act merely as a sous-chef. One creates a pasta sauce out of several cans of tomato paste, tarragon, and cream, while the other throws together a salad with greens, avocados, grapefruit, and her fabulous raspberry vinaigrette. Preparing a meal together can be like a ballet, as each surrenders to the other's ideas. The fly in the ointment is the woman who insists that certain foods can be only prepared one way—her way. Being reactive instead of proactive is offering me connection.

There is no dessert, the candles are burning low, the last bottle of wine is being opened, great yawns are replacing vivid conversation. Someone once said that a good husband is the workmanship of a good mother. So, for the moment, I take credit for how the boys have turned out, especially in their earnest endeavors at husbandhood.

If I had longed for felt satisfaction back at Christmastime, I am finally experiencing it. Gathering around a table, breaking bread together, offers those who partake a piece of something sacred. For now I am briefly liberated by the simple act of living. I watch the sideways glances the young couples indulge in as one thing or another is said and enjoy their ample displays of affection. I used to be envious of young love, but tonight I delight in its warmth.

And then my husband stands to deliver a toast:

"Here's to our wives and sweethearts.
May our sweethearts soon be our wives,
and our wives always our sweethearts."

I listen with my heart, reminded that some of my sons' behavior had to have been modeled after their father.

SAFE HARBOR

End of June

If it is woman's function to give, she must be replenished too.

—*Anne Morrow Lindbergh*, GIFT FROM THE SEA

It *is* early morning, soggy with high humidity, the kind of weather that defies lightness. Even so, I spring to my feet at the sound of the chirping birds and tiptoe down to the kitchen to prepare a Thermos of coffee. My older son and his wife leave today, having stayed long after the others to spend some quality time with me before departing on a Far Eastern bike trip.

Their sleepy heads appear just before dawn, and I walk them to their overstuffed little Dodge, bikes strapped to the roof, and hug them hard, holding on to my son for an extra moment. Then, like the ship captain's wife, I wave good-bye, a brave smile on my face and a lump in my throat. It's not that I want to hold on to them. It's just that I've not fully faced the inevitability of children's growing up and going so far away. I tend to linger around final moments, hoping to create an indelible impression, not only of what the experience looked like but of what it felt like as well. Endings have a way of plunging me into emotional wilderness, but not this time.

There are fewer tears now, perhaps because I'm beginning to realize they are not mine. They belong to each other; their "own little nation," I say, envisioning them huddled in their tent near some rice paddy. They hold the power of their destinies in their own hands. I can only offer Godspeed. It's a bittersweet reality, but I'm coming to understand that love blossoms when there is just the right amount of tenderness combined with a long leash.

It was good to have them home, but I'm surprised at how anxious I am to regain my solitude. For all the frivolity during our time together, you can't sustain celebration. Nor would I want to, since such joy and fun never come without effort. Although I didn't intend to edit my behavior, I did, nevertheless, minding my manners, holding my tongue, refraining from judgments.

Still, I feel a void, not because everyone is gone but because they are returning to lives that have well-worked-out agendas. It was strange bidding my husband good-bye, too, as if he were only going on a business trip, when, in reality, he was returning to his separate world, although he mentioned retirement more than once, liberally sprinkling his conversations with references to "we" and "us." Since we seemed to be reconnecting, I hesitated to spoil the momentary closeness with questions about the future. But there was something missing, evidence of distance that couldn't be denied.

I wonder now if it had something to do with not having sex. Not that I had necessarily wanted to make love, but I was troubled that it didn't even seem to be an option. I've been obsessed with sexual thoughts lately, longing for that part of my life to be restored, wincing at the sight of love scenes in movies, turning away when I see lovers embracing. I even found myself wondering what was going on between my sons and their wives behind closed doors each night.

Yet in truth, sex has never been high on my list of priorities. Thinking I want something is quite different from actually enjoying it. The myth around sex in this culture is that we should want it, that we are abnormal or repressed if we don't have it, so not partaking of it makes me feel like an outsider.

Perhaps I stopped being available for lovemaking simply because I didn't like it. It seemed fine for helping to pin down a man for marriage, even finer when I wanted children. Then it became a chore—a duty to perform after the dishes were done and the kids were put to bed. Pleasuring her man was what I had been taught a good wife simply should do.

Now, what seems hundreds of years later, I stand here wondering what I've missed. Many of my friends confide that they, too, are relieved that the need to do the "chore" is past. One quit sex because her husband failed to personalize it; for him it seemed any keyhole would do. Another couldn't bear her husband's snorting and sniffing. Another grew bored with her husband's idea of romance: lying in bed reading the swimsuit edition of *Sports Illustrated* while fondling himself, expecting her to become aroused by watching.

Sooner or later, grief and guilt over not having sex drive me to distraction. Why don't I let my ice-cube heart thaw and just get on with it? The worst that could happen is that it might be like before. Yet now that I've managed to reclaim some of my primitive self, who knows? What if, for once, I allowed my body to feel the passion my mind does? Or if, like the Chinese, I began to consider regular sex as paramount to good health and longevity? Would those be reason enough to consummate my longing?

Oh, well, no point to these speculations when there's no

one to make love to anyway. Perhaps just facing up to such unvarnished facts is a step toward a solution.

Today happens to be the summer solstice, a meaningful time for change, and with more daylight than I will see for another year, I'd best seize the hours with a vengeance.

Nearby is my bicycle with its bulbous tires and rusting chain, a workhorse of a vehicle that takes me on jaunts for mail and groceries. Perhaps a longer ride will still my mind and break up my melancholia. I will make it a symbolic journey, the farther the better, in honor of my children's longer one.

I take off through the woods, down our dirt path, and eventually onto pavement. I remember as a little girl heading off without ever having a destination—wonder-filled, expectant, hair flying just as now. My bike leads me, becoming an extension of my body, taking me back.

I am headed down Lovers Lane, now overgrown with wild pink roses and cornflowers. A meadow nearby is awash in purple clover. Gradually, all the colors, aromas, shadows, dips, and pockets become a blur that invites discovery. I'm on a two-lane, sparsely traveled road that cuts across the Cape. It's taking me inland, away from the beach traffic, past cranberry bogs, kettle ponds, and scrub-pine forests. Just now I understand why my daughter-in-law prefers bikes over other vehicles: "You miss nothing when you're moving two miles an hour," she says. "Even the smallest blade of grass can capture your attention." Just now it is the smell of bayberry, honeysuckle, and pine that captures mine.

My tongue touches my salty upper lip. I'm surprised at

how good the sweat tastes. All this moving, stretching, and breathing align my thoughts with my body's feelings. I wonder if I could share a long bike ride with my husband. What would happen if we had to depend on one another the way our son and his wife are about to do? We did once, when we were first married and living in Africa. Maybe we've lasted this long because we learned to be interdependent back then.

I stop thinking and pedal harder to make a hill. At the top I take my feet off the pedals, abandon all control, and race down the other side, skidding at the bottom on a sandy shoulder and braking in front of the Methodist Church, where a sign proclaims: THE OPPOSITE OF LOVE IS INDIFFER-ENCE. The message is haunting, even wounds me. I get off my bike and plop down onto the lawn, still moist and sweet-smelling from the early-morning dew. Sweat tickles my back as the drops, one by one, slide between my shoulder blades, I reach for my water bottle to take a couple of gulps before pulling my knees up to my chin and rocking out a kink in my back. I am still in recovery from the hour or so of hard riding, but I turn to the sign once more to muse over the word "indifference."

Had I become indifferent to my husband and marriage? I hate the thought. It denotes not caring, having little feeling, being cold and harsh. Am I that? I hope not. Perhaps we were simply tired souls who hadn't the energy for anything but inertia, both shutting down and keeping our feelings to ourselves.

But we were anything but indifferent to one another over Memorial Day, sharing easy conversation, exchanging knowing glances, seeing humor in our lives. Maybe separating was the sanest thing for two confused people to do, coming coincidentally as it did at menopause—hmmm, men-o-pause, a pause from men. Perhaps all women in long-term relationships should consider it. Primitive cultures insist on it, knowing a woman needs to regenerate, not unlike the starfish growing a new arm or the molting lobster growing larger and stronger within a new shell.

If I'm obsessing over indifference, it must mean I still care. Perhaps at one time I was indifferent, but no more, not about him or the marriage or any other aspect of my life. It's not that I don't ever want him to return home. It's just that I want it only if it is intentional, not a mere matter of convenience. If we are to have a future, it must be a collaboration, where each has a hand in the plot and contributes to the stage directions. I no longer have any interest in producing and directing the third act of our lives.

The carillon in the church steeple breaks my concentration with its melodious midmorning concert, a familiar tune:

> *"Morning has broken, like the first morning,*
> *Blackbird has spoken, like the first bird.*
> *Praise for the singing, praise for the morning,*
> *Praise for them springing, fresh from the word."*

I sing along, uplifted by the words, reminded of the way my favorite minister taught me how to pray, or rather, yield my thoughts: "Offer praise first," she said, "then thanksgiving. Follow it with petition, asking for your need to be met, and then conclude by relinquishing control." I find that once I do the first part, the reason for my prayer usually diminishes.

The little concert concludes when the bell in the church tower strikes ten. The day is young, and I have rebounded from a sense of loss to feeling as new as the morning.

What to do next? With no one around and no need to take a consensus, the sky's the limit. I hop back on my bike and head for the bike path, which takes me away from the tourist traffic and deeper into the interior of the Cape. Nostalgia works as a magnet and draws me five miles north to my reward—a general store that has been around as long as I can remember. Shoving my bike into a crowded bike stand, I hobble toward the front porch, where the same men who sit around the store's potbellied stove in the winter now sit on old church pews outside, drinking from bottomless cups of coffee, watching the world go by, and catching up on each other's business.

Once inside, I sit on a milk carton beside the newspapers, which are directly under the revolving ceiling fan. The breeze and the distraction of two little kids eyeing the penny candy and jars full of affordable toys make me forget that I am hot and sweaty. You can get your mail here, buy postage stamps, read the notices of upcoming events, pick up fruits, vegetables, freshly ground peanut butter, spices sold by the ounce, canned jelly made by a local housewife, homemade breads and muffins made by another, and general supplies such as lantern oil, sturdy pottery, and other staples necessary for a household. They carry one brand of most everything, not twenty, making it simple to choose. Nothing is complicated or fancy here, just practical and friendly. This is a place to linger, a microcosm of a small town; in fact, the general store *is* the town, that and several churches on nearby corners. I'm thinking, as I sit here and drink in the scene, how little it takes to get by, how simple life really can be, how pleasant to think only of necessities, eliminating the luxuries. Just now I recognize that this is everything I want—this is home. The Cape is where I belong, where I must stay. The kids may go far and wide and my husband may have other ideas, but as for me, this is contentment.

After buying a lemonade I'm ready for the return trip home, pedaling easily this time, in no particular hurry. Wind chimes, a gift from my children, greet me upon my return, along with a sinkful of last night's dirty dishes, soiled towels piled high in the back hall, and several workmen up on my roof!

"Hey, what are you guys doing up there?"

"Fixing a leak and then replacing half the shingles," one of them answers, as if he is puzzled by the question.

"Are you sure you have the right house?" I ask. "I didn't order any work to be done."

"Yeah, well your husband did ... called us a couple of weeks back. After this job we're supposed to insulate the attic and paint the trim."

Totally mystified now, I go to the phone and dial his number. "What's up with the workmen on the roof?" I ask my husband, barely saying hello.

"Oh, good," he answers. "I'm glad they showed up. They weren't sure when they'd be able to work us in."

"Work us in! What's going on?"

"I thought you'd be pleased," he says, surprised at the edginess in my voice.

"Well, I guess I am, but you could have warned me. Besides, your interest in this house is a huge turnaround from the water-heater incident. What gives?"

"We've got to preserve the cottage," he says. "It means so much to everyone, even the kids."

The conviction with which he is speaking has obvious underpinnings. Then he mumbles something about wanting to reinvest in us.

I'm not sure I like what I'm hearing, but nonetheless, here it is. He's contemplating returning, living here, being with me. In a daze, I fill him in on our son's departure and then say good-bye. For a moment or two I stand with the phone still in my hand. My mind races with questions. When is he thinking of returning? What is he planning to do here? What does he think it will take for us both to create a life here—to re-create one together? What do I really want? But then, all of a sudden, I find myself not wanting to know anymore. For now the cottage is being restored and that's enough, especially since I've only just decided that this is where I intend to stay. It's been a long day. For now I want to retain my praise for this grand solstice day, and let the future evolve as it will.

WILD AND SALTY

August

*If you can risk getting lost somewhere along the day you might
stumble upon openings that link you to your depths.*

—*Anonymous*

I *have* learned to pay attention to my instincts and take notice when I feel anxious—to remove the pebble from my shoe
before it blisters, get the chicken bone out of my throat—in
short, to be mindful of feelings and emotions and work with
them, not run from them. Such is the reason I find myself on
this early Tuesday morning being ferried by boat to the outer
bar, where I will stay overnight, going off alone before being
joined by another.

There is no doubt I was startled by my husband's talk of
retirement and reconciliation. Having spent the past year
shuttling between married woman and free spirit, I thought
it prudent to take stock of my wishes and desires before
yielding to something I hadn't bargained for. Taking a wild
and salty cure by spending twenty-four hours on a rugged
spit of land seemed the perfect tonic for my free-floating
anxiety: a place where I would stay present, buoy my spiritual
armor, and return satisfied that my hard-won autonomy was
intact.

The boat moves swiftly now. I grip my trusty old sleeping bag and backpack, remnants from more difficult experiences: trekking the Andes and hiking to the bottom of the
Grand Canyon, both gratifying adventures that tested my
will and stamina but, because I went with others, failed to
test my independence. This adventure isn't as dramatic and is

certainly not about miles hiked or mountaintops scaled, but as I will be completely alone with nature, I do expect it to be a deepening experience.

The twenty-minute trip passes quickly, and we soon pull into a little cove where disembarking looks manageable. I negotiate my way over the side of the boat, wade ashore carrying tent and sleeping bag, then return for food, water, and other supplies.

"See ya tomorrow, late morning," the captain says, backing his boat away, then adding an ominous note: "Remember, middle-of-the-night rescues are not part of my package. Hope the weather holds." With that, he's off, and the sound of his motor fades, removing the last din of everyday life.

I stand still, feet sinking into the muddy flat, and experience a familiar fear, nothing extreme, just a gnawing concern that comes over me when first I'm left alone in any situation, particularly one I have stubbornly seized upon despite warnings from well-meaning friends.

"Aren't you afraid something will happen to you?" a neighbor asked upon seeing me pack the trunk of my car.

"I certainly hope so," I answered defensively. "That's the whole point."

Pity that life teaches us to be so careful and guarded, I thought, as I drove away, but now, looking around at this utter wildness, I wonder if she knows something I don't. For sure, the weather is supposed to turn—it is hurricane season, after all—but not for another forty-eight hours. I've been forced into this window of time because of these predictions, but I also want to take advantage of the full moon.

A series of gentle waves washes over the tips of my

rubber boots, signaling not only a turning tide but my immediate task—getting my gear to higher ground. I spot a gawky
piece of driftwood, bare limbs sticking out all over, and prop
my stuff at its base. Then I survey this serene setting and the
360-degree view it affords. I adjust my breath to the ocean's
rumble, which at the moment is calm and unperturbed, and
set out to find a campsite. As I trudge up one dune and down
another, I am hampered by my boots in the soft sand, but the
combination works its magic and puts my high-gear personality into slow motion.

My eye is drawn to one scooped-out hollow, then another, until I choose a completely bald spot with no new
sprouts of dune grass in its basin and three sides of protec-
tive, towering mounds, a perfect spot in which to nestle my
dome tent.

In little over an hour my nesting place is set up. I've gone
from panic to peace—anxiety falling away, along with a
headache, muscles becoming mush, brain draining of all
complicated thought. Taking to a nearby perch with a natural
seat carved into the side of a dune, I'm further tranquilized
by the sounds of lapping water and wind.

Just beneath where I sit is a remarkable sight: a perfectly
drawn circle in the smooth sand, created by one blade of
swaying beach grass being moved by the wind. It is just as if
someone had taken a draftman's compass to draw a radius.
Fledgling beach grass is a marvel. I can only imagine how difficult it was for it to become so deeply rooted, so much of its
growth hidden, a survivor of storms, shifting sands, and wild
seas. Perhaps this is meant to be a sign for me, maybe even of
the marriage in which I have come full circle, engaging my

senses like so many tufts of beach grass to bring me to the center of myself. I feel as still and sure as the axis of a wheel, both in and out of relationship, wishing no longer to meddle with the workings of fate but to remain in the hub while the elements do the work.

Powerful messages are available in a place where strife is more common than peace, where impermanence reigns and all that lives is subject to change and erasure. I feel a kinship with this environment as I, too, have made *change* my friend.

I'm eager to walk, stretch, explore this paradise set in a circle of waves, to get to know her times and moods. Starting out on the protected side of the bar, I saunter along the edges of the shore, where the beach tapers and rough seas mingle with a tame bay. My feet must negotiate with the ever-increasing tide that washes over my footprints almost as quickly as I create them. I like the idea of taking sanctuary in a place where one's movements become an unsolvable mystery, with no clues left behind.

The idea of slipping away without explanation and having secrets has become a staple of my year by the sea. Soon I will be obliged to explain my daily routines to another. "I shall miss having secrets," I told Joan recently.

"Ah, but you must always retain some part of yourself which is nobody's business. The minute you let others in on your secrets, you've given away some of your strength."

Here, where much more is hidden than apparent, I am reminded that a companion to mystery is peace; that knowing less and wondering more offers expectancy. It has become my way to dispense with incessant seeking in favor of stumbling upon answers. In the words of Picasso, "I find, I do not seek." No longer desperate to know every outcome, these days I tend to wait and see, a far more satisfying way of being that lacks specificity and instead favors experience over analysis.

I plow on, sensing that someone is following me, a silly thought out here, but nonetheless I feel something lurking. The only creature that could possibly follow me is a fox or coyote, both of which hide from people, not stalk them. Still, I hear weird noises, even feel some vibrations, and after a few minutes see what I already felt, not on land but in the water. A parade of seals, temporarily washed off their sand-bar, have taken to the water for their daily exercise, swimming beside me as I walk, playing hide-and-seek until just now, when one makes eye contact with me, and I stop to hold its gaze.

"Hi there," I say, a broad smile splashing across my face as I talk to the air, attempting to carry on a conversation with the seals as my voice keeps them watching. "You guys have gotten me to do all kinds of crazy things since the first time we met," I say. "I've actually become a little mad."

With that, they all dive, then surface some fifty yards away, looking back at me as if to say, "C'mon."

I pick up my pace, fully engaged with their company, now honored by it, and find myself skipping, moving in sync with their arching dives, responding to their raw impulses. I catch myself believing the Celtic myth that in the dark pool of a seal's eyes there are spirits that call out to certain people.

No doubt the seals touched me back in October, urging me with their antics to be more playful, vulnerable, and free, insisting that I begin to look at what was missing in my life. Just now I am overcome by the reality that they did set me on a new path, that they have made a difference. Tears stain my cheeks, further reminding me how keenly alive I am just now.

We are nearing the tip of the island, where bay and ocean collide and water gushes. Waves ripple on either side of the point, careening, crashing, splashing, creating convoluted channels. The heaving surf is just beyond, now hissing through gleaming stones that are deposited upon the shore, and I stare at the sheer marvel of their survival, imagining the great mountain of which they were once a part, aware of their evolution from land to sea floor to shore.

I sit and grab handfuls of sand, letting the grains flow through my fingers, seeing in them my limitless future, a stark contrast from a few months ago when I was bored, counting the hours, staring into an hourglass that measured life in terms of a more prescribed amount of time. I am no longer just passing through the world, but digging deep and collecting moments. Time is a funny thing. Now that I am engrossed in life there is never enough time, but that was before I learned to stretch a moment to an hour and create multiple highs along the expanse of a day. I never saw the possibilities and promises that twenty-four hours actually offer.

The frothy whitecaps appear as a ruffled chorus line dancing across the surface of the sea, spitting, hissing, kicking all the way, acting very much like the woman I'm becoming, not content unless I'm tickling the rocks, slithering up the shore, embracing everything in sight. Catch the ocean as the tide rises and you find yourself amid a force that gets its strength from ebb and flow, that teaches the worth of filling up and emptying.

This afternoon's tide offers a pentimento of abstract patterns, garnished with shells, stones, and debris. The beach has become a canvas upon which an artist has created a collage, only to change his mind before the paint dries and compose a new overlapping image with the advent of the next wave. I, too, over the years have layered my basic frame, adapting to the demands of a culture, the ideals of a mother, designing and redesigning my persona, and now am finally scraping off the excess to have a glimpse of the original self.

I am so fortunate to have a friend like Joan who applauds my progress from the sidelines, helping me to see that whatever stage I'm in should be my project—that receiving and responding are true "tidal behavior," that whatever washes ashore should be greeted, picked up, sifted through, and held on to. As I contemplate living with another again, I must be ready to accept our differences and celebrate our similarities, to watch our new selves emerge and delight in what appears on my "shore."

Acceptance seems the biggest stretch that newly independent people must extend to one another. It is a strength I must acquire, or risk being estranged from the ebb and flow of the rest of my life. Like the tides that come and go at *their* will, not *ours*, we who frequent the beach must be mindful to time our swims and walks to the ocean's law. So it should be with the people who move in and through our lives.

Quickly this warm day is becoming a cool evening. It's time to head back to my temporary shelter, to collect driftwood on the way for tonight's fire. I feel a touch of hesitation as I turn my back and leave the passion of the pounding surf for calmer ground, even though I know that one cannot live on strong emotion alone. I head across the central corridor of my island, the only place that displays any sign of permanence, and where I will probably have the best chance of finding dry wood. It takes some doing for my eyes to adjust to the braided streams of light and shadow before I begin spotting random twigs, weathered boards, small logs half buried beneath silver dune grass and beige sand. My task is made easier when I come upon a twisted wreckage of storm fencing, which offers ample kindling for multiple fires. With arms weighted down, I stumble toward my little camp, happy to dump my load, collapse on my perch with cheese and a glass of wine, and watch day turn to night.

It was smart to bring mostly prepared foods—barbecued chicken, raw vegetables, bread. What's worth cooking if it means missing the sunset? I have never really taken time to truly watch the light show offered by the sun as it sets or the night as it develops. The sun, just disappearing, has left a painted sky of golds, pinks, oranges, and purples before becoming a melancholy blue, then turning to deeper tones of dusk. All is ripely quiet, and I lift my glass to me, a woman turned inside out, no longer wanting to become happy because, finally, I am.

My first impulse is to scavenge in my backpack for a flashlight so that I can read, write in my journal, record what I am experiencing. But then I see the moon turn on its soft white light, and I give over to the novelty of natural light, dropping my dependence on sight for the evening in favor of some of my other senses, as Joan's voice taps in to my consciousness: "The way to keep your senses alive is to use them."

Just then comes the background music of slurping surf, gull wings, and the snapping and crackle of burning wood.

I pull my knees to my chest, wrap my arms around my shins, and drink in the sweet, pungent aroma of driftwood as the sun, salt, and sea are burned from it. The wind creates a fickle flame that darts this way and that like fireflies. I'm hypnotized by the blaze, seeing the burn of struggle, the dance of aliveness, and knowing that the fire bears watching. I do not ever want the passion of my new ways to cool. The nourishment I feel can only be maintained if I stay close to the elements—fire, air, water, earth. If I surround myself with them, I shall always feel the stirrings of my soul.

With the night so luminous, not an inch of sky unused, I hesitate to turn in, wanting to luxuriate under the sequined heavens. I wrap myself in my sleeping bag and lie down, melting into the soft sand, while the ocean's murmur comforts me like a mother. Hours later I'm awakened by a chilling wind, forced to retreat inside my little tent like a snail into its moon shell.

The brightness of the morning stuns me. It seems as if I were only just basking in the moonlight. I've no idea what time it is, having left my watch on the mainland. Gathering clues from the chattering birds and the orange sun about to emerge, I would guess five-thirty. I crawl from the tent and quickly start a fire. As I wait for the water to boil, I huddle close by, in hopes of drying the damp night out of my clothes. Soon I am taking my first glorious sip of hot coffee, as the seals fish for their breakfast and the gulls wait for any scrap of food I'm willing to toss in their direction.

I am utterly content, tranquil in my aloneness, serene. Joan once told me that the root word in Greek for "alone" means "all one." That is precisely what I am experiencing, a sense of that sort of wholeness. Added to the peace of this morning is a quiet low-tide bay that boasts in its center a sandbar that has appeared three times in the past twenty-four hours. It teases me to venture out. I hesitate at first, the thought of chilly water making me shiver, but then, once again, I hear the words of my Navajo elder: "Listen to the muse when it's talking to you or it just goes on, and you miss its statement—that moment when you could have done something."

I put my coffee mug on the sand, strip to underpants and T-shirt, and wade in, searching the shallows for high ground, managing to stay ankle deep for a while. My eyes soon deceive me, and I sink to my thighs. No matter. At the very worst I'll be forced to swim. Intent now upon seeing what this momentary oasis offers, I push on, thighs moving the water aside, until at last I climb up on the sandbar, its surface a treasure trove of starfish and sand dollars, sea life that speaks of regeneration and eternity. I meander far out into the middle of the bay, dreaming about possibility, drinking in the moment, absorbing the grace of this tempo-rary world that allows me to experience what it means to be timebound. You have to hit such a place at just the right moment or risk missing it altogether, for as soon as the sand-bar appears, it begins to disappear again.

Standing on this island, I feel the perpetual motion of things—the tides, birds, seals, fish, shoreline, even myself. It seems to me that the task of the unfinished woman is to ac-knowledge her life as a work in progress, allowing each pas-sage, evolution, experience to offer wisdom for her soul.

As I finally turn back to walk to the other end of the bar, I see that water has already covered up half of it. There is no choice now but to swim to shore. I take off my underpants and T-shirt, with its bold slogan, THIS IS WHAT 50 LOOKS LIKE, and unceremoniously fling them on the bar to be left behind. I dive in and glide as far as my breath will take me.

Stripped bare, I can truly relate to the water as it em-braces my flesh. I flip onto my back and surrender myself to the currents as a school of silvery minnows flits over and under me. It feels good to be in my body without all the usual armor. I slide my hands down my sides, swaying in the gentle tide, held as if between the covers on a bed, a primal moment that allows me to see beyond my limits. Momentar-ily carried away by my fantasies, I don't notice that the cur-rent is moving swiftly now, pulling me away from shore. I re-vert to the side stroke, swimming quickly but remaining relaxed. As one thigh rubs against another, I feel a new confi-dence in my body, stroke by stroke.

Perhaps being sensual and sexual is nothing more than an attitude toward life. Could it be that the process of un-folding eludes many of us because, as my favorite writer, Nancy Mairs says, "most women carry their genitals as if they are in a sealed envelope." Maybe it's not for a man to open us; instead, we're meant to open ourselves and then relish what follows, with or without a man. It's about time I break my reliance on romance anyhow. As if to punctuate my thoughts, one wave slaps me, then another, as the ocean gathers me up and rolls me closer and closer to shore.

I emerge from the rigors of my swim, naked and unselfconscious, standing on the shore where the sun drys my body and offers color to my breasts, which have never seen the light of day. I feel like Aphrodite, whose lust for living and delight in the sensuous became the core of her being. "Take your dream by the hand and swim with it," Joan keeps telling me. "Let it float."

I see in the distance what must be my T-shirt drifting away, and with it all limitations created by ages and stages. Halfway to a hundred, I feel invincible, ready for new life. I walk back to my camp and step into my shorts and sweatshirt, glad that I thought to pack up my gear beforehand in order to be able to muse through the morning.

With a sudden string of ominous black clouds hanging over the sea and the wind picking up, it is as if on cue that I hear the motor of a boat in the distance.

I lug my gear to the cove and hop aboard, feeling part mermaid, part seal, knowing that something eternal has happened; that my truth depends on regular forays into the wilderness. I make a silent promise always to remember to strive toward the unimaginable.

We pass several seals, bottling just now, and I give them a wave of thanks for helping me reclaim my basic existence. Simple things will keep it so. I must live a little each day, greet the sun as it rises and revel in its setting, swim naked, sip coffee and wine by the shore, generate new ideas, admire myself, talk to animals, meditate, laugh, risk adventures. I must try to be soft, not hard; fluid, not rigid; tender, not cold; find rather than seek. I have been embraced by the sea, tested by its elements, emptied of anxiety, cleansed with fresh thought. In the process, I have recovered myself.

Embracing a husband and reinstating a relationship should be a piece of cake.

PORT OF CALL

September

When one has lived a long time alone,
one wants to live again among men and women,
to return to that place where one's ties with the human
broke, where the disquiet of death and now also
of history glimmers its firelight on faces . . .

—*Galway Kinnell, "When One Has Lived*
a Long Time Alone"

L*abor Day* at the fish market feels like Grand Central Station at rush hour. Summer people wander in and out all day long to pick up boxes of packed-for-travel lobster, scallops, swordfish, so they can take a taste of the Cape back to wherever they come from. Their faces display gloom, as no one wants to turn his back on summer. Some linger to talk about their fall plans, others have no time to talk, already in their harried, hurried mode, and then there are the few who are curious about what happens to us—the locals—after they leave.

"What's it like year-round?" one asks as I slap her cod onto a bed of ice, tucking bluefish pâatè in the corners of the box.

"It's quiet, that's for sure, but there's lots to do," I answer.

"Like what?" she presses, as if trying to believe that her suburban life is far better than life here.

"Empty beaches and bike paths, no lines at restaurants, stuff going on at the museums and libraries. It can even get hectic, if that's your pleasure."

She leaves with a wary look on her face as I wipe down the counters, quietly pleased that I didn't say too much, wanting to keep the joys of winter here a secret, lest we be invaded.

"I'm putting a sword steak in the cooler for you," the

owner says to me, displaying a beautiful cut on the palm of his hand. "Thought you might want to welcome your hubby home in grand style."

I'm taken aback. He doesn't often give his fish away, certainly not sword at $12.95 a pound. "Look forward to meeting him," he adds, "just to see if it's true, you having a husband and all that."

Time flies, this being the market's busiest day, save the Fourth of July. I leave at slack time, around two, and follow a caravan of cars home, rooftops covered with gear, bicycles hanging from their racks, boats being hauled to marinas for winter storage, all signs that summer is over.

My past Labor Days were fraught with much of the same bittersweet activity—stripping the beds, beating sand out of the hooked rugs, emptying the refrigerator, loading the car, always trying to accomplish the chores in record time so I could have one last walk on the beach. No longer. While everyone departs, I now simply wave good-bye. At long last, this day has lost its poignancy.

Yesterday I planted a hundred tulip bulbs, not because I'm suddenly interested in gardening but out of anticipation, knowing I'll be able to watch them bloom in April—that and to remind myself that I shall always be that enduring, blooming perennial I woke up to a few months back.

I hop into the outside shower as soon as I get home, rinsing off the smell of the fish market, wrap myself in an over-sized beach towel, and settle onto a chaise longue with a book and glass of iced tea, wanting to take advantage of the last few hours of single life. My husband will be arriving at six. I'm planning to meet him at a local watering hole. I've invited a variety of people there to drink to his future, dubbing the event a change-of-life party, wishing to ritualize his stepping over the threshold into this new life. Perhaps he'll be appalled at such an event, perhaps not. I figure this will be only the first of many surprises for both of us.

I doze for a bit, the sun both warming and relaxing my body, then pick some of my neighbors' Shasta daisies offered to me as they left this morning. I put them in a vase and then gaze around at the cottage, recalling what a comfortable refuge this has been for me this past year. Everything remains the same, except I've created a room of my own off the kitchen, with windows facing the woods, my only statement (to myself actually) that I must remain my own person. I've had the notion ever since a therapist friend showed me her sparsely furnished tower room with a view of the Hudson River. "I permit only objects and people of my choosing here," she said, "wanting pure space, with no negative energy, just for myself."

I feel a tad nervous as the day winds down—nothing serious, just the queasiness one feels before a first day of school or showing up for a new job. I step into my dress-up uniform—blue jeans and black linen blazer—comb my tousled hair, apply fresh lipstick, dab lemon-scented perfume behind my ears, and tell myself to calm down. You don't look half bad, I think as I peer into the mirror. A leathery tan accentuates my wrinkles, but the overall effect is handsome and hearty, a salty lady full of grit, sensitivity, and earthiness.

Once behind the wheel of the car, with a wad of my own hard-earned money in my pocket to pay for this little party, I open all the windows and let the wind blow in its unique freshness, then replay my husband's last phone call, when his voice sounded uncharacteristically up. No doubt he's done some work on himself—therapy, a few retreats, even yoga. He now has the voice of someone who has reinvoked his own passion. I'm anticipating greeting an unfinished man, a good soul, and an old friend, all the while knowing that my future and his remain a mystery still to be unraveled.

Main Street is dead, emptied of cars, summer obviously over. Now is the time when you recognize people in stores, take more than a moment to have a chat with them. Once at the restaurant I find a parking space right in front and go in, surprised to see so many of my guests already there: several fish-market employees, a woman photographer I hope to work with, the postmistress, two year-round couples I've gotten to know, Joan Erikson, and Josh Cahoon. Still to arrive are my plumber and his wife, two neighbors, and, of course, my husband.

The bartender has put out a tray of veggies and dip, "compliments of the house," he informs me. I indulge in light chatter while keeping one eye on the door and one on the clock—it's six-thirty. He must be stuck in holiday traffic.

Two glasses of wine later, the man of the hour appears, as if in a mirage, a little road-weary but excited just the same. After a lingering embrace that gives him a moment to adjust to the surprise, I introduce him to the unfamiliar faces and then retreat to the side to watch this six-foot-four-inch man relax into the spirit of the evening. His palpable presence warms my heart, as I remember how often he used to turn away from people—from the effort and intimacy involved—but not tonight. One of the guests, another retired man, approaches him with scissors in hand and ceremoniously cuts off his tie. Everyone cheers as my husband twirls it around as if it were a lasso and flings it to the rafters. I move closer and make a toast to his change of life, giving him a tide clock instead of the proverbial watch men are so often given at retirement.

We have endured, it would seem. A year ago in anger and despair I would have eagerly reached for divorce. But lethargy and exhaustion prevailed. Separation and solitude have healed us. It wasn't the marriage that needed to be terminated, rather the rote way in which we were existing within its walls.

There will be unknown jolts and instabilities as we live for a time on an unmoored raft, our days and ways as unstable perhaps as they were in adolescence. Fortunately, I no longer crave ease in life; that exquisite idleness so many people long for seems stifling to me now. I'm much more eager to delight in the ridiculous, just as we are doing at this moment.

In any case, the next few months will surely not be stolid or settled, and I've promised not to instruct or ask my husband what he is going to do with the rest of his life. I detest seeing wives ordering their husbands about, prematurely turning them into sniveling old men. I'll listen to his thoughts and ideas but hesitate before offering opinions. No one needs to be taught at this stage of life; rather, our own senses and sensitivities should carve out our paths. Falling into old patterns would only serve to diminish our spiritual growth.

In time the crowd dwindles, and we take a seat at a corner table to order some dinner. He wants his favorite, fried clams; I choose oysters on the half shell, after which he insists we share a split of champagne, our custom when having oysters.

"Baby, what a surprise!" he says of the party, melting me with my father's endearment, something he does from time to time now that my father is gone. "But how much did that cost?"

A typical question from a newly retired man who is unsure about his financial future, I think.

"It was *my* party," I answer, "paid for with fish-market earnings and an unexpected royalty check. Besides, your decision to change your life is a big deal. Haven't we always marked such events? Certainly the kids have had their fair share of parties. It's the least I could do."

He looks pleased and content. The afterglow of years permits us to be quiet together. Just as I feel a sense of peacefulness settling across the table, he interrupts the moment. "Remember how mad you got when I announced a few years back that I was at peace with myself?"

"How could I forget? Since I wasn't feeling peaceful, all I could think was, Why should you?"

"Right," he continued. "Of course, I didn't know what the hell I was talking about. I suppose I thought if I named the state of mind I was wishing for, it might come to pass. Well, guess what? Being at peace with oneself means being without passion, and that's what I've been missing—not just the sex stuff but the old adrenaline rush that comes when you're doing something crazy. Being stubborn and staid hasn't done much for me. I need to go back to the prescription I gave our marriage at the beginning—that we should always have adventures, both together and independent of each other."

"I'm coming to see that life is not a lesser thing than I imagined it to be," I say, thinking out loud just now. "Rather, it holds more than I have time to seize. The big secret is that everything doesn't happen in youth."

He nods. It occurs to me that the time for parting is past. If one or the other of us were going to jump ship, it would have had to happen before the kids were married, before the circle and tribe began enlarging and we began to see the potential for regeneration. I suppose there never was a good reason for us not to be together.

Separation has done its job—less of him has made more of me and vice versa. Funny how I focused on the sex issue, as if that should stop us from living together. A marriage has to have some flaws, some unresolved issues, some conflicts that can be worked through. Hopefully long-term marriages move beyond chemistry to compatibility anyway.

A moment of truth always brings with it an intensity that is delicious. Right now my cheeks have turned a deep pink as I return to a solid state of gratitude. If we both live consciously into each day, I'm convinced now that the most ordinary of our experiences will glow with meaning.

I am yawning with weariness as we pay the bill and begin to leave. "I have an idea for tomorrow," my husband says.

"Tomorrow," I say, startled. Thinking beyond right now is a jolt.

"Would you take me to see the seals?" he asks. "I want to

see why they mean so much to you. Perhaps they'll even speak to me."

"No doubt they will," I answer.

Like me, he is on a new path. I can only sit by and honor what is unfinished in him—in all of us.